R.D. VILLAM

Son of the Borderland: River of Blood

Copyright © 2025 by R.D. Villam

All rights reserved. No part of this publication may be reproduced, stored or transmitted in any form or by any means, electronic, mechanical, photocopying, recording, scanning, or otherwise without written permission from the publisher. It is illegal to copy this book, post it to a website, or distribute it by any other means without permission.

This novel is entirely a work of fiction. The names, characters and incidents portrayed in it are the work of the author's imagination. Any resemblance to actual persons, living or dead, events or localities is entirely coincidental.

R.D. Villam asserts the moral right to be identified as the author of this work.

R.D. Villam has no responsibility for the persistence or accuracy of URLs for external or third-party Internet Websites referred to in this publication and does not guarantee that any content on such Websites is, or will remain, accurate or appropriate.

First edition

*This book was professionally typeset on Reedsy.
Find out more at reedsy.com*

Contents

I Part One

1	Blacksmith's Apprentice	3
2	Lessons From an Old Story	13
3	Shining Black Stone	24
4	To Have Some Fun	29
5	The Right Person	36
6	Always Look Back	43
7	Chaos by the River	51
8	Life Changes	59
9	The Plan	67
10	If the Payment is Right	74
11	Luck Is On Our Side	86
12	You Don't Have to Promise Anything	94
13	The Red Hair	105
14	Roar	117
15	Stupid and Crazy	126
16	The Wrong Word	134
17	Big Wolf	142
18	A Little Madness	152
19	Prepare for the Unpredictable	163
20	The Ugly Necklace	170
21	Killing Something	179

II   Part Two

22	A More Honorable Path	191
23	Until the Time's End	199
24	To the North	212
25	The Fate of the Vallanir	225
26	I Will Give You Blood!	232
27	Promise	241
28	Allies and Murderers	250
29	For the Three of Us	260
30	Prayer and Hope	271

III   Part Three

31	The Next Fool	283
32	Legends	291
33	Values of Life	302
34	The Shaman's Hut	310
35	A Way Out	321
36	Behind the Waterfall	328
37	No Ordinary Man	340
38	A Better Plan	352
39	No Longer Yours	359
40	Unexpected Visitor	368
41	Family	378
42	Watch Over Her	392
43	A Gift From the Enemy	403
44	How the Gods Punish Us	413
45	Totally Stupid Boy	423
46	Nightmare	434
47	Forgiveness	443
48	Heiri Hardingir	457

IV Epilogue

49 Coming Home — 471
50 I'll Wait Forever — 477

I

Part One

1

Blacksmith's Apprentice

The town of Ortleg, 115 A.R. (115th year of the Age of the Alton Kings) or 24 N.E. (24th year after the founding of the Greater Elniri Empire)

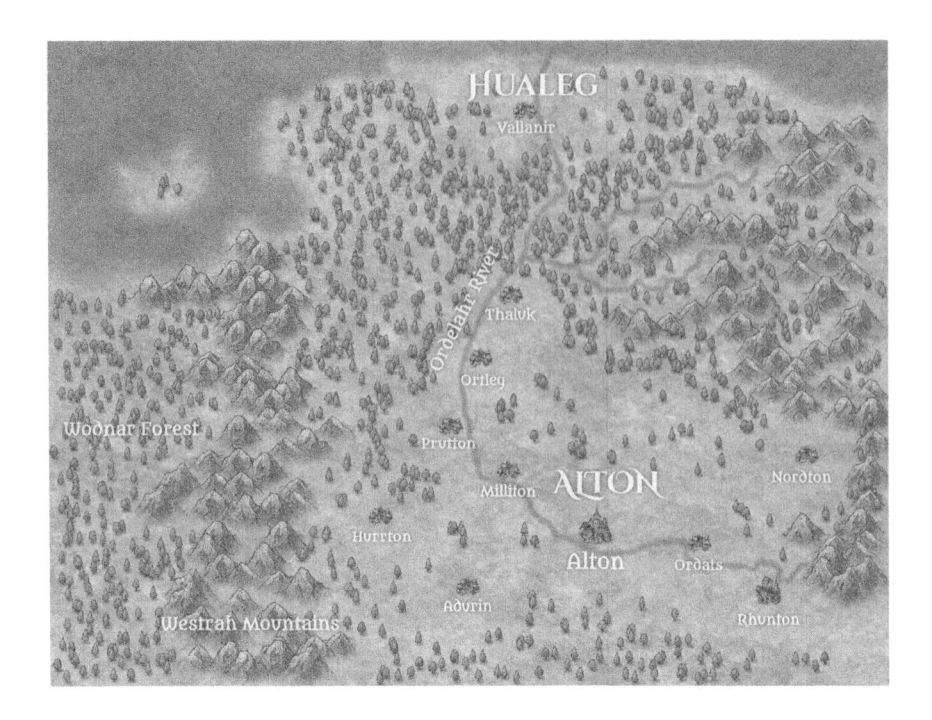

Clang. Schhinnng. Clang. The rhythm was the thing. Feel the heat radiating off the iron, even through the handle. See the orange-red glow pulse with each blow. Feel the shock travel up my arm, the satisfying *thud* as metal shaped metal. My mind wasn't exactly wandering, not like Uncle Bortez sometimes thought. It was more… buzzing. Thinking about the weight of the hammer, the way the steel resisted and then yielded, the sounds echoing off the stone walls of the workshop. It was familiar, solid work. But sometimes, under the rhythm, another beat started – a restless hum that whispered about… well, *other* things. Things beyond this heat, this metal, this village.

"William!"

Uncle Bortez's voice cut through the ringing hammer blows. I didn't stop immediately, caught in the swing, the momentum. The iron still glowed, a stubborn red. Almost there. Just a few more hits…

"William!" Louder this time. Definitely meant for me.

I let the hammer rest, the sudden silence almost deafening. I turned, wiping a bead of sweat from my brow with the back of my forearm, and tried to look like I hadn't just been miles away in my head. "Yes, Uncle?"

"The iron is still red! It's still too hard." He sighed, that familiar sound of patient exasperation I knew so well. "What a waste of energy! Reheat it if necessary. Wait for it to turn yellow. I've told you this a hundred times, haven't I? I know you like to bang things, but save your energy for more important tasks, okay?"

He was right, of course. The feel of the hammer was good, but I'd let the rhythm carry me away instead of watching the color. A sheepish grin spread across my face. "Sorry," I mumbled. It wasn't that the work itself was *bad*, just... sometimes my mind felt too full for it. "But tell me, what else is important besides work?"

Bortez looked momentarily stumped, a rare sight. "Why don't you find out for yourself? Look what your friends are doing out there!"

I glanced mentally towards the village fields and woods. "Farming, raising livestock, or gathering wood." I pictured the slow, repetitive tasks. Predictable. Safe. "All of that is good and can be exhausting, but honestly," I lowered my voice slightly, "it doesn't exactly spark much excitement, does it?"

He was quiet, then a chuckle escaped him. "Yeah, you're right about that."

A thought sparked, maybe a little mischievous. "But there are things that aren't. Spending time with the girls in the village, for example. Yeah, maybe I should do that. Uncle, can I take Muriel into town?"

Predictably, Bortez's expression clouded over as I mentioned his daughter's name. "Now that I think about it, you'd better stay here! You're more useful here."

I couldn't help but chuckle. His reaction was always the same. It made me happy for a moment, that easy banter, but then the restless feeling returned, a confusing knot in my stomach. Something felt... unfinished.

"Okay," Bortez sighed, surprising me. "That's enough for today. Time for you to rest."

"Close early?" I blinked. "What about the order from Mr.... the man in black... what's his name?"

"Mornitz? It's done." He nodded towards a shape wrapped in thick cloth in the corner. "He didn't ask for a scabbard. He said the sword was enough."

"That's too bad." I looked at the wrapped sword again. We'd both worked on it, but Bortez had done the crucial finishing. "This sword is exceptional."

"It is because the iron is exceptional and the person who worked on it is exceptional," Bortez chuckled, puffing his chest out slightly. "Maybe I'll make a scabbard for the sword as a bonus when I get back from Prutton. I don't think he'll be here for a few days."

We banked the forge fire, the oppressive heat slowly receding, and cleaned the tools, the familiar routine soothing. Outside on the patio, the air was cooler. Muriel had left spiced tea earlier, still steaming. We sat, the warmth seeping into tired muscles, easing the ache in my arms and back. Bortez watched me, his gaze steady. He always seemed to know when something was churning inside me. I opened my mouth, closed it again. How to start?

"Is there something on your mind?" he asked gently.

I took a breath. Best start with the truth I knew he'd accept. "Uncle, after my mother, you are the kindest person in the world. Your generosity to us is immeasurable. You gave me a job and taught me many things. I am very grateful to you." He was more than a mentor; sometimes, he felt almost like the father I'd never known.

He raised his eyebrows, surprised by my seriousness. I wasn't usually like this. "Because I don't have a son, William. That's why."

"Yeah. You even said you were going to give me the workshop," I chuckled, trying to lighten the mood.

"That's not something I can pass on to my daughter, is it?"

"Why not?" The question felt important. "It should be possible. I mean, yes, she's a girl and a little reckless, but she's also smart, a quick learner, strong, and always trying her best. And she's always happy to be here. You should have more confidence in your daughter. I don't understand why you always hesitate."

Bortez looked sharply at me. "Did you just talk to Muriel?"

"Everything I said was my own thoughts," I insisted, sipping the hot tea. "Besides, you should be the one talking to Muriel about this, not me. Don't you feel sorry for her?"

"What do you mean?"

"You rarely talk to her lately. You don't seem to care."

"What nonsense are you talking about?" he bristled. "I just don't want her working in the workshop like a man! She should do something... something more appropriate for her!"

"And what kind of work is that?" I pressed, maybe a little too hard. "Are there better job opportunities in this village or Ortleg for a girl like her? Maybe you just want her to stay at home and do nothing until it's time for her to get married."

"No, I don't think that way. And getting married is not that bad." He pouted, then sighed. "Um, well, I'll talk to her. Yeah, maybe she'll be able to run this workshop with you later. You know, you and Muriel are old enough, and maybe it's time for you two to get—"

"Uncle, I've been thinking," I cut in quickly, steering away from *that* particular track. It felt like the path laid out for me, the one I suddenly knew I couldn't take. I paused, gathering my courage. This was it. "I don't want to be a blacksmith for the rest of my life."

The air grew still. "What?" Bortez stared, his voice tight. "Hey, hey, wait a minute. What is this? It feels like just yesterday you said you wanted to be the best blacksmith in the world. Why? What's wrong? Come on, I think you're just bored. How about you practice making amazing swords again? Yes? I'll teach you a few more things later. Look, the forge is just the first step. The most important thing is the next step. Measuring the hardness and flexibility in every corner—"

"Yeah, yeah. Hard at the edges of the blade, flexible in the center." I knew the theory. I even enjoyed the challenge sometimes. But it wasn't *enough*.

"Well, talking is always easy, son," Bortez continued, his passion for the craft evident. "You should know that it is the art of making a good sword. Adjust the cooling appropriately so that we can get both hardness and flexibility. The grinding and the final process become easier if the previous process is successful." He loved this, sharing his knowledge. Usually, I soaked it up. But today, the restlessness was a physical ache.

"May I say a few more words, Uncle?" I interrupted gently.

He studied me, then nodded slowly. "Hmm... of course. Go ahead."

"I'm sixteen. I think I already know what I want to do with my life."

His eyes narrowed slightly. He looked concerned now. "And what is that?"

This was the leap. "Become a swordsman!" I raised my fist, the word tasting like freedom and action on my tongue.

Bortez gaped, then scoffed. "A swordsman? That's ridiculous. Do you know what kind of job that is?"

"I do. It's a job like... what Rogas does." The mercenary who swaggered through the village sometimes, full of stories and coin. "I practiced with him a lot. He said I have talent. Good enough to be a swordsman."

"A swordsman? Rogas? He's nothing more than a mercenary!" Bortez spat the word out.

"Merce... what?" The word was unfamiliar.

"Mercenaries! A group of people paid by the Alton Kingdom to fight robbers or enemy troops. Something like this also exists in the Kingdom of Tavarin, far to the south." He shook his head, disgusted. "Believe me, one day, both kingdoms will use these mercenaries to fight and kill each other, even though they may be from the same country. From the same village! I know that because I've made swords for them several times. Huh, a swordsman, he said?"

"Rogas always said that he was a swordsman," I said stubbornly. "Yeah, sort of. Besides, the pay is pretty good, you know? When he comes, he always treats people to food and drink." The money wasn't the main thing, but it didn't hurt.

"You mean being a swordsman can make you richer than being a blacksmith?" Bortez groaned. "What kind of stupid idea is that? They fight, they die, with no money." He paused, then shrugged reluctantly. "Well, they can get rich, if they're lucky, so it's possible. There's always a possibility. But to me, it's not that important."

"Which is more important: making the sword, or using it?" I asked.

"Making the sword, of course!" he snorted. "How can you use a sword if you haven't made one before?"

"What's the point of making something you don't use?" I countered.

"That's not what I meant. Being rich isn't important if it doesn't bring you anything good. Rogas came here with a lot of money, but for what? He just spent it on drinking and gambling. What a waste! Do you understand what I'm saying? Ah well, maybe you don't."

"I understand. I'm no kid." I bristled slightly. "And I don't like gambling either. But if I drink a little, it's okay, right?" I tried a grin, but the tension remained. "Uncle, do you think I am suitable for being a mercenary?"

He shook his head again, looking tired. "William, a year ago, a Tavarin merchant came and said you should become a stage performer in his country. He said you have a pleasant face and a beautiful voice. The audience would be happy to see you. Do you remember what your answer was? You said that you would think about it. But after two months, you forgot all about it. Just like now. You will soon forget what Rogas said." He leaned forward, earnest now. "To me, it's obvious that your talent is sword-making. When I was your age, I didn't understand this at all, while you've almost mastered all the techniques now. You will be great here. If you believe what I say."

His belief in me was a heavy weight. But it wasn't *my* belief. "Do you think I can't use a sword well? And become a swordsman? Or a mercenary?"

Bortez let out a long breath. "Okay, to be honest, you can. You're the strongest, most skillful boy I've ever seen. You can be whoever you want to be. I've seen you practice swordsmanship with Rogas, and if he's honest, he'll admit that you're much better than him. But you're still young, William. You will learn later about yourself, what is important and what is not, what is good and what is bad. What you want isn't always what's best for you."

I nodded, absorbing his words. He acknowledged my skill, at least. But he still didn't understand *why*. There was something else, something deeper driving this.

"There is one important thing, Uncle, that makes me want to master the sword as soon as possible."

He looked at me, suspicion returning to his eyes. "What is it?"

Here it was. The real heart of it. "I want to find my father," I said. "I need to know why he abandoned me and my mother. Or, if he's no longer alive, I need to know why. And if someone killed him, I need to kill that killer."

"Hey, hey, hey!" Bortez's eyes narrowed, his voice sharp with alarm. "What kind of talk is that? Who poisoned your mind about killing? Rogas?"

"I talked to Rogas about some things, and to other people." I shrugged. "I'll find out the rest myself."

"Don't listen to Rogas anymore! That worm, he doesn't know what he's talking about."

"But your job is to make swords," I pointed out. "You must be familiar with this killing business, right?"

"It's just a job!" he retorted fiercely. "Not that I enjoy it when my family or close friends have to deal with such things."

I shook my head, frustration rising. "Uncle, since childhood, I've always wondered who my father was and where he is now, but no one would answer. Not my mother, not even you. I always kept quiet when my friends gossiped about my father and mother. How dare they! If it wasn't for Mom's advice not to fight, I would have beaten them all. Now I'm not a kid anymore. Still, no one wants to tell me. If I end up finding out on my own, would it be wrong?"

"William," Bortez sighed. "Your mother forbade you to fight because she knew your strength would harm your friends! Besides... I think she has her reasons for not wanting to tell you about your past."

"That reason. Are you sure you don't know?" I watched him closely.

"I don't know! How many times have I told you? When you were two years old, you and your mother arrived in this village. Your mother didn't tell us where you two came from. She never spoke."

"People say I came from the north, from a distant land called Hualeg. How do they know?"

"They only guessed," Bortez said. "You know, because of your blue eyes and your big body."

"Do you think that's true?" I pressed.

"I don't know."

A grimness settled over me. "I've heard that the Hualeg people are cruel, savage, and love to kill. Do you think my father was like that?"

Bortez shook his head firmly. "They are not as bad as people say. Hundreds of years ago, it was the Hualeg people who came to build the villages here. That's why this area is called Ortleg. It's a Hualeg language that means 'red land'. Some people in this area are of Hualeg descent, mixed with Altonians. I mean, mocking those Northerners is like mocking themselves." He paused, looking at me intently. "But... William, do you really want to know about your father?"

"Every child wants to know who their father is. If you were me, you'd want to know too."

"Yeah, that's right." He conceded. "Then maybe you should ask your mother. But ask nicely!"

Ask Mom again?

"What if she still refuses to answer?"

"Yes, what if she refuses?" Bortez echoed, leaving the question hanging in the air.

I thought about it, about pushing her, about the look on her face.

I sighed. "I don't know. Maybe... I'll just accept it. I'll wait for her to explain."

"Good. You're a good boy, William." He patted my shoulder, relief clear in his expression. "Trust me, your mother knows what's best for you. She will tell you when she sees you are ready."

Ready? I *felt* ready. But maybe, for Uncle Bortez's sake, and for Mom's, I could wait. For a little while longer. The path forward still felt uncertain, but the desire for answers, for a life beyond the forge, burned stronger than ever.

2

Lessons From an Old Story

Uncle Bortez hitched up the borrowed wagon in the afternoon, loading the last of the metal tools the Prutton merchant had ordered. I watched him go, the familiar creak of the old wagon wheels fading down the southern road. I knew the way – across the Ordelahr River. He wouldn't reach Prutton until after dark.

Before leaving, he'd laid out the rest of his plan. After Prutton, he was heading further south to Milliton. Apparently, the Royal Army of Alton needed weapons – lots of them – and Uncle Bortez wasn't one to miss a potentially huge order. I remembered asking him once why he didn't just move the forge closer to Milliton, closer to the big buyers. He'd grumbled about higher taxes in the cities and insisted that good work speaks for itself, buyers would come to him even way up here. Maybe he was right.

He also thought Alton and Tavarin would be at war soon, despite the official peace. Little border clashes all the time, he said. Just a matter of time before something big happened. Or maybe it was the Elniri kingdom everyone whispered about, the one that crushed Terran to the east. Were they coming next? All this talk of war and troop movements mostly just meant more work for the forge, more coin for Bortez, as far as I was concerned. I didn't know much about war itself. If the kingdom called me up someday, I'd go, obviously. Maybe I could even learn to like it.

But thinking about war wasn't the point right now. Swinging one of

Bortez's practice swords in the empty workshop later? That was more for the satisfying weight in my hand, the whistle of the blade cutting the air. Fun. And maybe, just maybe, a little bit of warming up for finding out what really happened to my father. If he *was* dead, like Bortez hinted Mom believed.

My real questions lay north, in the past, not south towards Milliton and army contracts. So when Bortez had asked if I wanted to come along, I'd shaken my head. Staying here was much better. Because with Bortez gone for at least three days... Rogas was still in the village. And tomorrow, I could finally find him, get some *real* sword practice in, without worrying about Uncle Bortez catching me and lecturing me about wasting time or denting his practice blades. A grin spread across my face. Freedom.

I whistled cheerfully as I slid the heavy iron bars across the workshop door for the night. Just as the second bar clanged into place, a hand smacked my shoulder from behind. I spun around, annoyed at the interruption.

Muriel stood there, hands planted firmly on her hips, streaks of mud on her clothes and face. Her curly brown hair was escaping its braid, and her eyes, sharp as ever, glared at me. Honestly, she was cute, even covered in dirt. If only she didn't act like an angry badger half the time.

"What?" I asked.

"Has he left yet?" she demanded.

"An hour ago."

"Did you tell him?"

"Told him what?" I feigned innocence, though I had a sinking feeling I knew what was coming.

Her expression crumpled further. "Told him I wanted to learn how to handle swords, armor, or any of the more difficult things! The *real* work!"

I couldn't resist a grin. "Smart ass. Why would you want to do difficult work? The easier it is, the better."

"But have you told him?" she insisted, ignoring my teasing.

"Your father already knows," I said, remembering my conversation with Bortez earlier.

She shook her head vehemently. "Father won't understand unless you tell him clearly!"

"Your father knows best," I said, echoing Bortez's own words back at her, feeling rather wise for a moment. "When he sees that you are ready to accept everything, he will tell you." It felt like good advice when Bortez said it to me.

"That means you haven't told him yet!" she practically shouted.

"No need to shout."

She pouted, kicking at a loose stone. "I just want you to tell him! It's not that hard!"

"If it's not that hard, why don't you tell him yourself?" I laughed, then softened my tone. I didn't actually want her to stay mad.

"He doesn't want to hear me talk," she muttered, looking down.

"Calm down." I picked up the tray and empty cups from where we'd had tea earlier and handed them to her. "As soon as your father gets back, he'll talk to you. Maybe he'll even tell you something important."

Her head snapped up. "What's important?"

I just laughed again, enjoying her curiosity.

"Something like what?" she pressed.

"Here." I leaned in, tapping my cheek. "Kiss here first. Then I'll tell you."

"Hmmph!" Muriel growled, her eyes flashing. If her hands hadn't been full with the tray, I probably would have gotten a slap. Instead, she delivered a swift, hard kick to my shin.

"Ow!" I yelped, hopping on one foot. This time, the pain was definitely real. She spun around and marched off towards her house.

"Hey!" I called after her, rubbing my stinging shin. "Don't forget to take a bath! I know what you just did. You helped fix Master Benzo's wagon wheel, didn't you? Take a bath before dinner so you can be cute again!"

She glanced back over her shoulder and stuck her tongue out before disappearing around the corner. I burst out laughing. She really was something else.

Shaking my head, I grabbed a broom to sweep the stray leaves off the workshop porch. Mid-sweep, movement caught my eye. A man emerged from the deepening shadows at the corner of the lane, walking towards me.

He was tall, a bit taller than me even, with intense eyes under thick, dark brows. Dark hair, dark mustache, dark beard. He wore a long black coat that reached his knees, covering most of everything else. I recognized him instantly. Mornitz. The man who'd ordered the exceptional sword. Bortez had said he wouldn't be back for days. He was early.

"Good evening, sir," I said, trying to sound polite and professional, like Bortez would expect. I stopped myself from asking why he was early – his expression was sour, closed-off. Better tread carefully. "Is there anything I can help you with?"

"Don't you remember me?" he replied curtly, his voice sharp.

I swallowed my slight irritation. "I remember, sir."

"Where is Bortez?"

"My master is in Prutton. Business trip."

His eyes narrowed slightly. "Is my sword ready?"

"Yes, it is."

"Then what are you waiting for?" he snapped.

Okay, his attitude was starting to grate. A little bit of mischief sparked in me. Plus, Bortez's rule was clear. I managed a polite smile. "I'm waiting for your money, sir," I said smoothly. "May I see it before you see your sword?"

Mornitz glared at me.

I held up my hands placatingly. "I'm just delivering my master's message. First the money, then the goods."

He grunted, reaching inside his coat and pulling out a heavy leather pouch. It made a satisfying *clink* as he thrust it towards me. "Fifty sazets. Your master told you about the price, didn't he?"

"I will check it first, sir."

I took the pouch, walked over to the small table on the porch, and deliberately sat down. I tipped the coins out – a mix of silver and copper pieces. One by one, pushing them with my index finger, I counted, taking my sweet time. "One, two, three..." I could feel his impatience radiating off him, but I kept counting slowly, methodically. "...forty-eight, forty-nine, fifty."

I looked up, letting a grin spread across my face. "All right, there are fifty sazets. You have paid your payment. I thank you, sir. I will take your sword."

Scooping the coins back into the pouch, I tucked it securely into my pocket. I stood up, unlocked the bars and the workshop door again, and slipped inside. Straight to the back corner, beside the long metal-topped table. There was a small, hidden cabinet set low in the wall. I slid the panel open and dropped the pouch inside with a solid thud. Bortez always warned me – he'd once had payment stolen right off the table the moment he turned his back to fetch the goods. This Mornitz didn't seem like a common thief, but his intensity made me cautious. Better safe than sorry.

Fetching the wrapped sword, I brought it back outside and handed it to him. He unwrapped it carefully, examining every inch – the polish, the length, the balance, running a thumb cautiously near the edge, checking the engraving on the hilt. He gave a slow nod, a flicker of something that might have been satisfaction in his eyes.

"Good," he said, the word almost startling after his earlier curtness. "Your master is an expert." He actually smiled then, a brief, unexpected stretching of his lips. It changed his whole face for a second.

"Will you be staying long in Ortleg, sir?" I asked, curious now.

He shrugged, his gaze drifting past me for a moment before settling back on me. "I still have to... find some people. The kind that can fight."

"Oh. Mercenaries?" The word felt more familiar now after talking with Bortez.

"Something like that."

"For what?" The question slipped out before I could think better of it. "I mean, what would you pay them for?"

"For hunting down criminals."

"That's interesting," I said, genuinely intrigued. Tracking down bad guys sounded... exciting.

"Do you know where I can find them?" Mornitz asked, his eyes sharp again.

My mind immediately jumped to Rogas. "I know a soldier. His name is Rogas. He's in Ortleg right now." I thought of the other lads I sometimes sparred with, though none were like Rogas. Then, a bolder thought: "And I can do a little bit, too, if... um, how many men do you need?"

Mornitz looked me up and down slowly. "I only need one, the best. Better if you already know the person. Can you help me?" He reached into his coat again, but this time pulled out just two silver sazet coins, holding them out.

I stared at the coins, then at his face. Was that... for me? Just for finding someone?

"Y-yes, sir," I stammered, realizing the money *was* for me. I snatched the coins quickly, their weight solid in my palm, and stuffed them into my pocket alongside the pouch. Two whole sazets! "Of course, sir! I'll do you a favor!"

"Meet me at Horsling's Tavern in two days, after sundown. Do you know the place?"

"North of town," I confirmed immediately. Everyone knew Horsling's.

"Bring him—what's his name? Rogas? You two, meet me there. I'll give you three more if he comes with you."

Three more sazets! Just for showing up with Rogas? "Oh, we'll come, master! Don't worry about it." The words tumbled out in my excitement.

Mornitz gave another curt nod. "I will wait for you." He wrapped the sword back in its cloth, turned, and walked away, his tall figure quickly swallowed by the twilight.

I stood there for a long moment, the two sazets feeling warm in my pocket. Extra money, just like that! Mornitz wasn't just not a thief; he was generous! And his offer... hunting criminals with Rogas? Getting paid for it? It sounded like exactly the kind of action I craved.

But then reality settled back in. Bortez wouldn't be back for three days. I couldn't just take off on some mercenary job, even a short one, without his permission. He was my master, my uncle figure. And more importantly... much more importantly... there was Mom.

I couldn't leave, couldn't even think about leaving, until I talked to her. Really talked to her. Asking about my father wasn't just *a* priority; it felt like *the* priority now.

Mornitz's offer, the money, Rogas... it could wait. First, I needed answers.

Tonight. After dinner, when Mom sat by the fire with her knitting. That was the time. Her hands moved quickly, deftly, making blankets or clothes, her needles clicking softly in the quiet room. She always seemed calmest then, even though I knew the cold air sometimes made her cough, a reminder of the lung sickness the village healers couldn't fix. They said she worked too hard when she was younger, never rested. She was still beautiful, my mother, even with the grey starting to streak her long black hair, her tanned skin darker than most folk here. Strong, too. Never complained, never wanted help, turned down every man who'd ever asked to marry her after... well, after whatever happened before. Seeing her cough sometimes made my chest ache. How could I risk hurting her by digging into the past?

The last time I'd really pressed, maybe three years ago, she'd just gone quiet, that sad look in her eyes. I had to be careful.

Later, the fire crackled, casting dancing shadows. Mom's needles clicked rhythmically. I took a deep breath.

"Mother," I began, my voice quieter than I intended. "Can I ask you something? I hope it won't upset you."

She paused, her hands stilling over the yarn. She looked at me, her narrow eyes seeming to look right through me. "Have I ever been angry with you?" she asked softly.

I managed a small chuckle. "No." Never truly angry. Sad, sometimes. Worried. But not angry.

"Then you can ask me anything."

The permission hung in the air. I rushed the words out before I lost my nerve. "I want to know who my father is."

Silence. I held my breath, waiting for the deflection, the sadness, maybe even anger this time.

Instead, she smiled, a small, weary smile. "Why do you ask?"

Relief washed over me, making me slightly dizzy. "I want to know what he looks like," I said, seizing the first reason that came to mind.

"If you want to know what he looks like, look in the mirror." Her smile deepened slightly. "You'll see your father there. Your face is very much like him. Only your hair color is different. Your hair is brownish-black, while his hair is golden."

Golden hair. Like the Hualeg legends. So maybe the rumors were partly true. "Is he still alive? Or is he dead?"

This time, she closed her eyes. The silence stretched, filled only by the crackling fire. When she opened them again, the sadness was there. "He is dead."

I nodded slowly. Somehow, deep down, I think I'd expected that. It didn't lessen the hollow feeling, though. "Was he a good person?"

"He was the kindest person I have ever known." Her voice was soft but firm.

"If he was so kind a person, why are you afraid to tell me?" The question hung in the air.

She didn't answer that one.

"How did he die? And why?" I pressed gently.

She looked at me again, her gaze searching mine. "Why do you want to know?"

"Every child wants to know who his father is," I repeated the words I'd used with Bortez. They felt true.

"Yes," she acknowledged. "But after you know, what will you do?"

There it was. The heart of her fear. "Mother," I said carefully, "if you don't want to tell me now, I will accept it, but I will ask every year what happened in the past." I had to let her know this wouldn't go away. "Did my father do something wrong? Did he die because someone killed him?" I leaned forward slightly. "Because if that's the case, shouldn't I, as his son, avenge his death?"

Her breath hitched, her voice trembling when she spoke. "William, you said it yourself, the reason I didn't want to tell you. That day when I spoke to your father for the last time, he was the one who wanted us to leave and never look back. He didn't want you to know what happened. He understood that if you found out when you grew up, you would seek revenge."

He *didn't* want me to seek revenge? I stared at her, trying to process this. My father, the kindest man she knew, died – likely killed – and he forbade his own son from seeking justice? "He didn't want me to avenge his death?" I whispered. It felt wrong. Dishonorable. "Can you call me a devoted son, then?"

"Do you think your devotion will be measured by your revenge?" Her eyes, filled with a profound love and an equally profound sorrow, held mine. The question hit me like a physical blow.

"Your devotion to us is measured by your love," she said softly. "If you love your father and mother, then fulfill our request: don't look back."

"But... what happened?" The command felt impossible without understanding. "Why?"

"Your father didn't want you to know."

Frustration warred with the ache of seeing her pain. "Mother, you are the wisest person in the world, and I'm sure my father was, too. But how can I learn wisdom from you or my father if I am not allowed to know about your life experiences? Or know your happiness and sorrow?" I pleaded, leaning forward again. "You tell me not to look back, but... why should I do that if I don't know what wisdom lies in it? How can I believe in all sorts of rules and prohibitions if I don't know what troubles might befall me in the future?"

She closed her eyes again, and this time, tears escaped, tracing paths down her cheeks in the firelight. My chest tightened painfully. I hadn't wanted to make her cry.

"I really can't keep this from you," she whispered, wiping at her tears. "One day you will find out, and I don't want you to find out from anyone else. I'll tell you everything I know..." She opened her eyes, her gaze intense despite the tears. "...but you have to promise me that you won't disobey your father's orders and go back to his country for any reason. Do not go there. Just take the lessons from this story and forget the rest. Your life is still wide open before you. Can you promise that?"

I knelt quickly beside her chair, taking her hand. Her fingers felt frail. "Mother, I am a foolish son if I make you cry like this!" The words felt thick in my throat. "I promise. I promise to obey your orders and my father's.

Do not worry."

She took a shaky breath. "Then I'll start with the story of my life before I met your father. I never told him any of it..." She looked into the fire, her voice taking on a distant quality. "...My real name is Ailene, and I come from the land of Tavarin, far to the south."

And so she began. Ailene, daughter of a rich merchant in Tavar city, betrothed to a prince. A life of peace shattered by betrayal – an enemy merchant, a faithless prince, soldiers, death, escape. Fleeing north to Alton with her father, living as hidden merchants. Then, the attack in the north – Hualeg raiders. Her father killed.

"That's when your father came to the rescue," she said, her voice softening, a faint smile touching her lips. "He was also a Hualeg, but he was different. He freed me from the hands of those men. Your father's name is Vilnar..." Vilnar. The name sounded strong, strange. "...and he is the most perfect man I have ever seen in my life. Strong, brave, honorable. No one can compare to him."

She spoke of their marriage, a happy time living by the river, my birth. My birth name – Vahnar. It felt foreign on my tongue, a piece of a life I never knew. She explained changing our names to Elise and William when we came to Ortleg, for safety. Vahnar... I tucked the name away in my mind.

Then the story darkened again. The trip to Hualeg, Vilnar's homeland. His father and oldest brother dead. A feud with his other two brothers. Vilnar taking her and me away to escape the conflict. But his enemies caught up on the river. Vilnar fighting them off, ordering her to take me and flee south, promising he would follow.

"He promised me he would," she whispered, staring into the flames, "and I always believed his word. I rowed south for days until we finally reached our old house on the river. There I waited with you. For days. Weeks. Months. Until finally, I had to accept the fact that he was gone..." Her voice broke. "...and we both had to start our new lives without him. I then took you with me and arrived in Ortleg."

The story hung in the air, heavy with loss. "So that's it?" I asked quietly. "Is that all you know? Didn't you see what happened after you separated?"

A desperate spark of hope flickered. "Mother, maybe my father is still alive!"

She shook her head, the movement final, definite. "Your father is dead, William. If he wasn't, he would have caught up with us. He promised."

The hope died. An angry thought surfaced. "Who do you think were the men who attacked my father? My uncle and his men?" The ones from the feud?

Her gaze snapped towards me, sharp again. "Listen, son, it doesn't matter anymore."

"How can you say that?" The injustice burned. "Of course, it matters...."

"Then you don't understand why I'm telling you this story!" She turned away, her shoulders slumped, disappointment clear in her voice.

I froze, realizing I'd broken my promise already, pushing past the boundaries she'd set. I knelt again quickly. "I'm sorry, mother. I won't ask again." I gently touched her hand. "Believe me, you have nothing to worry about. I understand there are more important things than bringing up the past." The words felt like ash in my mouth, but I meant them for her sake. "It's just... I think I still need time to realize that knowing my father's killer isn't that important anymore."

How could it *not* be important? But her pain, and my father's last wish... it was a tangled knot I didn't know how to begin to unravel.

3

Shining Black Stone

The soft click of the latch as the door closed echoed the heavy beat of my own heart. I watched through the small window as William's silhouette disappeared into the dim light outside. Worry, a constant companion these sixteen years, tightened its grip around my chest. For a long moment, I simply sat, the half-finished knitting lying forgotten in my lap. Then, with a sigh that seemed to draw the very warmth from the room, I picked up the needles again. Their familiar click-clack, the creak of the old wooden chair, the crackle and pop of the fire – these were the sounds of my quiet life. But tonight, another sound intruded, faint but unmistakable from the yard: the *shhinnng* and *thud* of steel. William, practicing with that sword again, even now.

I didn't like that sword. Didn't like the way he spent hours with it, the almost obsessive focus in his eyes sometimes. Bortez was a good man, but had he given it to him? Or had William acquired it somehow from one of the old soldiers in the village? It didn't matter how it came to be his; it was his now. And every time he held it, it felt like a step closer to the kind of life I had desperately tried to shield him from – a life of conflict, of loss, the life Vilnar had fought to leave behind for his son.

But how could I forbid it? Forbid the sword, forbid the strength growing in him day by day? It would be like trying to forbid the tide from turning. It might hold for a moment, but eventually, nature takes its course. He was becoming a man. And perhaps... perhaps the sword had its uses. William carried so much coiled energy inside him, so many unspoken questions. Better he vent that fire against the cool night air than let it fester within, or worse, turn it on others. When he came inside later, weary from practice, the restless agitation would be gone, his breathing even, ready for sleep. It was a kind of peace, I supposed.

Yet, the unease lingered, deeper tonight than usual. Our conversation... it lay heavy on my soul. He had promised, yes, promised not to seek answers or vengeance in the north. But I knew my son. That quiet determination, once lit, burned with a steady, relentless flame. Could a promise made in the face of his mother's tears truly hold against sixteen years of unanswered questions, against the fresh, raw knowledge of his father's name and fate? The image of him journeying north, defying Vilnar's last wish, haunted the edges of my thoughts.

Guilt gnawed at me. Had I done the right thing? Telling him... unleashing that history... perhaps silence would have been the greater protection. Now the truth was out, a seed planted, and I feared the harvest. If he went north, if he broke that promise, how could I face Vilnar when my own time came?

Sleep offered no escape. I drifted, only to be jolted awake by visions of Vilnar's face, not smiling as I remembered him, but frowning, angry, his eyes accusing me of betraying his trust, of endangering our son with the past. Each time I woke, the ache in my chest felt deeper, the cough harder to suppress. I tried to muffle the sound in my blanket, praying William wouldn't hear in the next room.

It was useless. Sometime in the deep quiet of the night, the door creaked open, and William was there, his young face etched with worry in the dim firelight.

"Mother," he whispered, kneeling beside my bed, his voice thick with guilt. "I'm sorry I made you so sick!"

My breath hitched. "Please... don't say that," I managed, the words shaky. "I just... can't sleep."

"I'm going to find Master Kanlon. He has medicine..."

"No," I whispered, reaching out to touch his hand. His skin was warm, strong. "No need.... I just need you here tonight. Maybe I can sleep well... with you by my side."

He settled on the floor beside me, his presence a solid comfort in the darkness. And he was right; sleep came easier, though the dreams didn't vanish entirely. They changed.

Vilnar stood before me again, but the anger was gone, replaced by the gentle smile I remembered so vividly, the one that had captured my heart years ago. He reached out, his hand surprisingly solid, stroking my hair. *"Ailene,"* his voice was a warm echo in my mind, *"I am glad to see you again."*

Tears welled instantly. "What do you mean? Last night... you came... you were angry I told Vahnar..."

His smile deepened, full of love and reassurance. *"Those who came are not me. Guilt conjures harsh phantoms, my love. Don't believe them, don't think about them. You know I've never been angry with you and never can be."*

"I miss you..." The words were a sob. "I want to be with you."

"Ailene, we will be together again. Soon. But before that, I want you to do one important thing. Deliver my message to our son." His gaze grew serious, filled with paternal pride and hope. *"Tell him: be a man of honor who can keep his behavior in check and be a light to those around him, just like the meaning of his name, Vahnar Vallanir."* Vahnar Vallanir... the shining black stone of Vallanir. It resonated with a deep truth. *"Tell him not to hesitate to stand firm and uphold the values of truth and justice. He need not hesitate, for these values are already within him if he dares to seek them and if he always remains true to himself."*

My heart swelled with love, but fear followed. "He's still so young, Vilnar. I'm afraid he can't live up to such high expectations unless someone shows him the way."

"He will learn," Vilnar insisted gently. *"Yes, he will fall, but he will rise. That is the way he must walk. Soon he will be an adult. Ailene, you have given him the best advice, the best foundation. But the time will come when he will have to choose his own path, and we can only pray that it will be the best for him."*

I nodded, tears still flowing, but understanding dawned. "I will tell him."

"Wake up and tell him now. Tell him I love him very much and I'm proud of him."

A new fear surfaced. "When I wake up... will you leave me again?"

His smile was infinitely tender. *"I will wait for you here,"* he promised.

"Then wait for me."

I woke, not with a jolt, but with a profound sense of peace, of purpose. The crushing weight on my chest had eased. I turned my head, seeing William slumped beside the bed, asleep, his face still clouded with worry even in slumber. I gently patted his shoulder. "Wake up, William."

He stirred, blinking sleepily.

"I just met your father," I said, my voice calm and clear. "And he has a message for you."

Surprise flickered across his face, but I didn't pause. I told him everything – Vilnar's gentle appearance, his reassurance, the dismissal of the angry phantoms, the meaning of his birth name, the charge to live with honor, truth, and justice. As I spoke the words Vilnar had given me, I felt a lightness spread through me, as if sharing the message completed a final, vital task. The last vestiges of pain seemed to melt away.

When I finished, William's eyes were filled with a deep sadness. "Mother," he said, his voice low, "I wish my father could talk to me directly. I want to meet him, see what he looks like, hear what he sounds like."

"Oh, you will meet him, my Vahnar," I reassured him gently. "But later. In a long time from now." I took a soft breath, gathering my strength for the final truth. "Right now, I'm going to see him first. He's waiting for me."

His face went pale, confusion warring with dawning fear. "What... what do you mean by that, Mother?"

"William," I said softly, lying back against the pillows, feeling an immense weariness settle over me, but a peaceful one. "I'm going back to sleep." I reached up and stroked his cheek, memorizing the feel of his skin, the shape of his jaw – so like Vilnar's. "I've given you a lot of advice in my life. I will not say it again. You already know what is best for you." My voice was growing faint, but the love flowed strongly. "My love is always with you. Take good care of yourself. God bless us."

He didn't speak, couldn't speak. Tears streamed down his face, but he made no sound. I saw his love, his grief, clear as day. It needed no words. I smiled, truly at peace now. *Vilnar, I'm coming.* Silently, I said goodbye to my brave, beloved son. Then, I closed my eyes.

4

To Have Some Fun

The silence by the graveside was deep, pressing in on me even as Master Kanlon and some of the neighbors murmured condolences, their hands briefly heavy on my shoulder. I sat staring at the fresh earth, trying to pray, but the words wouldn't form. The village, the rustling leaves, the gentle breeze – it all felt distant, muffled, like I was underwater. Grief was a hollow space inside me, too vast for words. I'd barely spoken since finding Mom this morning, uttering only those two stark words to Master Kanlon: "She's gone." He'd understood, bless him, and handled everything else.

Remembering his kindness now, I looked up as he lingered. "Thank you…" The words rasped in my dry throat.

He nodded, his eyes full of a pity I couldn't yet process. "If you need anything else, let me know," he said gently. "We are all here for you."

"Yes, Master," I whispered back.

Slowly, they drifted away, leaving me alone. I sat on the ground, fingers tracing mindless patterns in the dirt. A small bird landed nearby, chirping, soon joined by another. They seemed so alive, so busy with their small concerns. Spring was bursting everywhere – green leaves, bird song, warm air. Just two days ago, I'd felt that same energy buzzing inside me, full of plans, ready to chase down answers about my father, maybe even follow Mornitz's offer. Now? It all felt like dust. Pointless.

Mom's death… it had swept in like a storm in the night, sudden and absolute. She was just... gone. And I couldn't do anything. For the first time, maybe, I truly understood there were forces stronger than my own muscles, forces that could steal everything without warning. A cold dread washed over me, followed by the sharp sting of regret. Had my questions pushed her too hard? If I hadn't insisted on knowing about Father, would she still be here, knitting by the fire tonight? The thought was a bitter poison.

My eyes felt dry, scraped raw. I'd cried from the moment I found her until the tears simply stopped coming sometime during the burial preparations. Now, there was just this strange, exhausted calm. Her last words echoed in my mind – Vilnar's message, her gentle smile, her final blessing. A different kind of ache settled in my chest, one of acceptance, perhaps.

"Mother," I whispered to the mound of earth, "take good care of yourself. You have nothing to worry about. I'm fine here."

I pushed myself to my feet, took one last look, and turned. Muriel stood a few paces away, waiting patiently. Her eyes were red-rimmed and puffy; she'd clearly shed the tears I no longer could. Her usual vibrant energy was dimmed, her hair escaping its braid. She looked like she'd been standing there a while.

"Your father isn't home yet?" I asked, though I knew Bortez wasn't due back for at least another day.

"Not yet," she confirmed, her voice trembling slightly. "He doesn't know... I'll tell him when he gets back."

I nodded, managing a faint, tight smile. It felt unnatural on my face. "Come on," I said, needing motion, needing routine. "Let's go back to the workshop."

Her swollen eyes widened. "Are you still going to work today?"

"I still have something to do," I said, needing the familiar weight of the tools, the heat of the forge, anything to fill the emptiness. "Besides, I'd rather do something..."

"You don't have to exert yourself. You can rest today."

"I'm fine," I insisted, needing her to believe it, maybe needing myself to believe it.

She nodded slowly, falling into step beside me. The few villagers still out offered quiet nods, murmurs of sympathy. I returned the nods, thanked them, kept walking.

Inside the workshop, the familiar smells of coal smoke and metal were strangely comforting. I went straight to the pile of iron pieces left over from the eastern merchant's order – some needing grinding, others still rough ingots needing the forge. Action felt better than sitting still.

Muriel, bless her, didn't just stand there looking lost. She moved to the furnace, her expression determined. "Can I...?"

"Go ahead," I said, grateful for her quiet offer to help. Watching her light the fire, her earlier enthusiasm flickered back, a tiny spark in the gloom.

"You don't mind if I try? Do you think my father will..." She hesitated, glancing towards the hammers.

"He won't know," I reassured her. "And if he finds out, he won't be upset as long as you do it right. I know him." I looked at her properly. "Can you do it?"

"Yes," she said, rolling up her sleeves with a firmness that belied her tear-stained face. She put on the face guard, the protective tarp, plugged her ears. She looked small under the gear, but when she swung that hammer, hitting the glowing iron Muriel had heated, the blows were strong, rhythmic. The clang filled the workshop. I worked the bellows, feeding the fire, the heat building around us. Sweat started to prickle my skin, Muriel's too. We exchanged brief, sweaty grins. Watching her, strong and focused, made the crushing weight on my chest ease just a little.

Clang. Clang. WHOOSH. Then, a loud *BANG BANG BANG* from the door cut through the rhythm. We both turned.

Rogas stood there, filling the doorway. Broad-shouldered, corn-colored hair and beard catching the light, his usual boisterous energy subdued, his eyes serious.

I walked over. "Rogas."

He nodded, his voice still managing to boom over the furnace roar. "William! I'm sorry! I just heard what happened. I want to offer you my condolences."

"Thank you," I said quietly.

"I heard you were looking for me yesterday," he continued. "Do you want to practice?"

Practice felt worlds away now. "I love to practice," I admitted, "but that's not what this is about." I glanced back at Muriel. She hadn't stopped hammering, but the blows seemed louder, more forceful. She definitely heard him, and I could feel her disapproval radiating even from across the room. She was probably hoping the noise would drive him away.

I gave Muriel a quick, hopefully reassuring smile, then turned back to Rogas. "Let's talk outside."

Out in the courtyard, the evening air felt cool against my heated skin. "Someone's looking for you," I said without preamble.

Rogas frowned, his expression shifting instantly from sympathetic concern to wary suspicion. It was strange how his face could change so quickly. "Who?"

"Mornitz," I said. "The man who ordered the sword? He came back. He's looking for a mercenary, someone good with a sword, to help him catch criminals."

Suspicion gave way to shrewd curiosity. "How much is he willing to pay?"

"I think it's not bad," I said, then found myself adding, "He gave me two sazets yesterday and promised three more if you agree to go with him." Why did I say that? It wasn't Rogas's business what Mornitz offered *me*. A flicker of annoyance at myself passed through me.

"What else did he say?" Rogas pressed.

"If you're interested, meet him tonight at Horsling's Tavern."

"When did he ask about it?"

"Two days ago."

"Why didn't he ask us to meet him that day?"

"Maybe he had somewhere to go. How should I know?" I shrugged, starting to feel impatient. My grief hadn't disappeared, it was just buried under the immediate task.

Rogas scratched his chin, studying me. "Well, let's see about that first. If the offer is good, I'll accept it. If not, I'll return to Alton and join the royal army again."

"Hmm... yes, good luck," I said, meaning it. Let him go chase criminals or join the army. It didn't matter to me anymore.

He raised an eyebrow. "Don't you want to meet him? Wouldn't he give you more money?"

I hesitated. The thought of chasing mercenary work felt hollow now. Mom's face, my father's message... it all pointed away from that life. "I don't," I said firmly. "I was interested at first, but now I'm not. You go, I'll stay."

"Hey," Rogas clapped a heavy hand on my shoulder. "I think you should go too. At least come with me to Horsling's Tavern and take the money from him. Three sazets! After that, you can go home. Come on now, this is good for you. A little fun!" He leaned in conspiratorially. "When someone is at their saddest, it's the perfect time to let go of the sadness and try to have some fun. Come with me, we'll relax there for a while. You'll feel better, trust me."

Just go for the money? Three sazets was a lot. It would certainly be useful now, with just me... The idea of "fun" felt wrong, alien, but maybe... maybe just getting out, getting the money, wouldn't hurt? "You want me to gamble with you, don't you?" I asked suspiciously.

Rogas roared with laughter. "You know I can help you with that! I'm an expert. But if you don't want to, you don't have to. We'll just have a drink. Agreed? I hear the drinks there are pretty good."

"I don't know," I mumbled. "I just know the place, but I've never been inside."

"Well, now's the time to find out."

A drink. The money. Get out of my own head for an hour. Maybe it wasn't such a bad idea. Maybe Mom wouldn't want me just sitting here in misery. Maybe Vilnar's message meant living, not just mourning. I nodded slowly. "Okay..."

"Good, let's go!" Rogas grinned broadly. "If we leave now, we can reach the tavern shortly after sunset."

"I'll tell Muriel first," I said, turning back towards the workshop.

"I don't think you need to tell her," Rogas started, then stopped himself with a low growl. "Okay. Hurry up. We have to leave soon so we don't get there too late."

Inside, the clanging had stopped. Muriel was pulling off her thick gloves, frowning darkly at me as I entered.

"Is the work done?" I asked, trying to sound casual.

Her frown deepened. "What's he doing here?" she asked flatly.

I sighed. "Sorry I left you to work alone."

"That's not the issue," she snapped. "I don't like him, and neither does my father. He says Rogas is a bad influence."

"I'm fine. You don't have to worry about me," I said, trying to keep my own voice calm. Bortez could be harsh sometimes. "Mornitz wants to see him. Rogas agreed to meet him at Horsling's Tavern. We'll both go there."

Muriel looked shocked. "That's the tavern north of town, isn't it? Isn't that a place for adults? If my father were here, he wouldn't let you go!"

"Well, I'm an adult," I retorted, feeling a prickle of defensiveness. "I can go wherever I want. Your father knows that. He even told me to enjoy myself outside instead of working all the time. Going to that place is a good example." I was twisting Bortez's words, but I didn't care right now.

She looked torn, clearly not buying my excuse but unsure how to argue.

"Don't worry, nothing will happen," I assured her more gently. "Your friends go out most nights too, even as far as Prutton. Maybe I'll meet them at the tavern."

"Then I'll come with you," she declared suddenly.

I stared at her. "You, come with me? What for?"

"To keep you from doing stupid things!"

"That's silly," I scoffed, feeling exasperated now. "I don't need you to take care of me."

"I'm coming with you!" she insisted, planting her hands on her hips, her earlier grief momentarily replaced by fierce determination.

"Are you serious?"

"Yes!"

I threw my hands up. Arguing felt like too much effort. "Well... whatever." I shrugged, tiredly. "Fine, as long as you don't do anything stupid. If your father finds out, he won't be happy."

Muriel stuck her tongue out, a flash of her usual self. "Well, I'm an adult too. So you don't have to worry about that either."

"I don't think so," I grumbled under my breath. "You're just a little girl, and now I have to take care of you!"

She actually laughed then, a watery sound, but a laugh nonetheless. "We'll see who takes care of whom."

5

The Right Person

Horsling's Tavern wasn't like the village alehouse. Rogas had filled me in on the walk up here, north of Ortleg into the rocky foothills where the kingdom of Alton sort of petered out. This place, surrounded by a few rough inns, was as far north as most respectable folk went. Rogas said royal soldiers rarely bothered coming out this far, which made it a popular spot for shady types heading north – bandits avoiding trouble down south, trappers emerging from the woods, merchants travelling with hired muscle. A tough crowd: risk-takers, gamblers, men who looked like they knew how to handle themselves and wouldn't hesitate to prove it.

Apparently, the only reason it wasn't total chaos was Master Horsling himself. Big fellow, Rogas said, beard down to his chest, loud laugh, but deadly in a fight. Killed plenty of troublemakers, or so the stories went. No one messed with Horsling or his tavern.

Knowing that helped a bit. Usually, I wouldn't mind a rowdy crowd; I wasn't exactly shy about sharing a bottle of wine and some loud talk myself. But tonight was different. Tonight, I had Muriel with me. The thought of Bortez finding out I'd brought his daughter – *his fifteen-year-old daughter* – to a place like this sent a wave of cold anxiety through me. What had I been thinking? And Muriel... even trying to look like a boy, there was something about her, an innocence that might stand out here like a beacon, attracting the wrong kind of attention.

I remembered Rogas's typically charming advice before we left. "If you dress like a woman looking for business," he'd said crudely, "you can't complain if they treat you like one. Dress like a sweet village girl, they'll wonder what you're doing here. Either way, trouble." Muriel had just snorted, ready to wear her usual clothes just to spite him, I think. We'd compromised: she wore my spare shirt, pants, and vest – all baggy on her – and tucked her fiery curls under a dark veil. She looked more like a skinny apprentice than anything else. I'd changed into my other set of clothes.

We'd arrived just as the sun was dipping below the hills. Inside, we found a dark corner booth, ordered some wine, and tried to look like we belonged. Or at least, like we weren't worth bothering.

After we'd nursed a bottle between the three of us (mostly Rogas and me, Muriel just sipped hers cautiously), Rogas started getting restless. "Where is this man?" he grumbled, wiping his mouth. "We've been here long enough. Sun's practically gone."

I scanned the room again. It was filling up. Maybe twenty, twenty-five people now. Loud laughter from a card game in one corner, where a couple of girls in low-cut dresses leaned over the players' shoulders. Men at tables talking low, others drinking heavily, smoke curling towards the rafters. No sign of Mornitz's tall, dark figure.

I shrugged, trying to appear unconcerned. "Maybe he'll show up soon."

"If he doesn't, I'm leaving," Rogas declared. "Forget this. Tomorrow, I head back to Alton. Find a proper place to stay first, though. Maybe find a girl to share it with." He shot a leering grin straight at Muriel. "Actually, maybe *you'd* like to come with me? Might enjoy yourself."

Muriel, who'd been unnaturally quiet, stiffened. Her face flushed crimson. Her hand tightened on her cup, and for a second, I thought she was going to throw the contents right in his face. I grabbed her wrist just in time.

"Hey," I said quickly, keeping my voice low, acutely aware of nearby tables turning quiet. "Don't listen to him. Rogas is a jerk, but he's just kidding."

"That's true," Rogas nodded, oblivious or uncaring of the tension. "You can make fun of me too if you want. Jokes like that are normal here." He grinned again, showing too many teeth. "Besides, I know you'd rather be with William, right?"

"Not a good joke, Rogas." My own anger flared. I grabbed the front of his rough-spun shirt. I could hit him. Easily. We might tear the place apart, but maybe he deserved it. But no... not here. Not with Muriel. He was just being an idiot, albeit a dangerous one when drunk.

Muriel, though, couldn't brush it off. Her face was scarlet, humiliation warring with fury. When my eyes met hers, she looked away quickly, staring hard at the tabletop.

I tightened my grip on Rogas's shirt. "Time to apologize."

He blinked, the grin fading slightly. "Um, yeah." He managed to look almost remorseful for a second. "Muriel, I'm sorry. Really sorry...."

I didn't believe him for a second. Men like Rogas needed a punch now and then to remind them of boundaries. Later, perhaps. Definitely not here.

Muriel turned her burning gaze on me, her jaw tight. "I want to go home."

"Now? Are you sure?" I asked, feeling a surge of relief. Yes, leaving early sounded like the best idea I'd heard all night.

"I like watching people play cards," she said stiffly, pointedly not looking at Rogas, "but I don't like sitting with losers like him."

"Hey," Rogas grinned, recovering quickly. "I already apologized."

"Shut up, Rogas," I snarled, letting go of his shirt. I turned back to Muriel. "Okay, if that's what you want, let's go."

"Hold on," Rogas protested. "Mornitz isn't here yet. How am I supposed to know who he is if you're gone?"

"It's your fault for causing trouble," I shot back. "You could ask Master Horsling. Describe him."

"Yeah, I can do that, but..."

"Shut up. There he is," I interrupted, spotting a tall, dark-coated figure pushing through the tavern door.

Mornitz exchanged a brief word with Master Horsling at the bar, ordered a drink, then scanned the room, his gaze sweeping past our corner without pausing, careful not to draw attention.

I almost called out, but Rogas clamped a hand on my arm. "What?" I demanded, shaking it off.

"Let me see him first," Rogas muttered, his eyes suddenly sharp, focused. That mercenary instinct, smelling potential profit, kicked in. "I don't want to deal with anyone who can't pay."

Greedy and arrogant, I thought, keeping the words under my breath. We watched as Mornitz found an empty table across the room and sat down, his face devoid of its earlier, unsettling smile. What was Rogas waiting for? My impatience grew.

A serving girl brought two large bottles of wine to Mornitz's table. Rogas let out a low chuckle. "He has good taste and money. Okay," he nodded at me. "You can go over there. I'll follow you."

Being ordered around by Rogas grated on me, but fine. Anything to get this over with. I stood up, squeezed past chairs and noisy drinkers, and navigated my way to Mornitz's table.

He looked up as I approached, his eyes narrowed. "Did you bring your friend?" he asked, his voice flat.

"Yes, he's in—"

Before I could finish, Rogas materialized beside me, sticking out a hand towards Mornitz with a broad, confident smile. "I understand you need help, sir?" He didn't wait for an invitation, pulling out a chair and sitting down.

Mornitz eyed him up and down, suspicion clear on his face, but gave a curt nod. "Only from the right person."

"I am the right person," Rogas declared, launching straight into a speech about his supposed heroic exploits with the royal army, laying it on thick. Mornitz listened impassively, his gaze unwavering. I just stood there awkwardly, completely ignored. I glanced back towards our booth – Muriel had stood up and was waving me over, frowning.

"Sir, I have to go," I cut in, needing to get out of there, needing to get Muriel home.

Mornitz gave another brief nod, still without a smile. Rogas grimaced slightly but managed a dismissive, "Thanks, William. I'll see you later."

As I turned away, Rogas was already continuing his tale, boasting about tracking down criminals in the South, practically claiming he'd single-handedly cleaned up the whole region. *Nonsense,* I thought, shaking my head as I pushed my way back through the crowd.

Outside, the cool night air was a relief after the smoke, noise, and stale alcohol smell. Muriel was waiting by the door. We started walking down the torchlit cobblestone path winding away from the tavern. Moonlight silvered the rocks, making the night feel less oppressive.

"You look upset," Muriel observed after a few moments of silence.

I sighed. "No, I'm not. Well, maybe a little."

"Why?"

The image of Mom's peaceful face flashed in my mind, followed by the sting of regret. "I just keep thinking about my mother."

Muriel's expression softened. "I think she's at peace now, happy in heaven."

"I know." I tried to return her gentle smile, but the sadness was a heavy cloak I couldn't just shrug off.

"If you're still sad," she asked, her tone shifting slightly, "why did you go to a place like that?"

"Rogas said when you're sad, you should have fun to feel better later."

She looked at me skeptically. "Do you feel better now?"

"Not really," I admitted.

"I told you Rogas was annoying and had a bad influence on you, but you didn't listen!"

A small chuckle escaped me. She sounded so much like Bortez sometimes. "Yeah, you're right. If I see him again, I might just kick his butt."

"Great! I'll join you!" Muriel raised a small fist, a spark of her usual fire returning, and we both laughed, breaking the tension a little.

"What did you want with the man in the black robe?" she asked after a moment.

"Mornitz? He's looking for mercenaries, and Rogas was interested." I hesitated, then added, "At first, I wanted to join him, too."

Her brow furrowed. "Why?"

"I wanted to see more of the world," I said vaguely. It felt true, but less urgent now. "But Mornitz only needs one person."

"And your work at the workshop?"

"I won't work in the workshop forever, Muriel." The words came out before I could stop them, sounding more definite than I felt. I looked at her earnest face in the moonlight. "One day, I'll leave."

She stopped walking, staring at me, shocked. "You mean you're going to leave us? Leave me and my father?"

"There are so many things I want to do," I tried to explain, feeling awkward. "I've told you. I want to see other places, other countries. They all sound interesting." I attempted a laugh. "But not now."

She wasn't laughing. "If you go..." she hesitated, chewing on her lip, "... can I come with you?"

"That's not possible," I said quickly. "Your father would kill me first."

"Yes, but when I grow up, I will!" she insisted.

"Your father needs you here," I reminded her gently. "Do you want to leave him?"

"We both need you here," she retorted, her voice catching slightly, "but you still want to leave!"

We walked on in silence for a minute, the unspoken things heavy between us. "Let's talk about something else," I said finally.

"Anyway," Muriel changed the subject readily enough, "I'm glad you didn't go with Rogas. I have a bad feeling about him."

I laughed lightly. "Why? If I got some money, I'd share it with you."

"I don't want your money!" she scoffed.

"At least I should get those three pieces," I mused aloud, remembering Rogas's persuasion.

"What three pieces?"

"Mornitz promised me three sazets if I brought Rogas to him."

Her eyes widened. "And he didn't give them to you?"

"No." Thinking back, he hadn't even looked at me when I left.

"Why didn't you ask him?"

"I don't know." I shrugged. "Maybe he forgot." Did he forget? Or did he just dismiss me once Rogas showed up? "Never mind, I don't need the money."

"Three sazets is a lot!" she protested.

I grinned, trying to lighten the mood again. "True. We could use it to book a room here."

Muriel growled and smacked my arm, hard. I winced, then laughed.

"But you're right," I stopped walking, the humor fading as her earlier words hit me. *Why didn't you ask him?* "Why *didn't* I ask him?"

"Exactly!" she said triumphantly.

"The money is rightfully mine!" Anger, clean and sharp, cut through the grief and confusion for a moment. He used me to get to Rogas and then dismissed me.

"Yes!" Muriel agreed fiercely.

"All right, then I'll go back and ask Mornitz for it." Without thinking further, I turned around.

"What?" Muriel looked horrified, grabbing my arm. "You're going back there? No! Next time, just speak your mind. Don't hesitate! That's all!"

"I'll go," I insisted, shaking off her hand. The injustice felt suddenly important. "We're still near the tavern. What's the problem? You don't want to come?"

"Oh, of course, I'm coming!" she declared, letting go and planting her hands back on her hips, her worry quickly morphing back into determination. "Again, so you won't do anything stupid."

6

Always Look Back

We turned, heading back north towards Horsling's Tavern, almost running now. My breath came in short bursts, driven by a sudden urgency. What if Mornitz and Rogas had already finished their business and left? Three sazets was three sazets, rightfully mine.

Reaching the cluster of buildings around the tavern, I told Muriel, "Wait here. Stay out of sight, maybe around that corner." To my relief, she nodded immediately, clearly having no desire to step back into that noisy, smoke-filled room.

Inside, the tavern was quieter than before. Only a few patrons remained, talking in low voices. My eyes scanned the room – no sign of Mornitz or Rogas. Damn it. Had I missed them? Unsure what to do next, I started to turn back, and my gaze met the steady eyes of Master Horsling behind the bar. He smiled, a knowing look on his rugged face.

Maybe *he* knew. I walked up to the bar.

Before I could ask, Horsling spoke, his voice a low rumble. "Your two friends just left. Saw them heading toward the river." He leaned forward slightly. "If you run, you may catch up with them. But be careful, boy. It can be dangerous out there at night." He paused, his eyes searching mine. "Do you have anything with you to defend yourself?"

I felt a chill despite the warm tavern air. "What do you mean, sir?"

"A sword, a knife, or something else?"

"No," I shook my head, confusion quickly turning to a prickle of fear. "I didn't bring anything." Why was he asking this?

"Then take this." He reached under the heavy wooden counter and produced a long dagger in a worn leather sheath. It was wickedly sharp-looking, nearly the length of my forearm. He laid it flat on the bar between us.

I stared at it, then back at his face. "You... want to lend it to me?"

"Yes."

"Just like that?" I couldn't quite believe it.

"Give it back when your business is done," he said, smiling faintly and giving his thick mustache a thoughtful twirl.

My hand hovered near the dagger, but I didn't touch it. "But... why should I take it?" My voice sounded thin. "Is something going to happen?"

He shrugged, a casual movement that didn't match the intensity in his eyes. "It's been a long time since anyone dared to cause trouble right around here. But time passes. Who knows, someday someone might try something foolish. It's better to be prepared."

"But... if it's dangerous, why didn't you suggest I just leave? Why give me the dagger?" It didn't make sense.

"Well," he leaned closer again, his voice dropping to a whisper, "you can go home and be safe. But sometimes... sometimes you should do something strange and unexpected, especially when you're young. It helps you learn more about yourself and discover paths you never knew existed."

Paths I never knew existed? What was he talking about? His gaze held mine for a long moment, something unreadable in their depths. Then he leaned back, smiling again. "So, what are you going to do? Are you going to take it?"

My heart hammered against my ribs. Fear clenched my gut – I wasn't a soldier, I'd never faced real danger. But beneath the fear, a spark of something else ignited – curiosity. *Learn more about yourself... discover paths...* Wasn't that what I wanted? Wasn't that why the thought of leaving Ortleg felt so strong? Maybe this... maybe this was part of it.

Taking a shaky breath, I reached out and closed my hand around the cool leather grip of the dagger. The weight felt solid, dangerous, real. "I... I will return the dagger later."

Master Horsling's smile widened slightly. "Calm down, boy. Maybe nothing bad will happen. But it's always good to be cautious." He paused, his eyes serious again. "And remember, don't act rashly. Always look back."

I froze. *Always look back?* But Father's message, through Mom... it was *never* look back. The contradiction jolted me. "Y-yes, sir," I stammered, tucking the sheathed dagger under my vest, hidden but heavy against my side.

"Go now," he urged. "Before it's too late."

Before it was too late? What did that mean? I left the tavern, my mind reeling, fear and a strange, reckless curiosity churning inside me.

A soft whistle cut through the night. Muriel emerged from the shadows of a side alley, tiptoeing towards me, a hopeful grin on her face. "Did you get the money?"

The three sazets felt utterly unimportant now. I shook my head, glancing nervously down the dark path leading west towards the river. "Rogas and Mornitz are gone, heading that way. But I will go after them. Maybe I can get my money there." It sounded like a weak excuse even to my own ears.

Muriel looked confused. "Go after them? Is that really necessary?" Her eyes dropped to the bulge under my vest where the dagger was hidden, then flew wide with alarm. "What's that? Why are you carrying a dagger?"

"Just in case. For protection," I mumbled, adjusting my vest, feeling caught out. "Don't ask too many questions, okay? Look," I lowered my voice, trying to sound firm, responsible, "it could be dangerous. Master Horsling seemed to think so. That's why I think it's better if you go home now. Let me go alone."

Her eyes widened further, fear replacing confusion. "If it's really dangerous, you'd better not go! What's the point? Three sazets isn't worth getting hurt! Come on! Let's just go home!"

"I have to go." The words felt true, even if I didn't fully understand why. Horsling's words, the sense of... something happening... I couldn't just walk away.

"Why?" she pleaded.

"I can't explain it yet. I'll explain it later." I met her worried gaze. "Go home, Muriel. I'll see you later." I hesitated. "I mean... you dare to go home alone, don't you? Don't worry, the streets closer to town are still safe, there are still people about. You'll be fine."

She didn't answer, just stared at me, her face a mask of confusion and hurt. But I didn't have time. I wasn't even sure what I felt myself – fear or foolish curiosity?

"Be careful," I said abruptly. It was meant for her, but as I turned and broke into a run, heading west along the dark, grassy path towards the river, I knew the warning was really for me.

The path followed the foothills, dipping towards the sound of water. I moved as quickly and quietly as I could, the borrowed dagger bumping against my ribs, my heart pounding a frantic rhythm. *Before it was too late.* Horsling's words echoed. Did he know something? Or was he setting me up? Why lend me a weapon if he meant me harm? It made no sense. Why would I even matter to him?

The murmur of the river grew louder. I slowed, crouching behind a thick bush at the edge of the tree line. Peering through the leaves, I saw them. Two figures standing on the riverbank, maybe fifty paces away. Moonlight struggled through the clouds, making shapes indistinct, but the builds looked right. Tall and dark-coated on the left – Mornitz. Broader, heavier on the right – Rogas. They were just standing there, looking out at the dark water. What were they doing?

I needed a better view. Staying low, I slipped between the massive trunks of ancient trees, edging closer. Yes, definitely them. Then I saw it – two pinpricks of light out on the river, growing steadily larger. Boats. Two boats, each with two figures huddled inside, rowing towards the bank.

"They're here," Mornitz's voice carried clearly in the night air.

"Wait a minute," Rogas suddenly sounded tense. "Can you explain to me again what your plan is, Mornitz? I don't understand why we need to take a boat across the river at this hour."

"The person we're after got away from us," Mornitz replied, his voice rougher now. "We have to hurry and catch up with him before it's too late."

Before it's too late. There it was again. My blood ran cold. Was *this* what Horsling meant? Did he want me to join them? Cross the river on some dangerous chase? Hunting someone? My hand instinctively went to the dagger hilt. Six of them chasing one person... seven, if I joined. This target must be dangerous.

Fear tightened its grip, but then that strange curiosity surged again, stronger this time, mixed with a reckless flicker of enthusiasm. *A defining moment.* Was this it? The unexpected path Horsling talked about? I was sixteen, my mother was gone... wasn't it time I decided things for myself? Maybe this danger was exactly what I needed to face to learn who I really was.

I nodded in the darkness, trying to convince myself. Okay. I'd step out, approach Mornitz, ask to join. I had the dagger. I knew how to handle myself. Supplies... I hadn't thought about supplies. Hopefully, it wouldn't be a long trip.

I took a breath, ready to move, but froze as Rogas suddenly spun, his sword flashing out, the point instantly at Mornitz's throat. The black-robed man gasped, stumbling back a step.

"Hey, you there!" Rogas bellowed towards the river. "Stop! Don't come here! Or I'll cut his throat right now!"

Silence fell, broken only by the lapping water. The men in the boats stopped rowing, their hands dropping to their sides, near their own swords. The boats began to drift slowly downstream.

Rogas let out a harsh chuckle, pressing the sword tip harder against Mornitz's neck. "Do you think you can fool me so easily?"

"I don't know what you mean," Mornitz replied, his voice surprisingly calm now, controlled.

"You want to take me across the river, right? Ha! No, my friend." Rogas shook his head. "I knew you wanted to trap me. Take me to a deserted place and then kill me! With the help of your men on the boat! You son of a bitch. I'm not that stupid."

"You're delirious," Mornitz scoffed. "Threatening people who can make you rich? That's foolishness number one. Thinking you can beat the five of us? Foolishness number two. You'll be dead soon if you keep this up. Put your sword away. Let's talk."

"Don't lie again!" Rogas snarled. "I know the man in that boat! He's the one who tried to kill me in the south! Do you think a thick beard can hide the scars on his face?" He yelled out towards the river, "Fool! I recognize you, you son of a bitch!" He turned back to Mornitz. "And you..."

He never finished. Mornitz moved with startling speed, twisting away from the sword point, his black cloak swirling. In the same motion, a blade appeared in his hand – Bortez's sword, the one I'd delivered just days ago – its tip clashing against Rogas's steel.

Mornitz grinned, a cold, predatory expression. "Okay, you're not stupid." He laughed softly. "But you're a dead man. You will die if you dare to fight us. Better you just surrender."

"You dog! Bastard!" Rogas spat, looking genuinely nervous now. "Bastards like you can't be trusted!"

Mornitz shook his head slowly. "Master Bellion wanted to see you alive when you were brought to him. He himself wanted to dismember your body. Of course... if you die here, he wouldn't mind."

"I will kill you first!" Rogas roared, lunging forward, swinging his sword with raw fury.

Mornitz parried easily. Rogas attacked again, a desperate flurry of blows, fast and powerful, but wild. Mornitz met each strike calmly, his defense flawless, waiting for an opening.

My heart leaped into my throat. I stood frozen twenty paces away, hidden, trembling. Rogas was my friend, whatever his flaws. I didn't know who Master Bellion was or why they wanted Rogas dead, but I couldn't just watch him get killed. I gripped the dagger, its handle slick with sweat, preparing to rush Mornitz from behind.

Then Horsling's words echoed: *"Don't act rashly. Always look back."*

Instinctively, I glanced back the way I'd come. And my blood turned to ice. Huddled behind the thick trunk of a nearby tree, eyes wide with terror, was Muriel.

Muriel?! Why is she here? Didn't I tell her to go home?

For a paralyzing moment, I couldn't move, couldn't think. Anger warred with absolute terror for her. I glared, trying to convey my fury and fear across the distance without shouting, without giving us away. Why couldn't she listen, just once?

My fear spiked as I saw the two boats, having drifted closer, now turning back towards the bank – right near where Muriel was hiding. If those men were halfway alert...

The moonlight broke through the clouds then, stark and bright. I frantically waved my hand, low to the ground, trying to signal Muriel to run towards *me*, away from the river. Her face was pale, eyes huge in the sudden light. She saw the danger, saw the boats nearing, and started to crouch, ready to run.

Too late. A man stepping out of the nearest boat – bearded, a jagged scar slashing one cheek – spotted the movement. He shouted, pointing directly at Muriel. His three companions instantly looked her way.

Scarface barked an order. He and another man turned back towards the fight between Rogas and Mornitz, while the remaining two started walking directly towards Muriel's hiding place.

A curse ripped through me. No time to think. I exploded from my hiding spot, slipping through the undergrowth, reaching Muriel in seconds and shoving past her, straight towards the two approaching bandits.

They were surprised to see me burst out of the darkness. One fumbled for his sword. Before he could draw, Horsling's dagger was in my hand, driving hard into his right hip, slicing clean through. He screamed, blood spraying hot in the cold air.

The second bandit reacted faster, swinging his sword wildly. I dropped low, the blade whistling over my head. Coming up, I lunged, stabbing upwards with all my strength. The dagger punched deep into his stomach. He cried out, stumbling back. I ripped the blade free, shoving him backwards onto his already downed companion. They lay tangled together, gasping, blood pooling around them.

Beside me, Muriel was crouched low, trembling violently. I stood over the fallen men, the bloodied dagger heavy in my hand, staring down at it. My breath hitched. I'd practiced swordplay for years, knew that being a soldier, a mercenary, meant spilling blood, maybe killing. I'd heard Rogas's stories – sometimes thrilling, sometimes horrifying. Listening had always brought that strange mix of excitement and fear.

Now, I felt it tenfold. Relief that *I* wasn't the one bleeding on the ground. Horror that *my* hands had done this. I'd known, the moment Horsling offered the dagger, that violence was coming. That I might hurt someone, kill someone. Or be killed myself. But knowing it and *doing* it...

The fight wasn't over. Nearby, Rogas was still battling Mornitz, but now the other two bandits, including Scarface, were closing in, backing him towards the cliff face. He was trapped. Cornered.

No more time for shock. No more time for wondering why. Help Rogas. Now. Before it was too late. Before I regretted standing here clutching a bloody dagger while my friend died.

7

Chaos by the River

The world narrowed to the frantic pounding in my chest and the slick feel of the dagger grip in my left hand. My right snatched the fallen bandit's sword from the ground – heavier than Bortez's practice blades, but balanced enough. I forced myself to ignore the awful, wet groaning sounds behind me, forced myself not to look towards the bush where Muriel was crying. No time. Only the fight ahead.

I ran towards Rogas, who was desperately holding off Mornitz and Scarface. Fear was a cold knot in my gut, but I tried to smother it, tried to conjure anger instead. Anger felt useful. Anger felt hot, sharp, something that could let me do what needed to be done without flinching. Was it truly anger? I wasn't sure. It felt foreign, ugly. But if it meant surviving, if it meant being cruel enough, I'd take it over the paralyzing fear.

This wouldn't be easy. They'd seen me take down two men already; they'd be cautious. The third bandit – the one who hadn't gone after Muriel – stepped forward to meet my charge, Scarface and Mornitz focusing on penning in Rogas near the cliff edge.

He cursed, swinging wildly. I met his blade with a jarring clang, channeling all my strength, all my years of hammering iron, into the blow. I didn't give him space to think, moving fast, violently, swinging again and again, forcing him back. My sheer explosive force seemed to surprise him; he stumbled slightly. That was the opening. My left hand, still holding

Horsling's dagger, darted out like a snake, slashing across his waist as he tried to regain his footing.

He yelped, trying to twist away, but his foot caught on a broken root hidden in the grass. He crashed backwards. Before he could even try to get up, the tip of the sword in my right hand punched through his stomach, grating against bone as it went clear through his back. A choked, muffled scream escaped him, his eyes bulged, his body spasming horribly before going still.

Three down. The sight of the blood, the finality of it... it barely registered this time. A terrifying numbness was creeping in.

I turned towards the remaining fight. Scarface looked desperate now, seeing his last companion fall, realizing he and Mornitz hadn't managed to finish Rogas quickly. When he saw me approaching, blade dripping, he raised his own sword, raw panic flashing in his eyes.

"Bastard!" he shrieked, his voice cracking. "You son of a devil! Who the hell are you? What are you doing here? We have nothing to do with you!"

I swallowed hard, my own heart threatening to leap out of my chest. I opened my mouth and roared – a raw, wordless sound torn from my lungs – swinging the sword in a wide arc as I advanced. It worked; he flinched back, momentarily terrified. Inside, I was shaking. *Don't show fear. Don't be careless. Don't blink.*

Mornitz, keeping Rogas pinned with his superior swordsmanship, glanced over. "Fool!" he snapped at Scarface. "He is only a kid! You have nothing to fear! Kill him! Quickly!" His cold eyes flickered towards me, and I felt a jolt, remembering I'd almost *joined* this man, thought him generous. *Generous?* He was a monster. The two sazets felt like blood money now, meaningless if I died here.

I leveled the sword, bracing myself. Two against two now. Rogas let out a harsh, barking laugh.

"Wow, your friend seems scared, Mornitz!" Rogas taunted, breathing heavily but grinning savagely. "Don't you feel sorry for him? Going to keep making him fight? How about just giving up? Instead of dying here!"

Mornitz ignored him, focusing on Scarface again. "Hey! What are you waiting for? Attack the boy! Don't you want revenge for the death of your friends?"

That did it. Scarface let out a long, ragged cry and charged, fueled by fury and fear. His sword swing was powerful, heavy. This one was tougher than the others. I felt the force of his blow vibrate up my arms. I dropped the dagger – useless in this kind of exchange – and gripped my sword hilt with both hands, meeting his frenzy with focused defense.

The clang of steel on steel filled the night air, loud, rhythmic – almost like the sound of the forge back home. That familiarity settled something in me, allowing me to move without hesitation, grimly focused. My sword became an extension of my will, whirling, blocking, pushing him back, step by relentless step, towards the dark, murmuring river.

He grew wilder, angrier, his movements becoming sloppy as panic set in. Slashes, thrusts – I parried them all, countering with heavy, hammering blows that drove him off balance. He gasped for breath, desperation in his eyes, forcing one last, badly aimed strike. I knocked his sword wide, sending him staggering. Seizing the moment, I brought my sword down hard across his upper back.

He roared in pain, twisting, trying to swing back even as he stumbled. I dodged easily and slashed again, low this time. My blade tore through his right thigh. He collapsed to his knees with a sickening sound, blood gushing, his sword clattering to the ground. A swift kick to his chest sent him rolling onto the grass, helpless, moaning.

I stood over him, chest heaving, the adrenaline surge leaving me trembling. My mind screamed to finish it – chop off his head, like Rogas would, like the stories told. End the threat. But looking down at the man, broken and bleeding at my feet... I couldn't. The raw anger faded, replaced by a sickening wave of pity, of confusion. Why should I kill him now? Was he truly my enemy, or just a pawn in someone else's game? Even if he was an enemy... did that mean I had to kill him like this? My hand tightened on the sword hilt, then loosened. I couldn't do it.

"William!" Rogas shouted, his voice sharp with pain and urgency.

I spun around. Rogas was grimacing, clutching his thigh – Mornitz must have wounded him during my fight with Scarface. He pointed frantically towards the river with his sword.

"Mornitz! He's escaping!"

I saw him – the black-robed figure scrambling into one of the boats, pushing off from the bank, grabbing the oars. He looked back, and even across the widening gap of dark water, I felt the pure hatred in his gaze directed straight at me.

Then, a bolt of panic – Muriel! She was near the boats! Where was she?

A flash of movement – she appeared from behind a willow tree, pale and shaking, running towards me. Thank God.

"After him, William!" Rogas yelled, hobbling a step before groaning in frustration. "Take the other boat! Don't let him get away!" He clearly couldn't run, couldn't pursue Mornitz himself.

"W-why?" The question stumbled out. My mind was reeling. "Why should I chase him? All that matters is that he's gone, and we're safe!"

"Safe? We're safe?" Rogas struggled upright, leaning heavily on his sword, his face contorted in a painful sneer. He limped towards me, stopping beside the still-moaning Scarface. "Are you stupid or what?" Without warning, he raised his sword high and brought it down viciously, silencing the injured man forever.

Muriel cried out, covering her face. I stared, shocked speechless by the casual brutality.

Rogas glared at me, his eyes hard. "They are your enemies! *That* is why you must hunt Mornitz! And not only that! If you get the chance, kill him!"

I shook my head, horrified. "But... he, Mornitz... he is a dangerous man! I don't think I can catch him and—"

"He's afraid!" Rogas interrupted fiercely. "He's afraid of *you*, William! Mornitz saw you beat those people! It's not you who should be afraid, it's him! He's scared, and he's a coward! He's not as tough as you think he is. Go after him!" His eyes blazed. Seeing my hesitation, his voice dropped, almost pleading, "Kill him..."

My jaw tightened. "No." The word felt solid, absolute. "He is not my enemy, and I am not his enemy. You are his enemy! He's after you for reasons unknown to me, and I don't want to know. I have nothing to do with any of this!"

Rogas stared at me as if I'd lost my mind. "Nothing to do with it? God, you're an idiot!"

"I'm just helping you! That's all!"

"Yes, you helped me. Thank you!" Rogas's voice dripped with sarcasm. "But do you think you can go home after this, live in peace, and pretend none of this ever happened? You and that girl think that?"

I looked at Muriel. She was watching us, her face white with fear. Rogas was right. A cold dread seeped into me. Killing four men... could I really just walk away?

Rogas shook his head, spitting on the ground in irritation. "Since tonight, Mornitz considers *you* an enemy. Thanks to your stupidity, he survived. One day he'll come looking for you, to your house, and bring more people with him. And do you think he'll just come to visit or order a sword? No, he won't! He will come to kill you! Don't you understand?" He leaned closer, his voice low and urgent. "The only way if you want to survive is to leave the city. Disappear for who knows how long until he finally forgets about you or doesn't care about you anymore!"

Leave Ortleg? Disappear? My mind spun. Was that the only way? Beside me, Muriel let out a small sob.

Rogas noticed, rounding on her. "Hey, are you crying because of William? Don't worry about him." His tone was harsh. "Don't you understand? You have problems too! If you go back to your house, Mornitz will find you one day. Maybe he'll kill you as well."

Muriel gasped, her eyes wide with terror.

Anger surged through me again. "Muriel has nothing to do with this! Why is she becoming a target?"

"What can you do?" Rogas replied with a cynical smile. "If Mornitz recognizes her face tonight, she'll be in danger!"

I spun towards Muriel. "Did... did Mornitz see you? Muriel! Did he see you?"

She looked wildly uncertain. "No..." Her lips trembled. "I... I don't think so. He didn't see me..."

"Are you sure?" I pressed desperately.

"It was dark..." She didn't sound convinced. "When he ran past me, I must have still been hiding. I... yes... I think so. He didn't see me!"

A sliver of relief, but it didn't last. The fear remained – for her, for Bortez, for myself. What if Mornitz *had* seen her? What if he came back? I could fight, maybe, but Muriel...

Rogas watched us, his expression unreadable. "If you think Muriel will be all right, that's up to you. But I have warned you. Yes, I hope she survives! Let the girl go home and forget about it. Right, Muriel?"

She stared back at him, silent, defiance warring with fear in her eyes.

Rogas ignored her. "Now, while she's home, we should leave right away, William, as far away as we can. And I mean right now. I'm sure Mornitz won't take me for granted anymore. He'll come with more men. We must be careful."

"Go... go where?" I felt completely lost, adrift.

"Hmm. Let me think about it..."

"To the south?" The idea felt desperate, grasping at straws. "The Royal Army..."

Rogas cut me off with a look of astonishment. "South? No, you won't. That's a bad idea. Before we reach the capital, they'll intercept us at Milliton."

"By Mornitz?"

"It's safer to go north. For now."

"North?" The word echoed strangely. North. Hualeg. My father's land. Mom's warning: *Do not go there*. What would happen if I disobeyed?

"Get the boat ready, William," Rogas ordered, pointing towards the remaining vessel bobbing near the bank. "We will set out."

"By boat?"

"Yes, by boat, of course!" he snapped, gesturing at his bleeding leg. "Do you think I can walk? Fool."

That was it. Fool? After everything? Something inside me snapped. I swung, my fist connecting hard with Rogas's jaw.

He staggered back, clutching his face, blood trickling from his nose. He stared at me, stunned disbelief in his eyes. "Why... why did you hit me?" he sputtered.

"Damn your injuries, asshole!" I yelled, trembling with fury. "You're lucky I only hit your face and didn't step on the wound on your leg! You caused all this trouble! Instead of apologizing, you kept bothering Muriel and me with your annoying words!"

"But... but you were also wrong!" he protested, sounding genuinely bewildered. "You were the one who brought me to Mornitz! For two pieces? Or three?"

"Bastard!" I raised my fist again.

"Hey, hey, I'm sorry!" Rogas flinched, raising both hands quickly.

I turned away, disgusted, tired of looking at him. My chest felt tight with anger, with fear, with guilt over Muriel being dragged into this nightmare. We stood in silence for a moment, the only sounds the river and Rogas's pained breathing. Then my eyes fell on Horsling's dagger, lying where I'd dropped it near Scarface's body.

The dagger. An idea sparked. Maybe...

I ran and scooped it up, the cool metal somehow calming the worst of my rage. I looked back at Rogas.

He held up his hands again. "I am sorry... for both of you. Do you understand? Isn't that enough?" His voice became urgent again. "Listen, you can be mad at me all you want, but everything I said is true, William. We have to go before Mornitz gets back."

I took a deep breath, shoving the dagger back into its sheath. "I'll take Muriel home first," I stated, my voice flat.

"We don't have much time!" Rogas argued, exasperated.

Muriel touched my arm gently. I looked down at her. She seemed calmer now, though still pale. "I can go home by myself," she said softly. "You don't have to worry."

"I won't be able to calm down if I let you go home alone," I insisted.

"I'm more worried about you..."

"Muriel... I'm sorry," I choked out. "It wasn't supposed to be like this..."

This was my fault. All of it.

"Hey, hurry," Rogas grumbled impatiently.

"Shut up!" I snapped without looking at him. I put my hand on Muriel's shoulder. "I'll take you back towards Horsling's Tavern. It's well-lit from there. After that, you can go home by yourself. This time, you *really* should go home. Don't follow me again."

"I'm sorry..." she whispered, fresh tears welling in her eyes.

"It's okay," I said, shaking my head, angry at myself. Why was *she* apologizing? "Come on, let's go."

"Hey, wait a minute. What about me?" Rogas yelped as we started to walk away.

"Wait for me here," I called back over my shoulder.

"How long? What if Mornitz comes back? I still can't escape! Do you want me to die?"

"Then just hide!" I yelled back, not slowing down. "Behind a tree, behind a rock, I don't care! If you die before I get back, I'll go north alone!"

I heard Rogas curse loudly behind me. "Then I'd better go now! I don't have to take care of you either, do I?"

"No problem!" I shouted, grabbing Muriel's arm and pulling her into a quicker walk. "That means I'll be looking for you later! You'll just have one more enemy!"

He let out another string of curses, but I didn't care anymore. Right now, only Muriel mattered. Getting her somewhere safe.

And then... then I had to figure out what to do about Master Horsling. The man who lent me the dagger. The man who sent me down to the river. He had some explaining to do. He owed me that much.

8

Life Changes

The walk back towards Horsling's Tavern was shrouded in a thick, suffocating silence. Muriel walked beside me, close but not touching, and I could feel the tremor that still ran through her. Neither of us spoke. What was there to say? The images from the riverbank played over and over in my mind – the flash of steel, the gurgling cries, the sickening spread of blood in the moonlight. We'd stumbled into a nightmare, and the shockwaves left us reeling.

My own thoughts were a tangled mess of fury and regret. Fury at myself. Why had I taken that dagger from Horsling? Why hadn't I just grabbed Muriel and run home the moment Rogas started his nonsense? My life in Ortleg... it was simple, predictable maybe, but it was *mine.* Working beside Bortez, teasing Muriel, even the quiet evenings with Mom... why had I thrown it away for a moment of reckless curiosity, for the weight of a borrowed blade?

Horsling's words echoed: *discover who you truly are.* What had I discovered? That I could kill a man? That I could stand shaking over bleeding bodies and feel... numb? Was *this* the path he spoke of? The path of a killer?

We reached the relative light spilling from the tavern windows. "Wait here," I told Muriel, my voice sounding hollow even to myself. "And—"

"Hide in a safe place," she finished for me, her voice surprisingly calm despite the fear still lingering in her eyes. "You don't have to worry about me."

I shook my head, managing a weak, humorless smile. "I'd rather worry. Worry makes us alert. I just learned that." I turned and pushed the tavern door open.

Inside, the boisterous energy was gone. Only four men remained, quietly finishing a card game at a corner table, their voices low. My eyes found Master Horsling instantly. He stood behind the bar, polishing a mug, his face unreadable. Did he know? Could he look at me and see the blood I'd spilled, the lives I'd taken?

I walked to the bar and sank onto a stool. He placed a cup of dark wine in front of me without a word. "Drink up," he said calmly. "You need this."

I stared at the cup, then at him. The wine smelled strong, inviting, but my throat felt tight. "Do you know what happened?"

"A rough night for you, I guess," he replied evenly.

"You guess?" My voice rose slightly. "No, you're not just guessing. You know what happened." I pulled the long dagger from under my vest and laid it on the smooth wood of the bar. The dried blood smeared on the blade looked obscene in the lamplight. "You knew what was going to happen, sir, and that's why you lent this to me."

"Are you accusing me?" His tone didn't change, no flicker of surprise or guilt. "Do you think I orchestrated all this? That I trapped you there?"

My hand instinctively hovered near the dagger's hilt. Could I trust him? "Am I mistaken?"

"Yes, you are mistaken," he said firmly. "I didn't know *what* was going to happen. I just sensed it."

"Sensed?"

He sighed, leaning slightly on the bar. "Listen, son. For you, I'll tell you a bit about myself. I've been through a lot of rough times, more than you can probably imagine. A guy like me wouldn't survive long here if I couldn't sense trouble coming. I'm not as strong as you think, but I have this little edge... this feeling. It's very important." He nodded towards the card players. "Those four? They look rough, maybe dangerous back home, but here? No evil intentions. Most visitors are like them. Maybe they're afraid of me." He chuckled softly, seeing my continued tension. "Come on, have a drink. It'll help. Aren't you thirsty?"

His words, his calm certainty, were strangely compelling. I needed to leave – Muriel was waiting, Rogas too – but I wanted... needed... to understand. I picked up the cup and took a cautious sip. The wine was strong, warming.

"Thank you," I managed, my voice a little less strained.

"Feeling better?"

"Yes..."

"They're harmless, these people," he continued, his gaze sweeping the room. "Cunning, maybe, but harmless. But," his easy smile vanished, his eyes hardening, "it felt different when I saw your friends talking earlier. They are dangerous."

"They are?"

"The soldier and the black-clad man. Both your friends, aren't they?"

"Only one is my friend," I corrected automatically. "The other one isn't. Are they both dangerous?"

"Both of them." A flicker of something – certainty, maybe distaste – crossed his face. "I don't know what they're up to, but the evil intentions radiating off them were... strong. When they left together, I expected something bad to happen. Someone was going to die, I thought."

My anger flared again. "Then you *knew* something was going to happen! And you let it happen!"

"What was I supposed to do?" he countered reasonably. "If two bad men decide to kill each other down by the river, is it my business to interfere?"

"What if your hunch was wrong?" I argued, leaning forward. "What if only one was really evil? Would you just let an innocent man die?"

"My guesses are rarely wrong," he said, a hint of arrogance creeping into his voice. "Besides, I *did* do something, didn't I? Because then you came back, right?"

I frowned, confused. "What do you mean?"

"You came back, looking for them. I thought... okay. *This* is the one. The variable. Let that be your business then. Let *you* take care of it." He actually chuckled.

"You wanted *me* to take care of it?" My voice rose again, incredulous. "You almost got me killed!" The card players glanced over. I took a deep breath, forcing my voice down. "You almost got me killed."

"But that didn't happen, did it?" He grinned, infuriatingly calm. "You handled yourself. Took care of some of them, I'd wager, judging by that blade. As I said, my guess was not wrong."

"I didn't kill them," I clarified, thinking of Mornitz and Rogas. "They're both still alive."

"Well, but... you killed people, didn't you?" he gestured at the bloody dagger. "There's blood on this."

The images flooded back – the impact, the screams, the blood. I glared at him, shame and anger churning. "You made me do it," I hissed.

"Don't be angry with me," he replied, his tone softening slightly. "I believe you can get through times like these. And then learn something."

"I don't think I've learned anything good from all this!" I snapped back.

"Try to get a good night's sleep tonight," he advised calmly. "You'll understand tomorrow."

"No, I don't want to hear any more of your nonsense!" I pushed back from the bar, standing abruptly. "I will give you back your dagger." I slid it across the counter towards him. "It helped me, so I thank you. But whatever the reason, you have changed my life, and I'm not sure it's for the better. I shouldn't have taken your advice."

Master Horsling didn't touch the dagger. He just smiled faintly. "Actually, I could have given you more advice. But given your circumstances, it's probably best not to. Let yourself prove whether what you say is right or wrong." He paused. "But... I'd like to say one more thing, if you don't mind."

"Say it."

He leaned forward again, his eyes searching mine intently. "I can sense *you*."

I held my breath, suddenly cold despite the wine. I stared at him, unable to look away.

"You are... different," Horsling said slowly. "There is something in you I have not felt for a long time, and that gave me the courage to lend you my dagger. But," he leaned back, the intensity fading, replaced by his usual hearty demeanor, "I don't need to tell you any more nonsense than that, do I?" He laughed. "Well, off with you. Take care of yourself."

I stood there, reeling from his words. *Different? Something in me?* What did he mean? I wanted to ask, demanded answers, but a deeper instinct warned me away. Some knowledge felt too heavy right now. "Thank you," I mumbled, feeling strangely guilty for shouting at him earlier.

"Is there anything still troubling you, boy?" he asked, his gaze sharp again.

"No, no." I shook my head quickly. "I... just have to go. My friend is waiting for me."

"Your friend?"

"Muriel."

His eyebrows shot up. "Muriel?"

"Yes, she's right there." I gestured vaguely towards the door.

"A girl? Your friend is a girl? And she's standing *outside* my tavern?" His expression turned thunderous. "Why didn't you bring her inside? Silly boy, what were you thinking, leaving her out there alone after what happened?"

"I was just afraid someone might recognize her here with me," I stammered, taken aback by his sudden anger.

He gave me a long, searching look. "Okay," he said finally, his voice calmer. "I see what you mean. You don't want anything to happen to her?"

"Yes."

"What are you going to do now?"

"I... maybe we'll part ways here." The thought felt like a lead weight in my stomach. "I better head north while she goes home, and hopefully nothing will happen to her."

Master Horsling took a deep breath, stroking his beard. "Are you sure?"

"I don't know," I admitted miserably. "I just want her to be safe."

"What are you afraid of?"

"Mornitz. The man in the black robe. I'm afraid he'll come back, come to the workshop one day. If I'm not around, I can't protect Muriel and her father."

"You should be more worried about yourself," he said bluntly. "Are you working in the workshop?"

"Yes. With Bortez."

"I know Bortez. He's a good man." He nodded decisively. "Well, here's my advice, and this time it's plain speaking. You're right, you should go north until things cool down, until it's safe. In the meantime," he met my eyes, "I'll take Muriel home myself right now. And my friends," he gestured vaguely, "will look after her and her father. If any strangers matching Mornitz's description come asking questions in your village, I will definitely hear about it, and I *will* do something. You do not have to worry on that score. I assure you, if Mornitz knew I was protecting Bortez and his daughter, he wouldn't dare harm them." He paused, his expression softening slightly. "But you... since you killed those men... I can't shield you from the consequences of that directly. I'm sorry that my actions put you in this position. If you want to blame me, I understand."

A wave of immense relief washed over me, so strong my knees almost buckled. Muriel would be safe. Bortez would be safe. "No," I shook my head, meaning it this time. "Everything that happened... it was my decision in the end. I will not blame you anymore." My voice felt thick with gratitude. "And you have done me a great favor if you will take care of Muriel and her father. I thank you, sir."

"Since my sensing got you into this, call it my responsibility," the tavern owner said gruffly. "Consider it help from a friend."

I went outside and brought him to Muriel. I explained quickly, briefly – Horsling would take her home, keep an eye out, she'd be safe. I was going north with Rogas, for now. It all happened so fast, felt so unreal, like we were just saying goodnight after an ordinary evening.

Muriel only had time to whisper, her eyes huge and fearful, "Be careful."

And I only managed, "See you later," before turning away.

It wasn't until I was walking back down the dark path towards the river, alone this time, that the weight of it truly hit me. North. How far? How long? When would I see Ortleg again? See Muriel? My throat tightened. I should have said more. Told her... told her to be careful, yes, but also to listen to her father but still chase her own dreams. Told her not to cry, that things would somehow be okay. Told her... something more than just "See you later." But the thoughts came too late, jumbled and useless now. I couldn't go back.

The sound of the river pulled me from my regrets. I pushed through the tall grass near the bank. The remaining boat bobbed gently. Rogas wasn't in it. And the bodies... they were gone. Panic seized me. What happened while I was gone?

"Rogas?" I whispered urgently into the darkness. "Rogas!"

"Shh!" A hissed reply came from nearby bushes. Rogas's annoying, familiar face peered out. "Not so loud."

"There's no one else here," I said, relief warring with irritation.

"Still, you must be careful!" he grumbled, emerging from the shadows. I saw then that he was burdened with extra swords – clearly looted from the dead bandits – and probably pouches of coin too.

"There could be people walking around here at night who suddenly appear," Rogas continued defensively. "Luckily, I hid the bodies."

"Where?"

He nodded towards a dense cluster of rocks further back from the path. It looked like hard work dragging them there, especially with his injured leg, which I saw he'd crudely bandaged.

"Eventually, people will find them," I said nervously. "Do you think they'll know we did this?"

"They won't, unless you brag about it everywhere." He eyed me suspiciously. "After a person kills more than one bandit, he usually gets cocky and babbles. Have you told anyone?"

"No," I lied quickly. No need for Rogas to know about my conversation with Horsling.

"Good. That means only Mornitz and his gang know about it. And that girl." He started tossing the looted gear into the boat. "Now you pray she doesn't talk about it to anyone."

"Muriel wouldn't do that!" I snapped.

Rogas just grinned cynically as he pushed the boat further into the water. "You don't have to be afraid. Someday, people might find out about the bodies and suspect you because you disappeared from your village, right? Most people won't care, but eventually, someone will connect the dots. But by the time they find out, you'll be far away, so what are you afraid of?"

"I'm not afraid!" I retorted, though it wasn't entirely true. "I'm just upset! I had a pleasant life in the village, and now everything has changed!"

"So what? Are you going to blame others or yourself?" Rogas jumped clumsily into the rocking boat and held out a hand to help me in. Once I was aboard, he shoved an oar into my hands. "Life always changes, whether you like it or not. Just face it and be thankful you're still alive. That's all that matters."

I sat heavily on the wooden thwart, gripping the rough oar. I looked back towards the dark shoreline, towards Ortleg, towards the life that felt impossibly distant now. My heart felt like a stone in my chest. The river current caught the boat, pulling us out into the darkness. With each dip and pull of the oars, the gap widened. Above, the stars glittered, cold and remote, utterly indifferent. Nothing up there had changed. Down here, for me, everything had.

9

The Plan

We rowed all night, the rhythmic splash of the oars the only sound besides Rogas's occasional grunt or muttered curse about his leg. The river flowed north, carrying us deeper into unfamiliar territory, further from everything I knew. By morning, my arms burned, my back ached, and exhaustion settled deep in my bones, but Rogas insisted we keep going. He sat in the front, peering ahead, agitated.

"We need to move fast, William," he'd urged for the tenth time. "Disappear completely."

"Disappear how?" I finally snapped, my own nerves frayed. The adrenaline from the fight had long since worn off, leaving only weariness and a hollow ache where my grief resided. "Do you even have a plan, Rogas, or are we just drifting?"

He actually laughed, a harsh, grating sound. "That's what's so exciting about an adventure! We don't know what we're going to find! We also don't know what we're going to do next!"

"This isn't an adventure," I said through gritted teeth, pulling hard on the oar. "We're on the run. We *have* to have a plan if we don't want Mornitz catching up to us."

"I have a plan!" Rogas insisted, suddenly serious again. "I've heard about the villages up here, further north. We'll go there. Find somewhere to lie low."

So we rowed on, hour after numbing hour. The sun climbed high, beat down on us, then began its slow descent towards the western hills. Finally, late in the afternoon, a village came into view, larger than I expected, nestled where our small river flowed into a much bigger one heading west – the Ordelahr, Rogas called it, the great river stretching far, far north. Orulion.

Fishing boats dotted the water near the docks, suggesting a busy place despite its remoteness. Rogas explained that Orulion's location made it a natural stopover, but because it was so far north, the Kingdom of Alton barely paid it any mind. They'd pulled their soldiers out years ago, he said, needing them more down south to watch Tavarin. The Hualeg, the northern nation... Rogas spoke of them with casual contempt, calling them distant savages, no real threat to the kingdom itself, leaving these northern villages to fend for themselves against raids.

Each time he mentioned the Hualeg, a familiar heat rose in my chest. My father's people. Insulting them felt like insulting *him*, insulting *me*. But what Rogas said about the raids... I knew from village talk that part was true. I bit my tongue, swallowed the anger. No one needed to know my blood ran half Hualeg. It felt like another secret to guard, another complication I didn't need.

As we tied up the boat at a rickety wooden dock, Rogas finally revealed his grand 'plan'. He glanced around conspiratorially, making sure no villagers were near, then leaned in, dropping his voice to a whisper.

"The village chief here is called Turpin. Or Taupin, maybe?" he muttered, scratching his beard. "Heard a few weeks back he's banding together with other chiefs around here. Forming their own little army to fight off the Hualeg if they attack again." He clapped me on the shoulder, his eyes gleaming with sudden enthusiasm. "And *that*, my friend, is our chance. We join this army." He pulled one of the swords looted from the bandits – *my* sword now, apparently – and thrust the hilt towards me, strapping the other to his own belt.

I stared at the sword, then at him. "Join them for what?"

"For the money, of course! What else?"

"But we came north to *hide*, Rogas!" I argued, keeping my own voice low but fierce. "If we join an army, stay in one place, won't Mornitz find us easily? Why don't we head east, follow the creek into the forests like you mentioned?"

He scoffed. "And do what? Hunt rabbits for the rest of our lives? How much coin do you think that brings in?"

"Why are you always thinking about money?" I shot back, exasperated. "I followed you because you said we could hide safely up here! Not to get rich fighting Hualeg!"

"You suggested joining Alton's army down south just yesterday!" he retorted sharply. "Same thing! We become soldiers. Difference is, villagers pay us now, not the king. And don't tell me you don't like money," he added tersely. "That's nonsense."

"You're the one who always talks nonsense!" My own anger flared, fueled by exhaustion and mistrust. "This morning it was run and hide, now it's stay and fight for money! Is this your 'plan'? Just do whatever benefits you right now, without a thought for anything else? No wonder people want to kill you!"

"Watch your mouth, brat," Rogas snarled, his eyes going hard and wild for a second. "Think you're tough now? I can still beat you."

"Then try," I challenged, my hand instinctively dropping to the hilt of the sword he'd just given me. My blood was up. "Sword or fists? I beat you easily before, remember?"

"You know nothing," he growled back, his own hand hovering over his weapon. "You're strong, yeah, but just a kid. I can still take you."

We glared at each other, the tension crackling between us. For a moment, I thought we really would fight, right here on the dock. Then, just as suddenly, Rogas's expression shifted. The anger vanished, replaced by a wide, calculating grin.

"Hey, hey," he said, holding up his hands placatingly. "Why are we doing this? We're friends, right? Partners in... well, whatever this is. Relax."

I didn't relax. I shook my head slowly. "I'll be your friend when I can trust you, Rogas. Before we go anywhere near this 'army', you tell me. Why do people want you dead? What *really* happened back there? And what were you planning with Mornitz in that tavern?"

"My story... it's long," he deflected, looking uncomfortable. "Not the right time. And in the tavern? What are you talking about? You saw! They ambushed me!"

"I think," I said slowly, watching his eyes, remembering Horsling's words about sensing intentions, "when you met Mornitz, you were planning to turn on him yourself. Rob him, maybe kill him. Figured that was easier money than working for him. Didn't you?"

He blinked, looking genuinely startled. Maybe even a little afraid. "What makes you think that?"

"I can sense it," I said coolly, mimicking Horsling's tone. "The stench of your bad intentions practically choked me back there. You can't lie to me."

"That's..." Rogas stammered, looking nervous now, actually seeming to believe I *could* read his mind. "I didn't want to do that! I really wanted the job!"

I just shook my head again, seeing the truth clearly now. "I guess, just like now, you always keep every option open, don't you? Good ones, bad ones. Then you just pick whichever helps you most at the moment."

He recovered quickly, flashing that infuriating grin again. "Well, aren't we all supposed to be like that? That's being smart! Prepared for anything!"

"Others call it being cunning," I retorted. "And they want to kill you for it. Like Mornitz did." I let my disgust show. "But you're right about one thing. Maybe I *should* keep more plans in my head from now on. And figure out who my real enemies are first."

"William, I promise I'll tell you everything," Rogas said quickly, glancing around. Our raised voices had attracted a few curious looks from further down the dock. "But not now. You have to trust me first. I've handled scrapes like this before. I'm still here, aren't I?"

"Only because I saved you yesterday!"

"It's because you were part of my luck!" he insisted, grinning again. "I rolled the dice, played the odds, and survived. Thanks to you showing up! Right? Now, let my luck help *you*. Stick with me, trust it, and we'll both come out ahead."

"You're still full of nonsense," I sighed, feeling too tired to argue further. "But fine. Fine. I'll follow your plan. For now."

"You won't regret it," Rogas laughed.

"I won't," I said, meeting his eyes, my voice hard, "even if I have to kill you later."

He looked surprised for a heartbeat, then threw his head back and laughed louder. "Look at you! Getting used to the idea already, aren't you? Threatening people! Haha! After the first kill, the rest get easier, right? It's always like that!"

I didn't laugh. I didn't know if I meant the threat or not. It felt like a bluff, a way to keep him wary. The thought of killing again made my stomach churn. But if he betrayed me? If Mornitz came back? What choices would I have then?

I followed Rogas into the village proper. Say what you will about him, the man could talk. Within an hour, stopping at a small waterside tavern, he'd charmed a couple of local fishermen, sharing stories (likely exaggerated) and buying a round of drinks.

One of them, Root – a friendly old fellow with kind eyes and a bushy white beard – ended up offering us a place to stay. "Got an empty cottage out back," he said, his voice raspy with age. "My son lived there, 'fore he left. Hasn't been home... hmm... two years now?"

"Ten years, Root," the other man corrected him gently. He had a similar beard but looked younger – Moor, Root's brother, we learned.

"Ten? Ah, time flies," Root chuckled, unbothered.

"Where did your son go?" I asked, curious despite my exhaustion.

"South," Moor answered, his expression clouding over. "Joined Alton's army. Nephew got tired of fishing, wanted excitement, better pay. Went south. Sent coin for a couple years, then... nothing."

"What happened?"

"Don't know," Moor sighed. "No word."

"He's dead," Root stated simply, matter-of-factly. It was shocking to hear a father say it so plainly, but he smiled faintly, as if he'd made his peace with it long ago. Though how could he have made peace if he couldn't remember when the boy left?

"We don't know that, Root," Moor insisted quietly. "Maybe he just moved on. Might come back someday."

"No, he won't," Root said firmly. "That's the risk of soldiering. He knew it. And," his eyes shifted to us, taking in the swords at our belts, "you two should know it, too. What are your names?"

"I'm Dall," Rogas answered smoothly. "And this is my brother, Tuck."

Tuck? I nearly choked. I shot Rogas a glare, then muttered my agreement.

"Yeah, you two should know that too," Root repeated.

"Should know what?" I asked.

"Being soldiers, you die faster," he replied bluntly.

"Only if we're stupid," Rogas countered.

"My nephew wasn't stupid," Moor said, a spark of anger in his eyes. "Strong lad, good with a sword. Still gone. If he really is dead..."

"What was his name?" Rogas asked casually.

"Boot. About your brother's age when he left." Moor glanced at me. "Did you know him?"

Rogas paused, his face blank for a moment. Then he shook his head. "No. Never heard of him."

Moor nodded slowly. "Suppose not. Long time ago." He looked at us more seriously. "Listen, young men. We know why you're likely here. Carrying swords like that. You aim to join Taupin's army, right?"

"That's the plan," Rogas confirmed easily.

"Then you know the risks," Root said gravely. "Up here, you fight the Hualeg. You know what they are, don't you? Giants, they say. Strong, cruel... maybe eat human flesh." Another uncomfortable jolt went through me. "You two look tough enough. Moor and I don't need to give you advice. We're just fishermen."

"Sir," I spoke up, wanting any information I could get, "if you know anything we ought to know, please tell us."

"Taupin will be glad of strong arms, that's all I can say," Root replied. "Want me to take you to him now?"

THE PLAN

"Let me take them," Moor offered, patting his brother's arm. "Want to go tonight?"

"We want to rest first," Rogas intervened quickly. "We'll see him tomorrow."

"Thank you for your offer, sir," I said, smiling gratefully at both brothers.

"Get some rest," Moor nodded. "And good luck."

"And may you live longer than I have," Root added with another chuckle, his eyes twinkling strangely.

Moor led us a short distance to Root's house, a sturdy wooden building smelling of fish and woodsmoke. Out back, as promised, was a small, weathered cabin. Inside, it was dusty, cluttered with old fishing gear and discarded items. Clearly empty for years. There was a single rough wooden bed frame against one wall. As soon as Moor left, Rogas claimed it, falling onto the thin mattress and snoring within minutes.

My own exhaustion was immense, but hunger gnawed at me. I went back to Root's house. The old man shared a simple meal of fish soup and dried fruit with me. When I offered him one of my few remaining sazet coins, he refused at first, saying he saw me as a son returned, welcome without payment. But I insisted, saying a son would gladly help his parents. He finally accepted with a warm smile.

Darkness had fallen completely by the time I returned to the hut. I spread a thin, dusty mat on the floorboards. Rogas's snores filled the small space, but I barely heard them. Sleep claimed me almost instantly, dragging me down into a heavy, dreamless dark.

10

If the Payment is Right

Sunlight sliced through a gap in the rough wooden shutters, prying my eyes open. For a blissful second, I didn't know where I was. Then it all came crashing back – Mom, gone. The bloody chaos by the river. Muriel's terrified face as I left her with Horsling. The long, exhausting night rowing north with Rogas. A fresh wave of anger washed over me, hot and bitter, directed mostly at myself. I was trapped in this mess, forced to flee my home, because I'd been reckless, because I'd listened to Horsling, because I hadn't just taken Muriel and gone straight back to Ortleg the first time we left the tavern. *This shouldn't have happened.* I should have been more careful.

Then Rogas's cynical words from the boat surfaced in my mind: *"Life always changes... whether you like it or not."* The man was infuriating, unreliable, possibly treacherous... but damn him, sometimes he was right.

I pushed myself up from the lumpy floor mat, my muscles protesting. The wooden bed frame was empty. Rogas was gone. Where?

I hurried outside. Root's backyard was cluttered with old, rotting fish crates, smelling faintly of the river. No sign of Rogas. I crossed the yard quickly, went up the narrow lane between Root's house and the neighbour's, and turned left onto the main path. There, on his porch, sat Root in his rocking chair, enjoying the morning sun.

He smiled as I approached. "You're awake. Come sit with me. I have tea and some bread, too."

"Thank you." The old man's simple kindness felt like a balm. I sat on the steps beside him. The bread was dry and coarse, sticking in my throat, but it filled the gnawing emptiness in my stomach. I washed it down with hot, weak tea. "Sir," I asked, trying to sound casual, "have you seen Ro— I mean, my brother?"

"Oh, your brother?" Root squinted thoughtfully. "He... what's his name again?"

"Dall." It felt stupid saying the fake name. "Yes, Dall. That's his name."

"Ah, Dall. Yes. Asked directions to Taupin's house bright and early. Headed off that way."

"Why didn't he take me with him?" I muttered, irritation flaring again. "He could have woken me up."

"That's what I asked him," Root chuckled, his eyes twinkling. "Said you looked like you needed the rest after your journey. Don't worry," he added, seeing my expression. "No need to get upset. You can catch up later. Whoever casts the net first isn't always the one who brings home the biggest fish. I know that, son, from all my years on the river."

He pointed me in the right direction, and after thanking him again, I set off.

Taupin's house, unlike most in Orulion, was across the wide Ordelahr River. Getting there meant taking a large, sturdy raft made of massive logs lashed together. Two quiet men operated it, pulling on a thick rope stretched across the water to guide it against the current. It felt strange, crossing that formidable river, heading deeper into the North.

On the far bank, a winding path led up from the landing towards a house nestled at the base of a low hill. As I approached, I heard noise – shouting, cheering. The courtyard in front of the house was packed, dozens of men forming a rough circle, all focused on something in the center.

My stomach clenched. In the middle of the circle stood Rogas, leaning casually on a sword, its tip resting on the packed earth. At his feet lay a young villager, groaning and clutching his stomach.

Idiot! Anger surged through me again. What had he done now? There was no blood, so maybe just bruises, but showing off like this? Drawing attention? We were supposed to be *hiding*. Did he have any sense at all? News of a stranger easily beating local fighters would travel. What if Mornitz heard? What was the point of coming north if Rogas was going to announce our presence to everyone?

A loud voice cut through the cheers, silencing the crowd. It came from a man seated on a stool on the far side of the circle – slender, older, with graying hair and a stern, authoritative air despite his simple clothes. This had to be Taupin, the chief.

"Our new friend seems to be an excellent warrior!" Taupin declared, his voice carrying easily. Applause broke out. "Five men have already tried, and five men have lost. Does anyone else dare challenge him?"

I shook my head in disbelief and annoyance. Rogas couldn't resist, could he? Of course, a seasoned mercenary would be better than local fishermen or farmers playing soldier, but did he have to prove it so publicly?

"Come on!" Taupin urged the crowd. "Doesn't anyone else dare?"

A low murmur went through the men, but no one stepped forward. Rogas grinned, looking insufferably pleased with himself as the young man he'd just beaten limped back into the crowd.

Then Taupin's sharp gaze swept the courtyard and landed squarely on me, standing awkwardly at the edge. "You," he pointed, his voice ringing out. "The young man who just arrived." Every head turned. I felt suddenly exposed, pinned by dozens of curious eyes. Even Rogas looked startled, his confident grin faltering as he saw me. "This is the first time I've seen you here. What's your name?"

My mind raced. "Will— ehm... Tuck," I stammered out the stupid fake name again. "My name is Tuck!"

"Tuck," Taupin appraised me, his eyes narrowed thoughtfully. "You're tall, well-built. Look like a strong young man. Don't you want to try? Don't you want to fight this man?" He gestured towards Rogas.

My heart thumped against my ribs. Fight Rogas? Here? Now? I shook my head. "No." The word came out too quiet. I cleared my throat and said louder, "No!" Then I panicked slightly. Was that rude? Would it cause suspicion? "Excuse me," I added quickly, "may I ask first? What for?"

Taupin threw his head back and laughed, a booming sound echoed by the men around him. "What for? I am building an army, boy! An army to protect our homes from those northern savages! I need strong, brave men. I need a leader, a deputy to stand beside me. Prove your strength, prove your courage! You can try if you dare. So," his gaze sharpened again, "do you dare to fight this man?"

I looked at Rogas. He was watching me, a mixture of surprise and challenge in his expression. All the frustration, all the resentment I felt towards him – for his recklessness, for dragging me into this, for nearly getting us killed, for his annoying jokes – it all boiled up inside me. Hiding? Caution? Right now, I didn't care. I wanted, more than anything, to wipe that smug look off his face. I wanted to hit him.

"Sir," I said, my voice ringing with sudden conviction, "do you think I'm afraid to fight him?"

Taupin chuckled again. "Are you afraid?"

"I'm not afraid!"

"Then why did you say no?" he laughed, clearly enjoying this. The crowd laughed with him.

Fine. If he wanted a show, I'd give him one. Forgetting completely about lying low, I pushed forward. "I will fight with him!"

The men parted to let me through. I reached the center, standing opposite Rogas. I forced a grin. "I will gladly defeat him, if I may," I said, loud enough for Taupin to hear. Then, quieter, to Rogas, "Do I have to use a sword?"

"We are not barbarians like the Hualeg," Taupin answered before Rogas could. "I don't want my men injured before the real battles begin. Take that sword." He pointed to the one lying near the last defeated villager. "The tip and edges are blunted. You'll only get bruises if you lose." He laughed again as I picked up the heavy, dulled practice sword. "Are you ready?"

I straightened up, gripping the sword. It felt clumsy compared to a real blade, but solid. "I'm ready."

Rogas eyed me, a wary smile playing on his lips. "Are you serious?"

"Of course," I shot back, meeting his gaze. "I'm just playing by your rules."

"I'm going to kick your ass," he sneered quietly.

"And I'm going to punch you in the nose one more time," I retorted just as softly.

Taupin's voice boomed over us. "All right! This is the last and decisive fight! Are you both ready?"

We both nodded.

"Begin!"

The crowd roared. I didn't hesitate, swinging first, putting all my strength and frustration into the blow. The blunted sword whooshed through the air. Rogas parried, the impact jarring both our arms, then lunged forward. I deflected his thrust with a powerful block that sent him stumbling back a step.

I pressed the attack, adrenaline singing through me now, grief and fear momentarily forgotten, replaced by pure, focused energy. I swung wildly, unpredictably – high, low, across – pouring out all the force I usually reserved for shaping iron. Rogas was skilled, experienced, he'd taught me moves I was probably using against him now, but he couldn't match my raw strength. He blocked desperately, sweat beading on his forehead. I drove him back, back towards the edge of the circle, then brought the heavy sword down in a crushing overhead blow. He tried to parry, but the force was too much. His sword clattered from his grasp, and he dropped to his knees.

Silence fell for a beat, then the crowd erupted louder than before.

I stood over him, chest heaving, pointing the blunted sword at his face. "I told you I would beat you."

He growled up at me, spitting dirt. "Put your sword away. We'll use our bare hands. Dare you?"

"No problem." I tossed the practice sword aside without a second thought.

He exploded upwards, ramming his head straight into my stomach like a battering ram. Pain exploded behind my eyes; the air rushed out of my lungs. I staggered back, stunned by the cheap shot. Luckily, I managed to stay upright. I threw punches, left and right, but we were too close, tangled together, my blows glancing off his shoulders. He didn't seem to feel them. He pushed back, then swung a heavy left fist that connected squarely with my jaw.

My head snapped back; the world swam for a second. Stars popped behind my eyes. Instinct took over. I blocked his incoming right fist with my left forearm, stumbling again. As I nearly fell, my hand shot out, grabbing a fistful of his thick hair, yanking his head down hard. My right knee came up, aiming for his face.

He must have sensed the danger. He surged forward again, burying his face in my chest to avoid the knee strike, leaving his stomach exposed. I drove my knee into his gut again, and again, feeling the impact, hearing his grunt of pain. I twisted, grabbing his head with my left arm, and swung my right fist with everything I had.

Crack. The punch landed flush on his nose. He staggered back with a cry, blood erupting, and collapsed onto the dusty ground.

I lunged, ready to finish it, but he threw up his hands, palms out.

"Hey, hey! Enough! That's enough!" he yelled, his voice muffled as he pinched his bleeding nose. "You broke my nose!"

I stood over him, gasping for breath, the red mist of fury slowly receding. "You already knew that," I panted. "You knew I had a reason to break your nose."

"Why? Do you really hold a grudge against me?" he grumbled, looking up at me.

"No," I said, shaking my head, the anger draining away, leaving me feeling shaky and slightly sick. "I just wanted to teach you a lesson."

"You're an arrogant brat," he cursed, but then, ridiculously, a bloody grin spread across his face. "You'll get a lesson later, too!"

A wave of weary relief washed over me. He wasn't truly angry. His nose would heal, crooked maybe, but he'd live.

Taupin strode forward from the crowd, his stern face beaming. "It's obvious you've won!" he declared as the villagers cheered again. He stopped in front of me. "I was looking for a leader for one of my fighting groups. You have proven you are the strongest and bravest man here today. I hope I can trust you. Will you accept?"

I looked at him, then glanced at Rogas, still sitting on the ground nursing his bloody nose. Leadership? Responsibility? After the chaos of the last few days, it was the last thing I wanted. And Rogas... despite everything, he clearly craved this kind of position, this recognition. Maybe it was better he had it. "I want to join your army, sir," I said respectfully, shaking my head. "And you can trust me. But I don't want to be a squad leader. Let him do it." I nodded towards Rogas. "I think he wants this job more."

Taupin considered this, stroking his graying beard. He turned to Rogas. "If that's the case, then I'll offer you the job. Are you ready?"

Rogas scrambled to his feet, wiping blood from his lip with the back of his hand, his sly grin firmly back in place. "If the pay is right."

Taupin nodded curtly. "We can talk about it. Now?"

"Yes. Right now."

"We'll talk at my house."

"I want my brother to be part of the discussion," Rogas added quickly. "He needs to know, too. If I become your deputy, then he becomes my deputy... or, your deputy's deputy."

Taupin looked from Rogas to me, puzzled. "He's your brother?"

"Yes," Rogas confirmed smoothly. "I'm Dall, he's Tuck. I think you can understand now, sir," he gestured towards his swollen nose, "why he wanted to punch me so badly. Because we're brothers."

Taupin just looked at him blankly for a second, clearly not understanding Rogas's bizarre logic, then shrugged. "I'm glad you're both here. Your strength is badly needed."

"Only if the payment is right, sir," Rogas reminded him shamelessly. "Don't forget that."

And suddenly, I understood. The showing off, the fighting, provoking me into a fight he probably knew he might lose... it wasn't just ego. It was all a performance to impress Taupin, to demonstrate fighting prowess (his own and, by association, mine), to increase his bargaining power for the pay. It was smart, in a twisted, Rogas sort of way. It was also incredibly annoying and dangerously conspicuous. I could only hope the news of two skilled strangers arriving and immediately causing a stir in Orulion didn't travel too far, too fast.

Taupin waved Rogas and me over to the porch of his house, away from the dusty courtyard where the villagers were still murmuring about the fight. Someone brought out cups and a steaming teapot. I sank onto a wooden bench, my muscles still buzzing from the exertion, my jaw aching where Rogas had connected. Across the courtyard, the men who Taupin hoped to turn into an army milled about – fishermen mostly, some tough-looking hunters maybe, but none looked like natural soldiers. They looked like men who worked hard with their hands, men who knew the river and the forest, not the battlefield.

Taupin poured tea, glancing at me over the rim of his cup. "Tuck," he said, using the ridiculous name Rogas had given me, "what do you think of them? Are they strong enough?"

Strong enough for what? Daily labor, yes. Facing Hualeg raiders? I shook my head honestly. "I don't know, sir. I don't really know what you're planning here. Building an army? Where are the weapons for this army?"

"In the warehouse," he replied readily. "Swords and spears, basic stuff, enough for about thirty men to start. Collected them over time. They'll have to do until we can get better."

"I've heard that the Hualeg are terrible," Rogas jumped in, clearly steering the conversation towards what mattered to him – the risk, and therefore the pay. "Do you know that?"

"Of course, I know," Taupin said grimly. "They attacked Orulion itself a few years back. I survived." His eyes hardened. "That's exactly why I'm doing this. We can't expect any help from the Kingdom when the wolves come down from the north. Alton's soldiers..." he spat the words out, "...useless when things get truly rough up here." He went on to explain his plan – contacting other northern village leaders, gathering men, heading to the northernmost village soon to set up defenses before the Hualeg raiding season might begin.

"How long will you stay up north?" Rogas asked, getting down to logistics.

"Until late autumn," Taupin replied. "About seven months from now."

Seven months. It felt like a lifetime. "Who will work the boats and fields here while you're all gone?" I asked, thinking of the hardship.

"We divide the tasks," Taupin explained with a sigh. "Some stay, some go. Our harvest will be smaller, the fishing less... but what choice do we have? We do this to survive."

"How many men will you gather in total?" Rogas pressed.

"Eleven villages involved, counting Orulion. Maybe ten fighters from each of the smaller ones. Should give us about a hundred men." Taupin looked at us expectantly. "Enough, I think. The Hualeg raiding parties are usually smaller than that. What do you think?"

Rogas shrugged noncommittally. "If you say so. But it's dangerous work, sir. Especially if your men are just fishermen who've never held a spear in anger. They'll get slaughtered without proper training."

"You can help us with that," Taupin said quickly. "Train them. Fight alongside them."

"Sure," Rogas smiled, leaning back, sensing his opportunity. His nose was already swelling up nicely. "I can make things easier for you. But you understand, sir... the more dangerous the job, the more skill required... the higher the pay."

Taupin's face fell slightly. "This village is not rich, Mr. Dall. We don't have coffers full of coin. We can feed you, house you – plenty of fish, you won't starve."

"You mean..." Rogas sat up straight, his voice sharp with disbelief, "you plan to pay us in *fish*?" He shook his head, looking at Taupin as if he were a simpleton. "We need money, Mr. Taupin. Sazets. Coin we can carry south eventually. We can't haul sacks of dried fish across the kingdom!" He leaned forward again. "And I know you have it. Don't tell me you don't. You collect fees, taxes, from every boat that docks, every merchant passing through. You collect coin, not fish! It's time you spent some of it protecting the people who pay you. I'm not asking for the moon, just a fair price for the risk and our skill."

Taupin looked distinctly uncomfortable now. "How much do you want?"

Rogas didn't hesitate. "Thirty sazets upfront, thirty at the start of each month, and thirty when we finish in the autumn." He glanced at me. "Oh, that's for me. For my brother, Tuck... twenty upfront, twenty a month, and twenty at the end. Hmm... yes, I think that's fair."

Taupin stared at him, aghast. "I'm not lying, Master Dall! I have some savings, yes, but nowhere near that amount! That's... that's crazy!"

"Okay," Rogas conceded smoothly. "So how much *can* you give?"

"Fifteen," Taupin said firmly. "Fifteen upfront, fifteen a month, fifteen at the end."

Rogas frowned, calculating. "So... thirty every month, for both of us?"

Taupin shook his head emphatically. "No. Fifteen sazets total. For both of you."

"What?" Rogas exploded, his face turning red under the grime and bruises. "Fifteen? For *both* of us? I could make more waiting tables back in Ortleg! We are experienced fighting men! We risk our lives, train your villagers, and you offer us fish scraps and pocket money? We—"

"We'll take it," I cut in sharply.

Rogas whipped his head around, glaring at me furiously. "Hey, you shut up! Let me handle this!"

"We accept!" I glared right back, then turned to Taupin, nodding decisively. "We accept your offer, sir. Fifteen sazets total per month is acceptable."

The village chief looked surprised, then visibly relieved. "I'm glad you understand, Mr. Tuck." He nodded, pleased. "So we agree, Mr. Dall?"

Rogas looked like he wanted to strangle me, but caught between my acceptance and Taupin's hopeful stare, he finally ground out, "All right. Fifteen! Ten for me," he shot me another venomous look, "and five for him."

"No problem," I agreed immediately, ignoring Rogas's glare. Let him keep the bigger share if it salved his wounded pride. Five sazets a month felt like a fortune anyway compared to the nothing I had now.

"Good!" Taupin smiled broadly, clearly happy to have secured us so cheaply.

Rogas grumbled under his breath, then added quickly, "Can we have our first fifteen sazets now?"

"Impatient, aren't you?" Taupin chuckled, but his expression turned serious again as he stood up. "Don't worry, Mr. Dall, I'll give them to you." He looked sternly from Rogas to me. "But listen carefully: as soon as you take my money, you become my men. You work for Orulion and the northern villages. You will *not* cheat me. You will obey orders, work hard, train these men well. No nonsense, no trouble-making, no disappearing acts. If you fail me..." his eyes hardened, "...then I will take back every last piece I have given you, one way or another. Do you understand?"

I nodded solemnly. "No problem, sir."

"Hey, we're professionals," Rogas said with a casual wave of his hand, though his eyes were wary. "We know the job."

Taupin looked unconvinced but nodded slowly and turned back towards his house to fetch the money.

The moment he was gone, Rogas rounded on me, his voice a furious whisper. "Next time, *let me* handle the money! You just cost us—!"

"No," I cut him off just as fiercely. "Next time, you run your plans by me *before* you open your mouth. I know what our work is worth, maybe better than you do right now. You greedy son of a bitch!"

"I was negotiating!" he hissed back. "You never just take the first offer! Basic tactics!" He snorted. "Okay, I get it. You did that just to piss me off because I left you sleeping this morning, didn't you? What a vindictive brat."

"Look around, Rogas!" I gestured towards the rough-looking villagers still lingering in the yard. "Have you seen this place? Did you expect Taupin to have sacks of gold hidden away? This village isn't rich!"

"You need to get to know guys like him better," Rogas whispered urgently, leaning closer. "Taupin's no simple village chief. He's a loan shark, I'd bet my share. Lends money to poor fishermen at killer rates, taxes everything that moves through here. He's got plenty tucked away, believe me. He could afford us."

"How do you know that?" I asked skeptically.

"I just know the type."

"That's just a guess," I countered, though a sliver of doubt entered my mind. "Maybe you're right, maybe not. But at least he's trying to protect these people. Do *you* actually care about them?"

"Of course I care!" Rogas exclaimed, looking offended. "If I'd gotten those thirty pieces a month, I'd have given twenty of them back to the poor folk here!"

I just stared at him. "Bullshit."

"I'm serious!" he insisted. "But how can I do that when I've only got ten?"

"Another excuse? You can still give some of your ten away now."

He shook his head, exasperated. "You're such a pain in the ass, Tuck."

"It's your own fault," I retorted. "If you really planned on giving money away, you should have said so. Maybe I wouldn't have interfered. But you didn't. So, we accept the deal. For the next seven months, we work for Taupin."

"Don't worry about it," Rogas said, that knowing, infuriating smirk returning. "That was the *original* plan, sure. But you've learned by now, haven't you? Everything can change in the blink of an eye. Something else might happen. Maybe our luck changes later. For the better."

"Or for the worse," I muttered irritably. He always had another angle, another possibility he wasn't sharing.

"Worse how? We die?" He laughed his harsh laugh again. "Hey, if we die fighting Hualeg before the seven months are up, we don't have to worry anymore, do we? Because we're already dead!"

I just looked away, towards the wide, slow-moving river, feeling trapped by circumstances, by Rogas's twisted logic, and by the long, uncertain months stretching ahead.

11

Luck Is On Our Side

The beam of light hitting my face through the shutter crack felt harsh, unwelcome. I woke with a groan, every muscle protesting yesterday's rowing and fighting. For a moment, I just lay there on the rough floor mat, the events of the past few days swirling in my head like muddy river water – Mom's peaceful face as she slipped away, the shocking brutality by the river, Muriel's tear-streaked face, the long journey north... and Rogas. Always Rogas, stirring up trouble. A familiar surge of anger tightened my chest. I was here, a fugitive in this strange northern village, because of a chain of events that felt both unavoidable and entirely my own damned fault.

Shouldn't have taken the dagger. Shouldn't have gone back. Should have stayed hidden.

But then Rogas's voice echoed in my memory: *"Life always changes... whether you like it or not."* Annoying, self-serving... but maybe true. Maybe pointless to regret what couldn't be undone.

I pushed myself up. The wooden bed frame was empty. Rogas was already gone. Again.

Sighing, I splashed some water on my face from a bucket outside and headed towards Taupin's house. As expected, Taupin had already given Rogas his instructions for the day – check the weapons, assess the men – and Rogas, equally predictably, had delegated everything to me before disappearing somewhere. Fine. It gave me something to do besides dwell on things I couldn't change. And honestly, I was curious about these northern villagers who planned to stand against the Hualeg.

I spent the morning inspecting the rough-forged swords and spearheads stored in Taupin's warehouse – functional, but desperately needing sharpening – and talking to the men who had gathered. Some handled the weapons with a clumsy familiarity born of hunting or perhaps past skirmishes; others looked like they'd be more comfortable with a fishing net. It was a mixed bag, raw potential at best.

I found Rogas lounging on the porch later, looking pleased with himself. "Well?" he asked.

"Some of them know which end of a sword to hold," I reported dryly. "That's a start. The weapons need work. If I had a proper grinder, I could fix them, but I suppose they'll have to manage."

"The weapons aren't the most important thing," Rogas declared, adopting a wise, experienced tone that always set my teeth on edge. "It's the spirit of the men. Are they eager? Committed? Or just a pack of shivering rabbits waiting to bolt?"

"I believe," I said, unable to resist a sarcastic jab, "that even rabbits might fight like lions if their leader sets the right example. If *you* can't manage that, maybe *I* should take the job. And the extra five sazets."

Rogas just laughed. "Still thinking about the money, eh Tuck? So you *do* want to be Taupin's number two?"

"If I have to," I said flatly.

"Be patient. Your time will come." He grinned that infuriating grin again. "For now, I still need those ten sazets."

I eyed him suspiciously. He always seemed to be scheming. "Looks like you've cooked up another plan already. What are you thinking about now?"

"You always assume the worst, William," he protested, though his eyes glinted. "I'm not up to anything!"

"That reminds me," I pressed, seizing the moment while we were relatively alone in a corner of the courtyard, away from the resting villagers. "You never answered me yesterday. What did you do? Why does those men want you dead so badly?"

Rogas shifted uncomfortably, rubbing his bruised, swollen nose. He watched the men eating and talking across the yard. "What do you want to know?" He hesitated. "It's... a long story. Don't know where to start."

"Who's Mornitz?" I prompted.

"Just hired muscle," Rogas shrugged, trying to sound casual, but there was a flicker of pride in his eyes – pride at being hunted. "Bounty hunter type. Someone pays him, he finds people."

"And Bellion? The name you yelled by the river. He's the one paying Mornitz?" The pieces started clicking together. "Mornitz said Bellion wanted you brought back alive so *he* could... deal with you. What did you do to him, Rogas? Rob him? Kill his son?" I threw the accusation out there, half-guessing.

To my surprise, Rogas's face went pale. "I didn't mean to do it!" he blurted out, then quickly shook his head, his expression turning sour. "That's not true! They don't know anything!"

Bingo. "So you *did* hurt his son?" I pressed. "Well, if someone hurt my family... maybe I'd hunt them down too."

"I didn't kill anybody!" Rogas insisted nervously. "Not... not *him*. I just... roughed him up a bit..."

"This son. What's his name?"

"Darron," Rogas spat the name out like it tasted bad. "And he's no innocent lamb, believe me. Arrogant bastard. Deserved a beating."

"Maybe," I conceded, "but fathers don't usually send bounty hunters after someone for just a 'beating'. You must have done more. Taken something important?"

Rogas sighed, finally seeming to decide to tell me at least part of the truth. "Look, it happened last summer. Near Nordton, down south. My troop ran into some raiders near the forest. Big fight. Bloody." He grinned grimly. "We won. Survivors scattered. We headed back towards Alton, then went to Milliton for some R&R. Next thing we know, we're attacked *again*. Same bastards. Came after us right in the city. We fought them off, but... lost a lot of good men." His face hardened. "Before the attackers fled, that scarred piece of shit you saw by the river – he left a message. Said 'Bellion won't forget'. Surprised me. Bellion's just some rich merchant in Nordton, never dealt with him. Then I found out – his son, Darron, was the leader of those raiders we fought in the forest. After that, I figured it was time to disappear for a while. Headed north. Ended up in Ortleg. Hoped they wouldn't find me way up there."

I tried to piece it together. "So this rich merchant Bellion runs a gang of robbers, led by his son? If he's a known criminal, why didn't you report him to your army commanders? Let the kingdom deal with him?"

"And get myself killed on the way back to Alton?" Rogas scoffed. "They'd be waiting for me. Safer up north."

"Safer?" I raised an eyebrow. "Mornitz found you easily enough once spring came. All your boasting and swaggering probably made it simple."

"Hey, I survived months, had some fun," he protested weakly. "Pretty good, I'd say."

"Sure. Until the snow melted."

He nodded thoughtfully, then actually laughed. "But my luck held, didn't it? Still here. And I think it's getting better. We'll make it through this winter safely too, you'll see."

"And after that? Hide forever?"

"Remember, William," he grinned, poking my shoulder, "you're on their list now, too. What about *you*? Going to hide?"

I looked away. "I haven't thought that far ahead."

"Well, *I* have." Rogas's eyes lit up with that familiar, dangerous spark. "I have a good plan for us. Want to hear it?"

Despite myself, I was curious. "What?"

"Look," he leaned in conspiratorially. "We work for Taupin for these seven months. Train his men. Fight the Hualeg if they show up. Earn our pay, earn some trust. Maybe not much money, but enough. Then... then we invite our new northern friends here, the best fighters, to come south with us."

"South? For what?" I frowned.

"To form our *own* army," Rogas declared, beaming. "A tough crew, loyal to *us*. And with this army, we march straight to Nordton, right to Bellion's doorstep. We take him down, take down Darron, take down Mornitz if he's still around. Destroy them all, root and stem! Wipe them out so completely no one even *thinks* about coming after us ever again."

I stared at him, stunned. The audacity of it... raising a private army to launch an attack deep in Alton territory? It was insane. It was terrifying. "Are you serious?" I asked incredulously. "Do you even know how strong Bellion is?"

"I know enough," Rogas replied confidently. "Give me thirty good men who follow my orders without question, and I can crush them."

I tried to wrap my head around it. A counter-attack. Taking the fight to them. It was... bold. "Hmm... well, if that's the case..."

"Pretty smart, isn't it?" he grinned, clearly expecting praise.

"Not bad," I admitted slowly. The core idea, eliminating the threat permanently, had a certain brutal logic. "But..." I looked him straight in the eye, "...I don't believe that's *all* you have planned. Just getting rid of them? I doubt it. After you beat Bellion, you plan to take his riches, don't you? You're planning to become a robber yourself!"

"Always thinking negative!" Rogas scoffed, though he didn't look surprised by the accusation. "Look, spoils of war are normal. And they're *robbers*, William! We'd just be robbing the robbers! We could even give some of it back to people they stole from before. Think of it! A noble act!"

Noble wasn't the word that came to mind. It sounded dangerously close to the chaos Bellion himself seemed to represent. I stayed silent.

"Now you understand, don't you?" Rogas pressed, clapping me on the back. "It's a good plan! Solid! You'll want in, I know it."

I shrugged, unwilling to commit, still processing. "As long as the pay is right."

He roared with laughter. "That's it! You're learning! Thinking like a mercenary now! Our future is bright, Tuck, bright!"

"As long as you don't play dumb," I muttered.

"No," he corrected, suddenly serious again. "As long as luck is on our side."

"Whatever," I sighed, pushing myself up. The sun was touching the western hills. The men in the courtyard were packing up, heading home or finding places to sleep on Taupin's porches. Tomorrow, we'd start getting ready for the journey north. "I'm going to sleep," I said. "If I'm lucky, I might have a nice dream. One that doesn't have you in it."

"Who do you want to meet in your dream? Muriel?" he teased. "Hey, I can help you with that."

"Shut up!"

He laughed again, but then caught my arm as I turned to leave. "Wait. Serious now. If you really wish for luck, I can give you something."

I eyed him suspiciously.

"Look at this." He dug into his pocket and pulled out a ring. It was made of some reddish-yellow metal, intricately carved. "My lucky ring. Whenever I wear this, luck stays with me. Always win at dice, never lose a fight... always get lucky with the girls." He winked.

"Hmm," I examined it skeptically. "If it's so lucky, why keep it in your pocket instead of wearing it?"

"I wear it a lot!"

"I've never seen it before."

"Your fault for not noticing," he retorted. "I'm serious. It's lucky. You want it? I'll give it to you."

I took the ring. It felt heavy, warm. Despite his nonsense claims, it looked well-made, maybe even valuable. "Yes, it's a nice ring. But if you give it to me, won't you lose your luck?"

"Nah, I got another lucky charm." He grinned, pulling out the necklace I *had* seen him wear – black cord, hung with three large, curved bear claws. "This one's even better. Ring won me ten sazets once. This necklace? Thirty!" He laughed again. "Problem is, wore them both together one time? Lost fifty! Crazy! Never wear them together now. So, the ring's just sitting there. Might as well offer it to you."

"You sound like you did yesterday with your plan," I said dryly. "Nonsense. I don't believe any of it. But... if you're really giving me the ring, I'd be grateful."

"It's yours."

"Okay, thanks."

"Put it on," he urged, watching me. I hesitated. "Then tomorrow," he grinned wickedly, "tell me what you did with Muriel in your dream."

Rolling my eyes, I slipped the heavy ring onto my finger. It felt strange, foreign. Probably wouldn't hurt, I figured. Who knew? Maybe, just maybe, Rogas wasn't talking complete nonsense this time.

Turns out, he was.

When I woke the next morning, the ring felt cold on my finger. I couldn't believe I'd actually half-hoped for some lucky dream, some sign. Instead, I'd slept like a log, dreamless and deep. Or maybe... maybe *that* was the luck? Waking up feeling rested, truly rested, for the first time since Mom... I looked down at the unfamiliar ring, then pushed myself off the floor mat.

Outside, the army was assembling. Thirty men from Orulion, plus Rogas, Taupin, and me. Weapons were distributed – those rough swords and spears from the warehouse. We boarded six sturdy river boats. There was no ceremony, no tearful farewells from the villagers who stayed behind, just grim determination. Everyone knew we might not come back.

As I took my place at an oar, a strange mix of feelings washed over me. We were heading north down the Ordelahr, the current pulling us swiftly along. North. The direction Mom had forbidden. The direction of my father's people, the Hualeg. I felt a deep unease disobeying her wish, yet... a undeniable flicker of excitement, too. I wanted to see this land, see the faces of these northerners, even if they were supposed to be the enemy.

The river flowed fast. By sunset, we reached the next village downriver, mooring the boats. The following morning, ten more men joined our ranks, swelling our numbers. We continued north, rowing by day, camping by night, stopping at villages nestled along the riverbank, gathering strength.

Days blurred into a rhythm of rowing, eating, sleeping. When we finally reached Thaluk, the northernmost village still standing in Alton territory, our army numbered eighty. Twenty more men from Thaluk itself joined us, bringing us to the full hundred Taupin had aimed for.

We made camp in a large, dilapidated stone building perched high on a cliff overlooking the river. From here, the view north was vast, empty. The Ordelahr snaked away through dense, dark forests until it disappeared into the haze.

That first evening in Thaluk, listening to the hushed conversations of the men, I overheard a story that sent a chill down my spine. Thaluk hadn't always been the border. There were once other villages further north, closer to Hualeg lands. They were gone now. Plundered, burned, swallowed by the wilderness. Thaluk only survived, the old man telling the tale said, because of these cliffs. They could see the raiders coming from miles away, giving just enough time to flee into the eastern hills, abandoning their homes and possessions to save their lives.

Looking out at that vast, silent forest stretching northward under the setting sun, the stories about cruel, giant Hualeg warriors suddenly felt terrifyingly real. This wasn't just a job for coin anymore. This was the edge of the world, and real danger lay just beyond the trees.

12

You Don't Have to Promise Anything

Day after day bled into the next here in Thaluk, perched on this cliff overlooking the vast northern wilderness. Half a month had passed since we arrived. Life fell into a rhythm: training with the villagers – trying to turn fishermen into fighters – patrolling the endless, watchful forest, and sometimes, when the gnawing boredom or the heavy weight of memory settled too deep, joining the locals hunting game or casting lines into the cold, swift Ordelahr.

On one patrol, following a stream eastward into the woods with five other men, one of the older fishermen started talking. "Not all Hualegs are bad, you know," he said, spitting into the water. "Years back, one used to come by sometimes. Traded fair. Gave us good coats for food, medicine. Good man. But," he sighed, "ones like him are rare as summer snow. Most just come to rob."

"When did they last come?" I asked, keeping my voice carefully neutral.

"Last summer," he grimaced, the memory clearly painful. "Five boats. Maybe fifty of them. Came up the river fast. Some of us made it to the woods." He shook his head. "Many didn't have time. Didn't survive…"

"Why did they kill?" The question felt thick in my throat. "Isn't robbing enough?"

The fisherman shrugged irritably. "How should I know their minds? Savages. Maybe they figure, why carry an axe if you don't bloody it on someone?"

I rowed on, silent, the fisherman's words stoking a cold fire inside me. A hatred for the violence, the senseless killing he described. And beneath it, shame. Shame that my own father came from these people. If these men knew my blood was half Hualeg... would they look at me with that same fear and hatred?

We continued our patrol, following the creek, climbing a low hill for a better view – nothing suspicious – then circling back towards the river as the sun began to slant west. Near the bank, nestled amongst the trees, stood a small, solitary log cabin.

An old man, hunched over with age, his beard a cascade of white, emerged as we approached. Bullock, they called him. Lived out here alone, gathering wood, herbs, whatever the forest provided. Spent his whole life here, people said.

"Well now!" he rasped, his voice thin but welcoming. "Visitors! Haven't seen folk out this way in ages. Come thirsty? Let me fetch you a drink. Been too long since I shared a cup with anyone."

"Thank you, sir, but we're just passing through," I said politely, though his eagerness tugged at me. "On patrol. We just wanted to ask if you've noticed anything... strange lately."

He peered at me. "Strange things?"

"Suspicious people," I clarified. "People from the north, maybe."

"Ah. The Hualeg."

He shuffled closer, his eyes, nearly hidden under bushy white brows, squinting hard as he tried to focus on my face. "Haven't seen anyone. Not for a long time. Northerners rarely come up this creek; they stick to the big river mostly. Just friends from the villages stop by sometimes."

"So, no one unusual around?"

"No, son."

I nodded. "I see." That seemed to settle it.

"Everything alright up at the village?" he asked, a hint of concern in his voice.

"We hope so. Just being cautious. Well," I started to turn, "if that's all, then goodbye, sir. We should be getting back."

"What's the hurry?" His thin, bony hand unexpectedly patted my arm. "Stay a while. Walk with me? I'd surely appreciate the company."

Looking at his lonely eyes, the eager hope on his face... I felt a pang of sympathy. How long had it been since he'd had a real conversation? "If you insist, sir," I smiled, despite my men shifting impatiently behind me.

"Ah, thank you, thank you!" His face lit up.

"Hey, Tuck," one of my patrol members spoke up respectfully but firmly. "We've been out since yesterday. Best we head back before dark falls proper."

"You go ahead," I told them. "I'll follow shortly. Just leave me one of the boats."

They agreed, nodding farewell to the old man, and headed back towards the riverbank.

Bullock led me to his small porch, gesturing towards a rickety-looking wooden chair. I sat down carefully. He disappeared inside his cabin for a moment, then re-emerged with two dusty bottles of what looked like homemade wine.

He poured us both a generous measure, beaming. "Like I said, son, it's been too long. Used to share a bottle regular, though. Every month or so, especially when *he* visited."

I took a tentative sip. The wine was surprisingly potent, sharp on the tongue. "Him?"

"Aye, the hunter fellow." Bullock settled into his own chair, peering at my face again in the fading light. "You don't know him?"

"Why would I know him?" I asked, confused.

"Because," the old man leaned forward, his voice dropping slightly, "your face is the spit of his. You two... could be brothers. Or..."

My breath caught in my throat. My mind flashed back to Mom's words: *Look in the mirror. You'll see your father there.* Could Bullock mean...? Vilnar? Here? A hunter? My heart hammered against my ribs, excitement warring with a sudden, fierce caution. Don't show anything. Don't betray the secret.

"Who is he?" I asked, forcing my voice to remain steady.

"A Hualeg," Bullock said, then chuckled. "Can you believe it? My best drinking buddy for years, a Hualeg! Hunted bear mostly, sold the skins in the villages. Lived up this creek somewhere for a few years. Then one day, just... gone. Never saw him again. Maybe went back north, settled down." He watched me closely, his old eyes sharp despite his claims of near-sightedness. "That was a long time ago," he continued softly. "But I don't forget a friend's face. And seeing you today... it's like looking at him again. Your face, your build, even your eyes." He nodded slowly. "So I'm sure you knew him. Why won't you admit it? Are you afraid? Afraid of a broken-down old man like me?"

I stayed silent, wrestling with myself. Why *was* I hesitating? Mom said my father was a good man, honorable, kind – not like the raiders these villagers feared. Bullock called him a friend. Why hide it? Was the shame of the Hualeg name stronger than the pride I should feel for the man Mom described?

Finally, I nodded, the admission feeling momentous. "Yes," I said quietly. "He... seemed to be my father."

Bullock's weathered face broke into a relieved smile. "I'm glad to hear it, son. Glad indeed. But why so unsure?"

"Because I never met him."

"Ah." His smile faded slightly. "So you don't know... if he's alive? Or... gone?"

"Yes," I replied, the single word heavy with all my uncertainty, pushing aside Mom's conviction that he was dead.

"And now," Bullock leaned forward again, his voice gentle, "now you want to know more about him?"

"Yes." The word tore from my throat, raw with years of suppressed longing. Tears pricked my eyes, and I blinked them back fiercely.

"I may not be much help. What is it you want to know?"

"Do you know where he used to live?" That felt like the first step.

"He mentioned his house once. Said it was up this creek." Bullock gestured eastward. "Not on the big river, but this smaller one. Never been there myself, mind you. But I reckon if you follow this water east, deep into the woods, you might find it."

Hope surged through me, fierce and bright. "Thank you, sir."

"What are you looking for there?" he asked shrewdly.

I hesitated. "Nothing," I lied, shifting uncomfortably. "Just... curious."

Bullock nodded slowly, stroking his beard, his eyes thoughtful. "Always felt I knew him well, your father. But maybe I didn't. Always wondered what truly happened to him." He looked at me again. "I think *you* know more than you're letting on, son. But... you're not ready to tell me yet."

"As soon as I know more myself, I'll tell you," I promised impulsively.

"I'm glad to hear that," Bullock replied, his smile returning. "Because it means you'll come back. Visit an old man. Be my friend. Like your father was."

The encounter left me shaken, buzzing with a renewed sense of purpose. I untied the small boat my patrol had left and started rowing east, up the winding creek Bullock had indicated. The desire to find my father's house, to uncover *something* tangible about him, burned stronger than ever, pushing aside Mom's warnings about the past. If I didn't do this now, didn't follow this lead, I knew I'd regret it forever. Maybe finding his home wouldn't give me all the answers, but it might help me understand him, understand myself.

The creek narrowed, twisting through dense forest. Boulders choked the banks, ancient trees draped heavy branches over the water. Was this the right way? The Ordelahr had countless tributaries branching east. Doubt gnawed at me as the sun dipped lower, painting the sky in shades of orange and purple. Maybe I should find a place to camp, try again tomorrow.

Then I saw it – a small cove, sheltered by large, moss-covered boulders. The water here was calm, still. Perfect place to pull ashore. As I steered the boat towards the bank and hopped out to tie the painter to a log, my eyes caught something through the thick bushes further inland. Wood. Faded, weathered wood. A house, almost completely hidden from the river.

My heart leaped. A certainty settled over me, deep and instinctive. *This was it.* Father's house.

I pushed through the undergrowth cautiously. The grass was knee-high, wild. The house itself was small, simple, built of sturdy logs, clearly uninhabited for a very long time. The path to the door had vanished beneath weeds. But then I saw something wrong: a window on the side stood slightly ajar, swinging gently in the breeze. Had someone been here recently?

My hand went to the sword hilt at my belt – the one Rogas had given me. I circled the cabin slowly, keeping my distance, peering through the open window. Dark inside. Empty furniture shapes, dust motes dancing in the fading light. No sign of life.

Satisfied it was abandoned, I moved back towards the front. I reached for the door, ready to push it open, and froze.

Standing about ten paces away, near the edge of the trees, was a girl. Roughly my age, my height. Long, thick braids the colour of ripe wheat fell over her shoulder. Her eyes, scanning me warily, were a startling, intense blue. She wore a heavy vest made of bearskin over simple clothes, and clutched in her *left* hand was a sword – a beautifully crafted weapon, much finer than mine. Its polished surface gleamed dully. Hualeg. The hair, the eyes... she had to be Hualeg.

Where had she come from? Had she been inside the house? Her stance was tense, balanced, ready. Definitely not friendly.

I decided to speak first, try to avoid a fight if possible. "Put down your sword!" I called out, keeping my voice steady. "Can we talk?"

She didn't reply immediately, just stared at me, her blue eyes narrowed. Did she even understand the Altonian tongue?

Then, to my relief, she spoke, her accent thick but understandable. She glanced down at her own fine sword, then back at me, lifting its point slightly. "Your sword," she said, her voice low and challenging. "Draw it."

My hand tightened on my hilt. "What do you mean?"

"Draw your sword!" she demanded, louder this time, taking a step forward.

Clearly, talking wasn't an option. With a sinking feeling, I drew my own blade. The instant my sword cleared its sheath, she charged. She moved with blurring speed, her left-handed attack coming from an angle I wasn't used to, the force of her blows shockingly powerful. I barely managed to parry the first strike, the impact jarring my arm to the shoulder. Another swing followed, then another, swift and unpredictable. I struggled to defend, constantly wrong-footed by her left-handed style. Every time I tried to launch my own attack, she shifted easily to her right, my blade whistling through empty air. Frustration boiled up inside me. Gripping my sword tighter, I put all my strength into a wide, sweeping blow, aiming to knock her blade aside.

Clang! The impact was solid. Her sword flew from her grasp, spinning end over end into the tall grass.

Not wasting the opening, I lunged forward, grabbing the front of her thick bearskin vest, shoving her backwards hard against the rough bark of a nearby tree. She hit it with a solid thud but didn't cry out, just glared up at me, her eyes blazing, already trying to fight back, to knee me.

"Stop it!" I yelled, pressing my left forearm against her chest to hold her pinned. Our faces were inches apart; I could feel the heat radiating from her, her breath coming in furious gasps. "Calm down!"

Surprisingly, she stopped struggling, though the defiance in her eyes didn't lessen. Seeing my chance, I lowered my sword point slightly, trying again. "Listen, we don't need to fight. I don't want to hurt you. Just tell me why you—"

Agony exploded in my groin. Her knee connected with vicious force, stealing my breath, making me double over with a strangled gasp. Nausea washed over me. Before I could react, her left hand clamped onto my right wrist, twisting, forcing my sword away. Her right fist slammed into my chin, snapping my head back. A second punch landed flush on my jaw.

Stars burst behind my eyes. The world tilted. My sword slipped from my numb fingers. As I stumbled, trying to regain my balance, a final, powerful kick connected with the side of my head. Darkness rushed in, swallowing me whole.

When I came to, the first thing I felt was warmth. A bonfire crackled merrily a few feet away. My head throbbed violently, and my jaw felt swollen, bruised. I blinked, trying to focus. I was leaning against something solid – a tree trunk. My body felt heavy, unresponsive.

Across the fire, the yellow-haired girl sat calmly, chewing on a piece of roasted meat. She watched me as I stirred, her expression unreadable. Then the memories flooded back – finding the house, the sudden fight, her surprising strength, the cheap shots that took me down. I tried to straighten up, reaching instinctively to touch my aching jaw. That's when I saw them – thick, rough bindings made from twisted plant roots secured tightly around my wrists. A quick glance down confirmed my ankles and knees were bound too.

Trapped. Helpless. A prisoner of this Hualeg girl. My mind raced. Would she kill me? Torture me? Or was this just... caution?

She finished chewing, swallowed, then pointed towards the fire with her knife. Several skewers of fish were propped near the flames, sizzling invitingly. "Fish," she said. "Eat."

The smell made my empty stomach rumble, but caution warred with hunger. I didn't move. What game was she playing?

"Take it," she repeated, her voice louder, impatient.

I shook my head slightly, trying to ignore the throbbing in my skull. "Who are you?"

She stopped chewing, her blue eyes fixed on me. She picked up one of the fish skewers and, without warning, threw it. It landed squarely in my bound hands, searing hot. I yelped, juggling the skewer frantically until the worst of the heat subsided.

"Hey!" I protested, anger flaring despite my predicament. "Can't you give it more nicely? It's food!"

"Eat," she commanded again, ignoring my complaint.

"If I don't want to eat, what are you going to do?" I challenged, testing her.

She picked up a waterskin, took a long drink. "I will be angry."

"Why would you be angry?"

"Because you don't do what I said."

"So what if you're angry?"

"I'll hit you." Simple. Direct.

A reluctant laugh escaped me. This was absurd. "So I have to eat. And then after I do that?"

She shrugged. "Do you want me to hit you again?"

"I mean," I clarified, trying to keep my frustration in check, "what do you want from me? Why did you tie me up?"

"I didn't want to do it," she replied, surprisingly.

"Then why did you?"

Her gaze hardened. "Because you came to this place. You shouldn't have." She stared at me intently. Then she repeated, flatly, "After you eat, you go."

"I'll go when I want to," I retorted stubbornly.

"You should go."

"Why?"

"Or my friends will kill you," she stated, her voice gruff.

My stomach tightened again, this time not from hunger. "Friends?" I nodded, trying to appear calm. "Are there many?"

"What?"

"Your friends. Are there many of them?"

"Many," she confirmed.

"Are they here?"

She looked me over again, considering. "Soon."

"Why are they coming?" I pressed, needing information.

"Because they want to." Evasive.

"Are you going to rob the villages again?" The question slipped out, sharp with the memory of the fisherman's story.

Her expression instantly darkened, anger flashing in her blue eyes. "You ask too many questions," she snapped. "I caught *you*. I ask questions."

"Well," I tried a different tactic, forcing a grin despite my aching jaw, "if you want us to talk, get to know each other, you could untie me first. We can talk as friends."

She just shook her head dismissively. "I already know you. So you eat, then leave. If you stay here until morning, you'll die."

Her threat felt chillingly real this time. *Hualeg. Friends. Coming soon.* I had to get back, warn Taupin, warn Rogas. But why was she letting me go?

Was she... not as bad as the stories? Not like the raiders? Or was this some kind of trick?

And why was *she* here, at my father's abandoned house? Was she just using it as a temporary camp? Or was she looking for something? She clearly wasn't alone, if her friends were coming. Where were they now?

My stomach growled again. Survival first. I picked up the fish skewer and started eating. It was surprisingly good, cooked perfectly. I glanced towards the dark shape of the cabin behind her. My father's house. I desperately wanted to look inside, search for any clue, any connection. But I knew she wouldn't allow it. She wanted me gone. And she was right – I *had* to go.

I finished the fish, took a long drink from the waterskin she offered, then nodded my thanks. Without a word, she drew her fine sword – *my* sword felt crude beside it – and sliced through the tough root bindings on my hands and feet with casual ease.

I stood up slowly, testing my legs, rubbing my sore wrists. I looked at her, standing confidently before me, her sword held loosely at her side. "You let me go," I said, needing to understand. "Aren't you afraid I might attack you?"

"No," she replied simply. "If you do, you are a fool."

"Of course," I couldn't resist a slightly bitter joke, "because you are still holding *my* sword. That sword." I gestured towards the blade she'd taken from me, now leaning against the tree. "I can't ask for it back, can I? But," I added, meeting her gaze, "I can attack you without the sword."

"Like I said," she repeated patiently, "you'd be a fool. Go away."

"You know," I found myself saying, "maybe I'll see you again later."

"Maybe," she replied tersely, offering nothing.

"And we will fight again," I continued, pushing it.

"Maybe."

"Maybe to the death."

She paused, considering this. "Yes."

The finality of her agreement sent another chill through me. "It could be... later, I'll have to kill you."

This time, she didn't answer, just watched me.

"Don't you regret letting me go?" I asked, genuinely puzzled.

She sighed, a barely audible sound. "No."

I shook my head, a strange mix of gratitude and something else – empathy? – stirring within me. "Hey," I said softly, "I'm the one who would regret it if I did that to you. I'm not going to kill you, not even hurt you! Tonight you did me a favor, letting me go, warning me. I won't forget it. So if we meet again, even if it's... the worst possible time... I'll be nice to you. I promise."

"You don't have to promise anything," she said flatly.

"That's up to me."

"Go."

I nodded, accepting the dismissal. I walked away from the firelight, around the bushes, back towards the dark riverbank. I untied my boat, pushed it into the water, and jumped aboard. As I picked up the oar, I looked back. She was standing there at the edge of the clearing, watching me, a silent silhouette against the fire glow. The moonlight caught her face, highlighting her strange, fierce beauty. I raised a hand in a half-wave, a smile I didn't quite understand touching my lips. She didn't respond.

As I rowed away, downstream now, back towards Thaluk, a heavy feeling settled over me. I desperately hoped my promise, my foolish words about fighting her again, wouldn't come true. I didn't want to meet her in battle. Despite everything, despite her being Hualeg, despite her beating me senseless... I wanted to know who she was. Maybe, somehow, I wanted to be her friend.

A ridiculous hope. She was Hualeg. By definition, she was my enemy now. Wasn't she?

13

The Red Hair

I rowed through the night, every splash of the oar echoing in the vast darkness. My arms screamed in protest, but fear kept me going, a cold knot tightening in my stomach with every mile gained downstream. The yellow-haired girl's warning – *my friends will kill you* – played over and over in my mind. What if they were already on the river? What if they patrolled these waters regularly? Facing one Hualeg warrior – a girl, no less – had ended with me unconscious and captured. Facing several, especially without my sword... I didn't want to think about it.

But the river remained empty, silent save for the whisper of the current and the cry of night birds. No sign of Hualeg boats, neither on the creek nor the wide Ordelahr. Maybe they were still far north. Maybe she'd just been trying to scare me off. Either way, relief warred with exhaustion as I pushed myself harder, desperation lending strength to my aching muscles. I reached the landing below Thaluk just before noon, the sun high and hot overhead.

Scrambling up the cliff path to the old stone building we used as headquarters, I didn't stop to catch my breath, didn't pause to think. I burst into the main room, finding Rogas, Taupin, and another man – Morrin, Thaluk's own village chief, short and stocky – huddled over a rough table.

Rogas looked up, a wide, relieved grin spreading across his bruised face. "Ah, Tuck! Back at last! Where have you been, boy? Gone three days! Hope you found something interesting out there."

"I just hope you didn't bring back any bad news," Taupin added, his expression wary.

"Other patrols returned," Morrin informed me gruffly. "West and north. Saw no sign of those barbarians. Hope the east is clear too."

I looked from face to face, the hope draining from theirs as they saw my expression. "Perhaps," I said, my voice rough with fatigue and dread, "they are near."

A heavy silence fell.

"We went east along the creek," I continued, trying to keep my voice steady. "All the way to old Bullock's cabin. He said he hadn't seen anything suspicious."

"That's good news, isn't it?" Morrin said, though he sounded hesitant. "But he's old. Half-blind, half-deaf. Can't rely on his word for much."

"My soldiers scouted around his house too," I went on, the next words catching in my throat. "Seemed clear. From there... we split up. I sent the five soldiers back here first, then I continued exploring further east."

"What do you mean?" Rogas sat up straighter, his easy grin vanishing. "Your men returned before you?"

"Yes," I confirmed. "They should have been back yesterday." A cold premonition washed over me as I saw the confusion on their faces.

"No one has returned from your patrol, Tuck," Rogas said slowly, his eyes narrowed.

"What?" My voice cracked.

"Your soldiers," Taupin confirmed grimly. "They haven't returned."

"Wait, wait," Morrin sputtered, starting to panic. "What's going on?"

I stared at them, the terrible possibilities crashing down on me. The missing boat. The Hualeg girl's warning. My men... "I don't know yet," I whispered, the words feeling like stones in my mouth. "But maybe... maybe they're nearby."

"Who?" Taupin demanded, his voice sharp with urgency.

"Hualeg raiders."

"Be clearer, boy! Don't just say things like that!" Taupin slammed his hand on the table.

Rogas gave me a hard look. "What did you find in the east, Tuck? Tell us."

So I told them. Rowing further east, finding the abandoned house, the fight. "A Hualeg was there," I said. "We fought. I lost."

Taupin winced. Rogas stared in disbelief, a sarcastic grin starting to form. "You lost? Seriously?"

"How?" Morrin asked, bewildered. "You beat everyone here! How could you lose?"

"My opponent was more skilled," I said flatly, pushing down the humiliation, the memory of her knee connecting, the punches. Carelessness was no excuse. I lost. "Does it matter? Do you want the rest of the story?"

"Yes!" Taupin urged impatiently.

"That Hualeg warrior captured me," I continued, watching their stunned faces. "Tied me up. But then... let me go."

Silence again. They stared as if I'd grown a second head.

"That's... strange," Morrin finally mumbled. "Hualegs know no mercy. They love to kill. Why let you go?"

"Are you sure it *was* a Hualeg?" Taupin questioned.

"Yes," I insisted. "But... maybe one of the good kind the fisherman mentioned? The warrior warned me before letting me go. Said the rest of the Hualegs – friends – would arrive soon."

Taupin and Morrin exchanged uneasy glances. Rogas just looked stunned.

"What did this warrior look like?" Rogas asked sharply.

"Tall," I described carefully, picturing her fierce blue eyes. "Yellow hair. Very good with a sword. Hits hard." I stopped there. For some reason, I couldn't bring myself to say the warrior was a girl. Maybe it was gratitude for her warning, for letting me live. Maybe it was shame, fear of Rogas's ridicule. Whatever the reason, the omission felt necessary right now.

"And you believe this warning?" Rogas pressed.

"I do." I sighed, the anxiety churning inside me again. "My squad... they haven't returned. It's possible they saw something, stopped somewhere along the creek. Or maybe..." the worst thought surfaced, "...maybe they met those Hualegs already."

"They should have been back by now," Morrin fretted.

"Yeah," Rogas said grimly. "Unless... something bad happened. Like they're dead."

"That's terrible!" Morrin exclaimed, paling.

"It wouldn't have happened if you hadn't split up!" Taupin rounded on me, his earlier relief forgotten, replaced by accusation. "If you'd stayed together, they'd be fine!"

"If Tuck had stayed with them, he'd likely be dead too," Rogas surprisingly defended me. He even managed a weak grin in my direction. "He was lucky. Understand, Tuck? Your famous luck is working overtime." He conveniently ignored that *his* luck hadn't prevented his own capture attempt. "Lucky you didn't die with your men – if they *are* dead. Lucky you ran into a Hualeg who let you go *and* gave you information."

"A Hualeg who defeated him!" Taupin snapped, still annoyed. "If Tuck had just won the fight, maybe he could have brought the prisoner here! We could have interrogated him! Gotten real answers!"

Enough blame. Enough speculation. "Look, sir," I interrupted, my own annoyance rising, "my men aren't necessarily dead. I'll go find them."

"Alone?" Morrin asked nervously.

"No," Rogas decided immediately. "Tuck, take ten soldiers with you."

"They could all be ambushed if Hualegs *are* out there!" Taupin protested.

"Then what do you suggest?" Rogas shot back impatiently. "We all sit here waiting like fools until the whole horde shows up on our doorstep?"

"We stay here! Defend this position, as originally planned!" Taupin insisted.

"We should have patrolled better from the start," Morrin muttered, shaking his head.

"That's exactly my point!" Taupin glared at me again. "You should have been more careful! Remember, I pay you well for this—"

"Then take your money back!" I exploded, shoving away from the table. Years of Bortez teaching me respect warred with the exhaustion, the fear, the injustice of being blamed for something I didn't understand yet. "Take it all back right now! I'll head south again! But don't be surprised if some of these men come with me when they realize dying up here for poor pay and confused leadership is a fool's game! Is *that* what you want, sir? I'm here to help! I'm the one out there *doing* something, risking my neck, not sitting here talking! So don't talk any more nonsense to me!"

Silence fell again, thick and heavy. Taupin and Morrin stared at me, stunned by my outburst. But Rogas... Rogas was grinning, a genuine, almost proud grin this time. It was unsettling, but right now, it felt like support.

"Ten soldiers, Tuck," Rogas repeated calmly into the silence. "Bring Thom and his usual crew." Thom was a steady fisherman, older than me, competent.

I nodded, the anger receding slightly, replaced by grim determination. "I'll go now."

"Are you sure?" Rogas asked, sounding almost concerned. "Don't you want to rest first? Eat?"

"I'll do that later," I said, already moving towards the door. "The sooner I go, the better."

Rogas nodded. "Remember," he called after me, holding up his hand, showing the bear claw necklace, "don't take off your lucky item. Seems to be working for you, believe it or not."

I ignored him, heading straight for the barracks. I forced down some dry bread and water, gathered Thom and nine other men I trusted from our training sessions, explained the situation quickly – missing patrol, possible Hualeg contact – and we headed back down to the river.

Back across the Ordelahr, then rowing upstream into the eastern creek. Exhaustion finally claimed me. I slumped in the boat, letting the others row and keep watch, falling into a heavy, uneasy sleep.

It felt like moments later when Thom shook me awake. "We're near the place you described, Tuck. Where the creek narrows."

I rubbed my eyes, instantly alert. "Seen anything?"

"Not yet."

"Keep moving. Slowly now."

The two boats crept forward, hugging opposite banks of the winding creek. We passed Bullock's lonely cabin – no sign of life. As the afternoon wore on, we reached the sheltered cove where I'd found the abandoned boat yesterday. Yes, there it was, still tied up where my patrol must have left it.

I scanned the bank. The bushes, the muddy footprints leading into the woods... it was the same place. "They went in there," I pointed. "Let's go."

"Are you sure, Tuck?" Thom asked, his voice hesitant. The other men looked tense, their hands tight on their weapons. They were older, most of them, but they looked to me for direction, simply because I could swing a sword better. The weight of that reliance felt heavy. I couldn't show doubt now.

"Don't be afraid," I said, forcing confidence into my voice. "Follow me. Keep some distance between each other – spread out. Stay low, use the trees. Watch, listen. See anything suspicious, alert the man next to you, or act fast if you have to. Got it?"

They nodded, looking slightly more determined. I led the way, stamping my own boots into the muddy trail, pushing cautiously into the dense forest. We moved slowly, scanning left and right, ears straining. The woods were quiet, too quiet. Large tree trunks offered cover, but also potential ambush points. I signaled the men to spread out further.

We kept moving deeper. Finally, the trees thinned ahead. Sunlight filtered through the canopy. I heard the faint gurgle of water – another stream, or maybe the same one looping back. We'd reached a clearing.

Peeking out from behind a massive oak, my breath caught. Lying face down near the stream bank was a body. The rough-spun tunic, the worn boots... I recognized them instantly. One of my men.

I glanced back, saw my search party had seen him too. Their faces were pale, eyes wide with fear. I looked back towards the stream. Another body lay crumpled near the water's edge to the left. A third lay sprawled near a cluster of rocks on the right.

All three. But where were the other two?

"I'm going to check," I whispered to Thom, who was closest. "You boys stay here. Cover me. Don't rush forward unless I signal. If there are enemies, let them show themselves first." Thom nodded uncertainly.

Clutching my sword, I stepped into the clearing. They looked like they'd been dead since yesterday. Killed with brutal efficiency. But maybe the killers were still nearby, watching. Crouching beside the nearest body, I saw the horrific wounds – deep, cleaving axe blows to the head and back. Grief and a cold, hard anger knotted inside me. Whoever did this...

Rustle.

The sound came from my right, from a thicket near the stream. I spun, sword ready. A figure burst out – tall, red-haired, with a thick, bushy beard flowing over a bearskin shirt. In his hands, he gripped a massive axe, its head as wide as his own. He grinned savagely from behind the beard and charged.

No time for fear. Instinct took over. I stepped back, letting his wild swing whistle past, then lunged forward, my sword clashing hard against the iron axe head. We locked together, straining, face to face. His eyes were bloodshot, breath stinking of stale wine.

My right foot found purchase on the slippery bank. I kicked out hard, catching him square in the groin. He gasped, doubling over slightly. Using the momentary opening, I slammed the pommel of my sword upwards into his chin. His head snapped back, defenses crumbling. I surged forward, bringing the sword down in a two-handed arc, shearing through his outstretched arm, then biting deep into his skull with a sickening crunch.

An angry bellow echoed from behind me. I spun again. Another Hualeg warrior erupted from the trees further down the stream, axe raised. And another behind him. And a third. All big, bearded, axes gleaming. Three new enemies.

Ignoring the pounding fear in my chest, I roared back, a wordless challenge. I held my ground, gauging the distance as the first one charged. At the last second, I dropped low, swinging my sword in a rising arc. His axe blade hissed inches above my head as my sword sliced deep into his exposed side. He went down with a grunt.

The second one was on me, his axe chopping downwards. Kneeling from the previous attack, I raised my sword just in time, parrying the blow with a ringing clang that numbed my arms. Twisting on my left leg, using it as a pivot, I spun my body around, coming up beside him in the blink of an eye. My sword swung horizontally, biting deep into his unprotected back. He staggered, roaring in pain.

I turned to face the third. He blocked my initial strike with the thick wooden handle of his axe. I pulled back, struck again, harder. Blocked again. On the third furious blow, his defense buckled. I saw the flash of terror in his eyes as he realized he couldn't hold me off. I sidestepped his clumsy counter-swing and drove my sword point deep into his neck.

The two I'd wounded earlier – the one with the slashed side, the one with the injured back – were struggling to rise, axes lifted weakly for one last stand. I moved faster. Two quick, brutal thrusts, and they lay still.

Silence descended, broken only by my own ragged breathing and the gentle murmur of the stream. I stood panting amidst the carnage, sword dripping red, scanning the surrounding trees, listening. Nothing. No more enemies.

Slowly, the adrenaline drained away, leaving me trembling, sickened. My second massacre in less than a week. Five more dead men at my feet.

I hissed towards the treeline where my men were hiding. Thom and the others emerged slowly, their faces pale, eyes wide as they took in the scene – the scattered Hualeg bodies, me standing among them covered in sweat and blood.

Thom swallowed hard. "Are... are you all right, Tuck?"

"Yes," I managed, my voice hoarse. "Why?"

"I just... want to know if what we did was right," he stammered, looking at the bodies, then back at me.

"What do you mean?"

"Do you... do you really need our help?"

I stared at him, bewildered, then annoyed. "Of course I need help! If you *can* help, that would be great!"

"But... you handled them. Easily. And you said wait until..."

"That was five enemies!" I snapped, my patience fraying. "What if there were ten? Twenty? I didn't handle it *easily*! I'd be grateful for help!

Just... come out when you see I'm in real trouble! Understand? Next time, I might not be so lucky."

We searched the rest of the immediate area. Inside the woods, not far from the clearing, we found the last two missing patrolmen. Also dead. Killed by axes. All five accounted for.

A heavy sadness settled over me. Taupin's angry words came back. Maybe he was right. If I had stayed with my men yesterday, maybe I could have made a difference. Maybe they'd still be alive.

But why were they *here*? This clearing was deep in the woods, away from the creek path. What lured them here? They wouldn't have recklessly pursued a single Hualeg scout, surely? It had to be something else.

"What now, Tuck?" Thom asked quietly, interrupting my thoughts.

"We have to find out why they died," I insisted.

"The Hualeg killed them," Thom said, stating the obvious. "Isn't that enough?"

"No," I shook my head. "That's *how* they died, not *why* they were *here*. It's not the right answer."

"It's enough for me," Thom replied firmly. "We should take our friends' bodies back to the boat and get out of here. Whatever brought them here, whatever provoked them... do you want that happening to us too?" He gestured towards the other soldiers, who nodded in agreement.

He was right, of course. Pushing deeper into these woods alone felt reckless. Relying on luck, as Rogas called it, wasn't a strategy. But walking away without knowing *why* my men died here felt wrong too. What if the reason they were lured here was the key to understanding the Hualegs' plans? What if ignoring it led to a bigger disaster later?

"Listen," I decided quickly. "I'm going to look around just a little more. You three," I pointed to Thom and two others, "keep watch here, cover my back. The rest of you, carefully take our friends' bodies back to the boat. Wait for me there. If I'm not back by sundown," I looked Thom straight in the eye, "you leave without me. Understand?"

"And how will you get back then?" Thom protested.

"I'll find a way. Walk back along the riverbank to Bullock's place if I have to. Borrow his boat."

"That's miles, Tuck! Through woods we don't know!" Thom argued. "You don't have to do this. It's too risky."

"Don't worry. I can hide if I need to. Just go. And be careful."

"*You're* the one who needs to be careful," Thom muttered, but he gave the orders for the others to start retrieving the bodies.

I turned and headed deeper into the woods, away from the stream, feeling Thom's worried gaze on my back. Going alone again. Ignoring my own advice about needing help. But the feeling that there was something more to find here, something important, was too strong to ignore.

I moved quickly now, slipping between trees, scanning the ground, trying to retrace my steps from yesterday, searching for anything out of place. Left here, right there... trying to remember the path towards the hidden house. Then, ahead, the canopy lightened again. Another clearing.

I peered cautiously through the bushes. Another small stream, wider than the last, meandering through the woods. Probably the same one, looping back. And voices. Soft, murmuring.

My breath caught. Sitting on the far bank were two large Hualeg men, similar in build and dress to the ones I'd just killed. And beside them... a girl. Reddish-auburn hair braided down her back, laughing at something one of the men said. She wore the familiar bearskin vest.

Not the yellow-haired girl. The clothes were similar, yes, but this girl's face was softer, more oval, her nose pointier. She looked younger too. And she was laughing, relaxed, completely different from the fierce warrior I'd fought yesterday.

Suddenly, her laughter died. Her head snapped up, her eyes locking directly onto the bushes where I hid. She saw me. I cursed silently – how? She said something sharp, low. The two men beside her instantly scrambled to their feet, drawing heavy swords, not axes this time.

They started towards the shallow stream, calling out. Not to me, but maybe to others nearby? Or maybe... calling for the ones I'd already silenced back at the other clearing. My heart pounded.

No time to wait. No time to think. The red-haired girl pointed straight at me. The two warriors splashed into the stream, heading right for my hiding spot. I backed up quickly, finding better footing behind a thick tree trunk. As the first Hualeg pushed through the bushes on the opposite bank, swinging his sword, I met his charge.

My blade crashed against his. I pushed him back, using the tree for leverage, then lunged, slashing his neck mercilessly. He crumpled without a sound.

The second warrior charged, swinging his sword wildly, three quick blows. I parried each one, dodging back between the trees, forcing him to follow into the more difficult terrain. He lunged again, his sword scraping against bark as I sidestepped. His momentary entanglement was the opening I needed. I ducked under his recovery swing and thrust my sword upwards, deep into his exposed side below the ribs.

He roared, stumbling back, clutching his side. He tried to raise his sword again, but I was faster. A horizontal slash across his neck, and he fell silent.

Two more dead. I looked towards the spot where the girl had been sitting. She was gone. Then I saw her, scrambling away down the riverbank to my right, brandishing her own sword but clearly trying to flee.

Without thinking, I gave chase, sprinting through the shallow water, closing the distance rapidly. Just as she glanced back in panic, I launched myself forward, tackling her low. We both crashed into the deeper part of the stream with a huge splash. Water surged over my head. I came up sputtering, grabbing for her, pushing her back, holding her head under the churning water. She struggled fiercely, kicking and clawing, but her strength was no match for mine in the water.

Then, abruptly, I came back to myself. What was I *doing*? Trying to drown her? A defenseless girl, even if she was Hualeg? Horror and revulsion washed over me. I immediately hauled her limp body out of the water, dragging her onto the muddy bank. She lay still for a terrifying moment, then coughed violently, spitting up water, her body trembling. She'd fainted.

Guilt churned in my stomach. I knelt beside her, looking down at her pale face, younger than I'd first thought, maybe Muriel's age.

"I'm sorry," I whispered, the words tasting like ash. Talking to an unconscious girl was pointless, I knew, but I needed to say it, needed to try and calm the turmoil inside me. "I'm sorry for doing this to you. You are my enemy. Your... your people killed my friends. But I will not kill you." My voice was shaking. "I will take you with me. We will... interrogate you."

Even that sounded wrong, cruel. What had I become?

14

Roar

I trussed the red-haired girl's wrists and ankles quickly with the same tough roots the yellow-haired girl had used on me. Hefting her surprisingly light body over my shoulder, I ignored her muffled groan. No time for second thoughts now. I had a prisoner, someone who might have answers. No need to push deeper into these dangerous woods alone.

I ran back through the forest, the girl bumping awkwardly against my back, the sky already darkening towards twilight. Reaching the clearing where I'd fought the first group of Hualegs felt like returning to a bad dream. The bodies were gone. My heart leaped into my throat – where were Thom and the others? Had something happened?

Then Thom's worried face appeared from behind a tree. "Tuck! You're back! Who... who are you carrying?" he stammered, eyes wide as he saw the unconscious girl slung over my shoulder.

"One of them," I grunted, lowering her gently to the ground. "Where are the others?"

"Took the bodies back to the boat already, like you said. We were just waiting for you. Come on!"

We moved quickly now, the forest growing pitch black around us. By the time we reached the riverbank where the boats waited, the last sliver of sun had vanished. Only one boat remained, Thom and two others waiting anxiously.

"The others went back first with our comrades," Thom explained as we scrambled aboard. "Told them not to stop for anything, not to get provoked."

"You weren't worried about me?" I asked, settling beside the still-unconscious girl.

Thom managed a tired grin in the darkness. "We had you, didn't we? Figured you could handle trouble." He hesitated. "Or... should I have been worried?"

I looked down at the captive girl, then back towards the dark woods where my patrolmen lay dead. "Maybe you should have," I said grimly. "And I think I know what happened to our friends yesterday. What provoked them." I nodded towards the girl. "Her. They must have seen her by the river, maybe fishing or resting. She ran, they followed, chasing her into the woods... right into an ambush."

Thom looked horrified. "You think that's how it happened?"

"Yes." It made a horrible kind of sense. "But finding proof isn't important now." We needed to get back. Warn Thaluk.

We rowed hard through the night, taking turns, not daring to light torches. The river felt vast and dangerous in the darkness. I'd killed six Hualeg warriors today, but how many more were out there? Was the girl's warning real? Were her friends truly nearby?

Exhaustion finally dragged me under again. I slept fitfully in the bottom of the boat, the hard wood digging into my back. When I woke, pale dawn light was painting the eastern sky. We were nearing Thaluk. The red-haired girl beside me was awake too, her eyes wide with fear and suspicion as she stared at me. Her mouth was now gagged with a strip of cloth.

"Gagged her when she woke up," Thom explained quietly from his rowing position. "Figured best she didn't scream when we reached the village."

Smart thinking. Even this far from the main river, a scream might carry, might attract unwanted attention. Better she stay quiet until we reached the relative safety of the headquarters.

We docked below the cliffs and carried her up the path. The village was just stirring. We took her straight to the old stone building. Rogas,

Taupin, and Morrin were already there, looking grim. I dumped the girl unceremoniously on the floor in front of them, then quickly recounted finding the bodies, the ambush theory, the second fight, and the capture.

"She can tell us," I finished, gesturing towards the bound, gagged girl. "How many Hualegs are coming. Where they are now."

"Are you sure she'll talk?" Rogas asked doubtfully, eyeing her.

Taupin frowned. "We need someone who speaks the Hualeg tongue to question her."

"Dorin can," Morrin spoke up immediately. "Lives west of the village. I'll fetch him."

"Yes, do that," Rogas nodded, then looked back at the girl with a coldness that chilled me. "Looks like she needs to talk. Or maybe I'll have to *persuade* her."

I stepped between him and the girl, glaring. "Don't be an asshole, Rogas! I caught her, she's my prisoner. We ask her properly. If I see you lay a hand on her, I swear I'll break your nose again, wound or no wound."

He flashed a mischievous, unsettling smile. "Think she can really help, Tuck? Talk or not, dead or alive, the Hualeg are still coming. We still have to fight. Maybe you should just take her to your room instead. Might be more fun."

Fury surged through me. I clenched my fist, ready to make good on my threat, when a frantic shout erupted from outside.

"Hualeg! Hualeg boats sighted on the river!"

Taupin and Morrin rushed out, Rogas right behind them. I shot one last worried glance at the girl – tied to a support pole now, her eyes wide with terror – then followed them out into the pandemonium.

Thom was running towards us, breathless. "Ten boats! Coming fast from the north!"

We didn't wait. We ran, sprinting up the path to the highest point of the cliff overlooking the Ordelahr. Thom was right. Far below, emerging from the hazy bend in the river north of the forests, came a flotilla of long, narrow Hualeg boats, oars flashing, heading south at speed. Ten of them. Impossible to count the figures crammed inside, but easily ten or more per boat. A hundred warriors? Maybe more.

Morrin cursed and ran back down towards the village square, shouting orders for the evacuation – women, children, old folks, into the eastern hills, now! Taupin turned to Rogas, his face grim. "Prepare the men! Battle stations!"

"Come on, Tuck!" Rogas yelled at me, already moving. "What are you waiting for?"

"You go down first!" I shouted back. "Organize the river defense! I'll follow!"

While they scrambled down the cliff path, I sprinted back to the headquarters. I couldn't leave the girl tied up, helpless, alone. I cut her bonds from the pole, slung her back over my shoulder – she struggled weakly this time – and carried her quickly to the small sleeping space I'd been given in a back room. I retied her hands securely to the heavy wooden bed frame.

"Listen," I panted, leaning close so she could see the seriousness in my eyes despite the gag. "I'm not going to hurt you. But you stay quiet, understand? Don't make a sound. I'll come back." I paused. "If your friends don't kill me first."

She made a muffled moaning sound, kicking her bound legs against the bed, her eyes wide with what looked like desperate urgency. Trying to tell me something? Maybe. But I couldn't understand, and there was no time. Ignoring her struggles, I turned and ran back towards the village center.

Chaos. Men grabbing spears, shields, shouting questions. Rogas was bellowing orders, dividing the hundred fighters according to the plan we'd vaguely discussed. About thirty to the cliff edge with Taupin and Morrin, ready with the boulders. Thirty more, including Thom's group and me, hidden amongst the rocks lining the riverbank below the main landing path – the first line of defense. The remaining forty or so, Rogas commanding, concealed along the steep path leading up to the village gate, ready for the second wave.

I took my place with Thom behind a large cluster of boulders near the water's edge, my heart hammering against my ribs. This was it. My first real battle. Not a skirmish, not an ambush, but a full-on assault. I looked at the tense faces around me. These fishermen, these hunters... they were counting on me, on Rogas, on Taupin. My actions here, my success or failure, would echo through the whole defense. Failure wasn't an option.

The guttural war cries of the Hualeg warriors drifted across the water now, closer, louder. A primal sound that sent shivers down my spine. I glanced up towards the cliff edge – Taupin and Morrin would be ready. I looked left and right at Thom and the others concealed beside me.

"Just do what I do," I told them, keeping my voice low but steady. "We hold here. We only engage if they get past the rocks on the cliff and make it ashore. Don't break cover early. And don't be afraid." Easy for me to say.

I peered cautiously around the edge of my boulder. The lead Hualeg boat, packed with maybe fifteen warriors, was drawing level with the base of the cliff. Now.

A thunderous roar echoed from above as the first massive boulders crashed down. Screams, splintering wood, the sickening crunch of rock on flesh. The first boat vanished in spray and wreckage. The second, close behind, met the same fate. Men floundered in the water, some sinking immediately, others swept away by the current, a few struggling towards the bank.

The remaining eight boats reacted quickly, veering sharply away from the deadly cliff face, swinging wide towards the gentler slope on our side of the river, aiming for the landing beach. The third and fourth boats were already grounding, warriors leaping out, axes and swords flashing in the sun.

My hand tightened on my sword hilt. *This is the time.*

Steeling myself, I waited until the first Hualeg warrior scrambled past the outer line of rocks. Then I sprang out, sword whistling, cutting him down before he even saw me. Behind me, our own war cries erupted as Thom and the others charged, spears leveled.

The riverbank became a whirlwind of brutal, close-quarters fighting. I moved like a machine, blocking, parrying, thrusting, my sword finding flesh again and again. Axes chopped, hammers swung, spears darted out. Men screamed, cursed, died. For a few desperate minutes, we held them, the narrow beachhead limiting their numbers, our defense furious.

But more boats kept landing. More Hualeg warriors poured onto the shore, pressing us back with sheer weight and ferocity. Our rough wooden shields splintered under their heavy axe blows. One of our men went down, then another. Then three more in quick succession. Out of our thirty, maybe twenty-five were left standing, falling back step by bloody step. And still the Hualegs came on.

We couldn't hold here. We'd be overrun. "Retreat!" I roared above the din. "Back! Up the path! Now!"

I signaled Thom. We became the rear guard, fighting desperately to cover the others as they scrambled back up the steep track towards the village gate. I parried an axe swing that would have split my skull, thrust my sword into the warrior's chest, then blocked a sword thrust from another. My ferocity seemed to momentarily stun them, giving us the precious seconds we needed. I turned and ran, Thom right beside me.

We sprinted up the winding path cut into the hillside, stones skittering underfoot. Behind us, dozens of Hualeg warriors surged in pursuit. I risked a glance back – twenty or more had almost reached the small plateau just below the village gate.

"Now!" I screamed, reaching the top.

As if summoned by my shout, Rogas and his forty men erupted from behind bushes and the low stone walls lining the path, charging downhill into the surprised Hualeg vanguard. I didn't hesitate. I stopped, spun, and plunged back into the fray, Thom and the others who'd retreated with me joining the counter-attack.

The narrow path became a slaughterhouse. Caught between Rogas's force charging down and us attacking from below, the Hualegs had nowhere to go. Spears found their marks, swords slashed, shields hammered. Bodies piled up on the steps. But the warriors behind kept coming, leaping over their fallen comrades, pressing forward three abreast, their war cries relentless.

Our spears broke, shields shattered. We were being pushed back again, fighting desperately to keep them bottlenecked on the path, away from the village proper. Then, a shout from further down the slope, near the river.

"Three Hualeg boats! Landing south of the village!"

My blood ran cold. A flanking attack. "Where are Taupin's troops?" I yelled.

"Coming down the cliff now!" someone shouted back.

"Send them here! Quickly!" We needed reinforcements on the main path desperately. "You!" I pointed at Thom and the handful of men nearest me – mostly the survivors from the riverbank fight. Maybe twenty in total. "With me! South! Now!" I looked at Rogas, locked in combat nearby. "Rogas!" I yelled, forgetting the fake names in the heat of battle. "Can you hold them here?"

He blocked an axe blow, then rammed his sword into his attacker's gut. "No problem!" he roared back, grinning savagely.

Trusting him – having no choice *but* to trust him – I turned and ran south, my twenty men pounding after me. We raced through the now eerily deserted village streets, the sounds of the main battle fading behind us. Down a grassy slope on the southern edge, towards the river again. Far below, three more longboats were beached, their Hualeg warriors – maybe forty of them – already disembarked, starting to run towards the village, slowed slightly by the marshy, muddy ground near the water.

They hadn't expected us. We had the high ground. Seizing the chance, I yelled, "Charge!" and sprinted down the slope towards them. "Pin them in the mud!"

I hit the first line of surprised Hualegs like a thunderbolt, sword flashing. All the fear, the grief, the anger, the confusion of the past days channeled into pure, focused violence. I fought with a speed and ruthlessness that shocked even myself, cutting down warrior after warrior. Behind me, Thom and the others formed a ragged line, their spears and shields holding back the Hualegs struggling in the sticky mud, preventing them from gaining solid footing on the slope.

Inspired by the ferocity of the counter-attack, my men fought like demons. The Hualegs, trapped in the mud, unable to maneuver effectively, became easy targets. It wasn't a battle anymore; it was a massacre. The muddy field ran red.

Suddenly, a long, piercing screech echoed from the direction of the village gate. A signal? Victory? Defeat? A jolt of fear shot through me. What did it mean?

The remaining Hualegs on the southern flank heard it too. They hesitated, then turned, scrambling back towards their boats, abandoning their attack. Confused but relentless, I chased after them, cutting down two who were too slow. One boat managed to push off, maybe ten warriors paddling frantically away downstream.

Panting, leaning on my sword, covered in mud and blood, I turned to the soldier beside me. "Go! Back to the village! Help the others! Hurry!"

Ignoring the burning in my lungs, the exhaustion threatening to pull me under, I scrambled back up the grassy slope, the remaining dozen or so men straggling behind me. My body screamed for rest, but dark thoughts pushed me onward. What if the signal meant Rogas had fallen? What if the main defense had collapsed? What if I was too late? Tears of fear and exhaustion pricked my eyes.

I reached the top of the hill, ran through the silent village streets again, the distant sounds of shouting growing louder. Still no sign of Hualegs here. Hope flickered. Maybe... maybe we'd held.

I burst through the village gate onto the plateau. And stopped dead, staring. My comrades – Rogas, Taupin, Morrin, the villagers – were cheering, shouting, jumping up and down, hugging each other, some weeping with relief and joy.

"We won!" someone yelled, seeing me. "Tuck! We won!"

Disbelief washed over me. Ignoring the men who turned to salute me, I ran past them, pushing through the celebrating crowd, scrambling up the path to the highest point on the cliff edge.

There, I could see it all. Far below, on the river, not three boats, but five Hualeg longboats were rowing raggedly away to the north, carrying the defeated remnants of their raiding party.

A tremor ran through me, starting deep inside, shaking my whole body. Relief, grief, terror, exhaustion, triumph – it all surged up at once. Unable to contain it, unable even to understand it, I raised my sword, raised my fist to the sky, and roared. A raw, primal sound ripped from my throat, echoing out across the valley, chasing the retreating Hualegs.

All the pain, all the fear, all the killing – released in that single, cathartic roar. I closed my eyes, tilting my face up, letting the bright sunlight warm my skin, feeling tears mix with the sweat and grime. Then I opened my eyes, looked down at the village, at the men who had fought beside me, and a wide, shaky smile spread across my face.

For a moment, dozens of eyes stared up at me in stunned silence. Then, a cheer went up. Men raised their own weapons, raised their fists, and roared back, their voices joining mine in a chorus of improbable, hard-won victory.

15

Stupid and Crazy

Victory felt hollow. Back in my small room in the barracks, the cheering outside seemed distant, unreal. I sat on the floor, leaning against the rough wall, just watching the red-haired Hualeg girl. She was tied securely to the bed frame, just as I'd left her before the battle. I'd taken the gag off earlier, brought her water and some leftover bread. She'd eaten and drunk silently, her eyes following my every move, wary but... less terrified than before. Maybe she sensed I didn't mean her immediate harm. At least she hadn't tried to spit at me or scream bloody murder. That felt like progress.

But what now? What did I do with her? My mind felt like muddy water, thoughts swirling sluggishly. Did she know her friends, her comrades, had been defeated this morning? That fifty of them lay dead down by the river or on the path? She must have heard the battle, the shouts, the eventual cheers of our victory. Was the quiet watchfulness in her eyes masking hatred now? Resentment?

The interpreter Dorin, the one man Morrin said spoke Hualeg, was gone. Fled south with his family when the alarm first sounded. Understandable, maybe, but it left me with a prisoner I couldn't even talk to. Was there any point keeping her?

Rogas, naturally, had his own charming suggestion when I'd mentioned my dilemma earlier. "She's your prize, Tuck!" he'd laughed, clapping me on the shoulder. "Spoils of war! Make her your slave. Or, you know..." He'd winked, his meaning sickeningly clear.

"Bastard!" I'd nearly hit him again. "What do you think I am?"

"Just saying," he'd shrugged, unfazed. "If they'd won, they'd do worse to the women here."

"But I'm *not* like them!" I'd shouted, the comparison making my blood boil.

"Yeah, whatever. She's your problem now," he'd said, wandering off.

So here I sat, her problem my problem. I sighed, running a hand through my tangled hair. I looked at the girl again, at her wary blue eyes. On impulse, I started talking, not caring if she understood a single word. Maybe just saying it aloud would help clear my own head.

"Just in case you understand," I began quietly, "and I don't think you do... but your comrades lost today. Badly. But I'm sure they'll be back. They always come back, don't they?" I shook my head, a weary frustration settling over me. "I don't want that. I lost friends today too... well, men under my command. You lost friends, family maybe. This victory... it doesn't feel good. Losing people never feels good. Haven't you ever thought about that? Why does it have to be like this? Raiding, killing... why not just come as friends? Trade? If you need something, we have things. Fish, wood, maybe grain further south. We need things too – furs, maybe metal from your northern mines? Why kill each other over it?" I scrubbed a hand over my face. "Maybe I'm a fool for wishing it could be different. But maybe not. Maybe you just need to think about it." I looked at her again. "If you could answer, if you could understand... I'd ask you what *you* can do to stop this. To make sure it doesn't happen again."

She stared at me, then suddenly spoke, a string of sharp, high-pitched sounds in her own tongue, gesturing emphatically towards the door with her bound hands. It meant nothing to me.

"That's enough," I sighed. It was useless. "Go to sleep now. Rest. Don't worry," I added, trying to sound reassuring, "I won't hurt you." I stretched out on my own floor mat. "We'll figure things out tomorrow. Maybe... maybe I'll just let you go free." The thought felt strange, risky, but also... right? "Rogas won't like it. Taupin and Morrin won't either. But I caught you, so I decide." I thought of the yellow-haired girl by my father's house. "Someone... your friend, maybe... the yellow-haired girl... she let me go two days ago. Warned me. Why shouldn't I do the same for you?" I closed my eyes, talking more to myself now. "If I'm lucky, maybe you'll go home and tell your people to stop the raids. Tell them there's another way. Then there'd be no more war. We could live like... like civilized people." I snorted softly at my own naivety. "If you're a good person, I'm sure you'll do that."

Peace with the Hualeg. Was it really possible? The idea felt huge, audacious. But my father... Bullock said he traded with southerners, lived peacefully among them for years. He found a way. Maybe... maybe that was the legacy I was supposed to continue. Not revenge, not hiding, but... building bridges? Could I do that? Become a man like him? The thought was both inspiring and terrifyingly immense. My head swam with exhaustion and confusion. Sleep finally claimed me.

It felt like mere moments later when a frantic pounding on my door jolted me awake. I grabbed my sword instantly, heart hammering, scrambling to my feet as I yelled, "What is it?"

A soldier burst in, breathless. "Sir! Tuck! They're waiting for you! Hualeg boat sighted again on the river!"

I'd expected another attack, yes, but *tonight*? After the beating they took just hours ago? It didn't seem possible. I raced out, following the soldier to the main briefing room, then hurried with Rogas, Taupin, and Morrin back up to the cliff edge, peering into the moonlit darkness.

"Long boat?" I demanded of the lookout who'd raised the alarm.

"Yes..." the soldier stammered, squinting. "I... I think so..."

"You're not sure?" Taupin snapped, his voice tight with tension.

I glanced at Rogas, then made a quick decision. No time for uncertainty. "Wake everyone!" I ordered, my voice carrying with newfound authority. The battle yesterday... something had shifted. "Fifty men to the main gate under Rogas. Thirty more down to the south river bend with Thom. We don't need more men on the cliff top – if it's just one boat, they won't risk the boulders again."

No one argued. Rogas gave me a sharp nod, already bellowing orders.

Taupin and Morrin hurried to organize the deployment. Maybe they were starting to trust me, or maybe they were just scared. It didn't matter. I headed back down to the riverbank with Thom and his thirty men, taking up defensive positions in the darkness behind the familiar rocks.

We waited. The river whispered past, cold and indifferent. Silence stretched. My ears strained, listening for the dip of oars, the guttural Hualeg voices. Nothing. The moon climbed higher, casting long shadows. Why no further sightings from the cliff? Why no sounds? Had they landed further up or downriver? Or... was there no boat at all?

Finally, a runner arrived from the village. "Last message from the cliff, sir. No enemy sighted. Master Taupin says you can stand down, rest again."

I hesitated. Could it have been a mistake? A drifting log mistaken for a boat in the dark? It felt too easy. I sent half the men back to the barracks but kept Thom and a dozen others with me, rotating watches through the rest of the night. But morning came clear and quiet. No attack. My fears, this time, had been unfounded.

Later that afternoon, after a few hours of much-needed sleep, I met again with Rogas, Taupin, and Morrin in the headquarters. The mood was tense, uncertain.

"I spoke to the lookout again," Taupin reported grimly. "The one who saw the boat last night. He admits... he wasn't as sure as he first claimed. Might have been shadows, the moonlight..."

"So the boat wasn't there?" Morrin asked.

Taupin nodded wearily. "Looks like it. Maybe they did go back north after all."

"Are you sure Hualegs are that weak?" Rogas scoffed. "They lose one fight and just give up, run home?"

"No," Taupin replied heavily. "That's not their way. Even if they went home, they'd just gather more warriors and come back stronger."

Morrin nodded in agreement. "It's only late spring. Months until winter slows them down. They came with maybe one-fifty yesterday. Next time? Could be twice that. They'll see this as a challenge now, an exciting war. I'm sure of it. Ask the village elders if you don't believe me."

Rogas laughed bitterly. "If they come back with three hundred, we might as well pack our bags now. No way we can win that fight."

"That's right." Taupin and Morrin both nodded glumly, then turned to me.

"What do you think, Tuck?" Taupin asked, his earlier annoyance gone, replaced by worried deference. "Should we evacuate Thaluk? Pull back further south, leave this village?"

Abandon Thaluk? After the fight we put up? It felt wrong. "They might not have many more men nearby *yet*," I argued, thinking aloud. "The hundred or so who escaped yesterday... they're probably still out there, licking their wounds, maybe watching us. They know our defenses now. That 'boat' last night? Maybe it *was* just a scout, testing if we were still alert. They won't have gone straight home defeated. They'll try again."

"True," Morrin conceded. "That fits their ways. The leader who lost face yesterday won't return home empty-handed if he can help it. He'll attack again."

"Or," Rogas offered another angle, "maybe they know Thaluk's too tough now. Maybe they *will* bypass us, head downriver, hit the easier villages further south."

"Possible," Taupin acknowledged worriedly. "And if they get past us, it'll be a disaster for the whole region."

"Then we should keep them here," I said firmly, an idea forming. "Bottle them up. Don't let them get past Thaluk."

The three older men looked at me expectantly.

"Do you have a plan?" Rogas asked, intrigued.

"Tie your fishing nets together," I explained quickly. "Every net you can find. Stretch them tight across the river, just downstream from here, anchored to strong stakes on both banks. Make it thick, strong. Their boats won't be able to push through easily." I warmed to the idea. "Want to make it nastier? Cut down some sturdy logs, sharpen the ends like giant spear points. Drive them into the riverbed just below the surface, hidden, angled upstream, behind the nets. Any boat that tries to break through gets holed, maybe sinks. We hit them while they're struggling in the water."

Rogas's eyes lit up. "That's a good trap! Vicious!"

"Yes, we can do that," Morrin agreed immediately.

"It would take time," Taupin fretted. "Three days? Five? What if the Hualeg come back before it's ready?"

"We try!" Morrin insisted. "It's better than just waiting!" Rogas and Taupin nodded agreement. "Tuck?"

"Of course," I said. "You men get started on the traps. I've just thought of another plan." I took a deep breath. "Something that, if it works, might delay their attack long enough for you to finish. Maybe even stop it completely."

"What is it?" Taupin asked warily.

"I want to make peace with them."

"What?" The word exploded from all three of them simultaneously.

"Impossible!" Taupin declared.

"Why not?" I countered, standing my ground. "I've heard stories," I added carefully, "of southerners trading peacefully with Hualegs in the past. It *can* happen."

"That was then, this is now!" Taupin argued vehemently. "You killed dozens of their warriors yesterday! You think they'll just shake your hand and call it even? Impossible!"

Rogas snorted, shaking his head in disbelief. "Okay, Tuck, I'll bite. *How do you plan to make peace with people who want to kill us all?*"

"The girl," I said simply. "My prisoner. I'll free her. Take her back to them as... a gesture."

Rogas burst out laughing. "A gesture? They won't care about one girl! They'll probably kill her themselves for getting captured! You think returning her makes them grateful? They'll likely kill *you* on sight!"

"Why not?" I insisted stubbornly, thinking of the yellow-haired girl letting me go. "Maybe they *will* be grateful. Maybe seeing one of their own returned unharmed will make them pause, reconsider. Maybe they'll break off the attack."

"You... you're joking, right? Dreaming!" Rogas laughed again, while Taupin and Morrin just stared at me like I was mad.

"Whatever you say," I said, my voice loud, firm, meeting Rogas's mocking gaze without flinching. "I don't care. I *will* go north. I'll take the girl, find her friends, and try to talk."

"You're completely crazy!" Rogas yelled back, genuinely angry now. "Suicidal! What soldiers here would be foolish enough to go with you on *that* mission? None!"

"I can row myself if I have to," I retorted. "Besides, bringing a troop would look like a threat. Alone is better. Stealthier."

"I can't let you go alone!" Rogas shouted, his chest puffing out. Then, surprisingly, his anger seemed to deflate slightly. "Look... take some men. Five? Ten? If anyone's crazy enough to volunteer. I'm not sure..."

"Five," I cut him off. "Five volunteers max. And I'll ask them myself. If no one wants to come, then I go alone."

Taupin looked horrified. "Tuck, think about this! The risk!"

"I know the risk," I said quietly. "If I'm unlucky, I won't be coming back."

"Exactly! And I don't want that!" Taupin pleaded. "I paid you to stay *here*! To fight! Not to get yourself killed on some impossible peace mission!"

"You paid me to protect this village," I corrected him calmly. "Maybe this *is* the best way to do that."

"But *how*?" he almost wailed, running a hand through his thinning hair. "Perhaps... more money? Would you stay for more money?"

I shook my head. "Keep your money for now, sir. I'll come back for my share later."

"Stubborn! You're throwing your life away!"

"Not really," I said, meeting his gaze evenly. "I'm good at taking care of myself. Do you think I'm stupid enough to just walk in there without a plan?"

"If not stupid, then crazy!" Taupin declared, shaking his head in defeat.

"Mr. Tuck," Morrin spoke carefully, choosing his words. "I truly don't understand. Yesterday, you fought like a demon, killed so many Hualeg. Now... peace? Why?"

"Because I don't want more people to die," I said simply. "On either side."

Taupin leaned forward again, his eyes narrowed with suspicion. "Are you sure... you're not hiding something from us, Tuck? Word gets around, you know. People talk. They say... they say you're Hualeg yourself. Part Hualeg, anyway." My blood ran cold. "Don't get me wrong," he added quickly, seeing my reaction. "No one holds it against you. In fact, they admire your fierceness! Say it explains how you fight! But... is it true? Is *that* why you want peace with them?"

I glared at him, anger replacing the cold dread. "My background," I said slowly, distinctly, "is none of your business."

"It is very much our business if it affects your decisions in protecting this village!" he shot back.

"Don't you trust me?"

"It's not like that! How could we not trust the man who saved us yesterday?" Taupin insisted, sounding frustrated now. "Of course, we trust your sword arm! We just... we don't want you making a rash decision based on... on sentiment, maybe... that puts us all in greater danger!"

"If you really trust me," I said, standing up, my decision made, "then trust me on this too. I am taking this risk for *all* of us. If I didn't care about protecting this place, protecting *you*, I wouldn't bother! I've told you my reasons. We'll see soon enough if I'm as stupid or crazy as you think." I turned towards the door. "Just have my pay ready when I get back, Mr. Taupin. I *will* be back for it."

16

The Wrong Word

Pushing off from the bank at Thaluk felt... final. The argument with Taupin, Morrin, and Rogas still echoed in my ears. Disappointment was a dull ache behind my ribs, but what had I expected? Applause? Of course, they thought I was crazy. Maybe I *was* crazy. But the thought of just waiting for the Hualeg to return, just building traps and hoping for the best... it felt like resigning ourselves to more killing, more loss. There had to be another way.

Now I just had to prove it. Prove this wasn't some suicidal fool's errand. Or at least, prove I could get myself – and the men who'd trusted me – out alive if it failed. I glanced back at the five soldiers rowing steadily behind me in the single longboat: Thom, steady as always; Mullen and Boulder, tough fishermen; young Spitz, quiet but observant; and Alend, another solid villager. Rogas had scoffed, said no one would follow me. He was wrong. Maybe it was foolish loyalty born from the heat of battle yesterday, maybe they truly believed in me, or maybe they were just as desperate for a different solution as I was. Whatever the reason, they were here, rowing north into danger because I'd asked them to. The weight of that trust felt heavier than any Hualeg axe.

Behind me, tied but no longer gagged, sat the red-haired Hualeg girl. My 'peace offering'. My prisoner. My responsibility.

My mind wouldn't quiet down. Was Taupin right? Was this desire for peace, this rejection of endless fighting, just some Hualeg sentimentality bubbling up from my father's blood? Yesterday I'd slaughtered men who might have been his kin. How could I possibly expect their comrades to welcome me now? Or was this truly me? Me wanting to be like Vilnar, the man my mother and Bullock described – someone who could bridge the gap, live between worlds?

A fine ambition. But utterly useless if I couldn't even speak their language. How could I make them listen? Was this whole plan just a dangerous fantasy? Were these men rowing towards their deaths because of my naive hope?

The doubts gnawed at me. I turned to face them, needing to give them one last chance. "Listen," I said over the rhythmic splash of the oars. "What we're doing... it's incredibly dangerous. You know that. You don't have to be here. If you're having second thoughts, if you get scared... just jump out. Swim back to Thaluk. No shame in it. You're free to go."

They stopped rowing for a beat, looking at me, then burst out laughing.

"Very funny, Tuck," Thom grinned from the front, wiping sweat from his brow. "Sure, we could swim back. Easy for you to say. But what about you? If *you* suddenly got scared, would *you* jump out?"

I managed a weak grin back. "If I jumped out and you all left too, who'd take *her* north?" I nodded towards the girl, who watched us silently, her expression unreadable. "She can't row herself home."

"Why not? Looks pretty strong to me," Thom joked.

"Hey, Tuck," Boulder, the burly, bald fisherman, spoke up gruffly. "You really taking her all the way north? Thought maybe you'd just drop her off somewhere upstream, let her find her own way back."

I smirked, trying to project confidence I didn't feel. "And miss all the fun? You've never been this far north, have you? Aren't you curious to see what's up here?"

"Not if it means getting my head split open," Boulder grumbled.

"You can always swim home," I repeated lightly. "All of you."

"And let you have all the excitement?" Thom laughed again, the others joining in. "No way. Besides," he winked, leaning closer, "if you ask me,

Tuck, that girl's a beauty, even tied up like that. She's your prize, right? If you're too noble for the slave idea, why not make her your wife?" He chuckled, clearly teasing.

I snorted dismissively. "First, she's not *mine*. Second, judging by the way she looks at me, she'd rather kick me than marry me. Can't you see the hatred in her eyes?"

"Nah, I don't agree," Thom insisted playfully. "That's not hatred. She likes you."

"Yes, that's true!" Mullen chimed in, grinning. "It's a look of love!"

"Like the look Ante gave *me* back in Orulion," Thom declared proudly.

Mullen snorted. "You're wrong there, Thom. Ante *hates* you."

Thom glared at him. "How do you know?"

"Because she told me," Mullen grinned.

"You? She wouldn't talk to *you*!"

"Oh, she did," Mullen smirked. "Right after she finished talking to *you*."

Thom flushed bright red and muttered a curse under his breath as the others roared with laughter. Their easy banter, even now, helped ease some of the tension. Then, abruptly, the red-haired girl spoke, a short, sharp burst of Hualeg words cutting through the laughter.

We all froze, staring at her. None of us understood.

She looked directly at me, ignoring the others, and spoke again, longer this time, her voice high-pitched, urgent. She pointed first at me, then gestured emphatically north.

"Want me to gag her again, Tuck?" Thom asked uneasily. "She's getting loud."

"I think..." young Spitz spoke up hesitantly from the back of the boat. "I think she said something about her tribe. *Ahruhr*. She said that word. It means 'tribe' in Hualeg."

My head snapped towards him. "You speak Hualeg?"

Spitz flushed slightly. "Just a few words, Tuck. My grandfather... he could understand it. He was part Hualeg, long ago."

A Hualeg descendant. Like me. A strange kinship flickered between us. "Did you understand anything else?"

"No. She speaks too fast. But... she kept saying *Valnir* after *Ahruhr*. *Ahruhr Valnir*. Maybe... the name of her tribe?"

Valnir? The name prickled my memory. Not Vilnar, my father's name, but close... *Vallanir*. The name Mom had told me. My father's tribe.

"You mean... Vallanir?" I asked slowly, watching the girl's face.

Her reaction was instantaneous. Her eyes flew wide, a huge, brilliant smile transforming her face. She let out an excited cry – "Vallanir! Vallanir!" – and actually thumped me hard on the chest with her bound fists.

I couldn't help but smile back, startled by her sudden joy. Seeing her relieved, happy, not angry or scared... it felt unexpectedly good.

"What does that mean?" Thom asked, bewildered.

"Maybe she's just glad we know her tribe's name? Glad she's going home," I guessed, trying to mask the sudden cold dread coiling in my gut. *Vallanir*. The men I'd killed yesterday... the men who killed my patrol... the girl I'd nearly drowned... they were from my father's tribe. My own people, in a way. Everything just got infinitely worse.

"I don't think that's it," Spitz murmured, looking suspiciously at the still-beaming girl.

I ignored him, not wanting to voice my own fear. "Let's keep moving," I said, forcing cheerfulness into my voice. "She looks happy. That's a good sign, right? Means she knows we're freeing her. Hopefully, she can persuade her friends to leave us alone."

Thom gave me a long look. "Honestly, Tuck, I'm still not sure about this plan. Or what's going on in that head of yours. You're being way too positive about this."

I just shrugged, turning my attention back to the river ahead. "We're getting near the edge of the deep forest now. Everyone, stay alert. Be careful."

The boat glided northwards, the river current aiding our oars. The banks grew wilder here, dense with ancient trees and tangled undergrowth. It felt... watchful. Too quiet. I glanced at the girl beside me. Her earlier excitement had faded, replaced by a nervous tension. She kept scanning the riverbanks, her eyes wide. My own nerves tightened.

"Wait," I whispered suddenly, holding up a hand. "Over there. Hide the boat."

Thom expertly steered us towards the right bank, nosing the boat into the shadows behind a cluster of large, water-worn rocks. I squinted, peering north through the gaps. About fifty paces ahead, on the *left* bank, half-concealed by drooping willow branches, was the unmistakable shape of a longboat's prow. Just sitting there, motionless. And where there was one boat hidden near a tributary junction like this... there were likely more.

"Go a little further," I breathed, needing a better look without exposing us.

"They'll see us, Tuck," Thom warned.

"It's okay. Just stay close to this bank. Don't get too close to them."

We edged forward along the rocky shoreline on our side. Reaching a small clearing that offered a slightly better view, we stopped again, holding the boat steady against the current. We could see the front half of the hidden longboat clearly now. Empty, it seemed. Waiting?

"Don't tell me we have to keep going, Tuck," Thom whispered anxiously. "This feels wrong. Could be a trap. Remember what happened to the patrol? Maybe they lure people in close..."

He was right. Charging blindly forward was suicide. We needed to draw *them* out. I stood up abruptly in our boat. The men stared at me, alarmed.

"What... what are you doing?" Thom hissed.

"I'm going to call them."

Before anyone could argue, I cupped my hands around my mouth and bellowed the only Hualeg word I knew that might mean something to them, the word the girl had reacted to so strongly: "VALLANIR!"

The name echoed across the water, startlingly loud in the stillness.

"VALLANIR!" I shouted again, pouring all my strength into it.

We waited, hearts pounding, scanning the silent treeline across the river. The red-haired girl beside me seemed to be holding her breath, trembling slightly. Then, from deep within the woods on the far bank, came an answering roar – not just one voice, but many. Followed by the harsh clang of metal on metal – weapons being readied. More cheers, fierce and guttural. The sound of a war party preparing to fight.

"Looks like you picked the wrong word, Tuck," Thom muttered grimly beside me.

Wrong word? Or exactly the right one to confirm they were here?

I waited. The hidden longboat slid out from behind the willow branches. Ten big warriors, oars digging deep. Then another boat appeared behind it. And another. And another. Five longboats in total, filled with armed Hualegs, fanning out across the river, blocking our path north.

"Gods preserve us," Mullen breathed from behind me. "Time to go, Tuck! They're coming!"

"And they don't seem to care about the girl!" Thom added frantically, nodding towards our captive. "Your plan failed, Tuck! Let's run!"

I looked down at the red-haired girl. Her face was deathly pale. She hid behind my legs, pressing herself against the side of the boat, clearly terrified of the approaching warriors. This wasn't the reaction of someone expecting rescue.

"Maybe... maybe they haven't seen her yet," I said desperately, though I didn't believe it. "When they see her, they'll understand..."

Thom shook his head frantically. "So, are we going or not?"

"Hurry if we're running!" Mullen urged, his hand already reaching for an oar. "Before it's too late!"

I raised my hand again, waving frantically towards the lead Hualeg boat. "Halt! Halt! We don't want to fight!"

"Say it: *Arnez!*" Spitz hissed urgently beside me.

"What?"

"*Arnez*! It means stop!"

"Ichst! Arnez!" the red-haired girl suddenly cried out, her voice thin with fear.

I looked down at her startled, then back at the closing boats.

"*Arnez!*" she repeated desperately, pleading with her eyes. "ARNEZ!"

Okay. Trust her. "ARNEZ!" I bellowed, putting all my force behind it. "ARNEZ!"

Miraculously, the lead boat slowed, oars lifting. The other boats behind it followed suit, their momentum carrying them closer, but they stopped rowing. The war cries died away, replaced by an tense, watchful silence across the water. We stared at the fifty grim Hualeg faces staring back at us across maybe a hundred paces of river. A big warrior in the first boat stood up slowly, waved an arm, and said something sharp in Hualeg. His boat began to move forward again, alone, towards us.

My men tensed, gripping their weapons.

"What does he want?" Mullen whispered nervously.

"Maybe... talk?" I guessed, my own heart pounding.

"Who can talk to him?" Thom demanded. "You, Spitz?"

Spitz looked like he was going to be sick. "I... I only know a few words!"

"You better drop that girl off quick," Mullen urged, pointing towards the rocky bank beside us. "Leave her there, and let's get out of here! Fast!"

Leave her? Just abandon her on the rocks? It felt wrong, cowardly. But he was right. Facing that lead boat, that giant warrior with the axe... it was suicide. And the girl herself... she suddenly whispered again, urgently, looking up at me with wide, terrified eyes. "Mornir." She tugged at my tunic. "Ireir. Ireir!"

"Spitz!" I snapped, needing the translation now. "Ireir! What does it mean?"

"Uh..." Spitz stammered, his face pale. "It... it means... run. I think. Yes, run!"

Run. The girl who'd attacked me, whose friends I'd killed, was telling me to run. I looked at the approaching Hualeg leader – tall, powerful, axe held ready, face grim under a thick red-brown beard. Fighting him here, on the water, was madness. Endangering my men, the girl...

"Turn around!" I shouted, making the decision instantly. "Back to the village! Row!"

My soldiers didn't need telling twice. Oars dug deep, the small boat spinning clumsily, then surging south, back the way we came, fighting against the river current now.

Behind us, angry shouts erupted from the Hualeg boats as they realized we were fleeing. Their oars churned the water, the five longboats leaping forward in pursuit. They had more rowers, more power, but our boat was smaller, lighter. And Thom knew this river like the back of his hand. He shouted directions, guiding us expertly through channels I hadn't even noticed, weaving between submerged rocks, scraping through narrow gaps. We gained some distance initially, the Hualeg war cries fading slightly behind us.

But then we hit a wider, straighter stretch of the Ordelahr. No more maneuvering. Just pure speed and endurance. And they were gaining. Their angry shouts grew louder again, closer. Looking over my shoulder, I could see the lead boat, maybe only fifty paces behind now, the big warrior standing in the prow, shaking his axe at us.

Far ahead, impossibly distant it seemed, I could just make out the familiar shape of the cliffs guarding Thaluk. If we could just reach the village, reach the defenses, reach the rest of our men... we might stand a chance. If the Hualegs didn't overtake us first.

"Row!" I yelled, pulling on my oar until my muscles screamed. "Faster!"

My comrades groaned, straining, sweat pouring down their faces, putting every last scrap of their strength into escaping the relentless pursuit.

17

Big Wolf

We rowed like madmen, muscles screaming, lungs burning, the small boat bucking as we fought the southward current. Behind us, the angry shouts of the Hualegs grew closer. The red-haired girl beside me was agitated, twisting against her bonds, looking like she desperately wanted to grab an oar herself, but we had none spare.

Suddenly, she shouted, pointing urgently towards the left bank ahead. "Vida! Asterein! Avenida!" Her voice was sharp, commanding, even in Hualeg. She rattled off more words I didn't understand, pointing again. "Asterein! Esperei lou din aszter! Kniir!"

"What do you mean?" I gasped out between frantic pulls on the oar.

"Kniir!" She pointed again, more insistently.

I squinted through the spray and my own exhaustion. On a jumble of rocks near the river's edge, a figure stood motionless, holding a long sword. Yellow hair caught the light. My heart leaped – it was *her*. The girl from my father's house. The one who'd beaten me, then let me go.

"She's telling us to go there," Spitz panted from behind me.

Thom glanced back, his face grim. We were all nearing our limit. The Hualeg boats were definitely gaining. We wouldn't make it back to Thaluk on the water. Landing, running for the forest – that was our only chance now. And maybe… maybe landing where *she* waited was better than landing blind.

"To the riverbank!" I yelled over the sound of splashing oars and distant war cries. "Head for her! Then run for the forest!"

"Are you sure this isn't a trap?" Thom shouted back, understandably wary.

The red-haired girl beside me practically vibrated with nervousness, clearly desperate for us to reach the other girl. Was it a trap? The yellow-haired girl *had* warned me, let me go... maybe I had nothing to fear from her. It was a huge risk, trusting these strange Hualeg girls, but what choice did we have?

"We're going there!" I shouted again. "Hurry!"

We put every last ounce of strength into those final oar strokes, angling the boat sharply towards the rocks where the yellow-haired girl stood waiting calmly. We scraped ashore just as the lead Hualeg boat was maybe thirty oar strokes behind. I sawed through the red-haired girl's bonds with my knife. We tumbled out onto the rocky bank.

The red-haired girl cried out – joy? relief? – towards the other, but the yellow-haired girl just gave a brief, acknowledging nod. Without a word, she turned and sprinted into the dense forest bordering the riverbank. We scrambled after her, abandoning the boat, plunging into the undergrowth just as the first pursuing Hualegs reached the shore behind us.

We ran blindly, following the flash of yellow hair through the trees, my soldiers panting hard behind me. We crashed through bushes, scrambled up a rising, rocky slope. Reaching a ledge higher up, I risked a look back. Below us, the river gleamed. Our boat, and the Hualeg longboats, looked small, abandoned. The pursuers had all disembarked, fanning out into the forest, searching for us.

Catching my breath, I looked ahead. The yellow-haired girl had stopped, waiting for us. And with her... my hand flew to my sword hilt... were three large Hualeg men, armed and watchful.

Before I could react, the girl held up a hand, calm but firm. "Calm down! This is not the enemy!" She spoke briefly to the three men in Hualeg, then turned back to us. "Hide yourselves. Wait for my signal."

Confused but trusting her command, my men and I quickly melted back behind rocks, thick tree trunks, dense bushes. I could hear the Hualeg pursuers crashing through the undergrowth below, their voices getting closer. I gripped my sword, heart pounding, watching the spot where they would emerge onto the narrow ledge.

One appeared, then two, three, more crowding behind them. I tensed, ready to fight, but remembered the girl's words – *wait for the signal.*

Suddenly, she leaped from her hiding spot like a striking viper. Her sword flashed, slashing deep into the lead pursuer's neck as she let out a sharp, piercing cry in Hualeg. That was the signal. I burst from cover, meeting the next Hualeg warrior head-on, my sword finding its mark. Thom, Mullen, Boulder, Spitz, Alend – they charged too, alongside the three Hualeg men allied with the yellow-haired girl.

The narrow ledge exploded into brutal chaos. Caught completely by surprise, trapped between our two groups, the pursuing Hualegs had no time to form a defense. It was a short, vicious slaughter. Swords flashed, men screamed, bodies tumbled back down the rocky slope into the dense forest below. In moments, it was over. Maybe a dozen of them lay dead, the yellow-haired girl and I accounting for more than our share.

We waited, panting, listening. Shouts echoed from further down the hill. More were coming. This next fight would be harder; they'd be wary now. But then, a long, ululating cry drifted up from the river valley, the same strange, triumphant signal I'd heard yesterday after the battle at Thaluk.

The yellow-haired girl let out a sharp exclamation, then turned and scrambled up the sheer rock face behind the ledge with the agility of a mountain cat. In seconds, she reached a higher clifftop, peering intently down towards the river far below.

Not wanting to be left behind, I followed her up, finding handholds and footholds, scrambling less gracefully but making it. I stood beside her, catching my breath, and followed her gaze. Down on the Ordelahr, the five Hualeg longboats that had chased us were moving again, rowing south. And further north, just rounding the river bend, five *more* longboats appeared, joining them. Ten boats. Heading south. Towards Thaluk.

"Five boats, plus five more," the yellow-haired girl said grimly beside me, her voice low. "One hundred and fifty Logenirs." She pointed south, towards the distant cliffs where Thaluk perched. "To your village."

My blood ran cold. "They're going to attack now? Again?"

"Tonight," she confirmed flatly.

"But... we just beat them yesterday!"

"Mornir and his men are hungry," she replied, using a name I didn't know – the leader, perhaps? "They won't waste time licking their wounds." She turned, her intense blue eyes meeting mine. "Your men will be defeated now."

"We beat that many yesterday, we can do it again!" I insisted, though my heart sank. An immediate second assault... could Thaluk withstand it? "I have to go back. Now."

I started to turn, looking for a way down, but her hand shot out, gripping my arm surprisingly strong. "With what?" she asked coolly.

"What do you mean?"

"How will you get to your village?"

"With my boat, of course!"

"Mornir must have destroyed it," she stated simply, nodding towards the riverbank far below where we'd landed.

I fell silent, the realization hitting me. Of course. They wouldn't leave us an escape route. Anger surged, hot and frustrated. "Then this is all a mistake!" I glared at her, forgetting gratitude, forgetting everything but the imminent danger to Thaluk. "I shouldn't have stopped here! I shouldn't have listened to the redhead!"

"Do you think my help was a mistake?" she replied, her voice still level, unmoved by my outburst. She gestured towards the red-haired girl, who had climbed up with her three companions and now stood watching us nervously. "You killed six of our men in the forest two days ago and then took my sister. That was a mistake. My men killed five of your soldiers before that. That was also a mistake. But *this*," she gestured around us, at the dead Logenirs below, "helping you escape Mornir... this is not a mistake."

Sister? The red-haired girl was her sister? And the men I killed... *her* men? My anger deflated, replaced by confusion and a heavy weight of responsibility. Her words hung in the air, undeniable.

"Listen," she continued, her gaze steady, "whatever happens down there... I have you to thank for bringing my sister back."

"Yeah," I muttered, feeling ashamed of my outburst now. "But it doesn't matter anymore, does it?" If Thaluk fell... "Thank you for your help," I said sincerely this time. "But I have to go. I'll get back to my village, even if I have to walk."

"Through the forest," she stated, "you will arrive tomorrow morning. Or maybe afternoon. You cannot travel fast in the dark."

"The main thing is that I get there."

"But it might be too late," she said softly. "And without you... the people in your village will lose."

I looked at her suspiciously. How could she know how important I was – or wasn't – to the defense? "You know about me?"

A faint, almost imperceptible smile touched her lips. "Enough to know everything I need to know."

"What do you know?"

"I can judge friends. And enemies," she said coolly. "I know which are big wolves, which are little dogs... and which are little dogs pretending to be big wolves." Her intense eyes held mine. "You... big wolf."

I stared at her, speechless.

She continued, "But even a big wolf cannot hunt alone always. Everyone in your village must act now. They can become wolves too, if they dare. But they must choose. To fight, or to leave. With you or without you, they must make their own decision."

She was right, but still... "It's my responsibility..."

She nodded, seeming to understand. "But you must know your limits. Go, then." She turned away slightly. "I am sorry. I wish I could help you more, but I cannot."

I hesitated. "How... how could you help me?"

"I wish," she said, looking out towards the south again, her voice tight with frustration, "I could take you in *my* boat, help you attack Logenir from behind. But I cannot. If Mornir sees me interfering further... our own tribe, further north... they will be in danger."

"Vallanir?" I asked quietly, testing the name.

Her head snapped back towards me, her eyes narrowed sharply. "You know?"

"Vallanir is your tribe," I stated, piecing it together now. The red-haired girl's excitement. The hostile reaction when I shouted the name. "And the people down there, the ones attacking my village... they are your enemies. Logenir, you called them?"

She nodded curtly. "They are Logenir. Outwardly, Hualeg look like Hualeg. But inwardly..." her expression turned fierce, "...they are our bitterest enemies. Since long ago. What else do you know?"

My mind raced. Vallanir. Logenir. Enemies within the Hualeg people. My father's tribe... fighting another. It explained so much, yet opened up a thousand new questions. Who was this girl? What was her position? What was the history between these tribes? But now wasn't the time. Thaluk was in danger.

"I... I have heard little about your tribe," I deflected, truthfully enough, "from your sister."

She studied me intently for a moment, clearly not entirely believing me, but let it go.

"I must go now," I said, turning towards the cliff edge again. I looked back at her. "Thank you. For your help. For everything." I hesitated again. "I hope... we can meet again. If I survive this." A sudden impulse seized me. "May I... know your name?"

She just looked at me, silent, unreadable.

"I'm William," I offered.

A pause, then, softly, "I am... Vida."

"Vida," I repeated. The name felt right somehow. "Your name is beautiful. Like... your face."

The words tumbled out before I could stop them. Heat rushed to my own face as I saw a faint blush rise on her cheeks. Cursing myself inwardly for the clumsy, ill-timed flirtation, I turned quickly and started scrambling back down the rock face before I could embarrass myself further. What was I thinking?

Reaching the ledge, I quickly explained the situation to Thom and the others – the Hualegs were heading for Thaluk *now*, we had no boat, we had to go overland, fast. Their faces fell, but they nodded grimly. We left Vida standing high on the clifftop, her sister and the three Vallanir men watching us from the ledge below as we plunged back into the darkening forest, heading south.

The journey back was a nightmare. The forest Vida had warned about was worse than I imagined – dense, pathless, choked with undergrowth. Rocks tripped us, steep slopes exhausted us, ravines forced long detours. We stumbled through dead ends, backtracking constantly, trying to keep heading south by the feel of the land and the faint stars occasionally visible through the thick canopy.

When true night fell, travel became impossible. The darkness was absolute. As Vida predicted, we couldn't move. We collapsed where we stood, huddled together for warmth and some small comfort against the fear, snatching a few hours of exhausted, dreamless sleep.

We were moving again before the first hint of dawn, pushing our bodies relentlessly. My muscles screamed, my head throbbed, but the thought of Thaluk, of Rogas and Taupin and the villagers facing that horde alone, spurred me on. Morale lifted slightly as the sun climbed, making navigation easier.

Around noon, pushing through a final thicket of pines, we stumbled out of the forest. And there it was, across a stretch of rough, rocky ground – the high cliff, and perched atop it, the familiar stone walls of Thaluk. We were back. Relief washed over us, so strong I almost collapsed. But the relief died instantly. Down by the riverbank, where our small fleet should have been, lay the ominous shapes of Hualeg longboats. Ten... twelve... maybe more. Beached, empty.

Apprehension seized us. We looked at each other, faces grim.

"Can you hear anything?" I asked, straining my ears. "Fighting?"

The five soldiers listened intently, then shook their heads. Silence. An eerie, unnatural silence hung over the village.

"That means... it's over?" Thom asked, his voice barely a whisper.

"Over?" Spitz echoed hollowly.

"We lost!" Thom choked out, burying his face in his hands. "They took the village! They're all dead!"

"All dead," Mullen repeated numbly beside him.

"Not necessarily," I said, trying to keep the rising panic out of my own voice. Hope felt fragile, foolish, but I couldn't give up yet. "We don't know that. We have to look first."

"You want to go *up there?*" Thom gestured towards the silent village, aghast.

My eyes scanned the cliffs. The main path up from the river was suicide, likely watched. But to the east... the sheer rock face I'd seen from the river. It looked almost impassable, but maybe... maybe there was a way up that side, unseen. "I will climb that rock face," I decided quickly. "Try to get into the village from the east, see what's happening. It's the only way up without being spotted immediately." I looked at my exhausted, frightened men. "There might still be something I can do. Will you come with me?" I added quickly, "You don't have to. Wait here if you think it's safer..."

"Of course we're coming!" Thom interrupted immediately, straightening up, his face set with grim determination.

Mullen nodded silently beside him.

"Wait," Boulder groaned, looking up at the towering cliff face with dismay. "Does that mean we're climbing... *that?*"

"You can stay here if you don't think you can make it," I said gently.

"I can make it!" he growled back, offended. "It sucks, but I can make it!"

Okay. We ran along the base of the cliffs until we reached the sheer eastern face. It looked even worse up close. Maybe fifteen spears high – twenty men standing on each other's shoulders? Almost vertical, treacherous rock, scored with narrow crevices and crumbling ledges. It looked impossible. But it was the only way.

I had to go up. There was no other choice.

Tightening the sword strap across my back, I scanned the rock face, picking out a potential route, visualizing the moves – handhold here, foothold there, shift weight... When I felt as ready as I'd ever be, I started climbing. Finding purchase in the rough stone, testing each hold before trusting my weight, I moved slowly, steadily upwards. Don't look down. Just focus on the next handhold, the next foothold. Pause. Breathe. Keep moving.

My soldiers followed below, finding their own paths, their grunts of exertion echoing softly up the cliff face. The climb was brutal. My fingers grew raw, muscles screaming, sweat stinging my eyes. But seeing the grassy clifftop just a few yards above spurred me on. Push through the pain. Almost there.

Then, a groan from below. "Tuck... Tuck..."

I risked a glance down. It was Spitz, clinging precariously, his face pale with exhaustion and fear.

"Tuck... I can't... can't get up..."

"Spitz!" I called down, trying to keep my voice encouraging. "Come on! You can do it! Look how close we are! Almost there!"

I pushed myself upwards again, calling out encouragement to all of them, trying to ignore my own burning muscles. Slowly, agonizingly, we gained height. Finally, my searching fingers closed around thick tufts of grass at the very top. With a final, desperate heave, I pulled myself over the edge, rolling onto the blessedly solid ground.

I lay there for a long moment, gasping for breath, grinning foolishly up at the clear blue sky. The sun felt warm on my face. Alive. We'd made it.

Checking quickly that the immediate area was clear – just scattered trees, no sign of Hualegs – I crawled to the cliff edge and looked down. "You're almost here!" I yelled to the others. "Just a little further!"

Thom scrambled over the edge next, then Mullen. Spitz followed, shaking like a leaf but managing a weak, relieved laugh. Boulder and Alend hauled themselves up last, collapsing beside us. We laughed then, all of us, a short burst of hysterical relief, patting each other on the back.

Catching my breath, feeling strength slowly return, I pushed myself to my feet. "Come on," I said grimly, the relief fading, replaced by apprehension.

"We need to see what's happening in the village."

18

A Little Madness

We scrambled over the clifftop, gasping for breath, muscles screaming from the climb. The silence from the village below was heavy, unnatural. Dread coiled in my stomach. We circled the eastern edge of the hill, following a narrow path between high stone walls that probably marked old property lines, until we reached the first few small houses on the outskirts of Thaluk proper. Empty. Doors hung open, cookfires were cold ashes. The villagers who hadn't made it to the hills must have been... dealt with.

"Do you have a plan, Tuck?" Thom asked quietly, his eyes scanning the deserted lanes nervously.

I nodded, forcing down the rising bile. "First, we see how bad it is. Find out how many Logenirs are still here. After that..." I met his gaze, my own hardening, "...we kill them. Or drive them out."

"Logenirs?" Spitz whispered beside him.

"Those Hualeg people," I clarified, the name Vida had given their enemies feeling right on my tongue.

"Are you sure we can do this?" Thom asked, glancing back at the exhausted men behind us. "Just the six of us?"

I looked at them – Thom, Mullen, Spitz, Boulder, Alend. Tired, scared, but they'd followed me back, climbed that cliff. "Yes," I said, hoping I sounded more confident than I felt.

Thom still looked doubtful. "I mean... maybe the others made it to the hills east of here?" He pointed towards the forest we'd just struggled through. "Shouldn't we try to find them first? Regroup?"

He had a point, maybe the smarter point. But the thought of those... Logenirs... occupying the village, desecrating the bodies of our friends... it ignited a cold rage in me. "Mullen, Spitz, you're with me," I decided quickly. "We check the village center. See if anyone's left alive, maybe trapped. Thom," I looked back at him, "you take Boulder and Alend, circle wide towards the eastern hills. Look for survivors. Find Morrin if you can."

"No," Thom said immediately, shaking his head. "I'm going with you, Tuck." The others – Mullen and Spitz – murmured agreement. Boulder and Alend looked relieved but nodded towards the hills. Fine.

"Okay," I conceded. "Boulder, Alend – you head for the hills. Find Morrin, find any survivors. Tell them what's happening. Thom, Mullen, Spitz – with me. Stay low, stay quiet."

We moved like shadows, slipping through overgrown yards, using walls and thick bushes for cover, edging deeper into the village. No sign of Logenirs yet, just an eerie silence. We reached the central area, darting behind a sturdy house near the main square. Then I heard it – voices. Rough laughter, slurred words. Hualeg tongue.

I peered cautiously around the corner of the wall. In the small courtyard of the house opposite, four Logenir warriors sprawled on benches, passing around wineskins, clearly relaxing after their victory.

"Drinking ale in the middle of the day?" Thom whispered beside me, disgusted. "No discipline."

"Good for us," I whispered back.

No time for hesitation. I gripped my sword, took a deep breath, and launched myself around the corner. My blade hissed through the air, slicing deep into the neck of the nearest Logenir before he could even register surprise. His eyes went wide, blood fountained, and he collapsed sideways.

The other three scrambled upright, surprise turning to alarm, reaching for axes leaning against the wall. Too slow. I lunged again, my sword punching through the second warrior's gut. Simultaneously, Thom and Mullen exploded from cover. Thom's spear took the third Logenir in the chest, while Mullen's sword silenced the fourth before he could even raise a proper shout.

Four down. Silent. Efficient. We dragged the bodies quickly out of sight behind some bushes, hearts pounding. We moved on, faster now, towards the cluster of larger houses near the cliff edge – Taupin's, Morrin's. Two more Logenirs stood guard near Morrin's porch. They went down just as quickly, just as silently, before they could raise an alarm.

From the slight rise near Morrin's house, we could see most of the village spread out below us. And my breath caught. Logenirs were everywhere. Dozens of them. Milling around the central square, lounging near the headquarters building on the cliff, patrolling the main road down towards the river. And... they were gathering the dead. Our dead. Their dead. Dragging them into grim piles in the center of the square.

We stood frozen for a long moment, horror washing over us. The disrespect, the sheer brutality of it... seeing our fallen comrades treated like that... sadness warred with a bitter, burning rage.

"There are so many..." Spitz whispered, his voice trembling.

"Bodies? Or those bastards?" Thom asked grimly.

"Both," Spitz replied, shaking his head slowly.

"Counted about forty Logenirs down there," Mullen murmured, his knuckles white where he gripped his sword. "And maybe... twice that many bodies."

"That means..." I thought aloud, forcing my mind to work past the horror, "...not all our men are dead. Some must have escaped with Morrin. And maybe not all the Logenirs who attacked are still here. Some might be out hunting the survivors."

"So what's the plan, Tuck?" Thom asked, looking to me.

I stared down at the occupied village, at the swaggering warriors who thought they'd won. The rage solidified into a cold, hard knot. "I'm not happy seeing them here."

"Who is?" Thom muttered.

"I'm going to kill them."

My men looked at each other, then back at me, expressions ranging from disbelief to alarm.

"Hey, Tuck, let's think straight here," Thom said carefully, like talking down a spooked horse. "There's forty, maybe fifty of them down there. Just four of us up here. You can't just... charge in. Unless you're crazy. We should find the others first, like you said. Make a real plan."

"You asked my plan," I repeated, my voice flat, calm in a way that scared even myself. "This is my plan. I kill them. Or at least... I drive them back north."

"Okay," Thom said slowly, humoring me. "How?"

"Kill their leader."

They gaped at me. Yes, maybe I *was* crazy. Maybe the killing, the grief, had finally broken something inside. But maybe, just maybe, a little madness was what we needed.

"Remember the Hualeg leader on the boat yesterday?" I pressed, ignoring their stunned silence. "The big one, reddish-brown hair? Vida called their tribe Logenir, said he was Mornir. He's their chief. If we take him out, the rest might fall apart. Lose heart, lose direction. Maybe they retreat." I looked at each of them, willing them to believe, or at least to follow.

"Well... maybe," Mullen conceded uncertainly. "But where is he? Don't see anyone looking like a chief down there."

"Probably resting in one of the houses," I guessed. "Taupin's or Morrin's, most likely. I'll find him. If I get a chance, I take it. If not... if not, I agree. We pull back, find the others, make a new plan."

"You're going down *there* now?" Thom asked, alarmed. "Into the middle of them? That's suicide, Tuck! Hey..."

But I was already moving, slipping away from the overlook, running low towards the next house, then the next, using every bit of cover. No time to waste arguing. If there was a chance, even a slim one, I had to take it now.

My target was Morrin's house – the largest, the most likely place for their leader to set up temporary command. I was halfway across an open space when I saw them – five Logenirs standing talking outside a smaller house nearby. As I scanned them, searching for Mornir, another warrior emerged from Morrin's doorway behind them, carrying a large basket overflowing with looted goods. He turned, heading back towards the main square, and his eyes met mine across the distance.

We both froze for an instant. Then I reacted, lunging forward, my sword swinging in a deadly arc. His head split open with a sickening crack before he could even drop the basket. The sound, the sudden violence, alerted the group of five. They roared, drawing weapons, charging towards me.

No escape now. No time for stealth. I met their charge head-on. Ducked under a wild axe swing, felt the wind of its passage, and gutted the warrior with an upward thrust. Spun away from a sword lunge, parrying frantically, then drove my own blade through the second attacker's chest. Slashed sideways, cutting deep into the third man's unprotected side as he tried to circle around me. Just as I turned to face the remaining two, Thom and Mullen were there, appearing as if from nowhere, their own blades flashing. It was over in seconds.

But the noise – the shouts, the clash of steel, the death cries – had done its work. More shouts echoed from the village center, from the cliff house. Logenirs were running towards us, alerted, weapons ready. Dozens of them. Even with my recklessness, even believing in Rogas's 'luck', I knew we couldn't win this. Not four against forty.

"Run!" I yelled, shoving Thom towards the way we'd come. "Plan failed! Get out!"

"Damn it! Of course, it did!" Thom muttered, scrambling beside me. "Why did you think it would work?"

We sprinted back the way we'd come, Mullen and Spitz close behind, ducking between houses, heading for the gap between the rocky cliffs leading out of Thaluk towards the eastern forest. Shouts and pounding footsteps echoed behind us, but we didn't look back. We pushed through bushes, leaped over low walls, scrambling down the grassy path until the sounds of pursuit faded behind us.

We finally collapsed, gasping for breath, hidden deep within the familiar woods. "Why... why aren't they chasing us?" Thom panted, managing a weak grin.

"Maybe they're afraid of a trap," I guessed, my own lungs burning. "Or... maybe they were ordered to hold the village, not pursue."

"Didn't see Mornir down there," Mullen wheezed, wiping sweat from his face.

I nodded grimly. "Looks like he's out hunting. Hunting Morrin, Taupin, Dall... the villagers who escaped. They must be in these woods somewhere." My gut clenched. "We need to find them. Stay alert."

My men nodded, their earlier fear replaced by weary resolve. We moved deeper into the forest, quieter now, listening, watching. It wasn't long before a figure suddenly appeared from behind a thick bush, startling us all into raising weapons before we recognized him.

"Boulder! What happened?" I demanded, lowering my sword, relief washing over me.

"Met up with the villagers!" Boulder reported breathlessly. "The ones who fled before the attack started. Morrin's with them. Some of our lads made it out too."

"Did you see Morrin? Taupin? Or Dall?"

Boulder shook his head. "Morrin's with the main group of villagers, further in. Said Taupin and Dall... drew the main Hualeg force away south, towards the lower woods, to give the rest a chance to escape."

South. Towards danger. My friends. "Then that's where we should go," I said immediately, already turning. "We have to help them."

"The Logenirs will be guarding the edges of those woods, Tuck," Thom reminded me urgently. "We can't just walk in."

"We should ask Morrin," Mullen suggested. "He knows these woods better than anyone."

I agreed. Boulder led us deeper into the forest, following hidden trails. Soon we reached a large clearing on a hidden hillside. My heart ached at the sight – dozens of women and children huddled together, faces etched with fear, guarded by a handful of village men and the few soldiers who had escaped. Morrin stood among them, his face grim.

Relief washed over me seeing so many had survived the initial onslaught. Morrin quickly filled us in. "Logenirs attacked just after sunrise. We held the path for a while, but... too many. Ordered the retreat here. Dall and Taupin... they took a small group, deliberately drew the pursuit southwards, giving us time."

"Take me to them," I demanded, urgency gripping me again. "Show me the way south."

"Tuck, it might already be too late..." Morrin began sadly.

"Maybe I can still do something!" I insisted.

He studied my face for a moment, then nodded slowly. "Okay. Calm down. We'll go together."

Leaving a dozen men to help guard the villagers, I set off again with Morrin and fifteen of the remaining village fighters, circling the slopes, climbing higher, then descending into the southern part of the forest. Morrin knew hidden paths, shortcuts through the dense woods. "Getting closer now," he murmured after a while.

I knew he was right when we started finding bodies – Logenir warriors, village fighters, sprawled amongst the trees, testament to a fierce running battle. Then I heard it – distant screams, the unmistakable clang of steel on steel.

Forgetting caution, I ran towards the sound, cresting a small hill. Below, in a shallow, wooded valley, the fight still raged. A dozen or so village soldiers, Rogas among them, stood back-to-back, completely surrounded by maybe three times their number of Logenir warriors. Behind Rogas, slumped against a tree, I saw Taupin, covered in blood, clearly badly wounded, maybe dying. And at the forefront of the Logenir attackers, bellowing orders, swinging a massive axe, was the burly, reddish-brown-haired warrior I'd seen on the lead boat yesterday. Mornir. The leader. The man I needed to kill.

No time for plans. No time for fear. I launched myself down the hill, sword drawn, aiming straight for the rear of the Hualeg line encircling my friends. My blade bit deep into the back of one warrior, then another, before they even knew I was there.

My sudden attack threw the Logenirs into momentary panic. Some turned to face me, others pressed their attack on Rogas's desperate group. The battle dissolved into a chaotic, swirling melee. Outnumbered, exhausted, fueled by rage and desperation, I fought like a cornered wolf, like the 'big wolf' Vida had called me. My sword became a blur, leaping, dodging, striking with deadly speed.

But even as I cut down warrior after warrior, I saw our own men fall. Alend, fighting bravely near me, went down with his skull split by an axe from behind. Mullen... brave, foolish Mullen... shoved me out of the path of another axe blow, taking the hit himself, collapsing with the weapon buried in his back. A roar of pure rage tore from my throat. I avenged him instantly, killing both his attackers, then plunged deeper into the fray, a whirlwind of destruction.

The Logenirs faltered, their numbers dwindling rapidly under the unexpected, ferocious assault from both sides. A long, wavering cry went up from somewhere in their ranks – a signal? An order? I paused, panting, realizing Mornir and the remaining handful of his warriors were trying to break free, attempting to flee back west through the trees.

"Twenty strong men! Follow me!" I yelled, my voice raw, pointing towards the fleeing Logenirs. "The rest of you, help the wounded!"

Shaking off my own bone-deep weariness, I chased after Mornir. A few of my comrades – fewer than twenty now – pounded after me. I caught one fleeing Logenir from behind, my sword slashing across his back. Pushing through bushes, I found another, then another, cutting them down ruthlessly.

The few remaining Logenirs cried out in terror now, scrambling frantically through the trees as if demons were on their heels. By the time we burst out of the woods near the village edge, only Mornir himself and two of his personal guard were left, sprinting desperately towards the main road. I pursued them relentlessly, ignoring the shouts of my own men falling behind, not even noticing dozens of other Logenir warriors – survivors from the main path battle? – closing in from the village side, trying to help their chief escape.

My vision tunneled, focused only on Mornir. Anger, grief, exhaustion – it all fueled a reckless charge. My comrades, seeing my fearlessness, surged after me, crashing into the reinforcing Logenirs with a boldness that momentarily stunned the enemy.

I fought through them, ignoring the blows glancing off my rough clothing, my sword a whirlwind of death. Thrust, parry, slash – every move lethal, every strike fueled by the loss of Mullen, Alend, the men by the river. The Logenir line shattered, scattering back onto the main road in disarray.

And there he was. Mornir. I launched myself at him without hesitation. He met my charge, his axe swinging in wide, powerful arcs. I dodged, parried, searching for an opening. He was strong, skilled, but maybe tired too. His axe nearly split me in two – I leaped aside at the last second, stumbling onto the grass.

As I fell, another Logenir warrior standing near Mornir swung his axe down at my exposed head. I rolled desperately, simultaneously stabbing upwards with my sword. It slid into his stomach; he gasped and collapsed. Using his falling body as a shield, I scrambled to my feet just as Mornir's axe crunched into the dead warrior's back. The axe stuck for a fatal second. I swung my sword hard against the handle, knocking the weapon from Mornir's grasp.

Disarmed, Mornir panicked. He drew a short sword, looking wildly around for support. Seeing his remaining troops broken, scattering, his courage finally failed him. He shouted something – desperately calling for help? – forcing me to engage two more warriors who rushed forward, giving him the chance to turn and run.

He sprinted down the rocky path towards the riverbank, the last few loyal Logenirs scrambling after him. By the time I cut down my final opponent and chased him down to the water's edge, it was too late. A single longboat – maybe commandeered from the villagers, or one that hadn't been destroyed – was already pulling away into the current. Mornir stood in the stern, glaring back at me, maybe a dozen surviving warriors rowing frantically north.

"LOGENIR!" I roared, shaking my fist, helpless rage consuming me. "COME BACK! LET ME KILL YOU ALL! LOGENIR!"

They didn't answer, just rowed harder, disappearing around the river bend.

Breathless, trembling, I turned as Rogas, Thom, and the other survivors reached the riverbank beside me. "What took you so long?" I snapped, the adrenaline still coursing, needing someone to blame.

Rogas shook his head wearily. "I think we've had enough—"

"We go after them!" I yelled, pointing at the empty river. "Take a boat! Gather everyone! We have to—!"

"William!" Rogas shouted, grabbing my shoulders hard, forcing me to look at him. His voice was rough, but steady. "That's enough! Do you hear me?" He shook me slightly. "That's enough, man. It's over. You understand?"

I stared at him, his words slowly penetrating the red haze of battle fury. Over?

"You won," Rogas said, a tired, wondering smile touching his lips. His eyes looked suspiciously moist. "We won."

Only then did it truly hit me. The silence. The absence of fighting. Victory. My chest heaved. My hands started to shake violently. I looked down at my sword, coated in gore. Then at the street, littered with the bodies of the men I had just killed.

The memories flooded back, sharp, brutal, vivid – the impact of blade on bone, the death cries, the terrified eyes. Anger, adrenaline, grief, fear, the strange coldness of killing... it all rushed out, overwhelming me. I dropped the sword as if it burned me. A strangled scream tore from my throat.

"Hey." Rogas put a steadying arm around my shoulders as my knees buckled. "It's okay."

I collapsed to my knees, covering my face with trembling hands. *Did I do this? Did I kill them all?* In the darkness behind my eyelids, I tried desperately to breathe, to calm the storm inside, to push away the horrific images I knew would haunt me forever. I had done this. This was the consequence. This is what I was now. A killer. A massive killer.

Through my ragged breathing, I heard Thom approach Rogas hesitantly. "Hey... why do you call him William? Isn't his name Tuck?"

Rogas laughed then, a strange, watery sound. He looked around at the exhausted, blood-stained soldiers gathering around us. "Guys." He gently but firmly pulled me back to my feet, keeping an arm around my shoulders as I swayed. "Now listen to me. I'm about to tell you something very important." His voice grew stronger, louder. "This young man," he gestured towards me, "his name is *not* Tuck!" He paused, letting the silence hang, building the moment like the showman he was. "In extraordinary times like these... you understand this is something that happens only once in your life? Something you'll tell your children, your grandchildren? These are the moments when you fought beside this young man... and *won*!" He looked around at their faces. "Now you should all know his real name! Listen! Remember this name well!" He paused again, grinning. "He, this young man's name... is... Tuck!"

A collective groan went through the crowd.

"Oops," Rogas grinned happily, slapping me on the back. "My mistake. His name is WILLIAM! William! Did you hear me? This is William! The conqueror of the Northmen!"

19

Prepare for the Unpredictable

Conqueror? What conqueror? Rogas revealing my real name like that... shouting it to the whole village... it felt strange, exposing. I didn't feel like a conqueror. I felt sick, exhausted, hollowed out. Ignoring the lingering back-slapping and congratulations, I stumbled away from the cheering crowd, needing silence, needing space. I ended up back down by the river, collapsing against the side of one of our remaining boats moored at the bank. Stretching my aching legs out, I tilted my head back, staring up at the faintly cloudy night sky, letting the cool breeze wash over my face. The gentle rocking of the boat under me was soothing. Sleep. That's what I needed. Sleep, and maybe forgetting the horrors of the past few days.

But rest seemed unlikely with Rogas around. I heard his booming laugh approaching, smelled the wine on his breath even before he clumsily climbed into the boat, nearly tipping us both into the water. He plopped down opposite me, grinning like an idiot.

"If you want to sleep, find another boat," I grumbled, not opening my eyes.

"Sleep?" he scoffed. "Now? We should be celebrating! Come on, William! Have a drink with the men! You earned it today, my friend, truly earned it. Or," he sloshed the wineskin he carried, "we can drink right here."

I opened my eyes, looking at his cheerful, oblivious face. "Celebrate what, Rogas? We won, yes. But forty-seven men didn't live to see it. Forty-seven dead since we got here." The number felt like a physical weight. "I don't feel much like drinking right now. You go ahead."

"It was a tough day," he conceded, his grin softening slightly. "Very tough. We lost good men. But look at the bright side! We smashed the Logenirs! Sent them running! They won't be raiding south anytime soon. Think of the villages downriver, the families safe now because of what we did today. Because of what *you* did today. You deserve a reward. Just a few sips?" He held out the wineskin again.

His argument, twisted as it was, held a sliver of truth. We *had* stopped them. Sighing, I took the offered skin, took a couple of long swallows – the wine burned, but dully – and handed it back. "Enough," I said. "Someone needs to stay sane and alert around here."

Rogas laughed heartily. "Don't worry about the Logenirs! They're terrified of you now! Saw it in their eyes when they ran. They won't dare show their faces near Thaluk again until next winter, maybe longer."

"One should prepare for the unpredictable, Rogas, not just assume the predictable," I replied wearily, shaking my head.

"Once again, you're right." He shook his own head, looking at me with a strange mix of admiration and amusement. "You brat, you really are something else. A special little bastard. Been all over, seen plenty of fights, but never seen anyone like you. What you did today... yesterday... That kind of fighting, that kind of... fury... men twice your age wouldn't dare. It's the stuff of legends. And you want to keep doing more? You sound like one of those heroes they sing about." He paused, his tone turning serious. "Sorry, don't mind me talking big, do you?"

"I'm used to your nonsense," I said flatly. "You always hide something behind the praise. What are you getting at now? That heroes in legends usually die young? That's what happens, right?"

He nodded slowly. "So you know that, do you? Great men, heroes... they often burn out fast."

"You think I'll die sooner than you?"

"I plan on living to be a hundred!" he declared with drunken confidence. "So, yes! But William, what I mean is... guys like you, the brave ones, the great ones... you gotta be *extra* careful. First, you start thinking you're invincible, underestimate the risks. Second, yeah, people love a hero, but heroes make enemies too. Jealous ones, scared ones, angry ones who hate you just for being who you are. Those enemies..."

"Wasn't it me," I interrupted dryly, "who just said 'no more wine'? Said someone needs to stay sane? Seems obvious I'm already more careful than you."

"That's why I said you're special!" he insisted. "Still vigilant, even after... that. Still thinking ahead. But listen," he grinned again, clearly enjoying his role as mentor, "there's always one thing. The thing that *makes* people great, maybe, but they don't always respect it enough. It's important. Know what it is?"

"What?"

"Luck!"

"Oh! Luck!" I feigned wide-eyed surprise. "Of course! How could I forget?"

He pouted. "You don't believe me? After that ring? You saw how it worked!"

I glanced down at the reddish-yellow ring still on my finger. Had it done anything? Impossible to say. But... maybe it hadn't hurt. "Maybe..." I conceded noncommittally, "I'm starting to believe."

"You should! That ring's been protecting you!"

"Hey," I frowned, "what exactly are you trying to tell me, Rogas?"

"I'm saying," he leaned forward, suddenly earnest again, "that after what you've done, the way you fight, the enemies you've made... you're going to find more trouble. Bigger trouble. The kind that kills you fast, no matter how good or lucky you *think* you are. That's what I'm saying!"

"Okay..." I waited.

"But," he lowered his voice conspiratorially, "I can help you. One last time." He fumbled at his neck and pulled off the black necklace with the three bear claws. "This necklace. My *real* lucky charm. I'm giving it to you."

My eyebrows shot up. "Are you serious?"

He pressed it into my hand. The claws felt smooth, heavy. "Here. Take it. With your reckless, crazy way of fighting, you need this more than I do. Think I'm joking?"

I looked at him, trying to read his face in the dim light. "What I mean is... do you *really* think this thing brings luck?"

"Wow," he sounded genuinely offended. "That's insulting! To me, and to you! Especially since I think *you* half-believe that ring kept you alive today!"

Maybe I did. A tiny part of me. "In that case," I said slowly, closing my hand around the necklace, "thank you. But... isn't it strange? You giving away your luck?"

"Don't need it anymore," he grimaced, looking suddenly weary himself. "I'm done, William. Done with big wars, ambushes, massacres... all of it. Too much for my soul. You can handle it. I'm finding something quieter."

"Hmm... serious? You're a mercenary. Fighting and killing is your job."

"Doesn't have to be big battles all the time," he argued. "Plenty of work as a town guard somewhere safe. Chasing off petty thieves. Simple patrols. Enough for me now. Safer money."

"Then..." I raised an eyebrow, "...you'll stay away from gambling, too?"

His grin vanished. "Hmm... well... right. Still need coin for that." He suddenly looked sly again. "Guess... I still need *a* lucky charm, huh?"

"So you want the necklace back?"

"No, no! It's yours!" he insisted quickly. "I'll just take the small one. The ring. We'll trade."

I couldn't help but laugh. "All right, Rogas. If you say so."

We exchanged the items – I gave him back the ring, and he watched as I held the heavy bear-claw necklace on my palm. Luck? Probably not. But it felt like... a connection. A strange sort of passing of the torch, maybe. A gesture from Rogas that felt more real than his usual bluster.

"Now..." he drained the last drop from the wineskin, "I'm heading back to the village." He stood up, swaying slightly in the gently rocking boat. "You sleep, wake up, whatever..." He paused, looking down at me. "Always be careful, William. Don't die too soon."

"Sure," I mumbled. "I'm fine here."

He hopped somewhat unsteadily onto the riverbank. "I'll post two guards nearby," he called back. "Just in case. For the unpredictable, right?"

I watched him disappear into the darkness, then looked down at the necklace again. Could this thing really bring luck? What kind of luck did I even need now? Escape from more battles? Or the strength to win them? The first sounded better, safer. But maybe... maybe it wasn't what I truly wanted anymore.

Leaning back, I closed my eyes. My mind drifted, inevitably, to the Hualeg girls. The red-haired girl, joyful but vulnerable. And Vida... yellow-haired Vida, beautiful, deadly serious, enigmatic. The one who called me 'big wolf'. Then my thoughts drifted south, to Ortleg, to Muriel. Stubborn, loyal Muriel. My promise to return. Three girls, three completely different worlds, unimaginable complications. I chuckled softly to myself in the darkness. Better to just sleep. Dreamless, if possible.

Taking a deep breath, feeling the cool night air, the gentle motion of the boat... rest finally began to claim me.

I woke to sunlight warming my face and the sound of quiet conversation nearby. I'd slept soundly, deeply. No enemies had come in the night. True to his word, Rogas had posted two guards near the boat; they nodded a greeting as I sat up, offering me bread and hot tea they'd brought from the village. Relief washed over me – a peaceful night, a peaceful morning.

But the peace shattered when I returned to the main camp. Taupin was awake, his wounds bandaged, directing cleanup efforts. Morrin was organizing patrols. But Rogas... Rogas was nowhere to be seen.

"Who saw him last?" I asked, gathering Thom, Mullen, and the guards Rogas had posted.

The guards looked at each other. "He told us to watch over you by the river," one said. "That was it. Haven't seen him since then."

"I checked his sleeping spot," another soldier chimed in. "Empty. And one of the smaller boats is gone from the landing."

Thom grunted, half-joking, half-serious. "Figures. Probably had enough of the glorious north, headed south to find a warm bed and a dice game."

"You mean he just... left?" Spitz asked, bewildered. "Abandoned us?"

"If he really wanted to leave, he would have said something," I insisted, though doubt gnawed at me. Would he? Rogas was impossible to predict. But leaving without his final pay from Taupin? That didn't seem like him. Unless... unless he planned this all along?

"Do you really believe that, William?" Thom asked, his skepticism clear.

I didn't answer. Maybe I didn't know Rogas at all.

"Well, if he's gone, let him go," Thom declared, clapping me on the shoulder. "Means William here is in charge proper now! Suits me better anyway! Right, lads?"

The soldiers around us nodded agreement readily. It seemed Rogas wouldn't be missed much. It felt strange, the command settling fully on my shoulders not through ambition, but through abandonment. Fine. Someone had to do it.

I turned back to the tasks at hand. Ordered the villagers who'd fled to the hills to return. Checked on the wounded – twenty-three men, some serious. Organized the burial detail for the dead. It was a long, grim afternoon digging the mass grave, laying our comrades to rest. No one spoke much.

Afterward, we started clearing debris, repairing damaged huts. Implementing the river trap plan – gathering nets, sharpening logs. Sending scouts north again, just in case. By sunset, the village felt marginally less like a battlefield, marginally more like a home again. The second night passed peacefully.

The next morning, the uneasy quiet continued. No sign of Rogas. No sign of Hualegs. Confusion started to set in. Had they truly gone?

I was overseeing the work on the river defenses when Boulder came jogging up from the southern path.

"William!" he called out, looking perplexed. "When I was checking the south watch post this morning... I met someone. Wants to see you."

"Who?" I asked, surprised. We weren't expecting visitors.

"That Hualeg girl," Boulder said, scratching his bald head. "The tall one. Yellow hair."

"Vida?" I straightened up, stunned. "Where?"

"Down the creek," Boulder replied, pointing south. "Same way we came back from the woods day before yesterday."

South? Not north? How had she gotten past our river guards without being seen? I turned to Thom, who was nearby organizing the net-tying. "Are you *sure* the guards are watching the river properly?"

He looked offended. "Sure I'm sure! But," he hesitated, "I'll check with them again. Maybe they were tired last night…"

"Tell them this is no small thing!" I snapped, my unease growing. "They were lucky it was her coming past this time, someone who seems… well, not immediately hostile. Tomorrow, it could be Logenir scouts, and we'll all pay the price for their carelessness!"

"I know, William. I don't like it either."

"I have to go," I told him. "You're in charge here until I get back." I turned to Boulder. "Take me there."

We took a small, swift boat, rowing south, away from Thaluk, then turning left into the familiar narrow creek winding into the eastern forest. The trees grew thick overhead, dappling the water in shadow and light. It felt quiet, secluded.

"Are you sure this is the right place?" I asked Boulder, scanning the dense foliage lining the banks.

"Yeah, saw her right around here this morning," he insisted. "Said she wanted to see you. Strange she's not here now."

I peered into the forest. Sunlight streamed through gaps in the leaves, illuminating patches of the forest floor. Why would Vida want to meet me here, in secret? Maybe she'd given up waiting, left already? Disappointment warred with suspicion. "I think we should go back—" I began.

WHAM!

Something incredibly hard slammed into the back of my head. Pain exploded behind my eyes, bright white, then instantly swallowing darkness. My consciousness winked out like a snuffed candle.

20

The Ugly Necklace

My head felt like it had been split open with an axe. I groaned, consciousness returning slowly, painfully. Thick tree branches swam into focus far above me. I was lying on damp, grassy ground. Trying to push myself up, I felt a sharp bite around my wrists – tied. Behind my back. Panic flared. I struggled, groaning again, managing to sit up. My head spun violently.

In front of me, a familiar, unsettling grin spread across a dark-bearded face. Mornitz. Still clad in those damn black robes.

"You're finally awake, boy," he said, his voice smooth, almost pleasant. "Good. Saves me the trouble of splashing river water on that thick skull of yours." His eyes scanned me up and down. "Though from what I hear, maybe 'boy' isn't the right word anymore. Playing the big man up in Thaluk, aren't you?"

Laughter nearby made me turn my throbbing head. We were beside a small river, deep in the woods. And we weren't alone. Beside Mornitz sat a young man – maybe a few years older than me – with thick, dark hair, a messy beard, and a distinctly crooked nose that gave his face a permanently irritated look. Behind him stood an old man, thin and gaunt, shrouded in a dark hood that shadowed an ancient, wrinkled face. He just stared at me, silent and unnerving. Two more rough-looking men stood behind them, laughing loudly – probably the ones who'd knocked me out.

My first coherent thought, amidst the pain and confusion: *Boulder.* Where was Boulder? Had they killed him? A cold dread settled over the panic. I had to assume the worst. I forced myself to focus on the men in front of me.

"What do you want?" I asked Mornitz, trying to keep my voice steady, my eyes darting between them, assessing the threat. "Looking for Rogas? He's gone. Disappeared from Thaluk."

Mornitz chuckled softly. "Then we'll look for him again. Everywhere. Until he's dead." His gaze turned cold. "But maybe we kill you first. Let him catch up with you later... in hell."

"Rogas is not the man we seek," the hooded old man suddenly rasped, his voice like dry leaves rustling. "He is no longer our concern."

Mornitz shot him an annoyed look. "He's still *our* business, Brenis! Until the day he dies." He turned to the crooked-nosed young man beside him. "He's the one who broke your nose, Darron, remember? Aren't you going to pay him back?"

"You don't need to mention my nose!" the young man – Darron – snapped, flushing red.

"Mr. Darron," the old man, Brenis, interjected smoothly, ignoring Mornitz. "We did not come all this way merely to chase that useless mercenary. If you allow yourself to be distracted by petty revenge, as Mornitz suggests, you dishonor yourself. Everything I have taught you will be wasted."

Mornitz shook his head angrily. "Think you're so smart, Brenis? Going to teach the boy forgiveness now? Master Bellion never made mistakes like that! He crushes anyone who gets in his way! That's why men fear him!"

"Do not listen to him, Mr. Darron," Brenis insisted calmly. "Do not waste your energy or time on base revenge. One day, you will be a greater man than your father. Believe me."

Mornitz laughed harshly. "Master Bellion already distrusts you, Brenis! Cast you aside! Why should anyone believe your counsel now?"

"He has not cast me aside. He still believes in my judgment," Brenis replied coldly. "If you do not understand, then be silent."

"Hey! Both of you, I get it!" Darron exclaimed suddenly, cutting them off, his face flushed with anger and frustration. "Stop talking like only the two of you know anything! I know what I'm doing!"

Mornitz just smiled that thin, unpleasant smile. Brenis nodded slowly, looking pleased.

Darron. Bellion's son. Rogas's story flashed through my mind – the fight near Nordton, the raid leader wounded and escaping. So this was him. And Brenis... his advisor? While Mornitz was just muscle, maybe? The situation felt far more complicated than Rogas had let on.

"Go ahead, Darron," Mornitz prompted. "Do what you think is right."

Darron turned his nervous, angry gaze on me. "William. Uh, that's your name, right?"

I just stared back, waiting. "What do you want?"

"Mm... my stuff," he stammered slightly. "I'm sure you have it. Where is it?"

"Stuff?"

"The necklace!" His voice rose, cracking slightly. "The bear-claw necklace Rogas gave you!"

The necklace? My mind raced. Where *was* it? I'd held it after trading the ring... Did I? But I genuinely couldn't remember it now. Had I lost it? Or...

"You mean that ugly necklace?" I shrugged, trying to look indifferent, buying time, formulating a lie. "I don't know. Rogas gave it to me two nights ago, down by the river in Thaluk. I was exhausted, fell asleep right after." A plausible story started forming. "When I woke up, the necklace was gone. Didn't notice until later. Then Rogas vanished from the village yesterday morning." I looked him straight in the eye. "I think Rogas took it back while I was sleeping."

"Are you lying?" Mornitz leaned forward, his hand resting on the knife at his belt. He looked at Darron. "Want me to cut off a finger? An ear? Make him remember?"

"I'm not lying, you idiot!" I retorted, injecting anger into my voice to mask the fear. "I don't know where it is! If I did, I'd give it to you! Why would I want some ugly bear claws?" Seeing disbelief still in their eyes, I pressed on. "Think about it! Rogas regretted giving it away almost immediately! He probably snatched it back first chance he got! You know how cunning he is! It's with him now, wherever he's run off to!"

Brenis suddenly stood up and crouched down in front of me, ignoring Mornitz and Darron. He brought his wrinkled face unsettlingly close to mine... and sniffed the air around me, like a hound casting for a scent.

I recoiled instinctively. What in the blazes was he doing?

After a moment, Brenis shook his hooded head, his ancient eyes fixed on mine. "The last person to hold that necklace... was you."

My blood ran cold. If they believed this... this *sniffer*... they had no more use for me. They'd kill me right here. Curses raced through my mind. Think! Think faster!

"Wait! Wait, I remember!" The words tumbled out, desperate now. "We were on the boat! Rogas gave it to me, I was half-asleep! I think... I think maybe it slipped out of my hand! Fell into the river! Right there by the bank where we talked!" Plausible? Maybe. "When I woke up, I forgot all about it! It was just an ugly necklace, why would I miss it?"

"Fell... into the river?" Darron cried out, his voice high with panic. He lunged forward, grabbing the front of my tunic, shaking me violently. "Then it's gone? Lost?"

"Easy!" I gasped, trying not to choke. "Take it easy! The riverbank there isn't deep! Just shallow, rocky! If you dive, look around between the rocks near where the boat was moored... you should find it!"

"And if the current took it? Drifted north?" Darron sounded hysterical now.

I grimaced, playing along. "Then... you'd have to look north, I suppose. But be careful," I added, unable to resist. "Heard there are Hualegs up that way."

"Kid, are you playing games?" Mornitz hissed, pressing the cold tip of his knife against my throat. "Think this is funny?"

I swallowed hard against the blade. "Look," I said, trying to sound reasonable, desperate. "I don't want trouble. I'd rather be friends. Doesn't matter who you are. Let's just forget what happened before. Let me help you. Untie me. I'll take you back to Thaluk, show you exactly where the necklace might have fallen. You can search safely. No one will bother you." I looked from Brenis to Darron, pleading with my eyes.

Mornitz scoffed. "Take you back? So your friends can ambush us?"

"I can ask them not to attack," I offered quickly. "I promise. I give you my word. No trouble from the village."

Darron hesitated, looking towards Brenis. The old man seemed to be considering it, weighing the options.

But Mornitz wasn't convinced. "He's lying! Planning something! You're crazy to trust him!"

"We may have little choice," Brenis murmured, his piercing blue eyes locking onto mine. "Can we trust your word, William?"

"I don't want to die here," I said simply, truthfully. "You don't want to die walking into Thaluk. I don't need to be your enemy. You don't need to be mine. Why make things worse? Let's just solve this necklace problem. I'm offering to help. Work together. You can trust my word. Be good to me, I'll be good to you."

Brenis nodded slowly. "I believe you offer this in good faith. Master Darron?"

Darron still looked torn, glancing nervously at Mornitz.

Mornitz seized the moment. "Take him to the boat! Keep his hands and feet tied! *I'll* handle things, Master Darron. If this brat tries *anything*, I'll kill him myself."

So they hauled me up, shoved me towards a small boat hidden nearby. A rough-looking bandit took the oars. Mornitz sat directly behind him, knife still readily accessible, watching me like a hawk. I was pushed into the middle, hands still bound tight. Darron and Brenis sat behind me, with the last bandit bringing up the rear. The boat pushed off, heading back up the creek, northwards initially.

My mind raced. Boulder had led me here, saying Vida wanted to meet. But Vida wasn't here. Only these bandits. And Boulder himself? Vanished. Likely dead, dumped in the river. How could Vida and these bandits be connected to the same place? Unless... unless Vida was never here at all? Had Boulder lied? Lured me into a trap? But why? Money? Or was he one of *them* all along? I remembered fighting alongside him, trusting him... could I be that naive? That poor a judge of men?

The creek twisted and turned. The sun shifted through the leaves overhead. We were definitely heading north, deeper into the woods, *away* from the Ordelahr, away from Thaluk. "Is this another way back to the village?" I asked, trying to sound casual.

Darron, sitting behind me, answered readily enough. "Mornitz found this creek route. And another hiding spot further up."

"Why not just take the Ordelahr? Faster back to Thaluk."

Darron laughed nervously. "And run straight into your patrols guarding the main river?"

My blood ran cold. "You know about the patrols already? We only set them up a couple of days ago."

"We were informed by—" Darron began, then stopped abruptly as Mornitz shot him a warning look.

"Master Darron," Mornitz cut in smoothly, "there is no need to share information with this boy. He is not your friend."

"I don't think it's a secret that should be kept," Darron mumbled petulantly.

I laughed, a harsh, bitter sound. "If people only tell secrets to their friends, Mornitz, I doubt anyone tells *you* much of anything."

"That's never stopped me getting what I want," he snorted. "Sometimes ripping open a belly works just as well."

"Shh!" The bandit rowing in front hissed suddenly, holding up a hand.

We rounded a sharp bend in the creek. The waterway continued left, but to the right, across a narrow strip of land maybe twenty paces wide, I saw the wide, familiar expanse of the Ordelahr River itself. A portage point. The bandits pulled the boat ashore, hauled it across the muddy ground, and launched it into the main river. I pushed along, hands still tied, Mornitz watching my every move. Back on the broad Ordelahr, we turned the boat south, towards Thaluk.

We hadn't rowed far when another boat suddenly emerged from behind a large rocky outcrop downstream, heading towards us. Small, familiar... the boat Boulder and I had taken from Thaluk. And rowing it... was Boulder himself. He looked up, saw our boat, saw me bound in the middle, and his face went utterly pale, his jaw dropping in shock.

So. He *had* betrayed me. And clearly didn't expect me to survive the encounter with Mornitz. A cold, hard grin touched my lips. "Shocked, Boulder?" I called out across the water. "Didn't think I'd still be breathing?"

"Wha... what happened?" he stammered, looking nervously between me and Mornitz.

"William is going to help us!" Darron announced cheerfully, clearly oblivious to the undercurrents. "The necklace fell in the river near the village. We're going back to look for it!"

"Are you crazy?" Boulder exclaimed, his eyes wide with panic. "Go back *there*? The village soldiers will kill us all if they see us coming upriver with him tied up!"

"That's what *I* said," Mornitz muttered darkly. "But I was outvoted."

Boulder suddenly stood up in his rocking boat, drawing his sword with a shaky hand. "You should have killed him back there!" he yelled, pointing his blade at me. "He's dangerous! Don't you know what he did? Killed maybe a hundred Hualegs like they were nothing! Like mosquitoes! If he gets a chance, he'll kill us too!"

"Hey," I snapped back, my voice dangerously low. "I can talk to the men in Thaluk. They won't attack you if I tell them not to. And *I* won't kill you either, Boulder." I let the contempt drip from my voice as I stared at the man who had been my comrade just hours ago.

"Put your sword down, Boulder," Brenis admonished sharply from behind me.

"Listen! Let *me* find the necklace!" Boulder pleaded frantically now. "You wait here! Hide! If I go back alone, they won't suspect anything! I can search the bank where he said it fell!"

Mornitz's eyes lit up. "Good idea!" he declared. "Then we won't need the boy after all."

My breath hitched. The situation had just turned deadly again. I had to do something. Now.

"You mean... we should kill him?" Darron grimaced, looking uncertain again, turning to Brenis for guidance.

The old man was silent, his hooded face unreadable, clearly conflicted.

"Are you sure?" Darron pressed Brenis again.

"It should be done!" Boulder exclaimed desperately from his boat. "Goddamn it! Should have done it back in the woods!"

Mornitz raised his knife, a cruel smile spreading across his face. "Well, doesn't matter. Then or now, the result's the same." He started to move towards me.

Cursing under my breath, I acted. Before Mornitz could take another step, I kicked upwards with both feet, slamming my bound legs hard into his chest. He staggered back with an grunt, colliding with the bandit behind him. Twisting violently despite my tied hands, I rammed my elbow sharply into Darron's ribs beside me. He gasped and collapsed sideways, clutching his side.

From the other boat, Boulder lunged, swinging his sword down towards my head. I threw myself sideways, rolling off the edge of our boat, hitting the cold river water with a heavy splash. Panic surged as I sank, hands tied behind me, feet bound. Kicking frantically, I desperately tried to orient myself, searching for the bottom. The river wasn't too deep here. Sunlight filtered down, illuminating the rocky riverbed below.

My feet touched rocks. Above me, the shadow of the boat loomed. Something flashed past my face – a sword! Perhaps thrown deliberately, aimed to finish me underwater. I twisted away just in time, watching the blade sink and wedge itself between two rocks nearby. An idea sparked – desperate, maybe impossible.

Using my bound feet, I pushed off the bottom, swimming clumsily towards the sunken sword. Pinning the blade against the rocks with my feet, I managed, after several agonizing attempts, to snag the tough root bindings of my wrists against the sharp edge. I sawed back and forth frantically, ignoring the scrape of steel against my skin, lungs burning, spots dancing before my eyes.

Seconds stretched into an eternity. Then, finally, the ropes parted! Freeing my hands, I quickly untied my ankles, kicked powerfully off the bottom, and surged towards the surface, gasping for air, dragging precious oxygen back into my starving lungs.

Treading water, I looked towards the boats. And froze, staring at a scene of shocking carnage. Boulder lay slumped over the side of his boat, a long knife buried deep in his chest. The two bandits who had been with Mornitz were also dead – one practically headless, the other disemboweled, spilling his guts into the bottom of the boat. Darron and Brenis were gone – overboard during the chaos, maybe?

And in the center of Mornitz's boat, two figures were locked in deadly combat. Mornitz, his face a mask of fury, desperately parrying the lightning-fast strikes of... Vida, the tall, yellow-haired Hualeg girl.

21

Killing Something

Vida. Where had she come from? She couldn't have just materialized. She must have been nearby, hidden, watching. She must have attacked the moment I went overboard.

And attack she did. She and Mornitz were locked in a furious sword fight right there in the rocking boat. Swords flashed, clanging loudly in the sudden quiet after the earlier chaos. Mornitz, despite his size and reach, was clearly outmatched. He fought with desperate fury, growling with effort, but Vida moved like water, fluid and unpredictable. Her blade danced around his defense, parrying his heavy blows with startling ease, her footwork agile even on the unstable boat deck.

With a sudden, sharp stomp first left, then right, she made the boat rock violently. Mornitz stumbled, losing his balance for a crucial second. Vida's sword darted in, piercing his side, near his ribs. He staggered back with a cry of pain, hitting the boat's thwart, his sword slipping from his grasp. As he fumbled for it, Vida leaped forward, her sword driving deep into his stomach this time. Blood sprayed. He fell back, groaning, clutching the wound. Without hesitation, Vida ended it, a swift, clean horizontal stroke that sent his head rolling into the bottom of the boat. Brutal. Efficient. Final.

She turned then, her chest heaving slightly, and shouted something sharp in Hualeg towards the riverbank. I followed her gaze. Two large Hualeg men – the allies I'd seen her with earlier – were wading into the shallows, axes raised, heading towards where Darron and Brenis were flailing, trying to keep their heads above water after being thrown overboard in the earlier scuffle.

"Vida!" I shouted, treading water frantically. She turned, surprise flickering in her intense blue eyes. "Please! Don't kill them!"

She paused, looking from me to the struggling figures of Darron and Brenis, then back at her men. After a moment's consideration, she gave a short, clipped order in Hualeg. The two men immediately lowered their axes.

Vida kicked Mornitz's body and the other dead bandits overboard with cold indifference, then rowed the few strokes towards me, offering a hand to haul me, dripping and exhausted, into the boat. "Thank you," I gasped out, collapsing onto the thwart, relief making me weak.

Suddenly, laughter echoed from the riverbank behind me. I turned. It was the red-haired girl – Vida's sister – beaming at me, looking utterly unharmed and surprisingly cheerful. She called out something in Hualeg, pointing towards the shore where my own small boat must still be hidden. I managed a breathless chuckle back; her relief was infectious somehow.

Meanwhile, Vida watched impassively as her two men dragged a sputtering, furious Darron and a stoic, dripping Brenis out of the water and secured them. She looked back at me, doubt clouding her eyes. "You do not want them dead? They tried to kill you."

"They're harmless now," I argued, though Darron's glare suggested otherwise. "Killing them solves nothing. It just brings more revenge from Darron's father down south. More danger for everyone. Too many people have died already."

"If we kill them here, the father will not know who did it," Vida countered logically, coldly.

"Do you really believe that?" I shook my head. "Killing doesn't solve things, Vida. It just makes bigger messes." I looked her straight in the eye. "Let them be my responsibility."

She studied me for a long moment, then gave a slight, almost imperceptible shrug. "Okay."

"Why *are* you here?" I asked, the question burning now. "How did you find me?"

"We travel," she replied vaguely. "Looking for something. We know many paths, see things others miss." She glanced towards where Boulder's body had presumably sunk. "We saw the bald man you traveled with earlier today. Waiting by the creek. He looked... restless. Wrong. Freya," she nodded towards her sister, who was now wading out towards our boat, "sensed danger. So we hid. We watched."

Freya? So that was her name. "Your sister... she *sensed* danger?" The idea resonated strangely, reminding me of Master Horsling. A chill traced its way down my spine as I remembered pinning Freya against that tree, nearly killing her myself. If she hadn't... If Vida hadn't intervened just now... I owed them my life.

Freya reached the boat, chattering excitedly in Hualeg as Vida helped her aboard.

"What did she say now?" I asked Vida.

Vida hesitated, a faint smile playing on her lips. "She says... she is glad she could help you."

I smiled back at Freya, feeling a genuine warmth, a gratitude that went beyond words. "Then I thank you, Freya. Looks like I owe you one."

Vida stared at me intently. "Do you mind? Owing us?"

I grinned, feeling some of my old self return despite the exhaustion and lingering shock. "What? Mind helping *you*? No! I'd be glad to do anything I can."

"Good." Vida nodded curtly. "We could use your help."

I looked at her, intrigued. Her turquoise eyes, so like Freya's, held a depth I couldn't fathom. They reminded me of my own blue eyes, a link to the Vallanir blood we apparently shared. That shared heritage, the fight we'd just survived together... it created a strange, unexpected connection. I wanted to know more about them, about Vallanir, about everything. But later. "Just tell me what you need," I said seriously. "When my own business is settled, I promise I'll help."

"Do you need help with your business now?" Vida asked unexpectedly.

"From you? Again?"

"Freya and I can help you bring these two," she gestured towards the sullen Darron and resigned Brenis, now guarded by Vida's men in the other boat, "to your village."

"You'd come to Thaluk?" The offer surprised me. "That's... great! But then I guess I'll owe you even more, huh?" I laughed.

"There is no need to count good deeds," Vida said simply. "I help you. You help me. It is balanced."

I nodded slowly. "I agree."

So we set off, the five of us – me, Vida, Freya, and our two unwilling passengers – in Mornitz's captured boat, heading south down the Ordelahr towards Thaluk. Vida's two silent warriors followed in the other boat, keeping a watchful distance.

As we rowed, I realized Mornitz must have used that hidden western creek Vida and I had met near – the one Boulder led me to – as a way to bypass Thaluk unseen, maybe to set up the initial ambush or to escape north after the battle. I'd have to tell Taupin and Morrin about that route; the villagers needed to know it existed.

My mind buzzed with questions for Vida and Freya. About Hualeg land, about the feud between Vallanir and Logenir, about my father's family. But I held my tongue. My father's departure from his tribe hadn't been peaceful, according to Mom. Revealing my identity as Vilnar's son might bring disaster, not friendship. Better to wait, to learn more first. And besides, with Darron and Brenis listening, now wasn't the time for sensitive conversations.

We reached Thaluk late that evening. The guards on the riverbank tensed as they saw Vida and Freya, their Hualeg features clear in the torchlight. Suspicious murmurs rippled through the soldiers who gathered as we brought Darron and Brenis ashore. I quickly explained that the girls were friends, allies who had saved my life. Thankfully, Thom arrived and backed me up, having seen Vida and Freya briefly during our escape from the riverbank earlier. His word helped calm the villagers' fears.

Dealing with Darron and Brenis was trickier. They were bandits, enemies who'd tried to kill me. But killing them now, in cold blood... it felt wrong. More bloodshed wouldn't solve anything, and might provoke Bellion further.

"These two are bandits from the south," I explained quickly to Thom, keeping my voice low. "They were looking for Rogas. When they couldn't find him, they came after me."

"Where's Boulder?" Thom asked, looking around, noticing his absence.

"He was one of them," I said flatly. "He led me into their trap. He's dead now."

Thom stared, dumbfounded, questions forming in his eyes. "He... he tricked you? All this time..."

I nodded curtly. "He lied to us all along. Forget him, Thom. He's not worth talking about."

"Okay." Thom swallowed hard, accepting it. He looked at the prisoners. "So, what should we do with these two?"

I glanced at Darron, who looked terrified, and Brenis, who met my gaze calmly, resignedly. An idea, harsh but maybe necessary, formed. "If they still see me as an enemy," I said loudly enough for them to hear, "maybe you should just kill them. Yes, that seems better. I could live more peacefully then. Can you do that, Thom?"

Thom grinned savagely, resting his hand on the knife at his belt. "With pleasure, William."

Darron yelped, paling further. Brenis shot him a warning look.

"You promised to help us!" Darron screamed hysterically at me.

"That was before your man Boulder tried to kill me," I replied coldly.

"Boulder was right!" Darron shrieked, losing control completely. "You *will* kill us as soon as you get the chance!"

Brenis raised a hand, silencing the younger man. He bowed his head respectfully towards me. "Master William," he said calmly, his voice steady despite the situation, "we apologize. What happened at the river... it was Mornitz's doing, and Boulder's foolishness. Neither Master Darron nor I intended you further harm. We genuinely regret the events. Let us return south, sir. We promise we will never consider you an enemy again. We swear it."

He sounded sincere. More sincere than Darron, anyway. "You seem reasonable, Brenis," I conceded. "But I'm not sure promises from bandits mean much. You still serve Darron's father." I let the silence hang, watching them. Then I made my decision. "But... killing you solves little now." I paused again. "You may go."

Darron stared, utterly bewildered. "Really?" he whispered, unable to believe it.

Brenis reacted instantly, nudging Darron hard and bowing low himself. "Thank you, Master William! You are... unexpectedly generous."

Darron hurriedly bowed too. "Thank you, Master!"

I nodded curtly. "And I'll help you find that necklace, too. So you remember... I don't *want* to be your enemy."

"We will remember, master," Brenis assured me earnestly.

"I'll never forget this!" Darron added fervently.

I almost chuckled. They seemed serious now, maybe terrified into honesty. Time would tell if it lasted. For now, I just wanted them gone. I sent Thom and a few soldiers down to the riverbank near the main docks. The sun was setting fast.

While they searched, I stood on the clifftop overlooking the river, Vida and Freya beside me. Darron and Brenis waited anxiously nearby with Morrin, Thom, and a few guards. Soon, a shout came from below.

"Found it!"

A soldier scrambled up the path and handed me the familiar bear-claw necklace. It felt heavy, inert in my hand. Rogas's lucky charm. I had never worn it, and still, I had escaped death again. Holding it now, after everything, it felt like just a piece of bone and cord.

"Here." I held it out to Darron. "Your necklace."

He took it reverently, with both hands, clutching it like a holy relic. "Thank you, sir! You are truly a good man!"

"It's yours," I said tiredly. "Now go."

"We... we can go now?" Darron asked, still seeming stunned.

"Unless you're afraid to travel by boat at night."

"No, no! Not afraid!" he assured me quickly.

"Then be on your way. Best we don't see you again."

"We will go now," Brenis bowed again deeply, pulling Darron with him. "I thank you, Master William. I promise you... our troubles with you and Rogas are finished. There will be no more conflict between us."

I gave them back the small boat Boulder had used. We watched from the cliff as they pushed off, lit a torch, and rowed quickly south, their small light soon disappearing into the vast darkness downstream. The villagers and soldiers who had gathered began to disperse, heading back to their homes or barracks, leaving the clifftop quiet again.

I stood there with Vida and Freya, looking out over the dark river valley, the wind sighing softly around us. After the bloodshed, the fear, the shouting... the peace felt profound, settling over my weary soul.

"If I were you," Vida spoke quietly beside me, breaking the silence, "I would not have hesitated to kill them. They tried to kill you." She looked at me curiously. "But you are not just forgiving. You helped them."

"I did what I thought was good," I replied simply. It felt true, even if it wasn't logical by warrior standards.

"Will it always be so? Forgive when they apologize?"

I shrugged. "The future... who can say?"

"One day," she warned softly, "that mercy could be fatal for you."

"It could," I acknowledged.

"What will you do now?" she asked.

I was silent for a long moment, gazing north into the darkness. "I don't know yet," I answered honestly. "Stay here until autumn, maybe, help rebuild, ensure the Logenir don't return immediately." Though after our victory, and with Mornir dead, Vida seemed confident they wouldn't attack again soon. "Then..." I smiled faintly, the thought a warm flicker in the gloom, "...maybe return south for a while. I'm not wanted by Bellion anymore, thanks to Brenis's promise – if it holds. I should be able to go home." Home. Ortleg. Muriel. Bortez. It felt like a lifetime ago. Had it only been weeks? Months? If I told Muriel everything... would she even believe half of it?

Freya said something beside me then, her voice soft in the Hualeg tongue.

I was starting to pick out a few recurring sounds, but I still turned to Vida. "What did she say now? Sounds like she's scolding me again?" I tried a small laugh.

Vida looked at her sister, then back at me, a strange expression on her face. "Hmm... no. Not scolding." She hesitated. "She has... a request."

"Really? What?"

"She wants you to come with us."

"Where?" I asked, though a part of me already knew.

"North."

My breath caught. North. Back towards the land my mother forbade me to enter. Back towards my father's origins. "Why?" I asked quietly. "Why does she want me to come?"

Freya spoke again, more insistently this time, looking straight at me.

Vida smiled slightly, a rare, genuine smile that lit up her face. "She says she likes you."

I laughed, startled.

Freya laughed too, a bright, cheerful sound. Vida joined in, her smile widening, and for a moment, the tension between us vanished completely. It felt... good.

"Okay," I said, sobering slightly, guessing there was more to it. "So you apparently need help. Why don't you just say it?"

"I was right," Vida teased gently, "Freya *does* like you." Then her expression turned serious again. "But you are also right. We do need help. And you... you are the one who can help us most."

"What do you want me to do?"

"Killing," she stated simply.

My stomach tightened again. More killing? "Killing?"

"Killing *something*," she clarified quickly.

I frowned, confused. "Something? A thing? Not... a person?"

"Yes." Vida nodded grimly. "A creature. But... I cannot explain it fully yet. If you agree to come, I can tell you more on the journey. You can see for yourself later. This *thing*... it must be killed."

"And you're sure *I* can help?"

Her gaze was steady, certain. "You killed six of my men in the woods, warriors who were supposed to help *me*. And you proved you can kill many more when protecting others. So yes. I am sure. You can help us. You *must* help us."

Her certainty was compelling. And the idea of hunting some *thing*, some creature, not people... it felt different. Maybe even... right? "Alright then," I said slowly. "Where exactly are we going?"

"Into the forest," she gestured northeast this time, away from the main river. "Deep into the wild lands."

"Can you tell me *why* you need this creature killed?"

"Later," she promised. "It is a long story."

I looked from Vida's serious, intense face to Freya's hopeful, eager one. I nodded slowly, the decision forming, feeling strangely inevitable. "Alright." A thought struck me. "Although... I thought maybe you'd want to take me all the way to Hualeg land itself."

"After this task is done," Vida said, "you may come to our country, if you wish it. Do you?"

"Does Freya want me to go there?" I asked, glancing at her sister with a grin.

"Do you want me to ask her?" Vida replied, her lips twitching.

"No, no need." I laughed. "What I mean is... is she the only one? What about you, Vida? Do *you* want me to come?" I held her gaze, teasing gently.

A faint blush crept up her neck again. "That is no concern of yours."

"Wrong answer," I grinned back.

Vida snorted softly, looking away for a second before meeting my eyes again, her expression serious but soft. "Okay. Yes. I want you to come with me."

"That's the right answer." I chuckled, feeling a surprising warmth spread through me. "Then I'm coming with you."

Vida held my gaze for a moment longer, then nodded decisively and spoke quickly to Freya in Hualeg.

Freya let out a whoop of joy, raising both hands in the air like a child. I laughed at her unrestrained delight, and soon all three of us were laughing together on the clifftop under the vast, starry sky.

The wind blew gently, cool and clean. I looked north again, towards the dark, winding river, the unseen lands beyond. My decision was made. North. Directly against my mother's dying wish. Guilt flickered, then faded, replaced by a stronger pull – curiosity, destiny, maybe just the need to keep moving forward, away from the ghosts of Thaluk. This was something I had to do. Master Horsling's words came back to me: *recognize yourself... something already inside you... the next path*. Maybe this was it. The land of my father, the path towards understanding who I truly was.

II

Part Two

22

A More Honorable Path

Seventeen Years Earlier

Smoke coiled towards the uncaring sky, carrying the stench of burned wood and something else... something sickeningly familiar. The fire had devoured everything. Houses, reduced to charred timbers and ash, skeletal remains scattered amongst the trampled grass. And bodies. Twisted, sprawled on the ground, by the rocks, near the wide Ordelahr riverbank. Men, women, children. This was the second village I'd passed today, and like the first, it was utterly silent. Utterly dead.

My arms moved with the steady, powerful rhythm born of years handling oars and axes, propelling my small boat against the current. Each stroke felt heavy, bitter. I glanced back at the pile of prime bearskins behind me, cured and ready for trade. Goods without a market. In any other summer, these villages would have welcomed me, traded eagerly for the thick pelts. Now... they were just a useless weight, a mocking reminder of the life I'd built here, now consumed by the savagery I thought I'd left behind. What was I supposed to do with them now?

But the bearskins were the least of my worries. A storm raged inside me – sorrow for the dead, worry for villages further south, cold anger, and a burning shame that gnawed at my gut. Shame because I knew, without needing to see insignia or banners, who had done this. My own people. Hualeg. I had ridden with raiders like these once, long ago.

Our lands, the lands of the Hualeg tribes, lie far to the north. A harsh, cold realm locked by ice for most of the year, shrouded in dense forests, reachable only by weeks of river travel. A hard land that breeds hard people. Three years ago, I still lived there, the youngest son of the chief of the Vallanir, the greatest of the tribes. Since the age of sixteen, I'd fought alongside my eldest brother, earning my warrior's respect against our blood enemies, the Logenir from the west.

Then, at eighteen, my other brother – ambitious, cruel – persuaded me to join a raid south. The journey downriver was filled with boasts and anticipation. The reality... was a horror I could never forget. Watching women and children cut down for a few trinkets, seeing the bloodlust in my own kin's eyes... it sickened me to my soul. I fought my brother, turned my back on the massacre, and returned north alone, stained by the violence I couldn't prevent.

But Hualeg law is rigid. A warrior cannot break ranks, cannot defy his chieftain or kin during a raid, no matter the reason. Despite my father's position, despite the whispers even among our own people that my brother's raid went too far, I had broken my vow. The council offered two paths. One: regain honor by killing Rohgar, son of the Logenir chief – my sworn enemy since boyhood battles. A task I could likely accomplish, but why? I felt no guilt for leaving the massacre, only for being part of it initially. I would not kill Rohgar simply to appease tradition. So I chose the second path: exile. Three years banishment from Hualeg lands. A deep shame for most warriors, but for me, it felt cleaner, more honorable than pointless murder.

Weeks I rowed south, leaving my old life behind. Deep in the vast forests of Alton, where the river ran clear and game was plentiful, I found a measure of peace I'd never known. I built a cabin on a quiet tributary creek, hunted, learned the rhythms of this southern land. Eventually, I began trading bearskins with the local villagers. Tentatively at first, then more openly as they came to know me not as a Hualeg raider, but simply Vilnar the hunter. I learned their tongue, shared their fires, drank their ale. Learned there was more to life than the swing of an axe, the clash of steel.

Years passed. My exile ended. I was twenty-two now. I could return north, reclaim my place. But the desire was gone. This land, these people, this peace... it had become my home.

Then the raids began again. Trickling at first, then growing bolder, more frequent, more savage. Hualeg warriors pushing further south than ever before, killing without reason, plundering meager villages. My anger returned, mixed now with that old, familiar shame. Which tribe was doing this? Vallanir? Logenir? Some other clan driven by hunger or greed?

Passing the first destroyed village today, I'd forced myself to row on, telling myself it wasn't my fight, stay hidden, avoid trouble. But seeing the second... this village... I knew these people. I'd traded here often, shared stories, laughed with them. Seeing *them* slaughtered... I couldn't turn away again.

Ahead, the roar of water grew louder. The waterfall. As high as a tall pine, marking the boundary of the southernmost village I knew. This must have been the raiders' latest target. I steered my boat towards the bank, my eyes scanning for danger. There. Three large Hualeg longboats, moored carelessly near the base of the falls. Much larger than the local craft. Confirmation.

I hid my own small boat behind a jumble of huge boulders near the shore, listening intently. Only the thunder of the waterfall filled the air. The village above must be silent, likely already ashes. My hand tightened into a fist. But rage without thought was death. I needed to see, to understand.

From beneath my boat seat, I drew my long hunting dagger, its blade honed sharp enough to skin a deer or fell a sapling. I secured it at my left hip. Then I reached for my true companion: the battle axe. Its handle, smooth from years of use, felt solid, balanced in my grip. The wide, heavy blade, currently wrapped in protective deerskin, could split a log – or a man – with a single blow.

Leaving the boat hidden, I didn't take the path. I scaled the wet, slippery rocks beside the waterfall itself, using holds known only to hunters and climbers, moving with practiced silence. Surprise was my only advantage. Reaching the top, I stayed low, melting into the dense trees bordering the village clearing as twilight deepened, casting long, deceiving shadows.

As I feared, the village was gone. Smoldering ruins, charred wood, the metallic tang of fresh blood heavy in the air. Bodies lay where they fell. My grip tightened on the axe handle, a low growl rumbling in my chest. I moved cautiously around the perimeter, checking the ruins, finding no survivors. Then I saw the campfire, down in a clearing near the swift-flowing river below the falls.

Six men. Hualeg warriors, gathered around the flames, feasting, drinking, their bloody weapons lying casually beside them. Six? Three boats should mean thirty men, maybe more. Where were the rest? Raiding further south? Or already gone?

I crept closer, hiding behind a thick bush, straining to hear their rough voices over the river's rush. I didn't recognize their markings, couldn't tell if they were Vallanir or another tribe.

"...back north tomorrow, or wait for Rohgar?" one grumbled between mouthfuls.

Rohgar. The name hit me like a physical blow. My blood enemy. Son of the Logenir chief. So these weren't Vallanir. They were *Logenir.*

The one who seemed leader – long red hair tied back, face hard – Togril, they called him – answered. "Rohgar said wait. Repair boats, gather food. He returns in ten days. If not, *then* we go back."

Another man spat into the fire. "He just wants us sitting here guarding his precious cargo! Afraid someone else will claim it if we return without him!"

"Someone from our village? Or one of *us?*" another laughed, and the others joined in, coarse and loud. Only Togril stayed quiet.

"Idiot orders," someone grumbled. "He's off having fun raiding south, we sit here bored for ten days!"

"Bored, while letting that treasure go to waste?" another shouted. "All for Rohgar?"

"Don't touch *her*," Togril warned, but his voice lacked force, conviction.

Her? My gut tightened. A captive? A village woman? Still alive? Could I save her? Six of them, battle-hardened Logenir... and Rohgar himself likely not far off, with two dozen more warriors. The odds were impossible. Even if I freed her, escape would be suicide. Better to retreat now, fade back into the forest, pretend I hadn't seen, hadn't heard...

"Hey, Togril," one of the men badgered him again. "Rohgar gets his pick of slaves down south, we get nothing? Not fair! Can't we have a little fun too?"

"Right! No harm done," another agreed eagerly. "When we're finished, toss her in the river. Tell Rohgar she killed herself. Easy!"

"Good idea!" came a chorus of assent. They were serious.

"What do you say, Togril?"

The leader stared into the fire, silent, clearly torn.

"Togril!"

"Damn you all," another soldier finally said, standing up with a lecherous grin. "If you won't decide, I will! I'll go get her!"

Cheers erupted. But Togril's sudden shout cut through them. "Shut up!" Silence fell. Then, a slow, cruel smile spread across Togril's face. "I'll go first!" The cheering started again, louder this time.

He disappeared into the trees near the riverbank. Moments later he returned, dragging a limp figure behind him – a woman, dark-haired, dressed in a long blue gown now ripped and muddied. He threw her roughly onto the ground by the fire. Tangled hair hid her face initially, but as he yanked her closer, pulling her up by one arm, I saw her eyes. Vacant. Staring. Filled with a horror that spoke of witnessing unspeakable things.

Something inside me snapped. Reason, caution, fear – all consumed by a white-hot rage.

As Togril reached down, tearing at the bodice of her gown, as his men cheered him on, I rose from the bushes, hefting the great axe, and roared my challenge.

"YOU BASTARDS! YOU DIE NOW!"

They scrambled in panic, grabbing for weapons, startled by my sudden appearance, my Hualeg war cry. Too late. I charged into the firelight, axe whistling. A swing right – the first man's head flew from his shoulders. A swing left – the second warrior nearly split in two.

The remaining three lunged, trying to surround me. I met their charge, axe a blur of deadly motion. A feint, a block, a skull-crushing blow. Another stumbled back, clutching his ruined chest. The last one turned to run – I lowered my head and threw the axe with all my strength. The heavy blade spun end over end, catching him between the shoulders, felling him like timber.

Five dead. Only Togril remained. He stared, paralyzed by fear and rage, then grabbed the woman's arm, hauling her towards the riverbank, using her as a shield. He fumbled for his sword, pointing it shakily at me. "Don't move!"

I froze, then slowly lowered my empty hands.

Togril started backing towards the river, dragging the woman, his eyes darting between me and my axe nearby. He was panicked, clumsy. Seeing my chance, I drew the long dagger from my belt in one smooth motion and threw it, hard and true.

He roared as the blade buried itself deep in his chest. He staggered back, lost his footing on the slippery bank, and plunged into the fast-flowing river, pulling the helpless woman in with him.

Cursing, I sprinted to the river's edge and dove in without hesitation. The current was strong, cold, pulling me towards the roar of the nearby waterfall. I swam desperately, searching the dark water. I saw Togril's body swept past, lifeless. Then my hand brushed against fabric, closed around bound wrists. I got a grip, fought the current, pulled her towards the shallows below the falls, away from the main current, finally dragging her limp, unconscious body onto the grassy bank.

She wasn't breathing. Panic seized me. I turned her over, struck her back hard, cleared her airway, then pressed rhythmically on her chest until she finally coughed, choked, and gasped, spewing river water. Relief washed over me, so intense I felt dizzy.

I swam back quickly to retrieve my hidden boat, grabbed dry cloaks, returned to her side. Gently, I cut her bonds, stripped away the soaked, ruined dress, dried her shivering body as best I could, and wrapped her tightly in one thick, warm bearskin cloak, then covered her with another. Her left calf was badly gashed, bleeding from the rocks below the falls. I cleaned and bandaged it carefully. She was so cold. I sat beside her, pulling her close, sharing my own body heat, holding her through the long, dark night as she drifted in and out of a troubled sleep.

Sunlight woke her the next morning. I was grilling some fish I'd caught earlier over a small, smokeless fire. She stirred under the heavy cloak, groaning softly as pain from her leg likely registered. She looked around, confused, fearful, then blushed deeply as she realized her state of undress beneath the cloak, her eyes darting towards me, then away.

"You're awake," I said gently, keeping my voice low. "Feeling better?"

She didn't understand my Hualeg words, of course. Just stared, clutching the cloak tighter.

I held out a piece of freshly cooked fish on a stick. "Here. Eat. Fish is better than venison when you're recovering, I think." I waited. When she didn't move, I added, "But if you want meat, I can hunt."

She hesitated, then slowly reached out a trembling hand, took the fish, and began eating with desperate hunger.

I pointed to my own chest. "Vilnar," I said clearly. "My name. Vil-nar. Understand?" I pointed to her face. "You? Name?" My gestures felt clumsy, but maybe she understood the intent.

She watched me for a long moment, her dark eyes searching mine, then nodded almost imperceptibly and whispered a name. "Ailene."

"Ah-lind?" I tried, the sounds unfamiliar.

She shook her head slightly. "Ai-lene."

"Ailene," I repeated, tasting the name. It sounded... beautiful. Like her. I smiled. "A lovely name."

She offered a small, tentative smile in return, the first I'd seen. It transformed her face, chasing away some of the haunted look in her eyes. My heart gave a strange lurch. Looking closely now, she wasn't from around here. The blue dress, though ruined, wasn't local style. Her features – the dark slanted eyes, smooth black hair, tanned skin – spoke of origins much further south. How had she ended up captive of Logenir raiders so far north? She couldn't tell me, and I couldn't ask.

Knowing she wouldn't understand the words, but hoping the intent was clear, I said, "Today, you rest. Heal. I will take my boat, go back to the village, get proper clothes for you. Tomorrow," I pointed south, downriver, "if you are stronger, I take you south. Find your family? Friends?"

She shook her head quickly, speaking rapidly in her own tongue, gesturing with her hands, her eyes pleading.

I watched, listened, but understood nothing except her clear reluctance to go south. "I'm sorry," I said gently. "I don't understand. But... going south seems best. Safest for you."

She fell silent, looking down, then finally gave a small, resigned nod.

Good. Settled then. She needed to get back to her own people. The north was too dangerous for a woman like her, alone.

I told myself that was the right decision, the only decision. But deep down, a selfish part of me wished otherwise. Wished she could stay. Wished I had more time with her, time to learn her language, time to see that smile again. I chuckled grimly to myself. Three years in the south, and Vilnar the Hualeg warrior was truly gone. Hualeg custom was direct – find a woman you desire, take her. But looking at Ailene, vulnerable and trusting beneath my cloak... that felt barbaric now. I was no longer just Hualeg.

23

Until the Time's End

The screams always jolted me awake. Even now, years later, they echoed just beneath the surface of sleep – the high-pitched terror of women, the desperate cries of children, the final moans of dying men. Firelight flickering on horrified faces, the coppery stench of blood, the heat of burning homes. My brother's men, *my* people, moving through the southern village like vengeful spirits, axes rising and falling. And that child, no older than five, clinging to his mother as she pleaded, pleaded for mercy that never came... until the axe fell.

I should have stopped it. Should have done more than just fight my own brother, turn my back in disgust, and flee north stained with their shame. *"We are Hualeg,"* my brother had sneered later, back in our father's hall. *"This is what we do."*

"No!" I had roared back. *"We are not like that!"*

"Aren't we?" he'd challenged. *"What will you do about it, little brother?"*

I hadn't had an answer then. Just rage, and later, the choice: kill Rohgar, the Logenir chieftain's son, to satisfy a blood feud I didn't believe in, or accept exile. I chose exile. Three years wandering the south, leaving the Hualeg name behind. And now... now the screams followed me even here, in this supposedly peaceful southern land.

I sat up, gasping, heart pounding against my ribs. The dream, vivid as always, faded with the waking light, leaving only the familiar ache of guilt.

But the sun was rising. A new day. Dwelling on the past achieved nothing. Ailene needed me. We had to leave today, push further south, away from the danger Rohgar and his Logenir warband represented.

Yesterday had been grim work. After saving Ailene, after tending her wound and sharing what little warmth I could offer through the night, I had returned to the ruined village below the waterfall. I spent hours digging a single, large grave, gathering the scattered bodies – villagers I might have known, Logenir warriors I had killed – men, women, children. I buried them all together, friend and foe alike, hoping their spirits might find more peace than mine.

Then I carried Ailene gently up from the riverbank to the village. Most houses were ash, but one stone structure stood relatively intact. We rested there. When she saw the raw earth of the mass grave, she insisted, though weak, on being taken closer. She knelt beside it, praying silently in her own tongue, tears tracing paths through the grime on her cheeks. Her sorrow was quiet, contained, but deep. Afterwards, unable to walk on her injured leg, she allowed me to carry her back to the stone house. She slept inside on a salvaged pallet; I stayed outside by the door, listening to the night sounds, my own sleep haunted by the ghosts of the past.

Now, after a quick breakfast of dried meat and river water, we set out again in my small boat. I rowed south, keeping close to the bank, my senses on high alert. Rohgar and his main force – maybe two dozen men still? – could be anywhere. Resting in the next village downriver? Camped along the bank? If I saw any sign, my plan was simple: hide the boat, wait, or if they were attacking a village, slip past on the far side of the river under cover, get Ailene further south, perhaps warn the next settlement if possible.

The first day passed quietly. The river flowed peacefully between steep, forested banks. Birds called, monkeys chattered high in the canopy. No sign of longboats, no smoke from campfires. Just the steady rhythm of my oars, the sun warm on my back, and Ailene sitting quietly behind me, watching the unfamiliar landscape drift by.

The second day felt different. Tense. The air itself seemed watchful. I felt it in my bones – the instinct honed by years of border warfare and solitary hunting. They were close. I scanned the banks constantly, letting the boat drift silently whenever I stopped rowing to listen. Ailene seemed to sense the change too; she sat straighter, her dark eyes wide, scanning the trees.

Around noon, I saw it – a thin plume of smoke rising from beyond a dense stand of pines ahead, where the river bent sharply. Logenir campfire. Then came the sounds, faint at first, then clearer: shouts, screams, the unmistakable clang of metal on metal. They were attacking the next village.

My plan had been clear: avoid conflict, get Ailene south. But hearing the sounds of battle... knowing Rohgar was likely there, slaughtering more innocents... something shifted inside me. This was my chance. My chance to stop Rohgar, to avenge the dead in the villages behind us, maybe even to finally silence the screams in my own head. My heart pounded, overruling caution.

I rowed hard towards the bank, nosing the boat into a thicket of reeds. Reaching under the seat, my hand closed around the familiar, comforting weight of my axe handle. I looked back at Ailene.

"Wait here," I said, knowing she wouldn't understand the Hualeg words, but hoping my tone conveyed urgency, reassurance. "I will be back."

Her eyes widened with fear as she saw the massive axe, its deerskin wrapping removed, the polished blade gleaming dully. But she didn't protest. Instead, she reached out a trembling hand, touched my cheek gently, and whispered something soft in her own language.

It sounded like a prayer. I managed a grim smile. "Thank you."

Then I leaped from the boat, axe in hand, and plunged into the forest, running towards the sounds of fighting.

Branches whipped at my face as I crashed through the undergrowth, ignoring the scratches, leaping fallen logs, driven by righteous fury. The screams grew louder, mingled with Hualeg war cries. I burst through the last line of trees onto the edge of a wide clearing bordering the village huts.

A fierce battle raged. A dozen of Logenir warriors lay dead or dying, but a dozen more pressed their attack, surrounding three figures fighting desperately back-to-back. Strangers. Southerners, by their dress and features. And gods, how they fought! Two wielded swords with blinding speed and skill, the third used a long spear like an extension of his own arm, darting in and out, keeping the attackers at bay. Their movements were precise, coordinated, covering each other flawlessly. I'd never seen fighting like it, not even among the best warriors of the Vallanir or Logenir.

But they were tiring, being pushed back towards the rocky foothills, the circle of howling Logenirs tightening around them. Leading the attack, bellowing orders, his red hair unmistakable even through the dust and gore, was Rohgar. My sworn enemy.

Seeing him there, directing this slaughter, brought back all the old hatred, the memory of past battles, the injustice of my exile. Vengeance, cold and sharp, rose within me. Without a second thought, I leaped from the treeline, raising my axe high, roaring his name, letting my own Hualeg war cry rip through the chaos.

"ROHGAR OF LOGENIR! IT IS I, VILNAR OF VALLANIR! YOUR DEATH HAS COME!"

My appearance, my name shouted across the battlefield, threw the Logenirs into confusion. They knew me. Knew my reputation. They hesitated, looking from me to Rohgar, momentarily forgetting the three strangers. That moment was all I needed.

I charged into their ranks, axe whistling. The first warrior fell, his shield splintered, his chest caved in. The second tried to parry; I smashed his axe aside and took his head clean off. I became a whirlwind of death, unstoppable, fueled by years of suppressed rage and a burning need for justice. Logenirs fell before me, screaming, trying to regroup, but their lines broke, scattering in panic.

Rohgar, seeing his men faltering, seeing me carving a path directly towards him, continued shouting orders for a moment, then turned and fled into the trees behind the village. Ignoring the remaining Logenirs, ignoring the three stunned strangers, I pursued him.

He stopped deeper among the trees, turning to face me, sword ready. The forest offered more room for his blade than my axe. He lunged, swift and practiced. I parried, the impact jarring my arms. He attacked again, faster this time. I gave ground, letting him press, waiting. Patience had never been Rohgar's strength. As I expected, frustration made him reckless. He overswung, a wide, desperate slash aimed at my neck.

I ducked under the whistling blade, pivoted, and brought my axe up in a vicious uppercut. The blade sheared clean through his sword hand at the wrist. His sword flew away. Before his scream of pain fully registered, my axe swung again, horizontally this time, biting deep into his side, nearly cleaving him in two. He collapsed without another sound.

I stood over him for a long moment, breathing heavily, the bloodlust slowly fading. Rohgar. Dead. The feud, the reason for my exile, ended here in this bloody southern clearing. A grim smile touched my lips – satisfaction not just for myself, but for the villagers he would never terrorize again.

Wiping Rohgar's blood from my axe blade on the grass, I became aware of the three strangers watching me from the edge of the trees, their expressions wary. The spearman – long black hair, cold eyes – looked particularly dangerous, his weapon still held ready. The grey-haired swordsman seemed more open, though cautious. It was the middle one, though, the one with light brown hair and surprisingly calm dark eyes, who caught my attention. He sheathed his sword slowly, deliberately, and raised a hand, palm open, speaking words I didn't understand, but his tone was even, questioning, not hostile.

A strange feeling, almost like recognition, passed through me. I felt... no threat from him. Without hesitation, I lowered my axe, resting the haft on the ground, showing I meant no further harm.

Then I remembered Ailene. Turning back to the strangers, I pointed towards the river, then made gestures – woman, boat, help. "Gentlemen," I tried, hoping the meaning was clear, "Wait here. Someone needs your help. On my boat."

The man with long black hair and the brown-haired leader exchanged puzzled glances. But the gray-haired man raised his hand slightly. "One moment..." he said, his Hualeg accented but clear.

He understood! Relief washed over me. Without waiting for more, I turned and ran back towards the river, leaping ditches, pushing through branches. I found Ailene where I'd left her, huddled fearfully under the cloaks in the boat.

"Ailene! It's alright! I found people! Southerners! They can help you!"

Her face lit up with a relief so profound it took my breath away. Before I could react, she threw her arms around my neck, hugging me tightly, burying her face in my shoulder. I stood frozen for a moment, stunned by the sudden contact, the unexpected intimacy. Awkwardly, I patted her back.

"Um," I cleared my throat, trying to regain my composure. "I'm fine. Now, you... you get on my back."

Carefully, mindful of her injured leg, I lifted her onto my back and hurried back through the forest, moving as swiftly as I could without jostling her too much. She clung tightly, her face hidden against my shoulder, shielding her eyes from the carnage we passed.

The three strangers were waiting where I'd left them. I gently set Ailene down on a patch of soft grass. "Gentlemen," I explained quickly in Hualeg to the grey-haired man, gesturing towards Ailene. "I found this girl in the village north of here. Attacked by those Logenir men. Her leg is injured." I hoped he understood the situation.

He nodded gravely. "We understand."

Relief flooded me again. "Her name is Ailene," I said. "Maybe you can help her find her family? Her people?"

The gray-haired man glanced at his companions, then nodded again. "We will try our best to help her. But first, that leg needs proper attention. If you permit," he added politely, "I have some skill in treating such wounds."

I hesitated only a second. These men, whoever they were, fought like heroes and carried themselves with honor. And this one spoke my tongue. They seemed trustworthy. "Yes. Please."

While the gray-haired man carefully unwrapped the crude bandage on Ailene's leg, cleaned the wound with supplies from his own pack, and applied fresh, clean dressings, I watched for a moment, satisfied she was in good hands. Then I joined the other two strangers near the village center where surviving villagers were emerging hesitantly from the forest, beginning the grim task of collecting the dead.

Later, as the sun dipped low, the burials complete, I found myself sharing a small campfire with the three southerners near the house where Ailene rested. The silent spearman built the fire then sat apart as before under a shady tree, sharpening his weapon, seemingly indifferent. The brown-haired man sat opposite me, offering a quiet smile. The gray-haired man sat beside me to translate.

As was custom, I spoke first, pointing to my chest. "I am Vilnar. Of the Hualeg people," I stated plainly, watching their reactions. "Like the men I killed today." I paused, then added, needing them to understand, "I do not regret killing them. They shamed our people. I have seen their victims in other villages. As a Hualeg, I felt... shame. My actions today... perhaps they show my regret."

The gray-haired man translated carefully. The brown-haired leader nodded slowly, his dark eyes thoughtful. Even the silent spearman glanced over briefly.

"We thank you, Vilnar," the gray-haired man said formally. "Your actions saved us, and these villagers. My name is Walter." He gestured to the brown-haired man. "This is my first brother, Fabien." Then towards the silent spearman. "And that is Claude, my second brother."

Finally, names for the faces.

Walter continued, "He doesn't talk much," nodding towards Claude, "but he's the best spearman in Estarath. We are knights of the Knight's Temple on Mount Hohn."

Knights? Temples? Estarath? All strange southern concepts, unfamiliar to me. "You are all brothers?"

Walter smiled. "We come from different lands, but in the temple, we become brothers. I joined my two brothers about a year ago. We travel, fight the darkness – the Elniri, criminals – and help people where we can. Today... today was unexpected trouble. We are grateful for your aid." He, Fabien, and even Claude inclined their heads in a formal bow.

Unfamiliar with the gesture, I bowed awkwardly back.

Fabien said something quietly to Walter. Walter turned back to me. "Vilnar, my brother Fabien... he greatly admires your skill in battle, and your clear sense of justice. He asks... if you would consider joining us? Become a knight? Help people not just here, but perhaps in other lands? We would be honored if you joined us."

Join them? Become a knight? The idea was startling. Travel? See more of this southern world? It held a certain appeal. "If I go south with you," I asked, thinking of Ailene, "could I also visit the village where Ailene is from? Do you know where she came from?"

Walter frowned slightly. "We spoke with her while I tended her leg. She is from Tavarin, a kingdom far to the south of Alton. Her father was a merchant; they travelled together. This summer was their first journey this far north. The... the Hualegs attacked the village you passed through yesterday. Her father was killed there."

My breath caught. I had suspected, but hearing it confirmed... poor Ailene.

Walter continued sadly, "She said she has no other family. Her father was all she had left. Now... she does not know where to go."

Deep sympathy welled within me. Condolences felt useless. What could I offer? An idea, bold and sudden, formed in my mind. It felt right. Hualeg custom was direct. Hesitation now felt wrong.

"Then," I began, trying to keep my voice steady, "in that case... could you ask her... ask her if she would stay here? Longer?" I paused, gathering my courage, meeting his curious gaze directly. "I mean... ask the girl Ailene... if she would marry me."

The words hung in the air. I rushed on before doubt could silence me. "We have only known days, I know. But tell her... tell her Vilnar will love her, protect her, always. Body and soul. I swear it by the gods of my people and the spirits of this land." My eyes dared anyone to question my intent. "Can you ask her this?"

Walter looked stunned for a second, then exchanged a quick glance and a few quiet words with Fabien. Fabien looked thoughtful, then nodded almost imperceptibly. Claude, predictably, just kept sharpening his spear, though I thought I saw a flicker of surprise in his cold eyes before he looked away.

"Look, Vilnar," Walter said gently, turning back to me. "Matters of the heart... especially after what she has endured... you cannot force such things. It must be her choice."

"I know," I insisted. "That is why I ask *you* to ask *her*."

Walter studied my face, saw the absolute seriousness there. He sighed, then managed a warm smile. "Okay, Vilnar. I will ask her." He stood up. "Good luck, my friend."

He disappeared into the house where Ailene rested. I was left pacing nervously by the fire, glancing towards the door, then up at the stars, then back at the door. Claude continued his vigil, staring impassively at the night sky. What did he see up there? Messages from his southern gods? Hualeg gods spoke through storms and ice, not quiet stars.

Fabien caught my eye, smiled encouragingly, and handed me a cup filled with a warm, spiced drink. I took it gratefully, downing it in one gulp, the warmth spreading through my tense body but doing little to calm the anxious waiting in my heart.

Waiting by the campfire felt longer than any battle I'd ever fought. Sharing a drink with Fabien, the brown-haired knight whose quiet warmth I found strangely comforting despite the language barrier, did little to ease the anxious pounding in my chest. Even Claude, the silent spearman, seemed less forbidding now, though he still focused more on his weapon than conversation. My gaze kept flicking towards the door of the house where Walter, the grey-haired knight who spoke my tongue, had gone to speak with Ailene. Had I been a fool? A blunt Hualeg warrior asking a gently bred southern woman to marry him after barely two days? What must she think?

Finally, the door opened. Walter emerged, Ailene leaning lightly on his arm. She moved slowly, favoring her bandaged leg, but her head was held high. I searched her face, trying to read her expression in the flickering firelight. Was that hesitation in her dark eyes? Or acceptance?

"Ailene wishes to give her answer now," Walter announced, his own expression carefully neutral.

She looked directly at me then, her gaze steady, unwavering. She spoke a few soft words in her southern tongue. I looked at her, then helplessly towards Walter for translation. To my utter confusion, Walter and Fabien suddenly burst into laughter. Even Claude, the stoic spearman, cracked a rare, wide grin.

"Alright, Vilnar," Walter said, clearly enjoying my bewilderment. "Ailene says you seem a very kind and honorable man." He paused, his eyes twinkling. "But she thinks perhaps you should shave off that thick Hualeg mustache and beard, so she might see your face more clearly."

I instinctively touched the thick golden beard that reached my chest. This? "Oh. This? No problem. Easily done."

"*But,*" Walter added, his smile broadening, "she says you can do that *later*. After you two are married."

My heart seemed to stop, then started again with a painful surge. "Does... does that mean she agrees?" I asked, my voice barely a whisper.

"Yes, Vilnar," Walter confirmed, his voice warm. "She agrees. She is very happy."

A wave of pure, incredulous joy washed over me, so strong I felt dizzy. A day that began watching my enemies die by my hand was ending... like this. With a promise of a future I hadn't dared dream of. I smiled, a wide, unrestrained grin splitting my usually stern face. I turned to Ailene, bowing my head slightly, searching for words. "Thank you," I managed, the simple phrase feeling wholly inadequate. "Thank you, Ailene."

Tears welled in her eyes, not of sorrow this time, but shining in the firelight. Slowly, hesitantly, she reached out and her small, warm fingers closed around mine. Emotion swelled in my chest, thick and unfamiliar. I, Vilnar of the Vallanir, who had faced down charging Logenirs without flinching, who had never shed a tear even when burying my own kin, found myself fighting desperately against the stinging pressure behind my own eyes. Gently, I lifted her hand, drew her closer, kissed her forehead, and then held her tightly as she trembled slightly in my arms.

The next morning, down by the river's edge, I took my sharpest dagger and, squinting into the reflected sunlight on the water, began shaving away the thick golden beard and mustache I'd worn since manhood. Ailene had said I could wait, but I wouldn't. Today was the beginning of our life together; I wanted nothing hidden. As the last whiskers fell away, I studied my reflection. Younger. Stranger. Smoother. Would she approve? We were so different – my northern fairness against her southern darkness, my height and bulk against her slender grace. But looking towards the clearing where she waited with the knights, I knew it didn't matter. What was between us went deeper than appearances.

There, on the banks of the Ordelahr, with birds singing overhead and the knights as our only witnesses, we were married. I swore my vows to the Wind God of my ancestors, she to the One God of her southern people. Soul and heart, bound together until time's end. A simple ritual, but more profound than any Hualeg council decree. Afterward, we shared a meal of grilled fish and roasted venison around the fire, a strange fellowship – three southern knights, a Hualeg warrior, and a woman from faraway Tavarin. For the first time since leaving the north, I felt a true sense of peace, of belonging.

As we ate, Walter spoke. "Vilnar, the Logenir threat here is ended, thanks to you. At least until summer returns, this region should be safe. We must travel south now. Claude," he glanced towards the spearman, "senses unrest there, trouble brewing. We must go where we are needed."

"How does he know what happens so far south?" I asked, looking at Claude with new curiosity. The man just stared impassively back. I nodded slowly. "Ah. The sound of the stars, perhaps."

Walter laughed, translating for the others. Fabien chuckled, and even Claude allowed another fleeting grin.

Remembering their earlier offer, I asked, "Your invitation... for me to become a knight like you... does it still stand?"

"I thought you weren't interested," Walter replied, surprised. He conferred briefly with Fabien, who nodded encouragingly. Walter turned back to me. "My brother Fabien is happy if you truly wish it. If you agree, you can become our brother this day."

"Does that mean I must leave? Go with you now?" I asked, glancing towards Ailene, my heart sinking slightly. "If so... perhaps I cannot. And besides," I admitted, "I know nothing of knighthood."

"You do not have to come with us now," Walter reassured me. "A knight can serve anywhere. It is good if you serve among your new people here. Knighthood is not about who you are, Vilnar, or where you are from. It is about *what you do*. Hold these values high: Truth. Justice. Honor. Loyalty." He met my eyes seriously. "You have already shown us the first three, by your actions and your words. The path requires learning, but we believe these values are already strong within you. As for Loyalty... we only ask that should your brothers ever need your aid, you will come willingly, without hesitation." He paused. "If you agree, you need only swear to uphold these values all your life. To love and protect the weak. You have great strength, Vilnar. Swear never to abuse it."

I listened intently, the words resonating deep within me. Truth. Justice. Honor. Loyalty. Protect the weak. These felt... right. Like principles I already held, but now given names, structure. "I understand," I said gravely. "If you believe I am worthy, I am ready."

That afternoon, I knelt on the riverbank, and Fabien, the quiet leader, touched my shoulders lightly with the flat of his sword, first left, then right. I swore the oath, binding myself to the four values, to my new brothers.

When it was done, Walter clasped my shoulder warmly. "Our paths diverge for now, Vilnar, but know this: there is always a place for you at our temple on Mount Hohn. Come when you can. We will welcome you with joy, for you are now one of us. Our brother."

I nodded, feeling a strange mix of pride and uncertainty. I watched them row away south down the great river, waving until their boat disappeared around a bend. Turning back, I saw Ailene watching me, her eyes filled with warmth and quiet support. A knight. Me. Vilnar the Hualeg exile, now a southern knight. Perhaps one day I *would* travel to this Mount Hohn, fight beside my new brothers.

But as I looked at Ailene, another feeling surfaced – a faint unease, a sense of being adrift between two worlds. I was a northerner. Shouldn't my place be in the North? The doubt lingered, a shadow at the edge of my newfound happiness.

24

To the North

Month after month passed. Time flowed like the river beside our cabin. In late spring, when the forests were alive with new green, Ailene gave birth to our son. Strong, healthy, with his mother's dark hair, but his eyes... they held the same startling blue as my own. I named him Vahnar. In the Old Tongue of Hualeg, it comes from *vahennarre* – the shining stone, the mythical gem harder and more beautiful than any other. My own name, Vilnar, comes from *villenarre*, the black stone, said to be the rough precursor from which the shining stone is born. It was my hope, my prayer, that my son would surpass me, that his life would be brighter, better.

Four years had passed since I walked away from Hualeg land. My exile was long over, but the desire to return had faded completely. Here, with Ailene, with Vahnar, hunting and trading peacefully, I found a contentment I never thought possible. My great battle axe lay gathering dust in a chest beneath our bed; I hadn't touched it since marrying Ailene.

Yet, I knew the past wasn't entirely buried. I was still Hualeg. The strength, the fierceness... it was still there, deep down, sleeping perhaps, but not gone. And I knew my people. Summer brought warmth, but it also brought the raiding season. Rohgar was dead, but other Logenir chiefs, other desperate tribes, might still venture south. The southern villagers lived in fear each summer, remembering Rohgar's last bloody campaign.

I shared their concern now. Not for myself – alone, I feared no one. But for Ailene. For Vahnar. If raiders came... Fortunately, our cabin was remote, hidden up this quiet creek, far from the main river routes the longboats usually followed. We were likely safe. Still, I stayed close that summer, hunting nearby, trading only briefly at the nearest villages.

As the season waned, I finally made a longer trip south, down the Ordelahr, to sell the accumulated bearskins and trade for winter supplies. Relief washed over me – no sign of Hualeg longboats, no rumors of raids further south. The journey back felt light, joyful. My boat, nearly empty now save for medicines, tools, and cloth for Ailene, moved swiftly upriver. I rowed and sang Hualeg hunting songs, eager to be home.

Turning into the familiar creek leading to our cabin, my song died in my throat. Far ahead, where the creek narrowed, a boat rested against the bank. Long, slender, unmistakably Hualeg. My heart sank. I quickly steered my own boat into the reeds, hiding it, my joy evaporating, replaced by cold dread.

The longboat carried only three men. Two rowed idly, while the third stood tall in the center, scanning the banks. Golden-yellow hair, braided neatly. A thick beard, tied impressively beneath his chin. Broad shoulders, powerful build – even larger than myself.

I recognized him instantly. Kronar. My oldest brother.

A cry almost escaped me. Kronar! The brother I loved most, the one who taught me the axe and sword, who stood beside me in my first battles, who argued against my exile. Seeing him here, so close to my home... memories flooded back, warm and welcome.

I wanted to shout his name, run to greet him. But caution, learned through years of exile and survival, held me back. Four years was a long time. Things change. Why was he here, so far south, with only two men? It wasn't a raid, surely – not Kronar's way, and far too small a force. I needed to understand before revealing myself.

I waited until their boat passed my hiding spot, then silently pushed my own boat back out and followed at a distance. As dusk began to settle, Kronar's boat pulled ashore, the men making camp. I hid my boat again further downstream and crept overland through the woods, circling around until I could observe their campfire unseen.

Spying on my own kin. It felt strange, dishonorable. This was the third time – first the Logenirs when I found Ailene, then Rohgar fighting the knights, now my own brother. What had I become?

One of Kronar's warriors spoke, his voice carrying clearly in the quiet evening air. "We have searched weeks. Risked southern villages. Do we continue?"

"He's been gone for years," the other added. "Could be anywhere. Far south, even."

Kronar shook his head, staring into the flames. "He is near here. The stories the southerners tell... they speak of a Hualeg hunter, golden-haired, trading bearskins. It must be him. He is close."

"But if he hides deliberately?" the first soldier argued. "If he does not *wish* to be found? Maybe he truly does not want to go home."

"We search this area one more week," Kronar decided, his voice firm. "If we do not find him by then, we return north. Autumn comes, then winter. Snow will fall, the rivers freeze. We must be back before then."

They were looking for *me*. Relief washed over me – Kronar wasn't here to raid or cause trouble. But why were they searching so diligently?

No more hiding. I stepped out from the trees into the firelight. "Brother!" I called out, keeping my hands open, away from my weapons. "I am here!"

All three leaped up, startled, hands flying to axes and swords. Then Kronar's eyes focused on my face. Recognition dawned, followed by shock, then overwhelming joy. He dropped his axe, spreading his arms wide, his booming laugh echoing through the trees.

"Vilnar! Little bastard! You live! Come here!"

The tension broke. Nothing to fear here. I hurried forward, relief making my steps light. He slapped my shoulder hard enough to bruise, I punched his arm playfully in return. We embraced fiercely, clapping each other on the back, laughing like boys again. He pulled me towards the fire, offered me roasted meat and strong Hualeg ale.

"Four years, Vilnar," Kronar said, shaking his head, his eyes searching mine. "Where have you been? What happened? Why did you not return when your exile ended? We waited! Father waited! I never agreed with that council ruling, you know. Not your fault entirely."

I shrugged, wiping grease from my lips – clean-shaven now, thanks to Ailene. "No need to speak of it, brother. The past is past. I came south, found a new life." I hesitated, then admitted, "Honestly, Kronar... I like it here."

His eyes widened slightly. "But... you will come home? Now? With us?"

I looked at my brother, searching for the right words, glancing briefly at his two curious warriors. "Why now, Kronar? Is something wrong? Something urgent?"

He looked down, his expression turning grave. "Father... wants you home, Vilnar. He is sickly. Growing weak."

The news hit me like a physical blow, though I tried not to show it. Father... old, yes, often ill even when I was young... but *sickly*? Weak? I loved my father, respected him deeply, even after the exile. He'd had no choice but to uphold the law. I missed him. Wanted to see him. But... go home *now*? What about Ailene? What about Vahnar, my son? Could I take them north? To that cold, harsh land? To the dangers of tribe politics, old feuds? It seemed... impossible. Unfair to them.

"I... I want to see Father," I said carefully. "But... I think later, Kronar. There are things here... things I must attend to first."

His eyes narrowed slightly. "Trouble, Vilnar? Are you in trouble?"

I shook my head quickly. "No, brother. Nothing like that. Everything is fine."

He nodded slowly, still watching me closely. "Alright. Attend your business. We will wait. When you are finished, we travel north together."

"No," I said gently but firmly. "It is... not a quick matter. It may take time. You should return north now, before the rivers freeze. I will follow later. When I can."

"Are you sure?" He still looked unconvinced. "Is it something I should know? I am your brother, Vilnar. I can help!"

I looked at him, my oldest brother, the one I trusted most in the world besides my father. "Brother," I said honestly, "you know I have always been straight with you. But this... this is something I cannot speak of now. Not yet. I promise you, I will tell you everything when the time comes for me to return."

He studied my face for a long moment, then sighed, finally nodding. "Well... I have always trusted your word, Vilnar, more than any other's."

"Thank you, brother." Relief washed through me. "Give Father my greetings. My love. Tell him... tell him I will come. Later."

"That news alone will bring him joy! It will be the best medicine!" Kronar clasped my shoulder again. "You know, little brother, you were always his favorite. Even when he had to punish you."

"Really?"

"Yes. So hurry home when you can. See for yourself!"

I just laughed softly. We talked a little longer, then parted ways. They would head north at first light.

I rowed home through the darkness, my mind filled with conflicting emotions – joy at seeing Kronar, worry for my father, love for the family waiting for me here. I reached our cabin well after midnight. Vahnar slept soundly in his cradle. Ailene was awake, sitting by the low fire, mending one of my tunics, waiting for me, as if she'd known I'd be late.

I had meant to tell her immediately about Kronar, about Father. But the sight of her face, calm and beautiful in the firelight, the quiet love in her eyes... it drove all other thoughts away. All that mattered was her, here, now. I went to her, knelt down, pulled her into my arms. She sighed softly, leaning against me, her head resting on my shoulder. We held each other in the quiet darkness, needing no words. Tomorrow. I would tell her everything tomorrow. Tonight, there was only this peace, this belonging. Nothing else mattered.

* * *

The morning broke clear and cool, birdsong filling the air around our small cabin. Vahnar gurgled happily as Ailene played with his tiny fingers after our simple breakfast. Kronar's words from the night before echoed in my mind – *Father is sickly. He wants you home.* I still hadn't told Ailene. Part of me wanted to shield her, to preserve this pocket of peace we'd carved out for ourselves just a little longer. After breakfast, filled with those small moments of laughter and warmth that had come to mean everything, I went outside to the woodpile. Chopping wood, the familiar bite of the axe into timber, the rhythmic swing – it helped clear my thoughts. Even in summer, the nights here could hold a chill; firewood was always needed.

Ailene came out after a while, carrying Vahnar bundled against her chest. She settled on the bench near the woodpile, watching me work, her presence a quiet comfort, an anchor. She smiled, and I smiled back between swings of the axe. Was now the time? Could I break this peace with news of illness and the long, uncertain journey north?

As if sensing my turmoil, she spoke first, her voice soft in her southern tongue – a language I now understood well after a year of listening, learning, loving her. "You were quiet last night after your trip south. Is everything alright?"

I stopped chopping, leaning the axe carefully against the woodblock. "The journey was... fine," I began, searching for her words. "The villages I visited... safe this time. Not like last year." I managed a smile. "Our coats are... hmm... all sold."

"That's good." She smiled back, shifting Vahnar, whose little hands were already reaching out, fascinated by the gleaming axe head. Careful, little one.

"But..." I took a breath, deciding there was no point hiding it longer. "Last night, on my way back... I met three men by the river." I sat down on a log beside her. "One of them... was my eldest brother, Kronar."

Her eyes widened slightly in surprise, but she waited silently for me to continue, her hand instinctively tightening on Vahnar.

"He came looking for me," I explained. "He told me... about my father. Back in Hualeg. Kronar says he is sick, growing weak. He wishes to see me." I paused, watching her face. "I told Kronar... I could not decide yet."

The silence stretched between us, filled only by the sounds of the forest and Vahnar's soft breathing.

"And then?" Ailene finally asked, her voice quiet.

I looked down at my hands, calloused from both axe work and, long ago, sword work. Then I met her gaze. "My decision depends on you, Ailene. I will not be parted from you, or from Vahnar. If you are willing to come north with me, then we will go. If you wish to stay here... then we stay."

She looked thoughtful, her dark eyes gazing past me towards the trees, considering the weight of my words. After a long moment, she said simply, "I leave the choice to you, Vilnar."

"But what do *you* want?" I pressed gently. "Is that truly alright? You must understand... Hualeg is far. A cold land, strange to you. Different people, different ways."

She paused again, then looked directly at me, her gaze steady. "If *you* truly wish for me to go with you, Vilnar... then I will."

"Aren't you afraid?" I asked softly, thinking of her father, killed by Logenirs, by Hualegs. Even though they were my enemies too, the name itself must hold terror for her.

Her chin lifted slightly. "Will you be able to protect me? Protect our son?" Her question wasn't born of doubt, but seeking assurance.

"Of course!" I answered immediately, fiercely. The thought of anyone harming them sent protective rage surging through me. "No one would dare touch my wife or son in the north! Not while I live!"

She nodded slowly, a small, trusting smile touching her lips. "Then I have nothing to fear. I will go with you, Vilnar. Wherever you go."

Relief washed over me, immense and profound, loosening a knot I hadn't realized I was holding in my chest. I took her hand, smaller and softer than mine, squeezing it gently. "Thank you," I whispered, gratitude filling me. "Thank you, Ailene. Together, then. Whatever comes."

We sat in silence for a while, watching Vahnar happily batting at wood shavings on the ground near my feet. The path ahead was uncertain, filled with potential dangers – my father's illness, the politics of the tribe, the harsh northern climate. But facing it together, with Ailene and Vahnar beside me... I felt ready.

We packed what little we possessed, secured the cabin, and took to the river again, this time heading north on the wide Ordelahr. For days upon days, we rowed through the seemingly endless dark forest that lined the great river's banks. The trees pressed close, their dense canopy blocking out much of the sun, creating an eerie, perpetual twilight on the water. Thankfully, the woods here were mostly quiet; few large predators ventured this close to the main river – bears sometimes, snakes perhaps, but mostly just shy wild cats and chattering monkeys high above. Still, I kept torches lit at the prow and stern day and night, a ward against the unknown shadows and any creatures they might hold.

I rowed mostly through the nights, letting Ailene and Vahnar sleep bundled under the furs. During the day, while they were awake, I rested, slept when I could. The journey was long, monotonous, grueling. I was grateful for Ailene's quiet strength; she never complained, despite the discomfort, the endless rowing, the strange and sometimes intimidating landscape. When my spirits flagged from exhaustion, she would sing soft, beautiful melodies from her southern homeland, her voice a calming balm. When her own worry showed in her eyes, I would sing the old Hualeg hunting chants, songs of strength and endurance. Sometimes, seeing my weariness, she would even take up the spare oar, her small frame surprisingly strong, helping me propel the boat forward. Vahnar watched us both, his bright blue eyes wide with wonder, laughing at our songs, his innocent joy a beacon lighting our long passage north.

After two weeks, the character of the forest began to change. The trees thinned, the landscape opened slightly, though the air grew noticeably colder, the sky a darker, grayer blue even at midday. We reached the great fork in the river – the left branch leading towards the Logenir territories, the right leading home, towards Vallanir lands.

I turned the boat right, feeling Ailene tense behind me. "Soon now," I reassured her, pointing ahead. "My village is not far. The village of the Vallanir. You will be safe there. Nothing to fear."

She nodded, pulling Vahnar closer, her other hand trailing in the river water beside the boat. "It's cold," she murmured, shivering slightly. "Like ice."

I nodded. "It grows colder here. In deep winter, this river will freeze solid, deep into the forests. Even the sea to the north freezes. Travel stops completely then. But," I smiled, trying to sound encouraging, "that is still three months away. Don't worry."

"The sky..." she looked up nervously. "Will it stay this dark?"

"The sun shines less brightly here, yes. And in the heart of winter, it barely rises above the horizon some days."

"Will it be terribly cold?" She huddled deeper into her cloak.

I smiled again, continuing to row steadily. "It is cold, yes. But we are born to it. Thick furs, good fires in the hearth... hardly anyone dies from the cold itself. We know how to live with it. You will get used to it, Ailene. And the crisp air will make Vahnar grow strong." I paused the oars for a moment, meeting her worried gaze. "Ailene. I do not want you to suffer. If... if you find the cold too hard, if this land is too harsh for you, I will bring you back south. Back to our cabin. Before the winter freeze sets in fully. That is my promise."

"I know," she whispered. "You told me before."

"I will say it again," I replied firmly.

We continued up the Vallanir branch of the river. The landscape felt starkly beautiful now, familiar to my eyes – rugged hills, dark pine forests clinging to slopes, the air crisp and clean with the scent of pine resin. As we rounded a final bend late that afternoon, my heart swelled with a complex mix of anticipation and apprehension. Home.

Wooden houses appeared along the riverbank, torches already lit against the gathering dusk, casting a warm, welcoming glow. Smoke curled from chimneys. Figures moved along the docks, securing boats for the night. Vallanir. My village.

I guided our boat towards the main dock, mooring it amongst the others. Helping Ailene and Vahnar out, careful of her footing, I led them onto Hualeg soil.

Villagers turned as we walked up from the docks, their gazes curious. Recognition dawned slowly on faces I hadn't seen in four years. Nods of respect, murmurs passing through the growing crowd. News of my return spread like wildfire. Men and women emerged from longhouses, warriors paused their tasks, all gathering to watch, to see the chief's exiled son return.

I walked steadily through them, head held high, Ailene close beside me, her face hidden beneath her drawn-up hood, Vahnar clutched protectively to her chest. We headed straight for the largest structure in the center of the village – my father's longhouse. Two stories high, built of massive timbers, symmetrical and imposing. The carved head of a great stag hung over the wide entrance.

Two guards stood at the base of the wooden steps leading up to the porch, their faces showing surprise, then recognition, then excitement mixed with caution.

"Greetings," I said formally. "I wish to see my father, the Hardingir."

"He waits for you, my lord," one guard replied immediately, bowing slightly. "Please, enter."

So, they had seen our approach. Father knew I was here. I took a deep breath, hoping for warmth, dreading potential conflict, and led my small family up the steps.

The great hall inside was brightly lit with torches, filled with people – twenty, maybe thirty – elders, kinsmen, their families, all gathered, waiting. The crowd parted silently as I entered, clearing a path towards the raised platform at the far end.

There sat my father, Radnar, Hardingir of the Vallanir. Older, yes, frailer than I remembered, but still large-framed, his presence commanding the room even seated. Beside him stood my brothers. Kronar, the eldest, taller even than me, his face breaking into a wide grin as he saw me. And to Father's left... Tarnar and Erenar. Tarnar, brown-haired, sharp-eyed, ever talkative, the brother whose southern raid led to my exile. Erenar, lighter-haired, quiet, his face an unreadable mask as always. Seeing Tarnar, a familiar anger tightened my gut, but I pushed it down. Now was not the time.

I stopped before the platform, bowing my head slightly. "Father. Brothers. I am glad to see you again."

Radnar struggled to his feet, aided by Kronar, his old eyes sparkling with undeniable joy as he stretched out his arms. "Vilnar! My son! Welcome!"

I stepped forward, embracing him. His frame felt thin under my hands, fragile, but his grip was surprisingly strong. Awkwardly, stiffly after so long, I returned the embrace, feeling a lifetime of complex emotions welling up – love, respect, resentment, relief.

Radnar pulled back, turning to the assembled crowd, his voice booming despite his frailty. "Vilnar! My mighty son, has returned! By Odaran's breath, I swear this is the happiest day of my life!"

A responding cheer went up. "We are all happy with you, Hardingir!"

I smiled faintly, acknowledging the welcome, then turned to my brothers.

Kronar clasped my shoulders hard. "I knew you would come back, little brother! Always believed!"

Erenar offered a brief, reserved nod. "Welcome, Vilnar."

Tarnar, however, just smirked, his eyes flicking past me to Ailene, still hooded beside me. "Hey, Vilnar," he drawled, his voice laced with mockery. "Looks like you brought a *squirg* back with you."

The derogatory term – used for southern captive women, implying they were fit only for slavery or death – struck me like a physical blow. Rage, hot and instant, surged through me. Tarnar hadn't changed. Still provocative, still trying to stir trouble. Remembering his silence, his lack of support at my council hearing four years ago... If he weren't my brother, standing here in my father's hall... But I clamped down on the fury. I had just returned. I had Ailene and Vahnar to consider. Recklessness now would achieve nothing.

Taking a slow, deliberate breath, I calmly reached over and drew back Ailene's hood, revealing her beautiful, proud face to the stunned hall. I put my arm protectively around her shoulders, drawing her closer. "She is a woman of honor," I declared loudly, my voice ringing with challenge, meeting Tarnar's gaze directly, then sweeping across the silent room. "Her name is Ailene. And she is my wife."

A collective gasp went through the hall. Silence, thick with tension and disbelief, followed. I felt Ailene tremble slightly beside me but held her firm.

Then, stroking Vahnar's dark hair as he peered out from Ailene's arms, I added, my voice softer but clear, "And this... this is my son, Vahnar."

The hall erupted in whispers, shocked murmurs, incredulous stares. A southerner? Wife to the Hardingir's son? Unheard of. Hualeg tradition allowed taking southern captives, slaves... but marriage? To a chief's son? I felt the weight of their judgment, their confusion, their potential hostility. But I stood my ground, meeting their eyes without flinching, waiting. Let them see who sided with Tarnar, who might stand with me.

Then Radnar raised a frail hand, calling for silence. When the murmuring subsided, he slowly walked down from the platform, approaching Ailene. He stopped before her, his old eyes studying her face intently. Then, a warm, genuine smile spread across his lips. He reached out and gently grasped her shoulders. "Well then," he said kindly, his voice carrying through the hall. "Welcome, daughter. My son's wife is also my daughter."

Relief washed over me, so potent I felt light-headed. "Thank you, Father," I said, my voice thick with emotion. "My wife... Ailene... does not understand your words yet, but she is very grateful."

"May I hold my grandson?" Radnar asked eagerly, his eyes fixed on Vahnar.

"Of course." Carefully, I took Vahnar from Ailene's arms and placed him in my father's. The baby, startled at first, reached out a small hand and slapped Radnar's wrinkled cheek playfully, then laughed, kicking his legs.

Radnar beamed, his gaze locking onto Vahnar's wide, blue eyes. "My grandson," he chuckled. "Truly a handsome boy. And strong! Mighty strength in you..." His voice trailed off. He fell silent, his expression changing as he looked from Vahnar back to Ailene, then to me, a strange, calculating look entering his eyes. He leaned closer, whispering so only I could hear, "Who *is* she, Vilnar?"

"What do you mean, Father?"

"The mother of your child," he whispered back urgently. "Who is she really? She carries herself... differently. She is no ordinary southern woman."

"I don't know her history," I answered honestly, though slightly annoyed by the probing question. "I found her captive, Father. Rescued her. She's my wife now. That is all that matters."

Radnar nodded slowly, still studying Ailene, then Vahnar. He whispered again, his voice barely audible, urgent, "When he grows, your son will be a special man, Vilnar. Marked. So... be careful, my son. Guard him well. Take good care of him."

Special? Marked? A chill traced its way down my spine, despite the warmth of the hall. Be careful? My heart pounded. I glanced quickly around – had anyone else heard? Kronar, Tarnar, Erenar? Their faces showed only curiosity, perhaps lingering surprise. Probably not. Better that way.

I looked back at my father, questioning him silently with my eyes. What did he mean? Radnar was known throughout Hualeg for his wisdom, his uncanny ability sometimes to see... potential, destiny... in the young. He had never used such words before, not about any child.

Fear, cold and sharp, pierced through my relief. Fear for Vahnar. If others suspected he was 'special'... enemies, rivals... they might see him as a threat, try to eliminate him.

Trying to keep my composure, trying not to show the sudden fear gripping me, I gently took Vahnar back from my father, holding my son close against my chest, feeling a fierce, overwhelming surge of protectiveness. Whatever the future held, whatever dangers awaited, I would guard him. With my life.

25

The Fate of the Vallanir

Standing in my father's hall, Ailene's hand warm in mine, Vahnar nestled against her chest, I felt the weight of unspoken questions in the air. The initial shock of our arrival had passed, replaced by cautious observation from the gathered elders and kinsmen. I knew this homecoming wasn't simple. Four years is a long time. Alliances shift, opinions harden. I needed to understand the currents beneath the surface, identify who remained a friend, and who might see my return – with a southern wife and child, no less – as a threat. Recklessness now could endanger us all.

My father, Radnar, must have sensed my thoughts, or perhaps simply knew the setting was too public for the conversation needed. "Have Tilda take your wife and child to your old room upstairs," he murmured, his voice low but carrying authority. "Let them rest after their journey. You and I... we need to speak privately."

I glanced over at Tilda, Kronar's wife, who offered a warm, reassuring smile. I'd known her since we were children; she was steady, kind. I nodded my assent. Ailene looked hesitant, but seeing my nod and Tilda's gentle gesture, she allowed herself and Vahnar to be led away up the heavy timber stairs. I watched them go, feeling a pang of separation already. I noted briefly that the other rooms on the second floor, once belonging to my brothers, stood empty – they had their own longhouses now. Only Father remained here, with his servants, in this echoing heart of the Vallanir.

Later, after the hall had cleared, the kinsmen returning to their own hearths, I joined my father in his private chamber. He moved slowly, leaning heavily on a carved staff, his large frame stooped with age and illness. I helped him settle onto his fur-covered sleeping platform, then closed the heavy shutters against the cool night wind and lit a single candle on the table beside him, casting flickering shadows across the room.

"Sit," Father requested, gesturing to a low stool, a faint smile touching his lips. "Sit beside me, Vilnar. Tell me of your life. These four years... what path did your exile take you on?"

And so I told him. Not everything, but enough. Of finding the quiet creek deep in the southern forests, building the cabin, learning to hunt the southern way. Of the villages along the Ordelahr, the people I met, the trading, the slow forging of a different kind of life. I spoke of the land, the changing seasons, the surprising richness I found away from the harsh Hualeg north. I spoke of Ailene briefly, carefully – how I found her in a village, how she came to be with me. I omitted the violence, the rescue, the battle with Rohgar and his men. That was a burden for another time, perhaps never.

He listened patiently, his eyes closed, occasionally nodding. When I finished, he sighed deeply. "I have wronged you, my son. The exile... though council law demanded it... I have often wondered if it was the right path. Perhaps it caused you needless suffering."

I reached out, gently patting his frail arm resting on the furs. "Father, believe me, it was the right decision. It changed my life, yes, but for the better. It taught me much. If I had not gone south..." I smiled, thinking of Ailene, of Vahnar asleep upstairs, "...I would never have met my wife. I would not have my son. My life would be less, not more."

A genuine smile touched his lips then, erasing some of the lines of pain and worry. "Vilnar," he said, his voice filled with affection, "you were always the son who brought me the greatest pride. Stronger than Kronar in your youth, smarter than Tarnar, more handsome than Erenar... and always," his eyes met mine, "the one the people loved most. They have not forgotten you, even after these years. You are the best son a Hardingir could hope for. My greatest hope, now."

His words were heavy with meaning. I sensed he was leading somewhere important. "Father," I asked cautiously, "what is it you truly wish to say?"

He took a ragged breath, gathering his strength. "Listen. My time grows short. I feel the winter in my bones, Vilnar, a deeper cold than any season brings. Soon, I will join your mother and our ancestors." My throat tightened. "And when I am gone," he continued, his voice low but urgent, "the fate of the Vallanir... it rests with you."

I shook my head quickly. "My mighty father will live many more winters. Do not speak like this."

"Time comes for every man, Vilnar. And I sense mine approaches. We must prepare."

"When that time comes," I countered gently, "you need not worry for the tribe. Kronar will lead. He is your eldest, a proven warrior. Strong, respected... feared, yes, but the people will follow him. Vallanir will be safe."

Father shook his head slowly, sadly. "Kronar is strong, yes. Feared, yes. But his strength lies in breaking things, not building them. He has made too many enemies over the years, Vilnar. Blood feuds simmer. Men hate him, wait for a chance to strike him down. Every night, I pray to the Wind God that he outlives me, but I fear..." His voice trailed off.

I stared at him, stunned. I knew Kronar was fierce, sometimes brutal, but I hadn't realized the depth of the enmity against him. Father's fears might be those of an old, sick man, but they couldn't be dismissed entirely. "Then... Tarnar?" I suggested, though the name tasted like ash in my mouth. "If something were to happen to Kronar..."

Father actually chuckled, a dry, rasping sound. "Tarnar? Come now, Vilnar. You never favored him, did you? Nor do many others. He has spirit, yes, I am proud of that fire in him. But he is hot-tempered, careless with his word, breaks promises as easily as dry twigs. Our people will not follow a man they cannot trust."

"What about Erenar, then?" He was quiet, yes, maybe overlooked, but intelligent.

Father paused, considering. "Erenar... he has a good mind. Learned much from the elders, skilled enough with a blade. But..." he sighed, "...he lacks presence, Vilnar. He keeps to the shadows, has never sought glory or proven himself in a way that commands true respect. Our people do not look up to him. And if our own folk doubt him, how will our enemies react? He needs... time. Opportunity."

"There is still time, surely?"

"Perhaps. If I live long enough to see him find his strength." He met my eyes again, his gaze heavy. "Do you understand now, Vilnar?"

I understood all too well where he was leading. "Father," I replied firmly, "you know I have never sought the Hardingir's seat. My path lies elsewhere."

He held my gaze, a flicker of defiance in his old eyes. "You may say that. But your heart knows differently. Your sense of duty, the justice that burns in you... it tells you that when I am gone, you are the only one who can truly hold the Vallanir together, guide us through the dangers ahead."

I frowned, shaking my head slowly, troubled. "Father, I came home because Kronar said you were ill. I am glad to see you still strong in spirit. But now... it seems you have plans for me already laid out." My old suspicion, the feeling that drove me into exile, resurfaced. "I have been gone four years. Why do you dare trust me with this burden now? What is truly happening here? What danger makes you speak of this so urgently?"

He took another deep breath, the effort visible. "I will tell you. Shortly after you left... a fragile peace was made. We and the Logenir divided the hunting grounds. For four years, an uneasy quiet held. But last summer... Malagar rose to lead the Logenir. Old Nokkar died, Rohgar had disappeared south..." (I kept my face impassive, revealing nothing of Rohgar's fate at my hands) "...so Malagar, Rohgar's younger brother, took the chieftain's seat."

"I know the name Malagar," I nodded. "Never met him."

"He is... cleverer than Rohgar," Father said grimly. "More ambitious. More dangerous. He was never satisfied with the land division. Now, he has spent months talking to the western tribes, whispering promises, offering rewards, inciting them against us. He gathers an army, Vilnar. Scouts report they move soon. Within days, I believe, they will attack."

So. War was coming anyway. Whether I had killed Rohgar or not, Malagar would have found his pretext. It didn't matter now. My actions in the south changed nothing here. "So..." I stared intently at my father, trying to read his deeper intent in the dim candlelight. "...you wish me to fight them? To lead our warriors against Malagar?"

He sighed, looking suddenly uncomfortable. "Your brothers... they are enough to fight Malagar's forces. Kronar would welcome your axe beside him, yes. But Tarnar, Erenar... they see this as *their* chance to win glory, to prove themselves. They will not thank you for returning now and stealing the light from them again."

I leaned back, the words stinging more than I expected. "I never thought... all this time... they believe I fight only for glory? To be the center of attention?"

Father shook his head wearily. "Do not trouble yourself with their jealousy, Vilnar. There are more important matters. Often, the dangers within the tribe are greater than those without." He paused, gathering strength again. "To lead, my son, requires support. Your name, your reputation... the common warriors, the people, they would follow you gladly. But the clan leaders, the powerful families... their backing is essential. And that support, amongst the Hualeg, often comes through alliances. Through marriage."

My unease grew. I waited, saying nothing.

"Kronar, as you know, is married to Tilda. Her father is Pradiar, our shaman, respected by all clans. A powerful connection. Tarnar married the daughter of the Brahanir chief, our oldest allies to the east. A necessary bond. Erenar... he sought the hand of the Drakknir chieftain's daughter, our northern allies. They wait to see how he proves himself against Malagar before giving their answer."

He paused again, taking a slow breath. "But our *strongest* potential ally, Vilnar... the Andranir, far to the north. Their chieftain, Patarag... he refused Erenar. I spoke with him myself. He said..." Father hesitated, "...he said he would only give his daughter to the greatest warrior in Hualeg." He looked directly at me. "You have heard of Patarag's daughter, Varda? Even as a girl, her beauty was sung of in all the longhouses. Many have sought her hand. All refused."

"Yes, I have heard the name," I replied curtly, a cold feeling spreading through me. I knew where this was going.

"Well," Father continued, his gaze unwavering, "Patarag fought beside you in the last great war against the Logenir, before the truce. He spoke highly of you. Was angered by your exile. He told me... if you ever returned... he would wish you to marry Varda. To bind the Vallanir and Andranir." He took another shaky breath. "And I... I told him my son Vilnar would be honored."

The room seemed to spin for a moment. He had *promised* me? Without asking? Before even knowing if I lived, let alone if I had... found someone else? The arrogance, the assumption... it was breathtaking. "Then what did you tell him?" I asked, my voice dangerously quiet.

"I said my son Vilnar would be happy to marry his daughter."

My jaw tightened. "Father, I understand you made that promise to Patarag *before* you knew I had married. But now... now that you know, fulfilling it is impossible. I already have a wife. I have a son."

"If you agree," he suggested, almost pleadingly, "Varda could be your First Wife. As tradition allows. Ailene... she could still be your wife. The second."

I shook my head, slowly but absolutely. "No, Father." My voice was firm now, the decision absolute. "I would do almost anything to honor you, to make you happy. But not this. Never this. I love Ailene. I love my son. I will *not* trade them, diminish them, for any alliance, any chieftainship."

He looked down, hesitating, then patted my hand where it rested on the furs beside him. "Do not be angry, my son. Please. Calm yourself. I... I knew you would answer thus."

"I am sorry if I disappoint you, Father."

"No." He shook his head again, meeting my eyes with weary resignation. "No, the disappointment is mine, in myself. I understood, even before I spoke. It was wrong of me. Making promises for others... an old man's folly. A fatal mistake for a Hardingir. My word is broken." He sighed. "Take it easy, Vilnar. I will send word to Patarag somehow. Convey your answer. I hope... I hope he takes it well."

"If you are reluctant, Father, let me go myself. I will speak to Patarag face to face."

He waved a dismissive hand. "No need to rush. Patarag does not even know you have returned. Let it be for now. Besides..." a faint smile touched his lips, "...I wish to keep you here. For a while longer." He settled back, closing his eyes. "We will see tomorrow. Perhaps... perhaps it is not as great a matter as I feared."

"Yes, Father." I watched him, my anger fading, replaced by a deep pity. "Do not worry yourself. Everything will be fine. Rest now."

I gently pulled the thick bearskin blanket higher over his frail body. The mighty Radnar, Hardingir of the Vallanir, feared warrior... now just an old, sick man, wrestling with politics and regrets. His wife, my mother, had died five years ago; her loss had clearly taken a heavy toll, accelerating his decline. Age and grief... no warrior could fight those forever.

I waited until his breathing deepened into sleep, then rose quietly. Peering through the shuttered window, I saw only the dark, deserted village square below. The night was late. Our conversation had lasted hours. Carefully, I blew out the single candle, plunging the room into darkness, and slipped out, closing the door softly behind me.

Back in the room Tilda had prepared for us, I found Ailene and Vahnar sleeping peacefully, wrapped together under the furs. I knelt beside them, watching the soft rise and fall of their breathing in the faint moonlight filtering through the window. I kissed Ailene's dark hair, then gently stroked Vahnar's head, his own hair dark like his mother's. My family. My heart ached with love and a fierce protectiveness. Bringing them here, to this cold land on the brink of war, surrounded by family intrigue and my father's cryptic warnings about Vahnar being 'special'... had it been the right decision? Or had I brought the only things I truly valued into terrible danger?

26

I Will Give You Blood!

"Da! Da-da! Da-da!"

A tiny fist scratched playfully at my nose, followed by surprisingly strong little feet kicking against my neck. I chuckled, opening my eyes from where I lay relaxed on the thick floor furs, propped against the edge of our sleeping platform. Vahnar laughed down at me, tugging at the remnants of my sideburns. "Hmm. You called me, son?" I let him have his fun, closing my eyes again, simply enjoying his presence, the familiar joy he brought to every morning these past five months.

Then, soft fingers slid beneath my thin sleeping shirt, caressing my chest. Ailene's warm breath ghosted across the back of my neck as she embraced me from behind. I leaned back into her warmth, remembering her shivering slightly during her first truly cold Hualeg night.

I opened my eyes again, twisting slightly to look at her. "Warmer now?"

"A little," she whispered, leaning closer, her dark eyes soft with unmistakable desire.

"I can warm you more." I caught her hand, lifting her fingers to my lips, kissing each one deliberately, letting my tongue trace the sensitive skin between them. Her breath hitched audibly.

A playful smile touched her lips, her pupils dilating. "Can you?"

"Of course," I murmured, voice dropping to a husky whisper.

I turned fully towards her, gently shifting Vahnar who had dozed off between us onto a softer pile of furs nearby, ensuring he was safe and warm. Then my attention was solely on Ailene. The morning light softened the lines of her face, highlighting the curve of her cheek, the darkness of her eyes that held so much strength and sorrow, yet still looked at me with undisguised hunger. I reached out, my calloused fingers tracing the delicate line of her jaw, brushing a stray strand of black hair back from her temple, then sliding down to caress the sensitive spot behind her ear. Her skin flushed beneath my touch, a soft gasp escaping her parted lips.

Slowly, deliberately, I pulled my own thin sleeping shirt over my head, letting it fall aside, watching her eyes travel hungrily across my bare chest. Then, meeting her gaze, I carefully helped her ease hers off, my knuckles deliberately brushing against her hardening nipples, feeling the sharp intake of breath that followed. Her breasts, full and perfect, seemed to beg for my attention in the cool morning air.

I drew her close, wrapping my arms around her, pulling her nakedness against my bare chest. She sighed softly, arching into me, her hardened nipples pressing into my chest as she melted into the embrace. Her hands roamed across my back, nails lightly dragging against my skin, sending shivers down my spine. Holding her felt like finding anchorage after a long storm. Her warmth seeped into me, chasing away the chill of the impending conflict. I buried my face in the curve of her neck, inhaling the faint, familiar scent of her hair, her skin, then tasting the salt of it with my tongue.

I tilted her chin up, kissing her deeply, passionately, my tongue exploring the familiar sweetness of her mouth as she moaned softly against my lips. My hands smoothed down her back, over the curve of her buttocks, pulling her hips firmly against mine so she could feel my arousal straining against the thin fabric still between us. She ground against me in response, her breath coming faster.

Carefully, I lifted her into my arms, carrying her to our sleeping platform. I laid her down gently amongst the thick furs, pausing to take in the sight of her naked body laid out before me – all curves and valleys I yearned to explore again with my hands, my lips, my tongue. I quickly shed the rest of our clothing, her eyes widening appreciatively at my fully aroused state.

I claimed her mouth again, one hand caressing her breast, teasing and rolling the nipple between my fingers until she whimpered with need. My lips traveled lower, taking one hardened peak into my mouth, sucking and lightly grazing it with my teeth while my hand slid between her thighs, finding her already slick with desire. She gasped as my fingers explored her most intimate places, her hips rising to meet my touch, seeking more.

"Please," she whispered urgently, her fingers tangling in my hair.

Mine was ready. Her legs wrapped around my waist as I finally joined our bodies in one smooth thrust. She cried out, her back arching off the furs, her nails digging into my shoulders. There was only her warmth surrounding me, her scent, the increasingly desperate sounds of pleasure escaping her lips with each movement. Each thrust deeper, each withdrawal slower, building a tension that threatened to consume us both.

Then, a soft knock sounded at the heavy wooden door.

"Vilnar." Kronar's voice, muffled but unmistakable, shattered the intimate bubble.

I froze mid-thrust. Ailene tensed beneath me, her eyes flying towards the door, then back to mine, pleading. Her inner muscles clenched around me involuntarily, nearly undoing my restraint.

"Don't stop," she whispered against my ear, her breath hot and urgent, her hips rising to meet mine in silent demand. "Please, don't stop."

Our eyes locked, and I saw the same desperate need I felt mirrored there. With a slight nod, I began to move again, more urgently now. Her inner muscles clenched around me as she approached her peak, her movements becoming more frantic, more demanding.

"Look at me," I commanded softly, and her eyes flickered open, dark with passion. In that moment of connection, I felt her shatter beneath me, her body convulsing in waves of pleasure, her cry of release muffled against my palm. The sight of her undoing was enough to trigger my own, a white-hot explosion that left me trembling and gasping her name like a prayer.

We clung to each other, panting slightly, hearts still racing in tandem. I managed a breathless smile down at Ailene's flushed face.

She giggled softly, the sound a welcome counterpoint to the interruption. "Is your brother still waiting?"

"You mean," I grinned back, tracing the curve of her lips with my thumb, "is he eavesdropping?"

She giggled again, burying her face against my shoulder for a second before pulling back slightly.

I cleared my throat, trying to regain some semblance of composure, and raised my voice, calling out towards the door. "Yes, Kronar?"

His voice came again, closer now, patient. "Have you three broken your fast yet?"

"Not yet."

"Food is laid out in the dining hall. Afterward, hurry. Come with me. There is an important meeting at the village hall. Father requires us. I will wait for you there."

"I will come," I replied, my mind already racing. An important meeting. Father. It could only be about Malagar and the Logenir threat.

Kronar's heavy footsteps faded down the corridor. Ailene looked up at me, her brow furrowed slightly. "What's wrong?"

I shrugged, pulling her close again, burying my face in her dark hair. "Just an important meeting. I don't know what about yet." It wasn't entirely a lie, but I knew enough from Father's words last night to guess. War was coming. No need to burden her with that fear just yet.

After we had dressed and cleaned ourselves, we went downstairs to the large dining hall. It was empty, save for the servants clearing away remnants of an earlier meal. Father and my brothers were already gone. The long, heavy table of dark wood dominated the room. Sitting there with Ailene and Vahnar, a wave of nostalgia washed over me. I remembered this table echoing with the boisterous laughter of four young brothers, the gentle reprimands of our mother, the deep, rumbling chuckle of our father in happier times. Before swords and axes became our constant companions. Before exile. Before death took Mother. The memory left a hollow ache. The hall felt too large now, too silent, too cold.

"W-wa! Wa!" Vahnar banged his fists on the table, reaching for a wooden spoon. I smiled, the present warmth pushing back the shadows of the past. I handed him the spoon, watching as Ailene carefully stirred the warm porridge she'd prepared for him. This warmth, this family... it was still here, if I chose to embrace it, to protect it. This was worth fighting for.

After we ate, I asked Ailene to return to our room with Vahnar. Kissing them both goodbye, I headed out towards the village hall.

Walking through the familiar paths, I felt a surprising warmth in the greetings I received. Father was right; the people hadn't forgotten me. Men and women, hunters and weavers, blacksmiths and elders – they nodded respectfully, many calling out welcomes, some even reaching out to clasp my arm in the old way. It felt good, better than the wary curiosity of yesterday. But I couldn't linger. The tense faces of the warriors guarding the entrance to the village hall told me the matter was urgent. My brief moment of pleasure faded as I stepped inside.

About twenty men were gathered, seated in a rough circle – clan elders, trusted warriors, the leaders of Vallanir society. Father sat at the head, looking frail but resolute. Kronar was beside him, along with Tarnar and Erenar. I greeted them all briefly with a nod and found an empty space in the circle, sitting quietly, listening.

The news was grim, confirming Father's fears. Malagar, the new Logenir chief, had moved his forces. They'd occupied the disputed northern hunting grounds, a clear provocation. From there, they could strike west towards the Drakknir, or south, directly at us. War was no longer a possibility; it was imminent.

Father leaned back, his expression a mix of weariness and anger. "Malagar has raised his war axe. Brave, perhaps. We shall see if he is also clever, or merely the greatest fool in the north."

Kronar spoke next, his voice calm, authoritative. "Scouts report Malagar has gathered warriors from his western allies – Logenir forces and several smaller tribes. Perhaps five hundred in total." He paused, letting the number sink in. "We have three hundred Vallanir warriors ready. The Brahanir chief sends word his hundred warriors march from the east, they should arrive soon. We will be outnumbered, but our men are better trained, fighting for their homes. I believe we can defeat them."

"Certainly! Victory will be ours!" Tarnar shouted, slamming a fist on his knee. "Malagar is even stupider than his brother Rohgar if he thinks he can best us!"

"Perhaps he is not so stupid," Erenar murmured quietly beside him. "We must be cautious."

Tarnar shot Erenar an irritated glance. "We'd win easily if the Drakknir send aid! Have you heard from them, Erenar? Will your future father-in-law help?"

Erenar looked briefly at Tarnar, his face impassive. "They send word they will join us on the battlefield. Another hundred warriors."

"A hundred? Why didn't you say so earlier?" Tarnar demanded.

"I was about to explain," Erenar replied coolly, "but, as usual, you preferred to speak before listening." Tarnar flushed red, sputtering, but fell silent.

Radnar ignored the sibling squabble, turning back to Kronar. "The Andranir, Kronar? Any word from Patarag?"

Kronar shook his head regretfully. "Not yet, Father. But they are sworn allies. They should come. Another hundred fifty warriors from them, and Malagar's numbers mean little."

"Yes, yes, enough talk of numbers!" Tarnar burst out impatiently. "I grow bored! When do we march?"

Ignoring Tarnar again, Father asked Kronar softly, "Your assessment? How will this play out?"

Kronar surveyed the room grimly. "It depends on Malagar's resolve. If they break after the first clash, losses might be kept under a hundred on both sides. But if they persist... if Malagar truly means to fight to the death... this could be the bloodiest battle Hualeg has seen in a generation."

Father sighed deeply, shaking his head. "I do not like this. War... it should not have come to this..."

"Vilnar could help us, if he is willing," Kronar said suddenly, turning his gaze towards me where I sat silently in the corner.

Every head in the room swiveled, all eyes locking onto me. I met Kronar's gaze steadily.

"Brother," I asked quietly, my voice cutting through the sudden silence, "do you truly wish to use my hands simply to kill our enemies again?"

A few men gasped softly. Father sighed again. Tarnar smirked openly, while Erenar frowned, looking troubled.

Kronar held my gaze, his expression serious. "Vilnar, this is not just about killing. It is about *your name*. Your reputation. Our enemies fear you. If they hear Vilnar has returned, if they see you leading the first charge... they might break before the battle truly begins. Think of the lives saved, brother. On both sides."

"Kronar, are you serious?" Tarnar laughed mockingly. "That doesn't sound like the Kronar I know! Usually, you relish the fight, want to kill as many enemies as possible! Why so soft now?"

Kronar's face hardened, his hand clenching into a fist. He pointed a thick finger at Tarnar. "Don't play games, little brother! This isn't about *my* desires! It's about the lives of *our* warriors! Our kin! Have you ever once cared about that?"

"Hey, why are we fighting amongst ourselves?" Erenar interjected quietly. "I don't think anyone here is wrong. Kronar speaks wisely, Tarnar speaks with passion, Vilnar asks hard questions—"

"Shut up, Erenar!" Tarnar snapped, clearly furious now. He jumped to his feet, glaring around the room. "What is wrong with all of you? This is a war council! We should be shouting for blood! 'Kill! Kill! Kill!' That's what warriors want to hear! While we sit here talking, Malagar marches closer! What are we waiting for?"

Silence followed his outburst. Many men looked down, uncomfortable, but some nodded slightly in agreement. Tarnar, sensing support, grew bolder, turning his smirk directly on me.

"And him," he pointed, "if Vilnar has lost his nerve after four years living soft in the south, why force him? Let him stay home! No one will blame him if he cannot face battle again."

"Tarnar!" Kronar growled, rising halfway from his seat. "You fool!"

I WILL GIVE YOU BLOOD!

That was enough. Tarnar's taunt, his implication of cowardice, his sneering reference to my past... the cold rage I'd been suppressing boiled over. I rose slowly to my feet, meeting his glare with my own, letting my fury show in my eyes. "Do you think so, brother?" I asked, my voice dangerously soft. "Do you truly wish to see blood? Do you wish to see the blood of enemies on the battlefield this time, Tarnar, not just the blood of helpless women and children you butchered in the south?" His face paled slightly. "Do you have the *guts* to witness real war?" My voice rose to a roar. "Alright then! I will give you blood! Follow me! But leave your sword behind – your childish skills are useless! Let *me* do everything! I will show you blood!"

Tarnar flinched back, his face crimson now with shame and fear, unable to meet my gaze. He actually took two steps backward, as if physically pushed by my anger. The hall was utterly silent, every man watching, remembering the Vilnar of old. No one in Hualeg crossed me when my rage was up. Except, perhaps, one.

I looked towards my father. He wasn't angry. He looked... worried. Deeply worried.

He struggled to his feet again, raising his trembling hands. "My children! My sons! Help me. No more quarrels between you." His voice shook with emotion. "You are all great warriors. Unmatched. United, you make our enemies tremble! Heed my words now." He looked at Kronar. "Kronar, eldest son. I entrust your brothers, all our warriors, to your command. I trust your decisions."

"Yes, Father," Kronar bowed his head. "Do not worry. I will do my best."

Radnar turned to my other brothers. "Tarnar. Erenar. Obey Kronar's orders without question. This will be your first true test in tribal war, greater than any border skirmish. Learn from it. Prove yourselves."

"Yes, Father," they both murmured, subdued.

Father sighed, relieved the immediate crisis between us was averted. He leaned back heavily in his chair. "And you, Vilnar." He looked at me, his expression softening slightly, but his eyes firm. "Everyone knows your strength. Your presence alone could change the course of the battle. But..."

he paused, "...you will not fight. No one doubts your courage, my son. But you must understand this. Besides," he added, almost as an afterthought, "you have just returned. Your place is here now. Accompany me. Keep your old father company. Do you understand?"

I bowed my head respectfully. "Of course, Father."

Radnar finally smiled again, genuine relief flooding his face. "Now I can rest easier. Go now, all of you. Prepare yourselves. Forget your quarrels. Remember your purpose. Let us pray the gods grant us victory." He dismissed the council.

Kronar immediately began organizing the warriors in the main village square. Weapons were checked, armor strapped on. As they prepared, the distinctive war horns of the Brahanir sounded from the east – our allies had arrived, a hundred strong warriors joining our ranks. Four hundred men now, ready for battle.

They lined up, spears bristling, axes gleaming, shields raised. Pradiar, the old shaman – Tilda's father – moved along the lines, chanting ancient incantations, sprinkling sacred water, praying for strength and victory from Odaran, Anthor, and all the spirits of Hualeg. The entire village gathered around, hands raised to the sky, their voices joining the shaman's prayers.

Then, with a final booming war cry, the warriors marched out, heading north towards the hunting grounds, towards Malagar and the Logenir. Confidence radiated from them, from the watching villagers.

But as I stood beside my father, watching them go, I saw the deep sadness etched on his face, the worry clouding his eyes. Was he simply afraid they would lose? Or did he sense something more? Did the wind blowing down from the north carry the scent of death, a premonition only an old, dying chief could smell?

A cold doubt settled in my own heart. Father's decision... keeping me here... was it truly wise?

27

Promise

A cold wind gusted along the banks of the Ordelahr, sharp enough to bite through my cloak and chill me to the bone. Autumn was settling deep into Hualeg lands; each day felt colder, the wind stronger. I pulled Vahnar tighter against my chest, shielding his small body with my own. Beside me, Ailene huddled deeper into her thick leather coat, her southern blood clearly feeling the northern chill more keenly than I.

The wind died down for a moment. I loosened my embrace slightly, looking down at my son. He was laughing, his bright blue eyes alight, utterly unaffected by the cold, kicking his sturdy little legs against me. A surge of pride went through me – a strong boy, my Vahnar. He hadn't been sick a single day since we arrived, adapting to the harsh Hualeg climate far easier than I'd dared hope.

Ailene, though... she never complained, her strength always humbling me. But I saw the faint pinch around her eyes sometimes, the way she sought the warmth of the fire. I knew this land was still hard for her.

"We should head back to the village," I said gently, turning us away from the river. "The sun is getting low. It will be colder soon."

She nodded, taking my arm, leaning against me as we walked along the rocky bank against the persistent wind. The familiar weight of her felt grounding.

"If the wind strengthens tomorrow – and it surely will as winter approaches – perhaps we should walk closer to the village," I suggested.

She rested her head briefly on my shoulder. "I love walking here, Vilnar. It is beautiful, in its own stark way. The trees, the rocks... the sound of the river is soothing." A pause. "It's nice..."

"But you miss our home?" I asked softly, already knowing the answer. Our quiet cabin by the southern creek felt like a lifetime ago.

"Yes," she admitted, her voice barely a whisper.

"Do you want to go home, Ailene?"

She was silent for a moment, watching Vahnar tug at my tunic. "Yes," she said finally. "But... it is up to you, Vilnar. We can go home when you think the time is right."

Her trust, her patience... it tightened my chest. "I want to go home too, my love," I said, meaning it with all my heart. But the words felt conditional, tainted by uncertainty I tried to keep from my voice. "Let us see how things stand in the village over the next week or two. My father... he may still need me here for a little longer. Kronar and my brothers have been gone fighting Malagar for a week now... news should come soon." I forced a hopeful tone. "Let me ensure everything is truly settled here, that Father is well and the Logenir threat is truly ended. Let me deal with... some other matters." The unresolved business with Patarag and the Andranir alliance felt like a shadow I couldn't yet mention to her. "Then, Ailene," I squeezed her arm, "then we will go home. Before the deep winter snows trap us here. I promise."

I hoped it was a promise I could keep. A week now, since Kronar, Tarnar, and Erenar marched north with our warriors and the Brahanir allies. A week of silence. No messengers, no returning scouts. The waiting was a torment, gnawing at my insides even as I tried to project calm for Ailene, for my father, for the worried village. Was the battle won? Lost? Was Kronar safe? My brothers? Everything depended on the outcome. A decisive victory, Malagar crushed... then, perhaps, I could fulfill my promise to Ailene, take my family south to the life I now preferred. But anything less... defeat, heavy losses, Kronar harmed... my duty would keep me here. And the Andranir situation still needed resolving. Too many uncertainties.

We reached the outskirts of the village, nearing the large village hall. We were heading towards Father's longhouse when a sudden shout pierced the quiet afternoon air, coming from the northern watch post.

"Our troops! The warriors have returned!"

Instantly, the village erupted. Doors flew open, villagers poured into the central field, faces etched with a mixture of hope and terror. Women whose husbands and sons had marched out clutched each other, scanning the northern path. I saw Father emerge from the longhouse, leaning heavily on his staff, his face pale with worry. Seeing his anxiety mirrored my own hidden fears tenfold. Something was wrong.

"Ailene," I said quickly, handing Vahnar carefully into her arms. "Take the boy back to the house. Now. Do not come out." I didn't want her, or Vahnar, to see whatever grim news was coming. She nodded, her eyes wide with understanding fear, and hurried away.

I pushed through the gathering crowd just as the first group of returning Vallanir soldiers appeared, staggering into the village square. Their expressions... were impossible to read. Not joy, not despair, but a bone-deep weariness, faces smudged with dirt and blood, eyes haunted. And behind them... more men, carrying rough stretchers bearing the bodies of their fallen comrades.

My breath caught. So many. I started counting automatically, a cold dread spreading through me. Ten, twenty, fifty... sixty... seventy bodies. Seventy men lost.

Wails broke out among the waiting families as recognition dawned. Wives seeing husbands carried lifeless, mothers seeing sons. The initial murmurs of hope dissolved into open weeping, bitter cries echoing through the square. Those whose men returned alive rushed forward, embracing them, tears of relief mingling with the tears of sorrow around them.

Then I saw them. Tarnar and Erenar, walking grimly behind the main group, their faces streaked with grime, their armor dented. Between them, carried by four other warriors, was a large figure on a stretcher, covered by a cloak, lying utterly still. Too still.

They brought the stretcher forward, placing it gently on the ground before Father and me. My blood ran cold. I knew, even before Erenar reached out a trembling hand and drew back the cloak.

Kronar. My eldest brother. His face pale and peaceful in death, a gaping wound visible on his chest.

"My son..." Father choked out, tears streaming down his ancient face as he collapsed beside the stretcher, embracing Kronar's lifeless form. A collective sob went through the crowd.

"Who...?" My voice trembled, thick with sudden, blinding grief and a surge of murderous rage. "Who killed him?" I clenched my fists, my eyes finding Tarnar's, then Erenar's, demanding an answer.

Tarnar looked away, his face pale, silent for once in his life. It was Erenar, ever composed even now, who met my gaze. "I will tell you everything, Vilnar," he said quietly. "But first... let us pay our last respects. To Kronar. To all who have fallen."

The hours that followed were a blur of grim ritual. Warriors prepared the funeral pyre, a great tower of logs built by the riverbank under the darkening sky. The seventy bodies were brought, washed, wrapped in shrouds, placed carefully upon the pyre, Kronar at the very top, facing the north star.

As night fell, the entire village gathered. Torches flickered, casting long, dancing shadows. Women and elders held flaming brands. I saw Tilda, Kronar's wife, standing numbly, clutching their small daughter – a yellow-haired girl, barely two summers old, maybe the only one present too young to understand, looking around with innocent curiosity. Pradiar the shaman began the ancient chants, his voice rising and falling, calling on Odaran the Sky Father.

"Take these brave souls to your side!" he cried, raising his arms. "They join their ancestors! Let their bodies be ash, their spirits your eternal guardians! In Valahar, glory everlasting, O Odaran!"

One by one, torches were thrown. Flames licked at the dry wood, caught, roared upwards, consuming the pyre, consuming the bodies of my brother, my kinsmen. The heat washed over my face, but I felt only a cold emptiness inside. Smoke billowed into the night sky, carrying the ashes, uniting the fallen with the wind, the river, the land they died defending.

Later, after the flames died down, after the mourners dispersed to their homes, Father summoned his three remaining sons back to his private chamber. The doors were barred. Guards stood outside.

Father sat slumped in his chair, staring blankly ahead. Tarnar stood by the cold hearth, still silent. I sat opposite him, simmering, questions burning within me. Only Erenar seemed fully composed, ready to report.

"We began well," Erenar stated, his voice flat, devoid of emotion. "Our five hundred – Vallanir, Brahanir, Drakknir – met Malagar's forces. We fought hard, broke their initial assault. They lost perhaps a hundred warriors, we lost thirty, maybe more among the allies." He paused. "Then... having won the day... the Brahanir and Drakknir commanders asked leave to return home."

"They *left*?" I repeated, incredulous. "Why?"

"We had repulsed the attack," Erenar said simply. "They saw their duty done."

"Duty done? This is war!" I slammed my fist on the table beside me. "Malagar wasn't destroyed! Why did you let them go?"

"It was Kronar who allowed them." Tarnar finally spoke, his voice low, defensive.

"Kronar?" I stared at him. "And now he cannot speak to confirm that, can he?"

"Then what do you expect?" Tarnar shot back, looking up at me, a flicker of resentment in his eyes. "Do you expect *us* to have died in his place?"

"What did you say?" I surged to my feet, fury blinding me for a second.

"Tarnar! Vilnar! Enough!" Erenar stepped between us again, his hand raised. Father moaned softly in his chair. "Vilnar," Erenar continued, his voice tight, "we are all grieving. Blame helps no one. Kronar made the decision. Perhaps it was a mistake. Perhaps... perhaps I should have argued more strongly." He looked down. "You were not there. You cannot know how it felt... watching him fall."

His words cooled my anger slightly, leaving only the bitter ache of loss and frustration. "I *wish* I had been there," I said grimly, sinking back down.

"To ensure things were done properly."

"If you wish certainty," Erenar replied stiffly, "ask the warriors who survived. They will tell you."

"Vilnar," Father murmured, "let it be."

But I couldn't. "There is more," I insisted, looking at Erenar. "The second day. You heard Malagar had ambushed the Andranir reinforcements. You gave chase. Kronar was killed breaking Malagar's trap. Why were the Andranir so late? Their lands are closer to the battlefield than ours!"

Erenar shook his head. "Why they were delayed, I do not know."

"Perhaps the summons reached them late," Father offered weakly, though his eyes flickered with uncertainty.

"Who led the Andranir?" I pressed.

"Federag," Erenar replied. "Patarag's son."

Federag. Patarag. The pieces clicked into place with sickening certainty. An alliance sought, a marriage proposed... and their warriors arriving too late? It smelled foul. "Father," I turned to him, my decision made instantly, "I will go to Andranir. Now. I will ask Federag, ask Patarag himself, why his warriors failed their allies."

"To Andranir?" Father looked alarmed again. "Alone? Are you sure?"

"If Patarag is true, there is nothing to fear," I stated.

"And if he is not? What if Malagar's whispers reached him?"

"Then I will deal with it," I replied coldly. I looked at my brothers. Tarnar looked away. Erenar met my gaze impassively.

"How many men will you take?" Father asked, still anxious.

"I go alone," I repeated. "If Patarag is innocent, a war party insults him. If he is guilty..." I left the implication hanging. "I trust no one else with this. But I ask that my departure be kept secret. For safety. Just in case." I looked directly at Tarnar, then Erenar.

Radnar sighed, defeated. "Very well."

"Do not worry, Father. No one else will know but us," Erenar assured him.

"Yes," Tarnar echoed quietly.

I nodded curtly. "I will leave tonight."

"Wait," Father held up a hand. "Tarnar, Erenar, leave us. Go home. Rest. I wish to speak with Vilnar alone."

My brothers bowed – "Yes, Father" – and filed out, leaving us in the dim, quiet room.

After the door closed, Father rose slowly, extinguished two more torches, leaving only one flickering weakly. He came and sat beside me, his presence frail but still powerful.

"Vilnar," he began, his voice heavy with sorrow, "I have just lost Kronar. My heart... it finds it hard to let you go again. Into danger."

I tried to smile reassuringly. "I will be fine, Father. Take care of yourself while I am gone. And please... watch over Ailene and Vahnar."

"Your wife and son are safe here. Do not fear for them."

"Then I can leave in peace."

He nodded, then sighed again. "Your great love for them... it shames an old man sometimes. Seeing you together... the way you speak to her, play with your son... When you were young, I did not... I missed so much. Now, only regret."

"Don't say that, Father," I murmured gently. "I am your favorite son, am I not?" I tried the jest again. "If you speak so to me, what would you say to my brothers?"

He sighed, the sound rattling in his chest. "It is that love that worries me, Vilnar." He leaned closer, his eyes searching mine. "When enemies see such devotion, they see weakness."

"You think they would harm Ailene or Vahnar to defeat me?" Anger flared again. "Let them dare!"

"Calm yourself." He patted my hand. "No, not while you live. Your love is also your greatest strength. Your rage, if they were harmed... no one would face it willingly."

"Then they are safe," I insisted, though his words planted a seed of unease.

"While *I* live, I will protect them," Father promised. "But if something happens to you in Andranir... and if my own time comes soon after... who protects them then?"

I stared at him, speechless.

"Ailene and Vahnar harm no one now," he continued gravely. "But the boy... when he grows? Stronger than you, Vilnar? And I believe he will be. I felt it when I held him. That power." He shook his head. "Can you imagine such a man in Hualeg? That potential makes him the greatest threat to our enemies. They will fear his future vengeance."

"Your words scare me, Father."

"Better fear now than blindness later," he replied sternly. "Fear keeps you alert. Alertness brings strength. Your strength lets you face fear."

I straightened, taking a deep breath. "I *will* be vigilant, Father. Believe me. I know what I must do in Andranir. I will not waste my life."

"Good." He attempted a smile. "Do not waste your life. May the gods protect us."

"Yes, Father."

"One more thing." He leaned closer again, his voice a low whisper. "Kronar is gone. Therefore... I have decided. You, Vilnar. You will succeed me. You will be Hardingir."

The world tilted. Me? Hardingir? Now? "Father... that is... a big decision. But Tarnar? Erenar? What will they say?"

He nodded grimly. "They will not like it. But the people... the warriors... they will accept you. Our allies will learn to accept you. They will bow to your strength, Vilnar." His eyes held mine, filled with conviction. "As long as *you* believe in yourself."

Could I? The weight felt crushing. Then I remembered Ailene. My promise. *Home before winter.* How could I be Hardingir here, and keep that promise? "Father," I said slowly, "perhaps... perhaps you should think more on this while I am gone. We will speak again when I return."

He seemed about to argue, then sighed, nodding wearily. "Alright then. As you wish."

"I am leaving now, Father. Take care," I said, rising.

I went back to our room. Ailene looked up as I entered, her eyes questioning. I told her everything – Kronar's death, the victory, the questions surrounding the Andranir, my need to travel north for a week or so to seek answers. I held her close, apologizing for leaving again, assuring her of her safety under my father's protection.

She listened calmly, her quiet strength a steady anchor. "Our life and death are in God's hands, Vilnar," she replied softly, touching my cheek. "Go. God will protect us all."

Her faith humbled me. I kissed her deeply, then kissed my sleeping son. Taking only my axe, dagger, and supplies, I slipped out into the cold Hualeg night and began the journey north, alone.

28

Allies and Murderers

The journey north to the Andranir village at the mouth of the Ordelahr took two grueling days of relentless rowing. The river flowed wide and cold here, the land flattening out towards the vast, blue northern sea dotted with colossal white shapes – icebergs drifting on the currents. Even in late autumn, the air held a biting chill I hadn't felt since leaving Hualeg years ago. I pulled my thickest bearskin coat tighter around me, the familiar weight of the battle axe hidden beneath it a grim comfort.

As I guided my small boat towards the Andranir docks, I saw them – warriors lining the shore, hands on sword hilts, watching my approach with vigilant, unwelcoming eyes. Villagers peered from doorways, whispering amongst themselves. Word of an approaching stranger, perhaps. Or maybe word of *me*.

Stepping onto the sturdy wooden dock, I faced the guards, keeping my hands open, away from my own hidden weapons. "I am Vilnar," I announced clearly, my voice carrying over the wind whistling off the sea. "Son of Radnar, Hardingir of the Vallanir. I wish to speak with Patarag, chief of the Andranir."

My name, my father's name, clearly registered. Surprise flickered across their faces, replaced by a mixture of awe and perhaps fear. Even after four years, the name Vilnar of Vallanir still carried weight in Hualeg. They exchanged glances, murmured amongst themselves.

Finally, one stepped forward, bowing slightly. "Lord Vilnar. Forgive our caution. We will inform the Hardingir of your arrival. Please, come with us."

They escorted me through the village – substantial and well-ordered, as befits the seat of a powerful Hardingir like Patarag, built strong against the constant sea wind – to a well-built guest house. Several guards remained outside as I waited within. It wasn't long before word came: Patarag would see me.

At the entrance to the chief's longhouse, a structure rivaling my father's own in size and authority, another guard greeted me respectfully but firmly. "Lord Vilnar, the Hardingir awaits. Before you enter, would you consent to leave your weapons with us?"

"Of course," I agreed without hesitation. I shrugged off my heavy coat, revealing the massive battle axe strapped to my back. I handed it over. The guard's eyes widened slightly as he took the unexpected weight, leaning it carefully against the wall beside the doorway. I pulled my coat back on, hiding the long dagger still at my belt, and entered the hall.

Patarag sat in a high-backed chair at the far end, flanked by his family and advisors. He was as I remembered him from past war councils – tall, leaner than my father, with a long white beard flowing down his chest, his eyes sharp and intelligent, radiating authority. To his right sat a younger man, large-framed with brown hair – Federag, his son and heir, I presumed. To his left, two women of striking beauty. One, older, likely his wife Freda. The other, younger, with hair like spun gold and eyes as blue as the northern sea... Varda. She met my gaze briefly and offered a small, knowing smile. Beautiful, yes, as the songs claimed. But my heart felt nothing. Only Ailene's face, her dark eyes filled with warmth, held beauty for me now. I gave Varda a polite, dismissive nod and focused my attention entirely on her father. Several other Andranir elders and warriors completed the assembly.

"Vilnar!" Patarag's voice was warm, welcoming, betraying none of the tension I sensed beneath the surface. "It is good to see you again after so long! Please, sit."

"Hardingir," I inclined my head respectfully. "Good to see you well." I took the indicated chair placed directly before him.

"And your father? Radnar? How does he fare? I heard he was unwell."

"My father is recovering his strength," I replied carefully. "He sends his greetings and thanks you for your prayers."

"Good, good." Patarag smiled. "Forgive my lack of introductions earlier. This is my son, Federag. My wife, Freda. And my daughter, Varda. You have not met them before, I believe, though perhaps your father has spoken of them."

He was steering the conversation directly towards the marriage alliance. Better to address it, but on my terms. "My father has told me much, Hardingir," I replied politely, "especially of your daughter's renowned beauty and spirit." I saw Varda smile faintly again. "And I wish to discuss that matter with you specifically, later perhaps. But first," I leaned forward slightly, letting my voice harden, "if you permit, there is a more pressing matter I must raise."

"Please," Patarag gestured, his expression becoming guarded.

I didn't waste words. "It concerns the recent battle. Against Malagar of Logenir." I let my gaze sweep the room. "You do not mind if I speak plainly here?"

Patarag hesitated only a second, then whispered something to his wife. Freda and Varda rose immediately, along with several others, filing out of the hall silently. Only five remained: me, Patarag, Federag, and two older warriors I recognized as Patarag's brother Aasrag and his son Aradril, the Andranir war leader. Patarag clearly wanted few witnesses for this conversation. Something *was* being hidden.

"Speak freely, Vilnar," Patarag said when the door closed. "Only those directly involved remain."

"I respect your discretion, Hardingir," I acknowledged. "Forgive my bluntness, but grief and anger sharpen my tongue. As you know, we won the war against Malagar. But the cost... was heavy. We lost many warriors. Including my brother, Kronar." I paused, letting the weight of that loss settle in the room. "As a warrior, I understand death in battle. But some things about this conflict trouble me deeply. Things that should not have happened." I met Patarag's eyes directly. "First: why did the Andranir forces arrive so late on the first day of battle? Our messengers were sent well in advance. Second: why, when Malagar ambushed your troops on the second day, did your army retreat so quickly, leaving my brother and his men surrounded? Vallanir warriors came because we received *your* plea for aid. We honored the alliance. Many died because of it. I hope you can provide answers."

A heavy silence descended. Federag shifted uncomfortably. Aradril stared stonily ahead. Aasrag looked thoughtful.

Patarag finally took a deep breath. "Vilnar. Your father and I... our tribes... we are more than allies. We are friends, bound by history and respect. Betrayal is not the Andranir way. I know you do not truly doubt our loyalty, only seek understanding. And you deserve it." He sighed. "We grieve Kronar's loss, and all your fallen warriors, as if they were our own. We wish things had happened differently. But the gods... they weave their own patterns." He leaned forward. "For the first matter – our late arrival. Your father's message *did* reach us later than expected. And fearing Logenir scouts on the main river, we chose the safer overland route, which took longer. That is the truth of it. As for the second..." he hesitated, "...there was... confusion. Miscommunication. The Logenir attack was fierce, unexpected. We did not know the main Vallanir force was so close, coming to our aid. We were heavily outnumbered. Federag and Aradril made the difficult choice... the *only* choice, they believed... to preserve our warriors. To retreat."

"Were there casualties among your men during this... retreat?" I asked, my voice dangerously quiet.

The four men exchanged uneasy glances. It was Federag who finally answered, his voice stiff. "None. We... we managed to withdraw safely before being fully engaged."

"So," I said, letting the implication hang, "you did not fight at all?"

"Of course we fought!" Federag bristled, flushing red. "We skirmished! But we retreated when we saw their full numbers!"

His answer, Patarag's smooth excuses... they felt thin, hollow. Like nonsense meant to placate a grieving ally. "Was it not *your* messengers," I pressed, my voice rising slightly, "who reached my brother Kronar, telling him you were under attack, begging for aid? The Vallanir army came because you are our ally! We *believed* you! Why did you not believe *us*?"

"It happened too fast!" Federag insisted, sounding flustered now. "The attack was sudden! Dangerous! We had little time... saving our men had to be the priority!"

"My brother Kronar and seventy Vallanir warriors sacrificed their lives honoring the alliance between our tribes!" I shot back, my control fraying. "An alliance *you* seem to have forgotten in your haste to save yourselves!"

Federag started to retort, his face now crimson with anger, but Patarag raised a calming hand. "Vilnar," the old chief said, his voice firm but placating. "Once again, we express our deepest sorrow and regret. Kronar's death, the loss of your warriors... it wounds us all. We hope... in the future... we will have the opportunity to demonstrate the true depth of our honor, our commitment to the Vallanir alliance."

His words were smooth, diplomatic. But they felt empty. "I will keep your promise in mind, Hardingir," I replied, letting a hint of ice enter my tone, glancing pointedly at the still-fuming Federag and the stony-faced Aradril. They glared back, clearly resentful of my directness, my challenge to their chief. They saw me as just a youth, perhaps, speaking above my station. Let them. Patarag, his brother Aasrag... they understood. They saw the future Hardingir of the Vallanir sitting before them, demanding accountability.

Patarag nodded slowly. "Vilnar. You can keep my promise."

"I will relay your words to my father," I said, rising. "He has always hoped the bond between our tribes would endure. Perhaps your message will bring him some comfort. Sirs, if you will excuse me."

"Vilnar, wait," Patarag said quickly. "Don't leave yet. Stay the night, at least. Rest from your journey. We would be poor hosts indeed if we did not offer hospitality. We have prepared dinner, a room. Allow us to show you proper Andranir welcome. Get to know us better."

I hesitated, studying his face, then glancing at Federag and Aradril. Their hostility was barely concealed. Was this genuine hospitality? Or a trap? Staying felt risky. Leaving abruptly might also be seen as an insult, confirming their suspicions. Trust Patarag? Or trust my gut? Against my better judgment, perhaps swayed by exhaustion, I decided to stay. A single night. It wouldn't hurt. And maybe... maybe observing them longer would reveal more.

Patarag seemed genuinely pleased. He arranged a special dinner, inviting his whole family back, including Varda. She was placed strategically near me, pouring my drink with a practiced, sweet smile, her blue eyes lingering perhaps a fraction too long on mine. Beautiful, yes. But cold compared to Ailene's warmth. As she leaned closer, offering spiced wine, all I could think of was Ailene's dark hair, her quiet strength, the feel of her hand in mine. Still, refusing hospitality entirely would be rude. I nodded my thanks, smiled politely back at Varda, and took a sip of the wine. Enough. Engaging further felt like a betrayal, even in thought. Across the table, I saw Patarag watching me intently, gauging my reaction to his daughter. He had a plan, clearly. And he would bring it up soon.

He did, after the meal, inviting me into a small, private chamber adjacent to the main hall. Just the two of us.

"Vilnar," he began, getting straight to the point. "Your father and I... we have spoken often about the future. About strengthening the bonds between our tribes. Alliances built on treaties can break. Alliances built on blood, on family... those endure."

His meaning was unmistakable. I decided to meet it head-on, politely but firmly. "Hardingir, I heard you refused my brother Erenar's proposal for your daughter, Varda. Did you not think that might offend my father, weaken our alliance?"

He waved a dismissive hand. "Radnar understood. Every father wishes the best match for his daughter. For Varda... the best warrior in Hualeg. That man, Vilnar, is you."

I shook my head. "Your praise honors me, sir, but I am unworthy. My past... the exile... I am not the noble figure you imagine."

Patarag laughed heartily. "Your exile only enhanced your name, Vilnar! Proved your integrity! When the truth of your stand against your brother became known, respect for you grew tenfold!"

"Your words are kind, sir. But for me, alliances, like marriages, must be built on trust."

He nodded gravely. "I agree."

"And trust requires honesty."

"Also agreed," he replied, watching me intently.

"Then let me speak honestly," I said, choosing my words with care, needing to refuse without causing insult, without jeopardizing the fragile alliance further. "Varda is, as all songs say, the jewel of the North. She deserves the greatest of men. I am... deeply honored that you would consider me. But Hardingir... I must decline. I am already married. I took a wife in the south. We have a son." I met his gaze steadily. "My only prayer now is that your daughter finds a husband truly worthy of her."

Silence. Patarag stared at me, his face slowly registering shock, then profound disappointment. He had clearly been certain I would accept, perhaps believing Varda's beauty alone would sway me, securing the alliance, ensuring his daughter's future beside the Vallanir's greatest warrior – perhaps its future chief.

I understood his ambition, the political necessity. But peace built on lies, on broken hearts... it could never be stable. "My lord," I added gently, wanting to salvage what I could, "I hope my answer... my situation... does not become an obstacle between our tribes. I believe trust, honesty, mutual respect... these can bind us just as strongly as marriage ties. Difficult times will come again. We will need each other. Let us face those times together, as true allies."

He didn't reply immediately, just sat there, stroking his long white beard thoughtfully. Finally, he looked up, his expression resigned but dignified. "Yes..." he said quietly. "Of course. Please," he gestured towards the door, "you must be weary. Rest well, Vilnar."

I nodded respectfully, relieved but also saddened by his disappointment. "Thank you, Hardingir." I went to the room prepared for me, leaving him sitting alone in the dim light. I had done what I felt was right, stayed true to Ailene, to myself. But had I damaged the alliance beyond repair? Only time would tell. Right now, all I wanted was to be home, with Ailene and Vahnar.

The next morning, after polite but brief farewells, I retrieved my axe and set off, rowing south with powerful strokes, eager to leave the Andranir village and its complex politics behind me. I rowed all day, pushing myself hard, wanting only to reach the familiar sight of my village.

Night fell again. Exhaustion finally forced me to stop. I pulled the boat ashore onto a rocky bank, securing it tightly, and collapsed onto the ground, intending only a few hours rest before pushing on. Praying to the gods for safety, sleep claimed me quickly.

"Wake up!" Ailene's voice, sharp with fear, echoed in my dream. *"Vilnar! Wake up!"*

My eyes snapped open. Darkness. Silence. Then... a faint splash nearby. Figures moving stealthily near the boat. Who? How?

Instinct took over before thought. I exploded upwards, kicking out blindly, connecting with something solid. A grunt, a splash as someone fell back into the river. I scrambled away from the boat, punching another shadowy figure staggering towards me. A sword hissed past my head in the darkness. I rolled left, into the freezing shallows, scrabbling for footing on the slick rocks. Using the surprise, I heaved upwards with all my strength, lifting the edge of my heavy boat, shoving it violently towards two more attackers lunging at me. They yelled as the boat crashed into them.

My axe! It had fallen into the river during my scramble. Plunging my hands into the icy water, I felt frantically along the bottom... yes! My fingers closed around the familiar haft. I ripped it free, water streaming from the blade, and spun to face my attackers, roaring a Hualeg war cry.

Six of them, silhouettes against the faint starlight, swords drawn, circling me now on the riverbank. I couldn't see their faces clearly, couldn't tell their tribe. But their intent was obvious. Kill me.

They attacked together. I met their charge, axe blurring in the darkness. Dodge, parry, strike. A head crushed. A sword arm severed. An axe bite deep into a shoulder. They were skilled, desperate, but my fury, my Hualeg battle-instinct, was fully awake now. Screams, curses, the clang of steel, the wet thud of the axe finding its mark. It was over quickly. Four lay dead or dying in the shallows, their blood staining the water dark, bodies drifting slowly northwards on the current.

I stood panting, axe dripping, scanning the darkness for the other two. They had turned, scrambling back into the forest, fleeing for their lives. Rage still burned hot within me. No mercy. Not for those who ambushed me in the dark.

I jumped up angrily and ran after them. As soon as I broke through the treeline, I saw them struggling through the undergrowth ahead. I caught up with the slower enemy first, my axe swinging down, silencing his panicked cry. Pushing through the bushes, I saw the last one running frantically not far ahead. Not wanting to miss the opportunity, I balanced myself, raised my axe high with both hands, and threw it with all my might. The heavy weapon whizzed through the air like a wheel of death, striking true, splitting the head of my final enemy before he could even look back.

Silence fell, broken only by my own ragged breathing. I quickly retrieved my axe from the fallen warrior and returned to the riverbank where the first four lay dead or dying in the shallows.

I looked down at the faces of my dead attackers, turning one over with my boot, trying to recognize their markings or features in the dim moonlight. Who were they? Who had hired them, sent them here to kill me in secret? They could not be from Vallanir; I recognized no one. A cold wave of regret washed over me then, sharp and bitter. I should have kept one alive. Should have captured one, forced answers from him before finishing him off. Now they were all dead, their secrets silenced forever.

My mind raced. Who knew I was here, alone, on this river tonight? Only my family back in Vallanir. And Patarag, Federag, the Andranir. Would Patarag truly order my death after accepting my refusal, after offering hospitality? It seemed... unlikely. Too dishonorable, even for Hualeg politics. If he wanted me dead, he could have done it easily, quietly, while I slept in his village.

Logenir? Possible. They hated me. But how would they know my route, my timing? Unless...

Unless someone from Vallanir told them. Or told the Brahanir, the Drakknir, allies who might resent my return, my potential claim to leadership... allies perhaps willing to do Malagar's work for him, or curry favor with Patarag by removing me? Tarnar? Erenar? Could one of my own brothers betray me so completely?

The thought made me feel dizzy, sick with a cold dread far worse than the river's chill. Betrayal from within...

My first thought, sharp and piercing: *Ailene. Vahnar.* If there was a traitor in our midst, someone willing to arrange my murder out here in the wilderness... then my wife, my son... they were not safe. Not even in my father's house.

Forgetting exhaustion, forgetting the cold, forgetting everything but the sudden, terrifying fear for my family, I shoved the boat back into the water and began rowing south again, harder than ever before, desperation lending impossible strength to my aching arms.

29

For the Three of Us

The black cloak of night still lay heavy when I returned to Vallanir the next afternoon, pushing my small boat hard against the current, driven by a gnawing unease born from the ambush. As I neared the village docks, that unease solidified into cold dread. The usual bustle was absent. People moved slowly, heads bowed, avoiding eye contact. Fear and sorrow hung thick in the air, heavier than the usual autumn chill.

"What's happened?" I demanded of the first villager I saw, an old fisherman mending nets. "What's wrong?"

He looked up, his eyes filled with pity, then looked quickly away. "My lord Vilnar... forgive me... it is your father. Hardingir Radnar... passed in the night."

What? The world tilted. Father... dead? It couldn't be. Just four days ago, yes, he was frail, but he was talking, planning, warning me... How? "Passed?" I repeated numbly. "How? What happened?"

"They say... they say he fell," the old man mumbled, still not meeting my eyes. "Down the stairs in the longhouse."

Fell down the stairs? My strong, proud father? Even frail, he moved with careful deliberation. An accident? Suspicion, cold and sharp, pierced through the shock. "Where is he now?" I asked, my voice tight.

"Taken to the funeral tower by the river, my lord. The rites... they will be held tonight."

Mixed feelings churned inside me – grief, anger, suspicion, a terrible sense of foreboding. I barely registered leaving the dock, walking numbly towards the river, towards the place where we sent our honored dead to the sky gods. My mind raced, yet couldn't seem to grasp anything. *Fell?*

The sun was already low, painting the sky in shades of blood orange and deep purple. A cold wind whipped along the riverbank. There, beside the newly constructed wooden pyre tower, lay my father's body on a simple table, prepared for the final journey. Only a few quiet figures stood nearby. I hurried towards him, my heart aching with a grief deeper than any I had known, even for my mother long ago.

His face looked calm in death, the lines of worry smoothed away, but so terribly old, so fragile. I reached out, stroked his cold cheek, tears finally blurring my vision. My fingers traced the line of his jaw, then moved down, instinctively feeling along his neck, the base of his skull beneath the white hair. Something felt... wrong. Not just the cold stillness, but... a subtle misalignment? A break? *He fell down the stairs.* Fatal for a man his age, certainly. But why? How? Was it truly an accident?

Footsteps approached from behind. I looked up, wiping furiously at my tears, my hand instinctively falling to the dagger at my belt. Two of Kronar's household warriors stood nearby, their faces carefully neutral.

"My lord Vilnar," one said respectfully. "We are glad you have returned safely. Lord Tarnar and the elders hold council now in the village hall. You are requested... summoned... to attend immediately."

Tarnar holding council? Already? A new wave of unease washed over me. My first thought wasn't of council matters, but of safety. "Where are my wife and son?" My voice came out harsher than intended, almost a growl.

The soldier hesitated. "They are in the Hardingir's longhouse, my lord. Safe. But Lord Tarnar stressed the meeting is most important, that you should attend first..."

Important? More important than Ailene? Than Vahnar? Rage, cold and swift, replaced the grief. Without a word, I pushed past the startled soldiers, leaving them standing by my father's body, and strode rapidly back towards the longhouse, towards *my* family. No one dared impede me.

Two different guards stood at the main entrance now, unfamiliar faces, looking nervous as I approached like a stormcloud.

"Where are they?" I demanded again. "My wife? My son?"

"Inside, my lord," one stammered, avoiding my eyes. "In your chamber."

"What are *you* doing here?" I fixed them with a glare.

They looked at each other uneasily. "Lord Tarnar's orders, my lord. For the time being... no one is permitted to see the lady Ailene."

Ice flowed through my veins. "You mean," I said, my voice dangerously low, "my wife and son are prisoners? Forbidden to leave? Forbidden visitors? Including *me*?"

"No! Not like that, my lord!" the guards flinched back, faces pale with fear.

"Damn you!" The rage exploded. I lashed out, slapping both men hard across the face, sending them stumbling back against the doorframe. "Bastards! What is the meaning of this?" But they were just soldiers following orders, too terrified to answer truthfully now. Shoving them aside, I stormed into the house, taking the stairs two at a time. *Is this where he fell?* The thought echoed grimly as I reached the second floor.

I didn't knock. I threw open the door to our chamber. Ailene was huddled on the bed, clutching Vahnar tightly, her eyes wide with terror. Seeing me, she let out a choked sob and scrambled towards me. I gathered them both into my arms, holding them fiercely, protectively. Ailene wept into my chest, great, shuddering sobs.

I held them until her crying subsided, stroking her hair, murmuring reassurances I didn't feel myself. "What happened?" I asked finally, gently tilting her face up. "Don't be afraid. Tell me everything. Let me handle this."

Through renewed tears, she recounted the previous night. Putting Vahnar to sleep, hearing a sudden scream from downstairs, then a heavy, sickening thud. Running out with a candle, finding Father lying broken, lifeless, at the bottom of the main stairs. Her own screams bringing servants, then villagers, then finally Tarnar and Erenar arriving from their own homes nearby. Confusion, grief, anger... then Tarnar's cold orders confining her to the room, guards posted, forbidden contact.

"Do they... do they think *I* did this?" she sobbed, burying her face against me again. "Blame me for your father's death? Vilnar, I swear, I did nothing! I heard the fall, that was all!"

"Ailene," I held her tighter. "Of course, I believe you! Never doubt that!"

She looked up, still pale, trembling. "Will they harm us? Me? Vahnar?"

I shook my head fiercely, gripping her shoulders, forcing her to meet my eyes. "No one will harm you. This is... a misunderstanding. You have nothing to fear. I will speak with Tarnar, with the elders. I will sort this out." I tried to inject confidence I didn't feel into my voice. "Wait for me here. Lock the door behind me. Don't open it for anyone but me."

"I understand," she whispered, hugging Vahnar tighter.

"I am leaving now." I kissed her forehead, then Vahnar's soft hair, my heart aching with love and a terrible fear. I stood up, turned, and left them, hurrying back downstairs, heading for the village hall.

This time, I didn't bother with stealth or quiet control. I grabbed my battle axe from where the guards had left it leaning inside the longhouse door. I shed my heavy outer coat, revealing the dried bloodstains and hastily bandaged wounds from the ambush – let them see I was not untouched by recent violence. Axe in hand, fury radiating from me like heat from a forge, I strode towards the village hall.

Villagers saw me coming and scattered, scrambling into doorways, their faces fearful. Let them fear. Let Tarnar fear. How dare they? How *dare* they cast suspicion on Ailene, confine her like a criminal? The guards posted outside the village hall took one look at my face, at the great axe gripped in my hand, and simply melted away into the shadows. None dared stop me.

I reached the center of the hall, the twenty or so elders and leaders seated in their council circle falling silent, turning wary eyes towards me. My gaze locked onto Tarnar, seated prominently near the center. I strode forward, stopped directly before him, and slammed the butt of my axe handle onto the hard-packed earth floor. *THUD.* The sound echoed like thunder in the sudden silence.

"TARNAR!" My voice boomed, filled with barely controlled rage. "Do you accuse my wife? Do you hold *her* responsible for our father's death?"

He went pale, visibly shrinking back in his seat. I remembered him mocking me as a boy, always trying to provoke me. He wasn't mocking now. The boy he knew was long gone, replaced by a warrior who had killed scores of men, whose fury was legendary even before exile.

Thankfully, before Tarnar could stammer out a reply that might have pushed me too far, Erenar spoke, his voice calm, placating. "Vilnar, please. No one accuses your wife. There has been... a misunderstanding. Fear and grief make people unwise. We are glad you have returned safely. Sit. Let us explain."

Still seething, I pulled a heavy bench forward with a scrape, sat down hard directly opposite Tarnar, rested my axe across my knees, and fixed my glare on him, waiting.

"Vilnar," Erenar began again carefully, "we have suffered much misfortune. First Kronar, now our father... the people are afraid. They whisper the gods are angry, punishing us." Pradiar, the old shaman, nodded gravely from his seat nearby. "Your wife, Ailene... she is a good woman, we know this. But..." Erenar faltered.

Pradiar continued smoothly, "She is a foreigner, Vilnar. An outsider. Some traditions are deep-rooted. Some believe... the presence of a stranger near the Hardingir at the time of his death... is an ill omen. A misfortune." He leaned forward earnestly. "Vilnar, I was Radnar's oldest friend. We faced much together. I accepted Kronar's death in battle. But Radnar... falling... it is a shock. We do not suspect your wife, truly. But caution seemed wise. Tarnar merely sought to keep her apart, safe from whispers, from foolish accusations, until calm returned. For the good of all, believe me."

His lengthy explanation, his talk of omens and gods' punishments, only fueled my fury. I growled low in my throat. "Punishment? Bad luck? Is that what you call it?" My voice rose again, harsh and grating. "Then tell me, Pradiar, tell me *all* of you – was it the gods' punishment or simple bad luck when *I* was ambushed two nights ago? Sleeping by the river on my return from Andranir? Attacked by six armed men who meant to kill me?" I let my eyes sweep the stunned faces. "Bad luck for *them*, perhaps, because I killed them all! Maybe I had the bad luck of not finding out who sent them before they died! But if you think the *gods* sent them to punish me, then you worship stupid gods indeed! It was *enemies*, Pradiar! Cowards who strike from the shadows!"

I looked around the silent, shocked room again. "And one thing troubles me greatly. I do not believe Patarag of the Andranir sent them. Nor Malagar's scattered Logenirs – they are too far west. Which leaves... Brahanir? Drakknir?" I let my gaze rest pointedly, heavily, first on Tarnar, then on Erenar. "Someone betrayed me. Someone told our supposed allies of my secret journey north. Someone wanted me dead." I gripped my axe tighter. "I swear by Odaran's missing eye, I will find the traitor. And I will show them no mercy."

Gasps echoed around the room. The implications hung heavy in the air. Betrayal. From within the alliance. Maybe from within this very room.

"Vilnar... these are very serious accusations," Erenar said cautiously, his composure finally cracking slightly.

"Are you accusing *us*, Vilnar?" Tarnar demanded, his voice shaky despite his attempt at defiance.

"You have nothing to fear, brother," I replied coldly, "if the accusation is not true."

"Perhaps *you* should be afraid," Tarnar shot back, finding a sliver of courage.

"Do you think so?" I met his gaze, letting my contempt show. "I will remember your threat, Tarnar. Perhaps you should remember the fate of others who have threatened me in the past."

Pradiar shook his head, looking deeply distressed, tears welling in his old eyes. "Oh, Radnar, my friend," he lamented, speaking almost to himself. "Decades we stood together, joy and sorrow! Now you leave us, and before your ashes cool, your sons fight amongst themselves! Our tribe needs a new leader! A strong hand to guide us through this trouble! If only you had guided us, named your successor before the spirits claimed you!"

His words hung in the air. Succession. With Kronar gone, the path was unclear, contested. Pradiar continued, looking around the room, stating the tradition, "Gentlemen, as custom dictates... if the Hardingir has not made his will known... then leadership passes to the eldest surviving son..." He looked towards Tarnar.

Before anyone could react, before Tarnar could swell with triumph, I cut Pradiar off, my voice ringing through the hall. "Father *did* make his will known. Before I left for Andranir. He spoke his decision to me."

Everyone stared, stunned again.

"Is that so?" Pradiar looked utterly bewildered. "And... who? Who did Radnar choose as his successor?"

I met the eyes of every man in the room, my gaze lingering on Tarnar and Erenar, before declaring firmly, unequivocally, "Me."

I hadn't intended to reveal it. Not now, not like this. The chieftainship... it wasn't what I wanted. A life with Ailene and Vahnar in the south, that was my desire. But seeing the suspicion cast on Ailene, hearing Tarnar's threats, feeling the instability, the potential betrayal... anger and perhaps a grim sense of duty forced my hand. I threw my father's decision into the center of the room like a challenge.

Chaos erupted. Shouts, arguments, disbelief.

"We cannot believe it!" Tarnar yelled over the noise. "There is no proof! No witnesses!"

"Vilnar," Erenar asked, his voice tight but controlled amidst the commotion, "do you have any proof of Father's words?"

"Unfortunately," I admitted calmly, meeting his gaze, "I do not. It was spoken between Father and son, alone."

"If there is no proof, no witness," Pradiar stated sadly, shaking his head, "then tradition cannot confirm your claim. The eldest son inherits..."

"Go ahead then, if that is your choice," I interrupted, my voice cold, letting the threat hang heavy in the air. "But my father *spoke* his will. I suggest... you all think very carefully before you choose to ignore it." I looked around again. "Whatever you decide, whoever you choose... know this: I *will* continue to hunt the traitor who sought my death. I will find them. I will kill them. Without mercy. And *no one* will stop me."

Unease rippled through the room. Men looked at each other nervously, confused, afraid. Only Tarnar continued to glare at me with pure hatred.

Erenar managed to regain control. "Gentlemen! Please! This is... a deeply complicated matter. Emotions are high. I suggest... I suggest we make no decision today. Let us first properly send our father's spirit to the heavens tonight. Let us rest, clear our minds, and council again tomorrow."

Rest? With calmer minds? Unlikely. Looking at Tarnar's face, at the fear and calculation in the eyes of the elders... tonight would be long, filled with whispers and plots. But everyone seemed to agree, relief washing over them at the postponement.

It was dark now. Time for Father's final journey. We went back to the riverbank. The villagers had gathered again, silent this time. Pradiar led the final prayers. Then, as Hardingir Radnar's remaining sons, we – Tarnar, Erenar, and I – took torches and together set the great pyre ablaze. Flames roared upwards, consuming the tower, consuming my father's body, sending ashes swirling into the night wind.

Afterward, I hurried straight back to the longhouse, back to our chamber. No guards stood outside the door now; no one dared interfere. Ailene looked up anxiously as I entered. I quickly recounted the meeting, the accusations, my claim to the chieftainship, the postponement.

She listened silently, her worries clear on her face. "What... what do you think will happen tomorrow, Vilnar?"

"Everything depends on their choice," I replied grimly. "If they are wise, they will choose me. Then I can settle this, find the traitor, secure our place, and you need not worry. But if they choose Tarnar..." I clenched my fist. "...then I may have to take the seat by force. Get rid of my enemies first. I have no choice, Ailene. It was Father's wish. And it is the only way to truly keep you and Vahnar safe now."

Ailene shook her head, tears welling in her eyes again. "Is this truly what you want, Vilnar?" she asked softly.

I frowned. "What do you mean?"

"To be Hardingir. Is that what *you* want?"

Her question stopped me short. I thought for a long moment. "No," I admitted slowly, the truth settling heavily. "No, it was... never what I truly wanted. But... Father wished it. And maybe... maybe it is my responsibility now. To the Vallanir. So it doesn't matter what I want. I must do it."

"Does your tribe *really* need you that badly, Vilnar?"

Did they? After today? After the suspicion, the hostility, the way they allowed Ailene to be treated? If they could disrespect my wife, my choice, were they truly *my* people anymore?

Ailene continued gently, her hand finding mine. "Because... there are two people here who need you more than anything else in this world. Two people who could not live if you were gone."

Her words struck me with the force of a physical blow. Ailene. Vahnar. In my anger, my pride, my focus on tribal politics and vengeance... had I forgotten them? Forgotten what truly mattered? My reckless challenge to my brothers, my claim to leadership... it wasn't just risking my own life. It was risking *theirs*.

I sank onto the edge of the bed, my earlier fury draining away, replaced by shame and a chilling fear. What had I done? Whether I won or lost tomorrow, whether I became chief or died trying, the cycle of violence would continue. If I killed Tarnar or Erenar, their supporters would seek revenge. If they killed me, Ailene and Vahnar would be helpless, targets themselves. To secure the chieftainship, how many would I have to kill? How much blood would stain my hands, stain my soul? What kind of life would that be for Ailene? For Vahnar? The thought was unbearable.

"You are right, Ailene," I whispered, kissing her head, pulling her close. "Gods, you are right. I... I did not think. My anger... my pride... I only thought of myself, my father's son. But I am... different now. I am your husband. I am Vahnar's father." I looked into her eyes, seeing my own fear reflected there. "You both need me. And the truth... the truth is *I* need *you*. I cannot live without you, without our son. Without you both, my life has no meaning."

"Vilnar," she murmured, holding me tight, "I know you wish to honor your father. Just as I pray our son will honor you. And as your wife... I will stand beside you always. Whatever you decide. In life, or..." she hesitated, "...in death. But..." her voice broke slightly, "...what about our child, Vilnar?

His future?"

I shook my head fiercely, my lips trembling. "I will not let you die here! I will not let Vahnar die here! That would be... the greatest failure. The greatest mistake." Shame washed over me again. "Ailene, I have made so many mistakes since returning. Bringing you here. Leaving you alone. Rushing to Andranir. Accusing my brothers, challenging them... I endangered us all." I crouched down before her, taking both her hands. "Therefore... I must make the right decision now. The best decision. For the three of us."

"What is your plan?" she asked quietly, hope flickering in her eyes.

I took a deep breath, the decision settling firmly, finally. "We leave. Tonight. Now."

"Go home?" she whispered.

"Yes. Home. To our cabin in the south." Relief flooded me as I said it. "But no one must know, Ailene. We must slip away unseen, or we will be in terrible danger."

"But... the meeting tomorrow? Your claim?"

"I don't care about it anymore," I said fiercely. "Let them choose Tarnar, or Erenar, or argue amongst themselves. Let them have their power, their feuds. They are my kin, my people... but maybe it is time I forget them, and they forget me. You and Vahnar... you are what is most important now. My only true tribe."

"But Vilnar... the journey south is long. We have nothing prepared."

"There is food in the pantry downstairs," I said quickly, my mind already working. "Venison, dried fish, supplies. Enough. I will load the boat while you gather Vahnar and our warmest cloaks. We leave immediately."

"Are you sure?" she asked one last time, searching my face.

I nodded, meeting her gaze with absolute certainty. "This time, Ailene, I am sure. This is the best decision I have made since setting foot back in this land."

I kissed her once more, then slipped out of the room. Making sure the corridors were empty, that no guards lingered, I went quickly down to the storage pantry, grabbing sacks of cured meat, dried berries, hard bread, waterskins. Back outside through a rear door, moving like a shadow through the quiet village towards the riverbank where my boat was moored. I loaded the supplies, then hurried back to the longhouse the same way. No one saw me. The village slept, exhausted from grief and uncertainty. The guards, if any were posted, must have been near the village hall, awaiting tomorrow's council.

In our room, Ailene was ready, Vahnar bundled warmly asleep in her arms, our few belongings wrapped in another cloak. Making sure everything was prepared, we crept out of the longhouse together, melting into the deep shadows, heading silently towards the river.

At midnight, under a sliver of moon hidden mostly by clouds, we pushed our small boat out into the cold, dark current of the Ordelahr and began rowing south. Away from Hualeg. Away from my past. Towards home.

30

Prayer and Hope

Day bled into night and back into day again as I rowed south, down the great Ordelahr, away from Hualeg, away from the ghosts and the gathering storms. My arms ached, my back protested, but the rhythm of the oars was steady, tireless, driven by the sight of Ailene huddled under furs in the boat, Vahnar sleeping peacefully against her chest. We were heading home – back to the quiet creek, the small cabin, the life I had chosen. Autumn deepened around us, the air growing sharper each day. Winter was coming; we needed to be south of the deep forests before the river froze solid.

For six days, the journey was blessedly uneventful. We spoke little, conserving strength, but sometimes Ailene would sing softly in her beautiful southern tongue, or I would hum an old Hualeg hunting chant. Vahnar would watch us, his blue eyes bright, occasionally laughing, filling our small boat with a warmth that defied the encroaching chill. In these moments, peace felt possible, the future hopeful.

But on the seventh day, the peace shattered. Some instinct, honed by years of survival, prickled the back of my neck. I stopped rowing, listening intently, scanning the dense forest lining the banks behind us. Nothing. Silence, save for the river's murmur and the wind in the pines. Yet... I knew. I could feel it.

"They are following us," I said quietly, my voice tight.

Ailene turned, her eyes wide with alarm, searching the empty stretch of river behind us. "Who?"

She saw nothing, heard nothing yet, but the tension radiating from me must have been palpable.

"People from my tribe, I think," I admitted grimly. "They must have realized we were gone. Come after us." My heart sank. I had hoped... foolishly, perhaps... that Father's command, or their own relief at my departure, would keep them from pursuing.

"But why?" Ailene whispered, clutching Vahnar closer. "Why would they still chase us?"

"Maybe..." I tried to sound reassuring, though I didn't believe it, "... maybe they mean no harm. Just want to talk." But I knew better. I pulled the boat towards the bank, into the shelter of overhanging willows. No, they wouldn't send two or three longboats – I could *feel* it was more than one boat – just to talk. Tarnar? Erenar? Sent by the council? Or acting on their own? It didn't matter. Their intent would be hostile. With over twenty warriors, maybe thirty... they came to drag me back, or kill me. And Ailene, Vahnar... they would be obstacles. Or worse, leverage.

Disappointment, bitter and cold, washed over me. Followed by a wave of sheer frustration. Was this my fate then? To be forever haunted by the blood feuds, the demands of a life I had tried so hard to leave behind? Was there no escape?

Then, looking at Ailene's frightened face, at the innocent trust in my sleeping son's features, the anger and despair coalesced into a single, hard point of clarity. *My* fate didn't matter. Not anymore. *They* were what mattered. Their safety. Their future.

I knew what I had to do. The final choice. The only choice.

Ailene watched me, her expression shifting from fear to a heartbreaking understanding. Tears welled in her eyes even before I spoke, as if she could read the decision in my soul. Nature itself seemed to hold its breath; the birds fell silent, the wind moaned through the branches like a lament.

I took a deep, shuddering breath, forcing my voice steady. "Ailene. Listen to me." I took her face gently between my hands. "I want you to take Vahnar. Take the boat. Row south. Now. As hard and fast as you can."

PRAYER AND HOPE

Her eyes widened in protest.

"I will stay here," I continued firmly, pushing past the lump forming in my throat. "Find out what they want. Delay them. Give you time to get away safely. Don't wait for me, Ailene. If everything... if everything is alright, I will follow. Catch up soon." Liar. "But whatever happens, you keep going south. Never look back. Promise me. Your life, Vahnar's life... it's wide open before you. Nothing to regret. Understand?"

She sobbed, shaking her head violently. "But... why? Why must it be like this, Vilnar?"

"Why?" The word echoed my own despair. "Don't think about why!" I said, louder now, needing her to be strong. "No regrets, Ailene! That is all that matters! Remember! No regrets! Do you understand?"

Through her tears, she finally gave a small, jerky nod. "Yes..."

I pulled her close then, kissing her with all the love, all the desperation, all the unspoken farewells crammed into one heartbreaking moment. Then I grabbed my battle axe from the bottom of the boat and vaulted over the side into the shallows. "I love you, Ailene," I choked out. "Take care of yourself. Take care of our son."

With all my remaining strength, I shoved the boat hard, pushing it out into the main current. Ailene sat frozen for a second, weeping, then seeing the boat drift, she grabbed the oars. "Row, Ailene!" I yelled, my voice cracking. "Remember my words! If Odaran and your God allow it... we will meet again!"

"I love you!" she cried back across the widening water. "I will wait for you!" Then she bent her head and began rowing south, pulling with desperate strength.

I watched until the boat was a small speck, until it disappeared around a bend in the river. Gone. I whispered softly to the empty river, "Go, Ailene. Live. Don't look back. Leave me... and I will be strong enough to let you go."

Tears I hadn't shed for my father, for Kronar, now streamed freely down my face. This might be the last time. The thought of never seeing Vahnar grow, never holding Ailene again... it was an agony beyond any physical wound. I regretted, suddenly, fiercely, not kissing my son one last time before pushing them away. I almost plunged back into the river, wanting to chase them, call them back... but I steeled myself. Their safety depended on my resolve now. The pursuers were closer; I could hear the faint rhythm of many oars now. This was the only way.

Closing my eyes, I offered a silent, desperate prayer. *"O mighty Odaran, Sky Father... I ask nothing for myself. But protect them. Protect my wife, my son. Grant them safe passage south, grant them a life of peace, beauty. Let my son grow strong, wise, good... better than his father. Let him be the light for his mother. Do not let him look back, do not let him carry the burden of what happens here. Let him be free. Let them both be free. Say goodbye to them for me, Odaran. Let them hear my love across the wind. Or... deliver the message through Ailene's own God, if you can't. Please do this... and I will face whatever comes in peace."*

A strange calm settled over me then. The prayer offered, the decision made. Father had said my love was my greatest strength. Now, I would prove it.

I scanned the riverbank, the surrounding forest. Rocks, trees, the narrowing bend ahead where the creek joined the Ordelahr. Not a perfect ambush site, but workable. The narrowing water would funnel their longboats, make them clumsy. I quickly climbed the bank, finding higher ground behind a massive, moss-covered boulder overlooking the river bend, axe held ready.

Soon, they came into view. Three longboats — as I thought, moving fast, side-by-side, packed with warriors – ten men in each, maybe more. Vallanir warriors. My kinsmen. Men I had trained with, fought beside. Their faces were grim, determined.

From the stern of the rearmost boat, a voice barked an order. "Faster! We must catch them before nightfall!"

Tarnar. My brother. His presence confirmed the worst. This wasn't a rescue party. This wasn't a negotiation. This was an execution. One final sign was all I needed.

I waited until the boats were almost abreast of my hiding place, then stepped out onto the rocky outcrop, hefting my axe, letting the afternoon sun glint off the polished blade.

"VALLANIR!" I roared, my voice echoing across the water. "Are you looking for Vilnar? I AM HERE!"

The reaction was instantaneous. Oars faltered, men shouted in surprise, turning to stare up at me. Panic flickered across faces. Hands flew to sword hilts. Swords were drawn. That was the last sign. The final proof of their intention. My own tribe, my own brothers, sent to hunt me down like a beast. Now, I would finish them.

A deep, tearing pain ripped through my heart. *"Father,"* I thought, the word a silent prayer, *"forgive me. Now I must fight them! My friends. My kin. The husbands and fathers of my people!"*

"HEEAAAAAA!!!" With a roar mixing rage, grief, and despair, I launched myself off the outcrop, aiming for the nearest boat, axe swinging.

Screams, death cries. My axe bit deep, shearing through shields, helmets, bone. I landed heavily amidst the chaos, regaining my balance instantly, becoming a whirlwind of destruction. Body parts flew. Weapons clattered uselessly. I carved a path from prow to stern, leaving only bleeding corpses and terror in my wake.

As the second boat scraped alongside the first, trying to board, I leaped across the gunwales without pausing, my axe already reaping its grim harvest. Swords stabbed at me, axes swung. Wounds opened on my arms, my chest, my legs, but I barely felt them, fueled by a berserker rage, a desire only to end this, end them all. I whirled, struck, killed, the deck slick with blood, until I stood alone again amidst the dead.

The third boat, Tarnar's boat, hung back slightly further out. Warriors on board threw knives, axes. I dodged, parried what I could. One knife grazed my side. Another buried itself deep in my left shoulder, near the chest. Agony, sharp and white-hot, momentarily stunned me. But the pain only inflamed my rage further. With a final, desperate surge of strength, I raised the great battle axe high above my head and hurled it with all my might towards Tarnar's boat.

It spun through the air, a terrifying wheel of death, smashing into the side of the longboat with incredible force, splitting timbers, sending warriors sprawling as icy river water poured in. Tarnar and the others panicked, struggling in the rapidly sinking vessel.

I pulled the knife from my chest, ignoring the gush of blood, and half-rowed, half-paddled the second boat towards them, grabbing two swords from fallen warriors beside me. As I reached them, some jumped into the freezing water, trying to swim away. Others lunged at me recklessly, swords swinging. I met them, sword in each hand now, parrying, thrusting, killing until the water ran red around me. I cut down those swimming nearby without mercy. No one would threaten Ailene and Vahnar again.

Finally, only one figure remained, struggling to stay afloat amidst the debris of the shattered boat. Tarnar. His sword arm was gone, severed at the shoulder by my thrown axe. He was bleeding heavily, dying. I reached down, hauled him into my boat. Stabbed through the waist with my own sword, he looked up at me, gasping.

Both of us fell into the bottom of the ravaged boat, slick with our mingled blood. Tarnar clutched the sword hilt buried in his stomach, his face pale, eyes wide with shock and pain. At that moment, seeing him helpless, seeing my *brother* dying by my hand, the battle fury drained away, leaving only exhaustion and a hollow ache. Yet, the betrayal... the pursuit... anger still simmered.

With immense effort, I pushed myself partly upright, ignoring the fire in my own wounds. I raised the sword still clutched in my right hand, its tip hovering over Tarnar's throat, ready to deliver the final blow. But seeing his face, stripped of its usual arrogance, looking only young and afraid now... I hesitated.

"Tarnar..." My voice was a ragged whisper. "My brother... why?" I coughed, tasting blood. "We left Vallanir... erased the past... wanted only peace... in the south. We were no threat to you. Why... why follow us? Why hunt us down like beasts? Why hate me so much?" The questions poured out, born of pain and bewildered grief.

Tarnar gasped, then managed a weak, bloody grin that looked grotesque on his pale face. "Mistaken... brother..." he choked out. "Hate...? Maybe...

rivalry. Always rivalry... You... always shone brighter... Father's favorite..." He coughed again, blood speckling his lips. "But hate...? I feared you more... Feared you coming back... taking what I thought... was mine by right..."

"So you sent them?" I demanded, the image of the ambushers in the dark forest flashing before my eyes. "Those men who ambushed me on my way back from Andranir? That was you?"

"No!" His denial was surprisingly forceful, his eyes widening with something that looked like genuine confusion, or perhaps indignation, even now. "That ambush... up north... By Odaran's pyre, Vilnar, I knew *nothing* of it! Swear... I thought *you* lied... made up that story... to accuse us..."

I stared down at him, searching his face. He seemed... honest. A dying man has little reason to lie about such things. But if not him... then who? And why this pursuit *now*?

"Then... why this?" I gestured weakly at the carnage around us, the dead Vallanir warriors floating in the river. "Why chase us now, Tarnar? Lead these men... our kinsmen... to their deaths?"

"Erenar..." Tarnar gasped, wincing as pain tore through him. "After you left... Erenar came to me. Said... said you were a danger now. Said your claim... Father naming you Hardingir... it would split the tribe. Said you'd return south... maybe raise forces there... to attack us later." He coughed again, weaker this time. "Said *I* should be chief... custom... eldest survivor... Said Vallanir needed *my* strength, *my* decisiveness... Needed me... to secure the tribe... by stopping *you* first. Before you reached the south." His eyes flickered with bitter self-mockery. "He played on my pride, Vilnar... my ambition... my fear of you... Gods, I was... such a fool..."

The pieces clicked into place, cold and ugly. Erenar. Quiet, overlooked Erenar. He hadn't needed to act directly. He'd used Tarnar's ambition, Tarnar's fear, Tarnar's long-held resentment of me... sent him here knowing full well what the outcome would likely be. "He wanted us *both* dead," I whispered, the realization settling like ice in my gut. "He knew you couldn't win here. He knew I would fight back. He gets rid of us both... and *he* becomes Hardingir."

Tarnar managed another weak, gurgling laugh. "Smart... Erenar... Always... the quiet one... Always... a trick..." He coughed violently, his body shuddering.

I looked down at my brother, my lifelong rival, now just a dying man manipulated into his final battle. The anger I felt towards him dissolved, replaced by a profound, weary sadness. Perhaps even pity.

"Do you think... Erenar planned it all?" Tarnar rasped, his breathing shallow now. "Kronar's death...? Father's... fall?"

I shook my head slowly, the effort immense. My own vision was blurring. "Don't know... Maybe not... Maybe... luck was just... on his side..."

"Then the gods... are on his side..." Tarnar laughed weakly, blood trickling from the corner of his mouth. "Luck... sign of the gods..."

"Don't believe it!" I objected, finding a spark of defiance. "He broke... all rules... all honor... The gods *will* punish him... one day..."

"Not... our business... now..." Tarnar whispered, his eyes glazing over. "Not mine... Nothing more... I can do..." He seemed strangely calm, resigned. "You always thought... me petty... arrogant... But now... I feel calm... No grudge... " His gaze focused on me, surprisingly clear for a moment. "Hope you... same... little brother..."

"What... do you mean?" My voice was barely audible now, strength failing fast.

"You... strong, Vilnar... You can still... survive this..." His voice was fading. "Find... your wife... child... Forget Erenar... Forget... revenge... Pointless..."

Forget? Could I? Find Ailene... Vahnar... Could I even move?

"And you?" I whispered.

"Leave me... there..." Tarnar rasped. "This sword... leave it... Pull out myself..."

I shook my head weakly, the movement sending waves of pain through me. "Can't... leave you..."

"Don't be... fool!" His voice rose with a final surge of weak energy. "No time... do what... supposed to do! Go! Find them!"

His eyes fluttered closed. His breathing stopped. Looking into his still

PRAYER AND HOPE

face, peaceful now despite the blood, I finally nodded, understanding his last wish. With agonizing effort, ignoring the fire ripping through my own body, I half-lifted, half-dragged my brother's body to the muddy riverbank. I laid him gently on the cold grass beneath the whispering pines. Blood flowed from my own wounds, mingling with his on the dark earth.

I looked down at him one last time. "Tarnar," I whispered, my voice thick with grief and regret. "I am sorry... for everything. It shouldn't... have ended like this."

He gave no answer. I imagined him gathering with Father and Kronar in Valahar, the Hall of Heroes. Hopefully... hopefully they would accept him.

"Goodbye..." I murmured, waving a hand I could barely lift.

Turning away, leaving my brother behind, I stumbled back to the boat, collapsing into the bottom, my heart aching with a sorrow too deep for tears. I had to row. Had to find Ailene. Find Vahnar. Hope... I clung to it. As long as I breathed, hope remained. Pushing past the agony, I found the remaining oar, began pulling weakly, desperately, south.

I rowed sitting up, then slumped forward, rowing lying down, pulling weakly. But the current fought me, my strength failed. Dawn broke, painting the sky in colours I barely saw. I couldn't fight anymore. The oars slipped from my numb fingers, drifting away.

Tears tracked paths through the blood and grime on my cheeks, but strangely, I smiled. No regret. If I didn't catch them, it meant they were safe, far ahead, rowing south towards the sun. Ailene... my strong Ailene... she would make it. She would raise Vahnar in peace, away from all this darkness. That thought brought a profound sense of release.

The morning sun touched my face. No warmth. I couldn't feel anything now. Numbness spreading. Father's words... *sensing the last moments*. My time had come.

I closed my eyes. Alone on the river, deep in the forest I had once called home, I surrendered. Darkness gathered, but in it, I saw them – Ailene, Vahnar, smiling, waiting.

I took one last, shuddering breath, and smiled back.

III

Part Three

31

The Next Fool

The snoring echoed again, louder this time, a deep, guttural rumble that seemed to vibrate through the damp stone floor of the cave. It emerged from the deeper darkness ahead, a sound both mundane and utterly terrifying in this eerie silence. I froze mid-step, the hairs on my arms prickling, a cold dread washing over me.

Don't be a fool, William. I knew better than to rush in. Vida had warned me, the Vallanir scouts had warned me – the beast in the Iddhurun cave was ancient, cunning, and deadly. It might sound asleep, but one careless move, one overconfident strike... and my skull would join the grisly collection scattered along the cave floor.

My eyes adjusted further to the gloom, picking out those grim warnings – human skulls stacked carelessly in niches, bones gnawed clean, separated from torsos still clad in scraps of rusted armor. Swords, axes, daggers lay everywhere, dropped in final moments of agony, now coated in mud and cobwebs. The remains of fools who thought they could conquer this beast. And now, standing at the threshold of its inner lair, I had the sinking feeling I was about to become the next fool in line.

"Shh," a soft whisper came from behind.

I turned, startled. Vida stood there, a tall silhouette against the faint light from the cave mouth. Even in the dimness, her yellow hair seemed to hold its own light. Her face was serious, ruthless, beautiful. She nodded curtly towards the side wall, then gestured for me to move forward, towards the opposite side of the central cavern ahead.

I hesitated, wanting to argue. Her plan made sense in theory – attack the creature from both sides if it was truly in the center, prevent it from focusing on one attacker. But crossing that open space, right under the nose of whatever was making that monstrous snoring sound... how could we possibly do it unseen?

"Come on," Vida urged, switching to the Altonian tongue she'd become surprisingly fluent in these past weeks traveling together. Her voice was a low hiss. "You did not journey all this way just to become a coward now, did you?"

"For the gods' sake, Vida," I whispered back frantically, "Can I say one thing?"

"What?" Impatience sharpened her tone.

"Why didn't you bring Svenar and Gunnar inside too?" They were Vida's two remaining Vallanir warriors, strong axe-men. "If all four of us were here, maybe our chances of *not* ending up as scattered bones would be slightly better!"

"I told you," she replied dismissively. "They stand guard outside the main entrance. With Freya and Adhril," (another Vallanir warrior who had joined them). "If this *thing* manages to get past us here, they will intercept it there. We surround it. Kill it."

I grumbled under my breath. "First, you didn't explain that clearly. As usual, you make your plan, expect everyone else to just follow. Second, I don't think this thing *escapes*. I think it *eats*. Probably eat you first. Your meat must be tastier than mine."

Vida snorted softly in the darkness. "Is this some kind of crude southern joke? Are you implying I am softer than you?"

I shook my head, exasperated. "You're really hard to joke with, Vida."

"Is this a good time for jokes?" she shot back.

"It feels like a good time to die!" I countered, my own fear making me irritable. "Seriously? You expect me to kill this beast with just this?" I hefted the sword at my hip – a decent blade, taken from a Logenir, but still just a sword. "No arrows? Not even a spear?"

"Arrows are useless," she stated flatly. "Skin like rock plates covers most of its body. Spears too – its weak point is the throat, beneath the jaw, hidden unless you are close. You can only kill it with a blade, at close range. And you," she added, a fraction softer, "are better with a sword than anyone I know."

"Your praise isn't exactly filling me with confidence right now."

"Hey." Her voice was firm again. "You *are* great. The best fighter here. You will not die. *We* will not die."

I muttered a curse, trying to force down the fear, trying to believe her certainty. She was usually right about these things. And hadn't I faced down Logenir warriors, dozens of them? Killed men in battle? This was just one opponent. An animal. Not as smart as a man, surely.

But then... why all the bones? These weren't foolish villagers who died here. These were warriors, judging by the gear. There was something more dangerous than human cunning in this cave.

Taking a deep breath, I pressed my back against the cold, damp cave wall, peering slowly around the edge of the rock formation to my left. The main cavern opened up before me. My eyes, fully adjusted now, could make out a large, dark shape hunched almost motionless in the center. Head? Body? Legs? Hard to distinguish clearly. Just a black mass, rising and falling slightly with that awful snoring rhythm. They said it looked something like a bear, but bigger, wrong somehow. I'd only ever seen bearskins before. Were bears truly this large?

Fear coiled again, cold and tight. Fear of the unknown. But as I watched the sleeping(?) shape, I realized the fear wasn't just a hindrance. It was a warning. A valuable ally, keeping me sharp, keeping me from doing something suicidally rash.

Okay. Time to move. I pushed off the wall, placing each foot with deliberate care on the sodden cave floor, trying not to make a sound. Both hands gripped my sword hilt. Breathe in, slow. Breathe out, slower. Focus. All attention on that black, snoring mass.

Step by silent step, I crossed the open space, reaching the relative safety of the rocks on the far side. Relief washed over me – I'd made it unseen. But the relief lasted only a heartbeat.

The snoring stopped.

The black creature's head lifted slowly. Two large, crimson eyes opened, pupils contracting, fixing instantly on *me*. A low snort, then a sound that started deep in its chest and erupted into a fearsome, guttural growl.

I cursed silently. *Fool. Just like all the others.*

The beast roared, a deafening sound that shook the very rock beneath my feet. The thick, shaggy black hair covering its body seemed to stand on end, revealing glimpses of something underneath – hard, dark green skin that shimmered faintly, like ancient, oiled scales. Now I could see its form properly. Four-legged, massively built, easily twice the size of a large pony, radiating power. Its head was blunt, muzzle short like a bear's, but its mouth peeled back to reveal oversized, viciously sharp fangs.

It leaped, impossibly fast for its bulk. Enormous claws, thick as daggers, slashed outwards from its front paws. I brought my sword up instinctively, trying to parry. The impact slammed into me like a physical blow, throwing me backwards hard against the unforgiving cave wall. Pain exploded in my back, lights flashing behind my eyes.

Before I could recover, another set of claws lashed out. I rolled desperately, sideways, under the creature's heavy body as the claws gouged deep grooves in the rock where I'd just been. I slashed upwards wildly with my sword, connecting with its front right leg. Blood spurted, dark and thick, but the creature barely seemed to notice, shaking its massive leg impatiently, forcing me to roll again to avoid being crushed.

Sharp stones dug into my arms, my back, my side. I grimaced, spitting out mud and grime. The beast twisted its huge body around, preparing to lunge again, those terrible red eyes fixed on me.

Suddenly, it shrieked – a high-pitched sound of agony completely different from its earlier roars. Its massive body convulsed, swaying violently left and right. I scrambled backwards, bewildered, then saw her. Vida. Somehow, silently, she had reached the beast, her own sword buried deep in the side of its thick neck, just below the jaw – the weak spot she'd mentioned.

She strained, trying to hold her grip, trying to drive the blade deeper, but the beast thrashed wildly in the opposite direction. With horrifying force, Vida was flung through the air like a doll, crashing headfirst against the far cave wall with a sickening thud. She collapsed onto the rocks below, motionless.

"Vida!" The cry tore from my throat. I started towards her crumpled form across the cavern.

But the beast howled again, a sound of pure agony and rage, halting me in my tracks. It writhed, trying desperately to reach the sword embedded in its neck, its massive claws scrabbling uselessly. It staggered, collapsed to its knees, then began crawling, dragging itself painfully across the cave floor… straight towards Vida. Towards the one who had wounded it. Even dying, it sought revenge. It reached her still form, raised a blood-streaked claw, ready to bring it down, to crush her skull.

No time to think. I sprang forward, sliding across the slick rocks on my knees, positioning myself between the descending claws and Vida's head, thrusting my own sword upward with every ounce of strength I possessed.

The tip pierced the tough pad of the beast's claw, grating on bone. I roared, pushing upwards with all my might as the creature's immense weight came down. It roared back, pain and fury mingling, trying to pull its paw back, trying to drag me with it. I held firm, driving the blade deeper, feeling tendons tear.

With a final, agonized bellow, it yanked its paw free, leaving my sword embedded for a moment before it too was ripped loose. Blood poured from the new wound. The beast stumbled back, crawling into the darkest corner of the cave, its roars fading into long, shuddering moans of pain.

Ignoring it for the moment, I scrambled to Vida's side. Checked her neck – felt a pulse, faint but steady. Ran my hands carefully over her head – no obvious wound, no blood matting her yellow hair. I breathed a shaky sigh of relief. Alive. Still alive.

Her eyelids fluttered open. She stared up at me, dazed, disoriented. Blinked slowly. Her lips parted. "What… happened to it?" she whispered, her voice weak, raspy. "Where... is it?"

"Over there," I nodded towards the shadows. "Are you alright?"

"Where is it?" she insisted, ignoring my question, trying weakly to push herself up.

I pointed again. "In the corner. Wounded badly." I gently pushed her back down. "Hey, calm down. Be careful. You hit that wall hard. Might have broken bones..."

"Kill it," she demanded, her eyes suddenly wide with urgency, her hand grabbing the front of my tunic with surprising strength, pulling my face closer to hers. "Kill it now, William."

"It's hurt," I reassured her. "Bleeding badly from your strike, and the paw... It'll die soon."

"No!" Her grip tightened, her eyes blazing with desperate intensity. "It will... recover. Heal itself. You have to kill it! Finish it! Right now!"

Recover? Heal itself? I stared at her, bewildered. What kind of creature *was* this? "Damn it, Vida," irritation flared through my fear and relief. "Are you hiding something from me? What *is* this thing?"

She didn't respond, just held my gaze, her eyes pleading, demanding.

I loosened her grip on my tunic, taking a deep breath, trying to remain calm despite the confusion, the nagging feeling she wasn't telling me everything. "Okay," I sighed. "Okay. I'll kill it. Make sure it's dead." I looked down at her sternly. "But Vida... you owe me an explanation. After."

Gathering my courage again, I stood up, sword ready, and stepped cautiously towards the dark corner. A low growl rumbled from the shadows. Two crimson points of light glowed menacingly – its eyes. I could just make out its greenish skin, pale now, shimmering wetly with blood.

A claw lashed out weakly from the darkness. Slow. Easy to dodge this time. I moved closer, circling towards its head, knowing this was my chance.

The beast let out one last defiant scream, mouth gaping wide, revealing rows of those terrible fangs, welcoming its end perhaps. I didn't hesitate. My sword slid past the teeth, into the gaping maw, driving deep down its throat, silencing the growl forever. Its breath ceased. It was dead. Finally.

I stood there for a long moment, gasping for air, heart hammering, sword still buried in the beast's throat. Relief washed over me – I'd survived. We'd survived. But then... the familiar unease crept back. Yes, I'd killed the monster. But I still didn't know *why*.

Vida said it killed people, the skulls were proof. But why was *she* hunting it? Why was it so important to kill? Helping Vida felt right – she was my friend now, my ally, she'd saved my life on the river. But doing this... killing something without fully understanding the reason... it felt too much like being a mercenary again, killing simply because I was told to, because I was good at it. Shouldn't friends be honest with each other?

A wave of dizziness washed over me, stronger this time. Not just exhaustion, something... different. The cave walls seemed to waver slightly. And a sound... a soft, sibilant whisper, seeming to come from nowhere and everywhere at once.

"William..."

I leaned heavily against the cooling flank of the dead beast, trying to clear my head. My heart raced, my chest felt tight. What was that? Lowering my gaze, trying to focus, my eyes fell on something nestled on the cave floor right beside the beast's open, lifeless mouth. A stone. Palm-sized, smooth, blacker than the surrounding shadows, yet seeming to... pulse? Emit a faint, inner light?

"William..."

The whisper again, closer now, clearer.

"*Do not take it... Do not touch it...*"

I ignored the warning whisper. My attention was completely fixed on the stone. It drew me, pulled at me with an invisible force. It felt... familiar somehow. Beautiful. The most beautiful thing I had ever seen.

I knelt down slowly, reaching out a trembling hand. Picked it up. It felt cool, smooth, heavy in my palm. A shimmering black stone. *Black stone... where had I heard that before?*

"William..." The whisper sounded again, soft, gentle, achingly familiar. Like...

Mother? Is that you? Are you here?

Before the thought could fully form, a searing, agonizing cold shot from the stone where my fingers touched it. Ice spreading up my hand, my arm, instantly consuming my entire body. It felt like thousands of frozen needles stabbing into me all at once.

I cried out, dropping the stone, stumbling back, but the pain, the *cold*, was everywhere, overwhelming, unbearable. My vision blurred, darkness swirling at the edges, rushing inwards... swallowing me whole. Consciousness fled.

32

Legends

My eyes snapped open. Branches, thick and dark, swayed gently far above me. My body ached, lying heavy in the bottom of a boat, rocking gently. Sunlight warmed my face, making me squint. A dull throb persisted behind my eyes. Groaning, I pushed myself into a sitting position, the world tilting slightly.

In front of me, three figures manned the oars – Svenar near the prow, Vida beside him, and Freya facing me near the middle thwart. Behind me, Gunnar and Adhril gave me solemn nods of greeting as I stirred.

Where...? How...? My mind felt foggy. The cave... yes. Vida and I went in. The fight with that monstrous beast... I remembered the terror, the struggle, dodging its claws, Vida being thrown against the wall... saving her... then driving my sword down its throat... the feel of its life draining away. But after that? A complete blank. How did I get in this boat? How long had I been unconscious?

"He's awake!" Gunnar's gruff voice broke the silence.

Freya immediately stopped rowing, turning fully towards me, her face breaking into a wide, relieved grin. "Thank the gods!" she exclaimed in clear, fluent Hualeg. "I was worried about you!"

I managed a weak grin back, then paused. I understood her perfectly. Every word. When did that happen? Hadn't I been struggling with the language just... before the cave? We *had* been traveling together for weeks, searching for the beast's mountain lair. I remembered trying to learn words from Freya... but fluent? Now? It felt deeply strange, unsettling.

"You must be hungry!" Freya said again, pulling me from my thoughts. "And thirsty!"

She knelt beside me, Vida and Svenar glancing back briefly. Vida... something felt important, something I needed to ask her about the cave, but the thought remained frustratingly out of reach.

Freya offered me grilled fish from a wooden box and a waterskin. My stomach growled fiercely. My mouth was painfully dry. I grabbed the waterskin first, drinking deeply of the sweet, tangy liquid until the ache in my throat eased. Then I devoured the fish ravenously.

When I finished, leaning back against the boat's side, feeling a little more human, I smiled properly at Freya. "Thank you."

She chuckled, studying my face intently. "Do you remember what happened? Are you truly okay?"

Remember? Up to a point. Killing the beast. Then... nothing. Okay? My head hurt, my body ached, but I was alive. "Of course," I replied, forcing confidence. "Full now, thanks to you."

She grimaced playfully. "Well, that's a good sign, I suppose."

"Yes." Her intense gaze made me feel awkward. I looked around. "So... where are we going now? Back home? To Thaluk?"

Freya raised her eyebrows slightly. "Home?"

Vida glanced back again, her expression unreadable.

A knot of unease tightened in my stomach. "We *are* going back, right?" I clarified, looking from Freya to Vida. "My part is done. I helped kill the beast. Right? So... I can go back south now?"

Freya's mischievous grin returned, but she didn't answer directly. "Oh, just happy!" she declared brightly. "You speak our language fluently now! Properly! So I finally have someone interesting to talk to on this long journey. Vida and the others," she sighed dramatically, "are *so* serious sometimes!"

Vida just shook her head from her rowing position.

"But..." The fluency still felt wrong, unnerving. "I've been speaking it... for a while?"

"Mmm... yes, a little," Freya waved vaguely. "But not like *now*. And we still have weeks of travel ahead! It gets lonely!" She laughed.

I managed a laugh too, playing along despite the confusion. "Hopefully, I can keep up with your chatter, Freya. And hopefully Vida won't get too angry."

"Oh, don't worry about Vida!" Freya assured me. "She's the best sister, protector, teacher... everything! She talks, yes, but mostly plans, this way, that way... tiring! Tell me about the south! The villages! The people!" She looked at me intently. "You."

"Me?"

"Yes. You."

"Why me?"

"You are... interesting," she stated simply. Then, abruptly, "Did you dream?"

"Uh, what?"

"While you slept so long. Did you dream?"

I frowned, searching the blankness in my memory after the fight. "I... I don't remember dreaming. Why?"

Freya laughed, a clear, crisp sound. "*I* dream when I sleep long! And remember them! Everything I see. And sometimes... sometimes they truly happen later." She smiled mischievously. "Do you believe me?"

"Believe you? Sure. Why not?" Her certainty was hard to dismiss.

"You don't think I am weird?"

"No," I said honestly. "Not weird."

"Do you like me?" she asked bluntly.

The question startled me again. "I... I don't see how anyone could *dislike* you, Freya."

She frowned slightly, parsing my clumsy answer.

"I mean, yes," I added quickly. "Of course I like you."

Her smile returned, wide and radiant. "Good! I like you too! If I dream something important again, I'll tell you first!"

"Why not tell Vida?" I smirked, glancing at her sister's back.

"I want you." Freya laughed again. "Don't worry about her! Her anger is quick. And if you can stand being hit occasionally, it's no problem!"

"Being hit? Good to know!"

She smiled warmly. "I like you."

"You... already said that."

"I like saying it again," she replied simply. "Because... I have seen you in my dreams."

I didn't know what to say. "Then... thanks again. Nice to be dreamed of." I tried to laugh, feeling lost with her chaotic way of talking. "But Freya, seriously. One question you *didn't* answer. Where *are* we going now?"

Freya hesitated, glancing back at Vida, who remained silent, rowing steadily. Freya shrugged slightly. "We are going to see a shaman."

"A shaman?" Irritation pricked again. Another secret mission? "Why?"

"Shaman, healer... wise woman," Freya amended.

"Why do we need one?"

"To check on *you*," she said, her face serious now.

"Check on *me*?" I asked, baffled. "Why?"

"You were... asleep... for a very long time," she replied carefully.

"That's normal. People faint! After a battle like that..."

"No, William," she interrupted gently. "It is not normal. And... do you truly think you were only unconscious for a day? Maybe two?"

The cold dread returned. "What do you mean?"

"You have been unconscious, William," Freya said softly, "for seven days."

"What?" The word felt ripped from my throat. *Seven days?* A whole week gone? Impossible! "Are you serious?" I yelled.

"Yes!" Freya looked genuinely worried now. "That is why we must take you to the shaman!"

"What for?" My mind reeled. A lost week? What happened? And the thought of some northern shaman poking at me, chanting spells... it was horrifying. "That's unnecessary! I'm awake! I feel fine!"

"Mmm... not necessarily," Freya muttered, looking unsure.

"What do you mean by that?"

"You still need checking," she insisted. "Inside maybe? Your chest? Your head? Maybe needs... opening?"

I stared at her, aghast. She had to be joking, trying to scare me. It sounded too gruesome. "Hey!" I raised my voice, appealing past her to Vida. "Since I'm the patient, *I* decide if I need checking!"

Vida finally stopped rowing, turning slowly to face me, her expression stern. "You had better come with us, William."

"Oh, really?" I challenged, bristling. "Why?"

"Like Freya said," Vida stated calmly, "perhaps something happened to you in that cave. Something we cannot see or understand yet."

"But I'm awake! I feel nothing strange!" Except the missing week and the sudden fluency in Hualeg...

"Let our shaman examine you," Vida insisted.

"No."

"It is for your own good!"

I looked at her set jaw, her determined eyes. Arguing was useless. But the lack of answers, the feeling of being managed... it infuriated me. "Are you hiding something from me again, Vida?" I demanded fiercely.

"What do you mean?" she countered, her voice rising to match mine.

Freya leaned back nervously between us.

"What happened in the cave?" I pressed. "*After* I killed the creature? Why was I unconscious for seven days? What aren't you telling me?"

Vida's brow furrowed slightly. "You... you truly do not remember anything after the beast died?"

"No! One moment I killed it, the next I woke up here! Why? What happened?" The blank space felt vast and terrifying.

Vida stared at me, then let out a slow breath. "That is why I said there was something strange. Why you must see the wisewoman." She spoke reluctantly. "You fainted in the cave. Right after the beast fell. We tried to wake you, but failed. Since the manner of your collapse seemed... unnatural... I told the others we should take you north, to see a wisewoman I know there. She is skilled enough to understand such matters. You do not need to be afraid of her."

Her explanation felt thin, incomplete. An unnatural collapse? Why? "Afraid? I'm not," I lied, deeply unsettled. "I just wanted to know why I *have* to go."

Vida seemed to hesitate, then continued, "The creature you killed, William... it was no ordinary beast."

"Clearly!" I snapped. "If it wasn't, why hunt it? Why risk our lives?"

"I explained the reason to you before," she said stiffly.

"You gave *a* reason! But not the whole truth! You're still hiding something!" I shook my head, exasperated. "Okay... if you won't talk, fine. But that means you don't trust me. Not as a friend. Even though I trusted *you*."

Vida looked thoughtful. "What more do you wish to know?"

"Everything!" I exclaimed, leaning forward again. "Why hunt *that* specific beast? What was it truly? What was its crime beyond defending its lair?"

"That reason is not enough?"

"It *was*," I admitted. "But not now. Not after losing seven days!"

Vida fell silent again, her jaw tight. I stared at her, waiting.

Freya spoke up gently. "Vida... tell him. Many know the stories. There is no secret. William deserves the truth." Vida shot her sister a warning look. Freya met it bravely. "What point hiding it now? He nearly died for us."

Vida looked away, a silent concession.

Freya turned back to me, her eyes bright.

"There is a legend in our land," she began, her voice taking on the dramatic cadence of a practiced storyteller. I settled back, listening intently, watching Vida out of the corner of my eye. She had resumed rowing, her face impassive, but I sensed she was listening too.

"A legend," Freya continued, "about a beast that lives deep within the eastern mountains. Ethrak, the Earth-Bound. They say it has lived there since the Beginning Times, shortly after the world was broken and the gods returned to the sky. For thousands of years of this new world, it slept, guarding its prize, unknown to humankind."

"Until one day," she leaned closer, her voice dropping conspiratorially,

"Signar the Bold, chieftain of the Vallanir, received a whisper on the wind – a message from the gods themselves, some say. A whisper of a divine relic, a weapon of immense power, still hidden here on earth. A weapon Signar believed he needed to unite the warring Hualeg tribes, to restore the glory of the Elder Days." Her eyes sparkled. "Do you know who Signar is?"

I grinned slightly despite the gravity of the tale. "Sounds like your great champion?"

"An ancestor," she nodded proudly. "A great Hardingir of the Vallanir."

"Lived about a hundred winters ago," Freya clarified. "The god – Anthor, the Thunderer, they say – whispered to Signar of this weapon, Anvasar. A hammer, more powerful than any axe or sword, for Anthor himself wielded it in the God Wars. With it, the legends claim, Anthor split the very earth, forging the path for the gods to return to the heavens when their war ended, lest they destroy this new world too."

I nodded slowly, picturing it. A god's hammer.

"But Ethrak," Freya's voice turned grim, "a monstrous beast born from the world's deep places, captured the wounded Anthor as he ascended. Anthor surrendered his hammer, Anvasar, as ransom for his freedom, a guarantee that Ethrak would be spared the world's final sundering, allowed to sleep undisturbed in the new world, provided it never troubled humankind. Ethrak agreed, took the hammer, and slept in its mountain cave for millennia, guarding the weapon."

She paused, letting the weight of the legend sink in. "Signar, hearing the whispers, believing Anthor's blessing was upon the Vallanir, sought out this cave, sought Ethrak, sought Anvasar. He promised the gods he would use the hammer only to unite the Hualeg, then return it to Anthor's realm." She sighed dramatically. "He found the cave. He faced Ethrak." Her voice dropped. "Unfortunately... Ethrak killed him."

I listened, captivated despite myself. This felt bigger than just hunting a dangerous animal.

"Signar's warriors returned with the tragic news," Freya continued. "His son, enraged, led another expedition to avenge his father and claim the hammer. He died too. All who went with him, died. The god's whisper, the blessing... it became a curse. Vallanir was weakened, lost land and standing among the tribes. Signar's quest was forgotten, his name remembered not for bravery, but for failure. Some even whispered it wasn't Anthor who spoke to him, but trickster spirits, enemy magic seeking Vallanir's ruin. That is the story most believe now."

She paused, taking a sip from the waterskin before looking at me again.

"But..." I prompted, trying to connect it to our own hunt, "you – Vida – you still believe the original legend? That Anthor spoke? That Ethrak guards a real divine weapon?"

"Yes. Vida convinced us," Freya stated simply, glancing back at her sister with absolute faith.

"She said that, and you just believed?" I asked, still skeptical.

Vida turned her head briefly, fixing me with an icy glare, then wordlessly resumed rowing.

"So what?" Freya challenged, loyal to her sister. "Should I not trust Vida?"

"That's not what I meant," I backpedaled slightly. "Just... it's a big legend to swallow whole."

Freya chuckled. "I believe because Vida is the smartest, most learned person in our tribe. She knows history, reads the old runes, studies the maps, speaks tongues even the elders have forgotten – like your southern speech!"

"Yes, that's true," I had to agree. "And she's also learned to fight and kill very effectively. Best in that field too, I think."

Freya laughed heartily at that. Behind me, I heard Gunnar and Adhril chuckle too. Svenar tried to hide his grin. Vida, pointedly, kept rowing, though I thought I saw the tips of her ears turn slightly red.

"Someone as smart as Vida must have good reasons for believing," I said, deliberately aiming the comment at Vida's back, hoping to draw her out.

"Yes," Vida's sharp voice cut through the air without her turning around. "I do."

"Alright," I pressed, pleased she'd finally responded. "Maybe you want to share those reasons? Explain why you risked everything, dragged us all out here?"

She fell silent again, the rhythmic splash of her oar the only answer.

Freya sighed dramatically. "Vida believes the legend *because* Ethrak exists. Because the beast in that cave *wasn't* just a bear, wasn't just any animal. It was ancient, powerful, unnatural. Its existence proves the core of the old story must be true."

"That's... still thin reasoning," I argued.

"Why?" Freya countered. "It seems you know something similar?"

"I want to tell *you* stories now," I said, leaning forward slightly. "Stories from the south. Some from my mother, which I believe. Others from tavern drunks, probably lies. They speak of the Ern – beings like angels, maybe, sent down when the world was young, covered by a sacred world-tree, Eviendares. The Ern taught the first humans many secrets – controlling water, wind, fire, earth."

Vida had stopped rowing again now, turning slightly, listening intently.

"Humans grew too skilled," I continued, watching Vida's reaction. "Too powerful. Jealousy arose among the Ern. War broke out – Ern against human, Ern against Ern, human against human. The Creator God grew angry, destroyed the world, remade it as it is now." I paused. "And similar to your legend, Freya, there are southern tales of great relic weapons lost in that destruction. Hidden somewhere – western forests, eastern mountains, across the southern sea. Many have searched. None have found anything. Maybe the stories are true, maybe not. But chasing legends... it seems like a way to waste lives. Like Signar. Like... maybe us, Vida?" I looked directly at her. "Risking death yesterday... for something that might not even exist?"

Vida met my gaze, her expression unreadable for a moment, then she actually laughed, a short, sharp sound. "You speak of wasting lives now, William? After the way you fought the Logenir? Like a blizzard, like a starving wolf? No one fights like that unless they embrace death already."

"That... that was different!" I objected, feeling my face flush. "I fought to protect people! To survive!"

"How is this different?" she countered coolly. "You fought yesterday to protect *me*."

"But the *intent* was different! We went there deliberately seeking a monster, seeking a legend! To kill!"

"My goal is more than just killing a beast," Vida stated, her voice low and intense. "It is more than Signar's ambition. The North is changing, William. Old threats rise again, new ones gather. Vallanir... my people... are caught in the middle. We need more than just courage to survive what is coming. We need... power. Hope. Anvasar could be that hope. I must try." She held my gaze. "Go ahead, denounce my quest if you wish. I do not care."

Her fierce conviction, her dedication to her people... it silenced my skepticism. "I am not denouncing your intentions, Vida," I said quietly, taking a slow breath. "I was... just asking. Trying to understand."

Her expression softened almost imperceptibly. "I know the risks are great. But sometimes... doing what might be right *requires* taking risks."

"Look," I said earnestly, "I apologize if I sounded critical. Truly. I was just... curious. Maybe trying to talk, like Freya said. That's all."

"I know," she replied tersely, though perhaps a fraction less coldly than before.

Beside me, Freya nodded, satisfied. "Well, talking like this is much more fun than just rowing in silence!"

"So," I asked Vida, needing to know, "is your mission over? You killed Ethrak. Did you find the hammer? Anvasar? Don't worry," I added quickly, "I don't want to see it. Just... is it done?"

Vida looked down, away from me. "I did not find it," she admitted quietly.

My stomach dropped slightly. "You didn't? Then... maybe it *was* the wrong beast after all?"

"The beast was Ethrak," she insisted. "But the weapon... it was not there."

"Then where is it?"

"I do not know." For the first time since I'd met her, Vida looked genuinely uncertain, doubt shadowing her eyes.

"What will you do now?" I asked gently.

She took a deep breath, her resolve returning. "I do not know yet. But... I must continue searching."

"Do you... want me to help you search again?" The offer surprised even myself.

She looked up, meeting my eyes, a flicker of surprise in her own gaze. "That..." she began, then hesitated. "That is up to you, William..."

We fell silent then, the only sound the rhythmic dip of the oars as Svenar and the others continued rowing us steadily north. Vida seemed lost in thought, wrestling with her failed quest. I tried to understand her fierce determination, her willingness to chase a legend for her people.

Freya finally broke the silence. "Hey! Enough heavy talk! Enough plans for now! Nothing we can decide yet anyway, right?" Her cheerful energy returned instantly. "Let's just enjoy the journey for now! Svenar, steer towards that sheltered cove ahead! Time for food and rest!"

Her command was casual, but practical. It surprised me again, though – Freya seemed to naturally take charge when Vida was preoccupied. Maybe she wasn't just the bubbly younger sister.

"We know a better place," Vida spoke up suddenly, shaking off her introspection. "Further ahead. Two more bends in the river." She picked up her oar again, looking directly at me, a strange hint of... something... in her eyes. Recognition? Shared knowledge? "A place I think *you* already know, William."

"Really?" I replied, puzzled. A place *I* knew, way out here? "Okay. But give me an oar. My body needs to move. Sitting idle drives me mad."

33

Values of Life

The steady rhythm of the oars resumed, carrying us further west. We traveled for what felt like a long time after leaving the beast's cave – perhaps the rest of that day (for me; for the others, more than a week!), maybe longer. My sense of time was still fractured after losing that week. When Vida had mentioned stopping at a place "two bends in the river" ahead, I'd assumed it was close. Apparently, a Hualeg warrior's definition of "bend" was different from mine.

It was late afternoon when we finally reached our destination. As Vida steered the boat towards the bank, a jolt of recognition shot through me, sharp and unexpected. I *knew* this place. The cluster of large, moss-covered boulders providing shelter from the main current, the narrow game trail leading into the dense woods, the clearing just beyond... and tucked back amongst the trees, almost invisible from the water, the weathered logs of an old, abandoned house.

My father's house. The place Bullock had described. The place where Vida had captured me just... gods, was it only two or three weeks ago? My mind struggled to reconcile the timelines. I felt a confusing mix of emotions – a deep, aching longing for a father I'd never truly known, mingled with a wary curiosity about Vida. How did *she* know this specific, hidden spot? Why lead us here?

Unfortunately, finding a quiet moment to ask her proved impossible. As soon as we made camp in the sheltered clearing behind the rocks, Vida became a whirlwind of practical activity – checking supplies, directing Svenar and Gunnar to scout the perimeter, sharpening her sword with focused intensity.

Freya, on the other hand, attached herself to me like a burr. She chattered endlessly, peppering me with questions about the South, demanding Altonian words for Hualeg objects – river, tree, fish, sky, fear, joy. Why the sudden, intense curiosity about my language? Was she competing with Vida's quiet competence? Or was she just... lonely, bored, genuinely trying to connect? Maybe all three. I answered patiently, trying to match her cheerful energy, though my mind kept drifting to the silent house hidden in the trees and the equally silent woman tending the campfire.

It wasn't until after we'd eaten – more grilled fish, hard bread – that I saw my chance. We sat around the fire, the flames casting dancing shadows, the three warriors talking quietly amongst themselves nearby. Freya was trying to teach me a Hualeg counting game involving pebbles. Vida sat slightly apart, staring into the flames, lost in thought. Now or never. It would have been better alone, but that seemed unlikely to happen.

Keeping my voice casual, still moving pebbles for Freya's game, I asked Vida, "Do you rest here often? On your travels?"

She looked up, her turquoise eyes meeting mine across the firelight. "We stayed here for some days before... before you arrived that first time."

I nodded slowly. "How did you find the house? You cannot see it easily from the river."

"We did not know it was here," she replied simply. "We sought only shelter behind the rocks. Svenar found the house later, looking for dry firewood. It was empty. A good place to rest, out of the wind."

"But... when I arrived that day... you were here alone?"

"We rested one night," she explained, her voice even, betraying no emotion. "The next day, the others," she gestured vaguely towards her warriors, "went east, searching for signs of the beast. I returned here first, after scouting a different path. Then... you came."

Her explanation sounded reasonable enough. Plausible. "Who do you think lived here?" I asked, glancing towards the dark shape of the cabin through the trees, its windows like empty eyes. The door and shutters looked broken, weathered by time and neglect. Could it even be repaired?

"Just a hunter, perhaps," Vida shrugged dismissively, turning back to the fire.

I finished the last crumb of my fish, took a long drink from the waterskin, trying to appear relaxed, thoughtful, not like someone whose heart was pounding with unanswered questions about his own past tied to this very spot.

"Do you have more questions, William?" Vida asked suddenly, her gaze sharp again, catching me off guard.

"Huh?" I shrugged, flustered. "I... I was just thinking. Trying to make conversation. You don't mind me asking things, do you?"

"No problem," she said coolly. "But if you have no more questions for me right now... it is my turn to ask." Her tone was flat, but beneath it, I sensed danger.

"Go ahead," I said warily. "But... take it easy, okay?"

"Why did you come to this house?" she asked directly, her eyes fixed on mine. "That day I found you?"

The question hit me like a physical blow. Tell the truth? About Bullock? About seeking my father? No. Too dangerous. Too much revealed. I fell back on the story I'd prepared, the partial truth. "My job... my orders from Taupin... were to patrol the eastern creeks. Check for any Hualeg signs near the river."

"Why were you alone?" she pressed immediately. "Patrols usually have at least two men."

"That's normal for scouts sometimes," I lied, feeling increasingly uncomfortable. "Besides... the others... they were supposed to follow me back to the village. Faster boat." I let a trace of bitterness enter my voice. "Unfortunately... they were then killed. By your men."

"Yes," Vida replied dryly, unmoved. "We have spoken of this. You also killed *my* men. We have both expressed regrets. It is done."

Done? Was it ever truly done? I nodded anyway, looking down at my hands, remembering the feel of the sword, the blood. I doubted Svenar, Gunnar, or Adhril felt it was truly 'done'. Their grief for their fallen comrades was buried deep, but it was there. Hualeg vengeance could simmer for years, generations even.

"So," Vida concluded, apparently satisfied for now, "there is nothing strange about either of us being near this house that day. Or do you have other questions?"

"Mmm... no," I mumbled, feeling defeated.

"Very well." She dismissed the topic curtly. "Then it is time for sleep. We have far to travel still, and we have lingered long enough on this river."

"About that," I seized the chance to change the subject, "how much longer? To reach this... shaman?" The word still felt strange, ominous. "Sorry if I ask again."

"Two weeks travel, maybe," she estimated. "Perhaps faster if the winds are favorable further north."

"And after that?" I held my breath. "After I see this shaman... am I free to go south? Back to Thaluk?"

Vida considered me for a moment, her expression unreadable. "You can go," she said finally.

Relief washed over me, so strong it almost felt like suspicion. Was it really that simple? "Look," I felt compelled to add, "I know you probably want my help again... with whatever comes next. And I *will* help," I said quickly, seeing her expression tighten slightly. "But... I wish I still had the choice, Vida. To decide for myself."

"I understand," she nodded slowly. "And... thank you."

"And if I do decide to go home... I'll need a boat. Supplies."

"We will see you safely to the nearest southern village where passage can be found," she promised.

"Even if it means delaying your own journey? Taking you out of your way?"

"Yes," she confirmed, her gaze steady. "That is the consequence. You need not hesitate when the time comes. I give my word."

"Thank you," I said again, meaning it, though a tiny sliver of doubt remained. Her promises felt... conditional sometimes. She nodded back curtly. "Any other questions?"

Before I could answer, Freya piped up brightly from beside me. "*I have some questions for William! May I?*"

"About what?" I grinned at her, relieved the tense interrogation from Vida was over. Freya's questions were usually easier, less... loaded.

"About your father and mother!" she declared cheerfully. "Are they from the south, too?"

The grin vanished from my face. My blood ran cold.

Freya looked at me expectantly. Vida watched me too, her expression carefully neutral, but her eyes sharp. They were waiting.

"Of course," I stammered, forcing a casual tone. "Where else would they be from?"

"Where exactly?" Freya pressed innocently.

Think fast. Deflect. "If I tell you about mine," I countered, trying a playful smile, "you have to tell me all about *your* parents first." I didn't want them knowing about Vilnar, about my Hualeg blood, my connection to *this* tribe, Vallanir. Not yet. Not until I understood more. It felt too dangerous.

"Oh, I don't mind telling stories!" Freya began eagerly. "My father..."

"I think that is enough talk for tonight," Vida interrupted firmly, cutting her sister off mid-sentence.

Freya turned, looking annoyed. Vida simply stared back, an unspoken command passing between them. A moment of silent challenge, then Freya turned back to me with a theatrical sigh and a shrug. "My sister has ordered," she said, leaning closer and pretending to whisper, though Vida could clearly hear, "so we must obey. We can talk more tomorrow? In peace? What do you think?"

"Hmm... okay..." I managed a weak smile, grateful for Vida's intervention this time.

"Hey," Vida said sharply, her gaze sweeping over all of us. "I said enough talking. Sleep now."

We obeyed. Everyone found their sleeping spots – Vida and Freya near the house wall, me a little distance away across the dying fire, the three warriors taking turns on watch.

I lay wrapped in my cloak, staring up at the stars through the gaps in the branches. Sleep felt far away. Maybe because I'd slept for seven days straight? Everyone called it unconsciousness, fainting... but maybe it *was* just sleep? If so, why sleep now?

Eventually, exhaustion claimed me. And I dreamed.

Darkness. The cold, damp smell of the cave. I walked alone down a long, twisting corridor, my sword heavy in my hand. Reaching the central cavern, the huge, monstrous beast was there, waiting. The fight replayed itself – the dodging, the terror, Vida's intervention, her fall... then my final, desperate lunge, driving my sword deep into its gaping mouth, silencing its roar forever as it collapsed into the shadows.

Then, from a dark corner of the dream-cave, a figure emerged. Tall, broad-shouldered, radiating power. Golden hair, golden beard, eyes as blue and piercing as a winter sky. He raised his right hand. In it, nestled against his palm, pulsed an object, glowing with a soft, internal light. His sharp gaze fixed on me, pinning me where I stood beside the dead beast. His voice echoed, deep and commanding: "Stay down and take it. Take it!"

An unseen force seemed to press me down. I found myself kneeling, trembling, reaching out towards the glowing object, compelled to obey...

Then, another voice, soft, urgent, filled with love and fear, whispered right beside my ear – *Mother's* voice. "Don't take it, my son. Don't go there. It is not for you..."

The conflict tore at me – the command, the warning... My mother... I cried out her name, tears suddenly streaming down my face in the dream... and woke with a gasp, my heart pounding violently against my ribs.

I sat bolt upright, looking around wildly. The pre-dawn chill hung heavy in the air. The campfire was just dying embers. Vida and Freya slept soundly nearby, as did Gunnar and Adhril. Svenar sat leaning against a tree, on watch, his eyes reflecting the faint glow of the coals. He saw me stir and lifted his chin in a silent greeting.

The dream... it clung to me, vivid and disturbing. That golden-haired man... the glowing thing... Mom's warning... What did it mean? Fear and a profound sadness churned inside me.

Svenar nodded towards the waterskin beside me. I gratefully took a long drink of the cool water. "Bad dreams?" he rumbled softly, his voice like shifting rocks. "Don't let them eat you up, boy. Spoil the morning."

I managed a shaky laugh, wiping sweat from my brow despite the chill. "You, Svenar? Giving advice? I thought your only skill was scaring people into silence."

He offered a rare, fleeting grin, showing surprisingly white teeth in his thick brown beard. He took a sip from his own skin. "Even silent rocks have heard whispers on the wind." He paused, looking out towards the first faint hint of light in the eastern sky. "The rivers in the south... they are not as beautiful as the poets claim, you know." His voice turned unexpectedly somber. "That journey we took... down south... I had many nightmares after. Still do sometimes. Like... like the land itself haunted me. Cannot remember the shapes I saw after waking, but the *feeling*... it lingers." He shook his massive head. "Maybe... maybe because I do not yet deserve it."

"What don't you deserve?" I asked, intrigued by this glimpse into the stoic warrior's mind.

"Valahar," he stated simply. "Odaran's feast hall. Not yet."

I frowned. "You don't deserve to die? Go to the warrior's afterlife?"

He looked at me then, his gaze deep, ancient. "Only those who have truly slain their enemies deserve that rest."

"And... who are your enemies, Svenar?"

"All those I hate," he growled softly. "All those who deserve to die by my hand."

"Okay..." I said slowly. "Can you be more specific? The Logenirs?"

"Yes," he spat the name out. "They are one. The main ones."

I nodded. "I'm sorry, Svenar, but that sounds... strange. You only deserve death after you kill people who you think deserve death? Say that happens, doesn't that mean you *both* deserve... death? Will you continue the fight in Valahar, then, in front of the gods?"

He actually chuckled, a low rumble. "The true battle never ends, boy. Not here, not there. Not ever."

"That sounds crazy, honestly," I admitted.

"What?"

"Well," I sighed. His fatalistic warrior code felt alien, bleak. "For me... I need to know where things end. How they end. Like... this journey we're on now... it *must* have an end."

"Perhaps you expect too much from life, boy," he replied, turning back to watch the lightening sky.

"Really?"

"Everything repeats," the philosophical giant stated. "No true beginning, no true end. A fighter lives, fights, dies... then fights again in the halls beyond. It is the way."

"Hey, you two!" Freya's cheerful voice cut through the pre-dawn gloom. She was sitting up now, rubbing sleep from her eyes, Vida stirring beside her. "What deep secrets are you discussing so early? Are you drunk already?"

Svenar just grunted, offering no reply.

"Svenar is teaching me the true values of Hualeg life," I grinned back at Freya, the disturbing dream and Svenar's grim words already starting to fade slightly in her bright presence. "Very interesting. And speaking of interesting things, Freya... before we start rowing later, I want to ask you something important."

"Sure!" she replied brightly, instantly awake now. "Or maybe *I* can tell *you* about some other life values? Ones I am sure you will enjoy much more?" She laughed, her eyes sparkling mischievously.

Beside her, Vida just frowned.

34

The Shaman's Hut

We ate breakfast quickly – dried meat, hard bread, washed down with cold water – the usual quiet efficiency of Vida's camp routine. Then, just as I finished rinsing my bowl in the river, Freya bounced over, her energy a stark contrast to the quiet watchfulness of Vida and the stoic silence of the warriors packing the boat.

"William!" she grinned, her eyes sparkling. "Come, let's walk a little." She pulled me away from the others towards the edge of the dense forest lining the riverbank.

I hesitated. "Where? We need to get ready to leave." Disappearing into the woods alone with her... I glanced back instinctively towards Vida, who was supervising Gunnar securing supplies in the boat.

"Just over here," Freya insisted brightly, tugging my arm again, clearly oblivious or indifferent to my reluctance. "Just by the trees. More private!"

With a sigh and a feeling of mild irritation mixed with curiosity, I let her lead me the twenty paces or so into the dappled shade beneath the first line of ancient pines, just out of direct sight and easy earshot of the others by the boat.

She turned to face me, hands on her hips, grinning expectantly. "Well? We are safe here. No serious warriors listening." She winked. "You can ask now. Your important question?"

Right. My question. I pushed aside the awkwardness of the situation she'd created and focused on the reason I'd wanted to talk to her in the first place. I paused, trying to find the right words, then began, "You said... you can sometimes see things? In dreams?"

She tapped her chin, mock-thoughtful. "Sometimes. Glimpses. Something like that."

"Well," I took a breath, the images vivid again. "I had a dream last night. It felt... strange."

I told her – not all, but enough. The dark cave, fighting the beast, killing it by thrusting my sword into its mouth, the sudden appearance of a golden-haired man with the glowing object, his commanding voice echoing 'Stay down and take it.', my compulsion to kneel, and then a woman's warning, 'Don't take it' before I woke up. Then I finished, feeling foolish laying out a mere dream. "But... it probably doesn't mean anything, right?"

"You don't think it's important?" Freya stared at me, her playful manner gone, replaced by intense seriousness.

"I... I'm not sure."

"If it wasn't important, you wouldn't feel the need to tell me," she stated confidently. She smiled faintly. "You sense something, and you want to know what it means."

"Do *you* know what it means?" I asked.

She shook her head. "It was *your* dream, William. Only you hold the true key. I can only guess... maybe you are being offered power? Or guidance? Or perhaps you wish for connection... to the man you saw?"

"I don't wish for anything," I objected. "Except maybe answers."

Freya grimaced playfully. "Everyone wants *something*."

"Maybe," I conceded. "But the man... I don't know him, yet he felt... familiar. Close."

"Why?"

"I don't know."

"Maybe," she offered again, her tone thoughtful, "because he *is* close to you, but you do not know him yet."

"How?"

She laughed suddenly. "I am just talking! Trying to make you think!"

I laughed too, relieved. "You can't help trying."

"Hey, what I said *is* important!" she insisted, poking my arm. "Think about the *feelings*! You will understand later! Another value of life!"

"Uh. Okay..."

"So," she tilted her head, "was that it? Or is there anything else you wanted to ask me while we're alone?"

"I don't think so," I grinned, starting to edge back towards the river.

"Wow, disappointing," she grumbled dramatically. "And here I thought you lured me into the woods for something *really* important."

"*You* dragged *me* here!" I protested. "What did you *expect* me to ask?"

She struck her pose again, eyelashes fluttering. "Something like, 'Freya, will you marry me?'"

I froze again. Still joking? Or... testing me? My face felt hot. "It's... getting late in the morning," I stammered, turning decisively this time. "Vida will be impatient. We should go." I started walking quickly back towards the boat.

"Coward," she called softly behind me, mischief back in her voice.

"Yeah, well, who wouldn't?" I retorted over my shoulder, forcing a laugh. "Your sister might make me row all day without rest if we delay too long!"

"No!" she laughed, easily catching up. "Coward because you don't have the courage to say what you truly want!"

I just shook my head, pointedly ignoring that comment, and quickened my pace towards the camp. Freya's laughter followed me. When we reached the clearing, Vida looked up from cleaning her sword, her gaze sharp and questioning as she took in Freya's lingering amusement and my likely flushed face. Thankfully, she said nothing.

We packed up quickly and continued our journey along the river, heading west now along the main branch. The landscape felt subtly different here, less wild perhaps. By noon the next day, we rounded a bend, and I saw it – another familiar sight. A small, sturdy wooden house nestled near the bank, a thin curl of smoke rising from its chimney. Bullock's house.

A wave of warmth spread through me. The old man had been kind, offered friendship when I had none. "Vida," I said, "can we stop here? Just for a moment?"

She looked towards the cabin, then at me, hesitation clear on her face. Doing anything unplanned seemed to go against her nature.

"He's a friend," I explained quickly. "An old man who lives alone. I passed his house on my way east... it's only polite to greet him now I pass again. We won't stay long."

She considered it, then gave a curt nod. "Briefly."

As I stepped out onto the bank, Vida stood up too. "I will come with you."

"No need," I objected. "Bullock... he might be wary of strangers, especially Hualeg."

"He need not fear *me*," she stated flatly, ignoring Freya's slight frown from the boat. "And I wish to know who this southern friend is." She clearly didn't trust me entirely yet. Shrugging, I led the way to the door, Vida following silently behind me.

I knocked. After a moment, the door creaked open, revealing Bullock's weathered face. His eyes widened slightly in surprise seeing me, perhaps even a little fear seeing Vida behind me, but then a genuine smile spread across his face.

"You!" he exclaimed warmly. "Lad! Come in, come in! Forgive the mess..."

"Thank you, Bullock, but we can't stay," I said quickly. "Just passing through again. Came from the eastern mountains," I gestured vaguely, "heading further north now. Saw your smoke, had to stop and greet you."

Bullock nodded, his gaze shifting curiously to Vida.

"This is Vida," I introduced her quickly. "She travels with me. You have nothing to fear, sir," I added reassuringly, "she is Hualeg, yes, but from a good tribe."

"The good ones..." Bullock began, his eyes twinkling, "like..."

"Like me," I interrupted smoothly, laughing, cutting him off before he could say 'like your father was'. I didn't want Vida piecing things together yet.

Bullock caught my meaning instantly and just nodded again, though his eyes held a spark of amusement. "So," he asked, changing the subject, "did you find what you were looking for? Over there in the east?"

Did I? I thought of the empty house, the unanswered questions. "More or less," I replied vaguely. "There was... some trouble back in Thaluk first, but that's settled now. Then I helped Vida hunt a dangerous beast in the mountains. That is done too."

He nodded slowly. "So, all is well then? Good. Glad to hear it. May you find what you truly seek, lad, whether it's in the east, or perhaps later, further north."

I grimaced slightly. "Honestly, Bullock, I'd rather just be heading south."

"Ah," he chuckled softly. "Well, sometimes a man finds out what he truly *wants* isn't always what he truly *needs*. You'll figure it out, son." He clapped me briefly on the shoulder. "Now, forgive my asking again, but more importantly... how much of my potent brew do you need this time? A long journey to the mountains and back... supplies must be low." His eyes twinkled playfully.

I laughed, relieved the awkward moment had passed. "Two bottles, if you can spare them? I can pay, of course."

"Nonsense, lad! Two bottles are a gift between friends!" he declared. "Told you I made too much! Need someone to share it with!"

"Then make it five bottles total," I countered, pulling out the few southern coins I still carried, "so I can properly pay you for the other three."

He eventually agreed, bustling inside and returning with five clay bottles stoppered with wax. He refused payment for two but accepted coin for the other three. "Got five more aging nicely," he mentioned. "If you want them..."

"Keep those, sir," I smiled, stowing the bottles carefully in my pack. "Perhaps we can share them when I return this way."

We said our goodbyes, and Vida and I returned to the boat. We continued our journey, rowing hard. That night, we reached the place where the river split – the mighty Ordelahr, Vida called it. Left led south, back towards Thaluk, towards the life I knew. If we turned that way, I could likely be back within a day or two. Morrin would welcome me, I was sure. But our path lay right, north, up a branch of the river I didn't recognize, deeper into Hualeg lands.

Fear, cold and familiar, returned as we turned north. My mother's warning – *never go to the land of the northerners, your father's land* – echoed in my mind. But Vida had assured me the shaman's house wasn't actually *in* Vallanir territory itself, just nearby. Maybe... maybe this didn't count as truly breaking my promise to Mom? I hoped so.

For days we rowed north, resting eight or ten hours each night, rowing from dawn till dusk. The river twisted and turned, sometimes wide and slow, sometimes narrow and fast, forcing us to navigate carefully around hidden rocks. On the seventh day after leaving Bullock's, the terrain changed again. The river widened into a broad, sunlit expanse, the banks rockier, the dense forest thinning out, replaced by larger, more scattered trees. It felt brighter, more open.

"Are we out of the deep forest?" I asked Vida, squinting against the sunlight. "Are we near Hualeg villages now?"

She shook her head, her eyes scanning the banks warily. "Still forest land. But different. More open. More dangerous."

"Dangerous?"

"Now we must be more careful," she stated grimly. "Ahead lies another fork. The right branch continues north towards Vallanir lands. The left branch leads west, towards Logenir territory, and the other western tribes." Her hand rested near her sword hilt. "The Logenir often post observers here. If they see us..."

"After we destroyed Malagar's war party near Thaluk," I recalled, "might they be waiting for you here for revenge?"

Vida shook her head again, though her vigilance didn't lessen. "Unlikely they'd risk open war here. Vallanir usually posts observers too. Each side watches the other. If Logenir gathered force, we would know, counter them. But," she added darkly, "lone boats... carelessness... they might still try something if they think they can get away with it. Especially if they recognized *you*."

"Great." Just what I needed. "Where is this shaman's house then?"

"Not far past the fork," she replied. She turned to the warriors. "Be alert.

But maintain speed. We must reach the hut before dark."

We rowed on, tension palpable now. Eyes scanned the banks, searching the shadows between the large tree trunks. Perfect hiding spots for archers. Did Hualegs use bows often? I hadn't seen any in the fights near Thaluk, but as Vida said, that situation was different. This felt much more precarious.

We reached the fork and turned right, heading deeper into the territory bordering Vallanir lands. Suddenly, Freya, sitting near the prow, hissed softly, pointing subtly towards the left bank we were leaving behind. Everyone tensed, shields ready, scanning the trees. I thought I glimpsed movement, a shadow detaching itself from a large oak, but then it was gone. We continued rowing hard, putting distance between us and the fork. Nothing happened. Maybe just a lone Logenir scout, deciding not to risk engaging our larger party.

Soon after, Vida steered the boat towards the right bank again. The terrain here was hilly, the trees growing close together again, casting the area in premature twilight. "We stop here," she announced, standing and preparing to jump ashore. "The wisewoman's hut is up on that hill. Hidden. Hard to find after dark, so we must hurry."

"We're all going?" I asked, still hesitant about leaving the relative safety of the river.

Vida shook her head, already outlining the plan. "This riverbank is too exposed at night. If we all go up, the boat might be found, destroyed. Stranding us. If only some go up, those left guarding the boat here would be easy targets for ambush." She looked decisive. "We cannot stay here. The best option is this: William and I will go up the hill now to find the shaman. Svenar, Gunnar, Adhril – you and Freya take the boat, return to Vallanir."

"Wait a minute!" Freya protested instantly, jumping up. "Why only you two go up? Why can't *I* come?"

"Freya," Vida's voice was firm, leaving no room for argument. "If there is trouble on the hill, if William and I must fight, how could we protect you as well? You go with the warriors. Go home. If needed, you can bring more help. That is the best way you can support us now." Seeing Freya open her mouth to argue again, Vida added coolly, "Remember your promise, sister, when you asked to join this journey. I am the leader here."

I watched the silent battle of wills between them. Freya looked mutinous, but Vida's stern gaze, her reminder of rank and promises, clearly won. Freya subsided, looking thoroughly annoyed, but she turned back towards the boat. Without another word, she and the three warriors pushed off, heading north.

Vida turned and started climbing the steep hill without looking back. I scrambled after her, trying to keep up with her brisk, ground-eating pace. We moved quickly, silently, between the trees. Somewhere nearby, I could hear the rush of falling water – another stream, not the main river.

Just as the last rays of sun disappeared below the horizon, we reached it. Nestled in a small, hidden clearing near the crest of the hill stood a modest wooden hut. It was small, maybe the size of Bullock's place, blending almost perfectly with the surrounding forest. Strange white symbols were painted on the trunks of the trees encircling the clearing – wards against spirits, perhaps? Or just trail markers?

The place felt utterly deserted. No smoke from the chimney, the door and shutters tightly closed. Vida looked around, scanning the trees, then walked to the door and knocked several times. Silence. She tried the latch; the door swung open, unlocked. She peered inside, then entered. I waited outside, feeling increasingly uneasy.

She reappeared a moment later. "She is not here."

"Where could she be?"

"Some belongings remain. Food stores seem recent." Vida sounded thoughtful. "Perhaps just gone gathering herbs, delayed. We will have to wait." She gestured for me to come inside. "You will not like the cold out here when night falls fully."

I didn't feel cold yet, sheltered by the trees, but she was probably right. I ducked through the low doorway into the hut.

It was even smaller inside than I expected – just one main room, maybe four paces by six. Cabinets lined the walls, filled with small clay pots, bundles of dried herbs, strange-looking tools. A short, square table stood near the door, no chairs. At the back was a stone fireplace, cold now, with sleeping mats and blankets neatly rolled beside it.

Vida lit a single candle from her pouch, placing it on top of a cabinet, casting flickering shadows around the small space. The air immediately felt warmer, cozier. "I hope Helga does not mind me using her candle," Vida murmured, sitting cross-legged on the floor behind the low table.

She took out her waterskin, pouring some into two simple wooden mugs she found on a shelf. We had eaten on the boat earlier, so this felt less like a meal, more like... waiting. I sat down opposite her, taking the offered mug.

"Why not light the fire?" I asked, gesturing towards the hearth.

"Smoke," she replied curtly. "Can be seen for miles from the chimney. The Logenir scouts do not know this place is here, but smoke might draw unwanted attention."

That made sense. Embarrassingly obvious, really. I nodded, feeling slightly foolish for not thinking of it. We drank in silence for a while, the only sounds the faint sighing of the wind outside and the crackle of the candlewick. The silence stretched, growing awkward. I wanted to ask her things – about this place, the shaman, why *I* needed examining – but couldn't find the right words.

Finally, feeling drowsy from the long day's rowing and the relative warmth, I asked, breaking the quiet, "Will... will the shaman return tonight, do you think?"

"If Helga does not come tonight, then hopefully tomorrow," Vida replied, looking at me across the table, her expression unreadable in the dim light. She took a deep breath, then said quietly, "William... I am sorry."

I blinked, surprised. "What? Sorry for what?"

"For... bringing you here. For all you have endured because of my quest..."

I shrugged, uncomfortable with her apology. "I'm fine, Vida. Truly." Besides, much of it was my own doing.

"I have not... told you everything I know," she admitted, her gaze dropping to her mug.

My heart gave a slight jump. Was she finally going to explain? "Why not?" I tried to keep my voice casual, not wanting to spook her. "I'm happy to listen whenever you want to talk. Seriously. You can trust me, Vida. I hope you know that. I consider you my friend."

She looked up, considering my words. "I could not have said this with Freya and the others present. They... they would find it difficult to understand. Or perhaps, to believe."

This sounded important. Confidential. "They couldn't understand, but *I* can?"

"Yes," she said simply, looking doubtful again herself. "Because you... you have experienced it."

Experienced *what*? The memory loss? The strange fluency? The dream? "Alright," I urged gently, leaning forward slightly, trying not to seem too eager. "Then please, explain. Before I die of curiosity!"

She looked like she was about to speak, opened her mouth slightly, then hesitated, shaking her head. "Later," she decided firmly. "When we meet the wisewoman. She can explain things better than I."

"Okay," I sighed, slumping back, trying to hide my intense disappointment. "Now I'm dead." I managed a weak grin.

"Sorry," she murmured again.

"Hey, stop that," I protested gently. "Stop apologizing. It makes my skin crawl." I forced another grin. "Don't worry about it. I can wait. Waited seven days unconscious, what's one more day awake, right? Even if I have to wait my whole life for you to explain, that's okay!" I laughed, trying to lighten the mood. "Honestly, Vida, just knowing you *intend* to talk eventually makes me happy. Come on, let's have another drink."

"You have had enough," she countered, though without real heat.

I laughed again. "You think I'm drunk? On water? This is nothing!"

"Perhaps," she conceded, a tiny smile touching her lips for a second. "But you are tired. You should sleep."

"What about you?" I yawned, stretching my aching arms.

"I will wait a while longer. Perhaps she will return soon." She looked towards the door. "I will wake you later, if you wish to take a watch."

"Okay," I agreed readily. "But don't wait too long. You need rest too, Vida."

Nodding my thanks, I walked over to the sleeping mats near the cold hearth, pulled a rough blanket over myself, and lay down. Exhaustion washed over me instantly. Letting go of all the questions, the confusion, the lingering strangeness of the dream, I closed my eyes and fell immediately into a deep, dreamless sleep.

35

A Way Out

I drifted awake sometime deep in the night, instantly aware of two things: the profound darkness inside the shaman's hut, and a steady warmth pressed against my left side. Holding my breath, not daring to move, I realized it was Vida's back against my arm. She slept deeply, her breathing even and peaceful beside me on the narrow sleeping mat.

My first instinct was to ease away, carefully, so as not to wake or embarrass her when morning came. But then I hesitated. Why should *I* move? I hadn't sought this closeness. If she had shifted towards me in her sleep, it was likely just for warmth against the mountain chill. We weren't doing anything wrong. No one else was here to misinterpret it. Let her sleep. Trying to ignore the disconcerting intimacy of her presence, the faint scent of pine and something uniquely *her* in the darkness, I closed my eyes again, seeking sleep myself.

It was useless, of course. Sleep remained stubbornly out of reach, my mind too aware of the warrior woman sleeping soundly less than an arm's length away. Finally, I opened my eyes again, scanning the pitch-black room. Vida must have extinguished the single candle before she lay down, likely conserving it. Good sense, but it made the small hut feel colder, darker.

Was it just the cold that made her edge closer? She was Hualeg, a northerner like Svenar and the others. Surely she was more accustomed to this chill than I was? And why hadn't she woken me for a watch, as she'd suggested? Vida always seemed so disciplined, so focused on duty. Did she deem this hidden hut completely safe? Or had she looked at me, finally succumbing to sleep after days of exhaustion and stress, and felt... reluctant to disturb me? Many possibilities. Beneath the warrior's hardness, maybe she was just... a normal girl, sometimes unpredictable.

Wait... what is that smell?

A faint, unfamiliar scent drifted through the darkness. Sweet, slightly cloying. Hadn't noticed it before falling asleep. Was it one of the shaman's herbs? A leaking potion maybe? It seemed to be growing stronger, almost pungent.

And... was that a sound? Beyond the wind sighing outside? I strained my ears, filtering out the night noises... yes. Whispers. Just outside the hut's thin wooden walls.

"How many inside?" a low voice asked. Hualeg tongue.

"Two," another voice replied. *"Sound asleep. Like babes."*

My blood ran cold.

"The girl?" the first voice pressed.

"Yes. And another. A southerner, by the look of him earlier. Don't know him. When will we get a chance like this again?"

"The door?"

"Barred inside. Simple log bar. Easy work from out here."

"Good. Tell the others. Get ready."

Bastards! My body went rigid. Who were they? Logenir scouts, tracking us somehow? Or someone else? What did they want?

My hand moved slowly, silently, finding the reassuring grip of my sword beside my sleeping mat. Don't move yet. Don't give yourself away. They were still outside, preparing. Better to wait until they came *in*. Surprise them in the confined space. Gods, I hoped that was the right decision. One mistake now...

But Vida? Should I wake her? She was still sleeping deeply beside me, likely breathing in that sweet, heavy scent... *A potion?* To keep us unconscious? That explained why they weren't worried about noise. And why Vida hadn't woken me.

Footsteps scraped just outside the door. A faint scratching sound, then a metallic click. In the utter darkness, I could just make out the shape of the heavy wooden bar securing the door from inside... lifting upwards, impossibly. Pulled by a wire threaded through a crack? It lifted clear, then fell to the floorboards with a dull *thud*.

The intruders didn't hesitate. They clearly believed us incapacitated by the potion – which, somehow, hadn't fully affected me. Maybe my position near the floor, maybe sheer luck...

The door creaked open, letting in a gust of frigid night air and faint starlight. I kept my breathing even, feigning sleep, watching through slitted eyes. Two figures slipped inside. One carried a sword, moonlight glinting briefly on the blade. The other held a coil of thick rope. They moved towards the sleeping mats. Towards Vida. Towards me. Behind them, a third figure filled the doorway, holding aloft a flickering torch, casting dancing, monstrous shadows within the small hut.

"*Tie up the girl,*" the torchbearer ordered softly in Hualeg. "*Kill the other one.*"

Okay. Enough waiting.

With a silent surge of adrenaline, I pushed myself up from the mat, sword already in hand, lunging forward in the same motion. The man with the sword barely had time to register my movement before the tip of my blade punched deep into his stomach. His eyes went wide with shock and agony; his own sword clattered uselessly to the floor. The man beside him, the one with the rope, let out a sharp scream of alarm, shattering the silence.

I ripped my sword free from the first man's gut and swung it viciously in a low arc, slicing deep into the second man's side as he fumbled for a weapon. Both men collapsed, groaning, onto the floor near Vida's sleeping form.

I leaped over them just as the third man at the door reacted, dropping the torch – which immediately set the dry floor rushes alight – and grabbing for the sword at his hip. Too slow. I cleared the small table in a single bound, my sword thrusting forward, plunging straight into his exposed neck. He gurgled, collapsing in the doorway.

More screams erupted from *outside* the hut now. How many more were there? Gods, was I supposed to fight them all *here*? This tiny hut was a deathtrap, rapidly filling with smoke from the spreading fire. Terrible decision.

I spun around, crouching beside Vida, shaking her shoulder urgently. "Vida! Wake up! Vida!"

I muttered an apology under my breath and slapped her cheek, hard. She stirred, moaning, eyes still closed, trying to turn away. I grabbed one of the waterskins from the table – still half full – and poured the cold water directly onto her face.

That worked. She gasped, sputtering, her eyes flying open, filled with shock and panic. She winced immediately, pressing both hands to her head. "What...? Aaarrggh! My head..." She seemed dizzy, disoriented. Drugged by the scent?

"Vida!" I shook her again, trying to cut through the fog. "Listen! Attackers! We have to get out! Now!"

Her eyes widened further, but she still looked pained, confused.

"The hut's on fire!" I pointed towards the flames now licking greedily up the wooden wall near the door. "Come on! Move!"

I hauled her upright. She let me pull her, weak and unsteady on her feet, but seemed to faint again, slumping against me. I quickly grabbed her travel bag, slung it over my own shoulder, checked her sword was secure at her hip, then half-lifted, half-dragged her towards the doorway.

"Okay..." she gasped, rallying slightly, leaning heavily on me. "Wait... How many... outside?"

"I don't know! But we..." Before I could finish, another shadow lunged through the smoke-filled doorway.

I let go of Vida momentarily, shoving her back towards the relative safety of the hut's interior, and met the attacker's charge. A sword swung towards my neck. I ducked low, twisting, bringing my own sword up in a parrying block that scraped harshly against his blade. He stumbled back from the force of the block. I pressed forward instantly, finding an opening, my sword biting deep into his gut. He collapsed with a strangled cry.

I spun, scanning the darkness outside the burning hut. One warrior stood near a large tree about ten paces away, watching warily. Three more were emerging from the forest edge, spreading out, clearly intending to surround me. More could be lurking in the shadows.

No time for careful tactics. No escape back through the burning hut. I had to attack first, break their cordon. I leaped towards the nearest enemy on my left. He was ready, blocking my initial strike. From the right, another closed in. I whirled, my sword a flashing arc in the firelight, clanging against both their blades, forcing them back a step.

I sensed the warrior on my right was weaker, less confident. Feinting left, I dodged his clumsy swing, jumped inside his guard, and brought my sword down hard from above. He tried to block, failed. My blade sliced through his shoulder, biting deep into his collarbone. He screamed and fell.

Roaring a challenge, ignoring the pain in my own bruised body, I turned on the remaining two. They looked startled, frightened now, backing away into the shadows. Then, they turned and bolted, disappearing back into the dense forest.

I started to give chase, wanting to capture one, get answers, but then I heard Vida's weak voice from the doorway of the now fiercely burning hut.

"William..." She stood swaying, holding her head, her face pale in the flickering firelight. She had her bag slung over her shoulder, her sword at her hip. She winced, clearly still in pain. "We... have to go..."

"Let me go after them," I argued, glancing towards the forest where the attackers had vanished. "Just grab one! Find out who they are!"

Vida shook her head vehemently, though the movement clearly cost her. "Don't. Foolish. They must have... more friends... waiting. Near the river, maybe. Or... maybe this was bait. Lure you out." She stumbled forward, pointing towards the back of the burning cabin, away from the main path down the hill. "There... a path... back here. Helga... she once said... our way out... if danger comes..."

Trust her. I had to trust her. Nodding, I rushed back to her side, supporting her staggering steps as we circled around the burning hut into the dark forest behind it. The undergrowth was thick here, tangled, scratching at us as we pushed through. Vida, despite her dizziness and pain, seemed certain of the direction, breaking through thickets, climbing over fallen logs, leading us onto higher ground.

I wasn't sure at first, using my sword to hack at obstructing branches, clearing the way for her limping steps. But after a while, the bushes thinned, the trees grew sparser. We emerged onto a more open, rocky plain. The night sky was visible again above us. It looked like we'd reached the edge of a steep drop, a cliff maybe. I could hear the distant rush of a waterfall somewhere below in the darkness. Then, another sound drifted up on the wind – faint but unmistakable. Dogs barking. They were tracking us.

Vida didn't hesitate. She ran towards the cliff edge, grabbed onto the thick branch of an overhanging tree, and swung herself down onto a narrow ledge barely visible below.

"Vida! Where are you going?" I called out, peering down into the darkness. "Down the cliff? It looks dangerous!" How deep was the drop?

Just then, the first drops of cold rain began to fall, quickly turning into a downpour. The rocks underfoot grew slick. Following Vida down that narrow ledge in the dark and driving rain... it felt suicidal. But the barking dogs sounded closer now. We had no choice.

Taking a deep breath, I followed her over the edge, finding precarious handholds and footholds on the wet stone wall, the darkness plunging away to my right. The rain plastered my hair to my face, making the rocks even more treacherous. We descended slowly, carefully, the roar of the waterfall below growing louder, masking any sounds of pursuit.

So far, so good. We'd made it maybe halfway down the cliff face. The rain seemed to be easing the dogs off our scent. I felt a brief moment of calm, a flicker of hope that we might actually escape this.

Then, the patch of ground beneath my right foot, which had seemed solid rock, suddenly crumbled. It felt soft, yielding. Before I could react, before I could shift my weight, my footing vanished completely. My body scraped against the rock face as I slid downwards uncontrollably, plunging into the darkness below.

36

Behind the Waterfall

Darkness... then pain, a dull, throbbing ache centered behind my eyes. I groaned, trying to shift, feeling solid, dry rock beneath me. Dry? But I remembered... falling. The rain-slicked cliff face, the ground crumbling beneath my feet, the terrifying plunge into darkness... then hitting water? Yes, cold water. I must have hit my head on the way down, knocked myself out. Lucky it wasn't rocks below...

Slowly, cautiously, I opened my eyes again. Still dark, but not completely. Faint light filtered through a shimmering curtain of falling water just nearby, illuminating a small cave space. Hidden behind a waterfall. Safe, for now. My body lay on a large, flat rock, shielded from the spray by another wall of stone. A small, quiet stream trickled past the edge of the rock ledge deeper into the cave's recesses.

Then I saw her. Not far to my left, Vida sat with her back partially towards me, wringing out her wet tunic. Her long yellow hair, usually tightly braided, was loose, cascading down her bare shoulders and back.

My breath caught sharply in my throat before I could stop it, an involuntary gasp in the quiet cave.

And that small sound, or perhaps just the shift in the air, made Vida freeze for an instant. Slowly, she turned her head, her turquoise eyes locking onto mine across the dim space. She knew I was awake. She knew I'd likely seen her state of undress.

Heat flooded my face. Mortified, I quickly shut my eyes again, whispering desperately, idiotically, "I didn't see your body! I didn't see anything!"

"Shut up!" Vida's sharp retort cut through the roar of the waterfall. She sounded more annoyed by my foolish outburst than embarrassed.

"Sorry..." I mumbled, keeping my eyes firmly closed.

"If you are awake, just open your eyes," she sighed, sounding weary now. "No one forbids it."

Alright, if it's allowed... I thought, feeling immensely foolish. Slowly, cautiously, I opened my eyes again. Relief washed over me – she was facing me now, pulling her damp tunic back over her head, settling it into place.

Her next command, however, startled me. "Take off your clothes."

"W-what?" I stammered, completely bewildered.

"Your shirt," she clarified impatiently, gesturing towards my own soaked and muddy tunic. "Wring it out until it is drier. Do you wish to freeze all night in wet clothes?"

Oh. Right. Practical. Of course. Feeling incredibly stupid, I mumbled an apology and sat up fully. My head swam for a second from the lingering ache, but otherwise, the fall didn't seem to have broken anything major. I pulled off my tunic and undershirt, rolling them tightly, wringing out surprising amounts of cold river water onto the rock floor. Vida watched me impassively, making no move to look away, which only increased my awkwardness.

I cleared my throat, needing to break the silence. "So... we're safe here?"

She was quiet for a moment, staring towards the curtain of water. "Yes. So far," she replied finally. "The dogs... their barking faded during the rain. They do not know we fell, or where we landed. But," she added grimly, "when it grows light, when the rain stops fully, they will search again. Mornir's men. They will find the cliff edge where we went down. We should hide here a while longer."

"How long?" I asked, dread creeping in.

"Until Freya returns with Svenar and the others. A day, perhaps two."

"A day or two?" I stared at her, shocked. "Stuck *here*? What are we supposed to eat?"

Vida just shrugged, unconcerned. "We will see. Fish from the stream, perhaps. You do not mind waiting, do you?"

"Well..." A strange impulse made me grin despite the situation. "If you mean, do I mind being trapped alone in a hidden cave behind a waterfall with you for a day or two... then of course I don't mind." It was a stupid joke, meant only to lighten the heavy mood, maybe provoke a reaction other than her usual sternness.

She looked at me, a flicker of surprise in her eyes, then replied evenly, "Yes. Why not?"

I laughed, startled by her unexpected agreement. What did *that* mean?

"But Freya," Vida added, her expression turning serious again, "if she finds out we were... together like this... alone... she might be angry."

"Angry? Why?"

"Do you truly not know what she wants from you, William?"

I frowned, confused. "What are you talking about?"

"She wants you to be her husband," Vida stated bluntly. "She thinks you *should* be her husband."

My mind reeled. Freya? Wanted to marry me? I remembered her playful teasing – *"Something like, 'Freya, will you marry me?'"* – but I'd dismissed it as just... Freya being Freya. "Wait a minute," I stammered. "That... that's not funny, Vida. Your jokes aren't funny."

"You think I am joking?" she asked, her gaze steady, serious.

I looked at her face, searching for any hint of humor, finding none. Suspicion warred with disbelief. "Yes... because... it feels strange. Hearing this from *you*. You don't usually... talk like this."

"I am telling you what I know. What Freya feels. What she believes is her right."

"Her *right*? This is serious? But... how old is she? Fifteen? She must be younger than me!"

"Old enough to marry, by Hualeg custom," Vida replied flatly.

"Marriage isn't just about age!" I protested.

"I will not comment on that," Vida said coolly. "You have your southern views. I merely explain *our* ways. It is not a strange matter for us. You... took

Freya from the riverbank after the fight where our companions died. You carried her away from her kin, her protectors."

My jaw dropped. *So, this is really serious.*

"In our country," Vida continued relentlessly, "our women hold positions of respect. Especially those of noble blood, like my sister. If a man dares to do what you did – taking a highborn girl away, even if you intended no harm – that man owes the woman a debt. She now has the right to demand recompense. She could demand your arrest, or even your death." Vida paused, letting the weight sink in. "But you are lucky. Freya... likes you. Therefore, she will ask you to marry her instead. It is her right to claim you. If you refuse... it is a grave insult. To her, to our family, to the Vallanir. An insult that could still end with your death."

Panic seized me. Not fear of dying – I could run, fight – but fear of this... this cultural trap. They thought I'd kidnapped Freya? That I *owed* her marriage?

"Listen!" I argued desperately. "I already apologized! For capturing her! And she forgave me! We talked about it! Why does marriage suddenly come into it now? Marriage shouldn't be forced! Fine, maybe that's your tradition here, but I'm from the south! Those rules don't apply to me!"

"The rules apply to those who interact with our people, southerner. Especially within Hualeg lands."

"But I don't have to follow them! I don't have to go back to your village with her!"

"So you will run away?" Vida's voice was dangerously quiet now. "Go back south alone? And in doing so, insult Freya, shame her, in front of everyone?"

"I wasn't going to insult her at all!" I protested hotly.

Vida just looked at me, waiting. "Then what *are* you going to do, William?"

I stared back, speechless. Trapped. Everything I'd done, every choice made since meeting Vida and Freya... it felt impossibly complicated now. I looked down at my hands, then glanced miserably back at Vida.

"Do you... have any suggestions?" I asked finally, hating the feeling of helplessness.

"No one can force you to marry," Vida replied, her tone softening slightly. "Honestly, William, who *is* strong enough to force you to do anything? No one. You are too strong." A faint, almost imperceptible smile touched her lips. "But... in Hualeg... a man of honor does not simply run from responsibility. When accused, he faces it. Defends himself. Apologizes if wrong. And speaks what is truly in his heart." She met my eyes again. "If you are not ready to be Freya's husband, if you do not desire it, then you must tell her so. Explain your reasons plainly. Hope she understands, accepts your wish, and releases her claim upon you."

A glimmer of hope. "So... you think if I talk to her... explain..."

"Do *not* speak of it until *she* raises the matter," Vida warned sharply. "Or you will shame her further. She will not ask you now, not alone. She will likely wait, take you before our father, our elders, in the village. Then she will make her claim formally. *That* is the time, the place, to speak your heart honestly."

My relief faded. A formal confrontation? In front of her whole tribe? "Is *that* the main reason you brought me north, Vida?" I asked, suspicion returning. "Not just the beast, but this? To face Freya's claim?"

"That is *Freya's* reason, perhaps," Vida replied curtly. "My reason remains what I told you: I needed your help to kill Ethrak. And you gave it. Please do not misunderstand *my* intentions." But her eyes flickered away for a second, and I felt again that she wasn't telling me everything.

"Okay," I sighed, accepting the uneasy truce for now. "So the point is, I have to go back with you to your village eventually?"

"It is your choice," she repeated quietly. "As I said, no one forces you."

"Fine," I said, my jaw tightening with resolve. "Then I *will* go with you. When the time comes. I will face Freya, face her father, face anyone. I will speak my mind. Tell them what I truly want." I paused, then added deliberately, meeting Vida's gaze across the dim cave, "Or *who* I truly want... if marriage is indeed forced upon me."

Vida looked back at me, her expression unreadable in the shadows. "Maybe..." she murmured, her voice almost inaudible, then fell silent, not continuing the thought.

"Honestly," I pressed on, emboldened now, wanting, needing clarity from *her*, "I've never thought about marriage. Not really. But if I *have* to choose now, if custom demands it... then of course I will choose the woman I truly... care for."

Her gaze flickered again. "I do not know what is in your head, William. But... good luck to you."

"Hey, it's my future!" I protested, trying to lighten the mood again, trying to provoke a reaction. "It *has* to work out!"

Vida just shrugged noncommittally. "Of course..."

Her sudden silence, her withdrawal, annoyed me. "Aren't you going to ask?" I challenged softly. "Ask me what I might say? In your village? About what I want? Or *who* I might want as my wife?"

"I do not need to know that," she evaded, looking away towards the waterfall.

"Maybe you *do* need to know," I persisted gently, "if that woman... is you."

We locked eyes then, the air crackling with unspoken tension. I held her gaze, offering a tentative grin. Vida just snorted softly, a sound of dismissal, maybe embarrassment.

"I do not wish to speak of this," she stated flatly.

"Why not?" I leaned forward slightly. "It's a much more interesting conversation than talking about tribal customs or beasts. More interesting than talking about Freya, even. Let's talk about *us*, Vida. You first, then me. Do you... do you have a lover back home?" I grinned again, pushing deliberately now.

"That," she snapped, her eyes flashing, "is none of your business!"

"Let me make it my business," I replied softly, feeling reckless. "Because, Vida... I like you..."

"Shut up!" Her voice was sharp, warning. "Do you want me to hit you?" She actually clenched her fists, glaring at me.

I laughed, maybe a little nervously, but exhilarated by finally breaking through her reserve. "Vida the beauty, threatening me again! Alright," I held up my hands in mock surrender, still grinning, "if getting hit means you might finally accept me, then I'm ready."

Her fist shot out faster than I could react. The blow connected squarely with my jaw, hard enough to snap my head back, sending stars exploding behind my eyes. Pain flared, sharp and intense. Damn! She hit like a blacksmith's hammer!

I staggered back, almost hitting my head on the cave wall behind me. Through the ringing in my ears, I dimly registered her left hand swinging back for another blow – *left-handed*, I remembered belatedly, that's why I hadn't seen the first one coming properly.

This time, though, despite the pain, I reacted faster. My hand shot out, intercepting her left wrist, stopping the punch mid-air. Her right hand came up instantly, aiming for my face again. I caught that wrist too. Without thinking, driven by instinct and maybe something more, I pulled her towards me, off balance, until we were pressed close together, her struggles surprisingly strong against my grip, her face inches from mine, eyes blazing with fury.

"You hit me?" I gasped out, the pain in my jaw making speech difficult. "That *hurts*, you know!" Anger warred with a strange sense of triumph. Then I grinned again, recklessly. "But... I thank you, Vida. Because surely that means you *are* ready to accept me now?"

She glared, spitting fury. "Let go! Or I will bite your nose off!"

"Damn, your threats *are* getting worse," I chuckled, though my heart was pounding. I loosened my grip, letting her pull away. She stumbled back, breathing heavily, leaning against the cold stone wall, retreating into the deepest shadows where I couldn't clearly see her expression.

I sat down heavily on the rock ledge again, rubbing my jaw. "I'm sorry," I said after a moment, my voice still rough. "If I angered you. Yes, I exaggerated. Pushed too hard."

She didn't reply immediately. So, I continued, "You were the one who brought up the subject. Then I said what I want. Isn't that what a man should do, according to you? Speak his heart? I don't understand why you are so upset. Is it... always like this? You never let anyone know you? Or is it just... me? If it is, I will not speak of it again."

"Freya," she said softly from the shadows, "is my sister."

I waited, trying to understand the weight she put on those simple words. What did that mean in this context?

"Yes, she is," I agreed with that one. "But that doesn't make *her* the most important thing... to *you*, does it? For any person, the most important thing should be themselves first. What *you* want, Vida. What *you* feel. What is in *your* heart. That should matter most. Or... in Hualeg... can women like you not say what they truly desire?"

"We can," came her quiet reply from the darkness.

"So why didn't you? Why won't you?"

"I chose not to."

"Why?"

Silence again. Then, finally, "You would not understand."

"Wouldn't I?" I challenged gently. "Alright. So that means... I cannot expect anything? From you?"

"What do you mean?" Her voice was barely a whisper now.

"You know what I mean," I replied softly, laying my own feelings bare. "I like you, Vida. More than like. But I cannot expect... you feel the same?"

The silence stretched, long and heavy, filled only by the roar of the waterfall outside. When she finally spoke, her voice was thick with an emotion I couldn't decipher. "I... do not know. I do not know what... we can do. About this. Maybe... maybe we will never have the chance."

"Never have the chance?" Annoyance flared again, masking a sudden, sharp disappointment. "That's ridiculous! Why do you talk as if we're going to die tomorrow? Yes, it's possible! Anything's possible! But..." I sighed, frustrated. "Fine. If that's how you truly feel, then perhaps we shouldn't speak of it again."

I let my gaze linger on the shimmering curtain of the waterfall at the cave mouth. Outside, the first hints of dawn were painting the sky, the rain had stopped. Had we really talked, argued, fought... for hours? Or did I wake much earlier than I thought?

I stared out through the falling water, my heart heavy, my thoughts tangled. Anger? Disappointment?

Yes. But something else too...

"We should get out." I tried to suppress my feelings.

"No," Vida's soft voice came from behind me. My arm was suddenly clasped by her hand.

I turned my head, surprised by the touch. "What now, Vida? We still have to check the situation outside."

"Don't," she whispered, her grip tightening slightly on my arm. "Not yet. It is still dangerous out there."

"I'm hungry. We need to find something to eat."

"Later. Please... do not go now."

I stared at her, confused by her sudden plea, her unexpected touch. She pushed her way out from the shadows, coming towards me, moving fully into the faint light filtering through the waterfall. Her eyes were wide, her expression unguarded, vulnerable in a way I'd never seen before. Her fingers, still holding my wrist, loosened their grip, moved slowly upwards, tracing a line along my arm, my neck, finally resting gently against my cheek, sending a jolt through my entire body.

My heart hammered wildly against my ribs. My body felt like it was on fire.

Something rose uncontrollably inside me as she slowly, deliberately, leaned her body against mine, her head resting against my chest. "Stay here today," she whispered against my skin, her breath warm.

"Vida..." My voice was rough, strangled. I was utterly confused, unsure how to react, how to control the fierce turmoil gripping me.

She hugged me tighter, her breath coming faster now against my neck. I returned the embrace instinctively, pulling her close, letting my body respond even as my mind reeled. She lifted her face then, looking up at me, her turquoise eyes dark with emotion.

Then I saw them – tears, glistening at the corners of her eyes, threatening to spill down her cheeks. "Vida? Why...?"

"This..." she whispered, her voice thick with unshed tears, "this might be the only time we can be together..."

Before I could ask what she meant, her lips found mine, kissing me with a desperate, heart-wrenching intensity that shattered my confusion, ignited something fierce and overwhelming within me. Startled, I responded instinctively, returning the kiss with equal, maybe greater, emotion, pouring all my own tangled feelings – frustration, anger, longing, fear, tenderness – into the embrace.

We clung to each other then, tight, desperate, letting go of all the unspoken words, all the barriers, all the fear and doubt. Nothing else mattered in that moment. Nothing left to hold onto, nothing left to deny.

"I love you, Vida," the words escaped me in a ragged whisper against her lips.

"I love you, William," she breathed back against mine.

The roar of the waterfall faded into a distant hum as the world narrowed to just us. The cool air against my bare chest was instantly warmed by the heat radiating from her body pressed against mine. My fingers finding the hem of her tunic, pulling it gently upwards. She raised her arms, allowing me to slip it over her head.

The sight of her bare shoulders in the dim light stole my breath. Her skin, still slightly damp, shimmered with a soft glow. I reached out, my fingertips tentatively tracing the line of her collarbone, down to the gentle swell of her breasts. She gasped softly, her eyes closing, her head tilting back slightly. Encouraged, I cupped her breasts in my hands, feeling the rapid beat of her heart beneath my palms. Her nipples, already hard, pressed against my skin, sending a jolt of pure sensation through me.

Vida's hands were equally eager, exploring my chest, my stomach, her fingers dipping beneath the waistband of my trousers. I sucked in a breath as her touch sent shivers down my spine. We stumbled back slightly, leaning against the cool, rough surface of the cave wall, our bodies still locked together.

Undressing the rest of the way felt like a clumsy dance, our fingers fumbling with fastenings and wet fabric. There was an urgency to our movements, a desperate need to be closer, to shed the last barriers between us. My trousers and her remaining undergarment were soon discarded on the rocky floor, leaving us completely bare in the dim light.

The sight of her naked body, so close, so real, was breathtaking. Her curves were soft and strong, her skin smooth and inviting. I reached out again, my hands tracing the line of her hip, down her thigh, feeling the goosebumps rise on her skin. She mirrored my touch, her hands exploring the length of my manhood, pulling me closer until there was no space left between us.

We kissed again, deeper this time, our bodies pressed together from chest to thigh. I could feel the heat radiating from her core, the soft brush of her curls against my skin. A primal urge surged through me, a need to connect with her in the most fundamental way.

I shifted slightly, my knee nudging between her legs. She gasped again, a small, involuntary sound that fueled my desire. I cupped her face, looking into her eyes, searching for any sign of hesitation. But all I saw was a reflection of my own longing, a raw vulnerability that mirrored my own.

With a trembling hand, I reached down, gently exploring the soft folds between her legs. She was wet, slick with desire, and I felt a surge of triumph mixed with a healthy dose of nervousness. This was new for both of us.

"Vida..." I whispered, my voice hoarse.

She met my gaze, her eyes dark and trusting. "It's alright, William."

Taking a deep breath, I guided myself to her entrance. It was tight, unfamiliar, and I paused, unsure. She squeezed my hand, offering silent encouragement. Slowly, carefully, I pressed forward. There was a moment of resistance, a sharp intake of breath from Vida, and then I was inside her, a sensation both exquisite and overwhelming.

We stayed still for a moment, our bodies adjusting to this new intimacy. I could feel her heart pounding against mine, her breath coming in short, shallow gasps. I leaned down, kissing her softly on the lips, her forehead, her cheek.

Then, slowly, I began to move. The friction was intense, unfamiliar, but incredibly arousing. Vida moaned softly, her hands gripping my shoulders, her body arching against mine. Our movements were clumsy at first, a tentative exploration of rhythm and sensation. But as our desire grew, our movements became more confident, more urgent.

I lost myself in the feel of her body around mine, the soft sounds she made with each thrust, the way her nails dug into my back. The world outside the cave, the threat of Mornir's men, Freya's claim – all of it vanished, replaced only by the intense connection between us.

The air grew thick with our mingled breaths, the scent of damp earth and burgeoning desire filling the small cave. I pushed deeper, faster, the sensations building to a fever pitch. Vida cried out, her body clenching around mine, and I felt the wave of my own release wash over me, a powerful, shuddering climax that left me breathless and weak.

We collapsed against the cave wall, our bodies still intertwined, our breathing ragged. The roar of the waterfall seemed to fade back into focus, a gentle lullaby to our shared intimacy. I held her close, my face buried in her hair, feeling the slow, steady beat of her heart against my chest.

The silence that followed was comfortable, filled with a sense of profound connection and vulnerability. I gently kissed the top of her head.

"Vida," I murmured, my voice still rough.

She shifted slightly, looking up at me, her eyes soft and filled with a tenderness I had never seen before. A faint smile touched her lips.

"William," she whispered back, her voice equally soft.

The clumsiness of our first time had been overshadowed by the intensity of our emotions, the raw honesty of our connection. In that hidden cave, behind the curtain of falling water, we had found something precious, something real. And as the first rays of dawn finally pierced through the waterfall, painting the cave in a soft, golden light, I knew that my life had irrevocably changed.

37

No Ordinary Man

The roar of the waterfall outside the cave mouth had faded to a dull, constant hum, a backdrop to the quiet intimacy that enveloped us. Hours had passed since the first light of dawn, hours since Vida and I had surrendered completely to the overwhelming feelings that had finally broken through our defenses. We lay entwined on the smooth, cool rock of the cave floor, her body warm and soft against mine, her yellow hair fanned out across my chest. The air was cool, damp from the persistent rain outside, but where our skin touched, there was only heat.

My mind felt blissfully empty for a long while, focused only on the steady beat of her heart against my ribs, the soft rhythm of her breathing, the lingering scent of her skin. Every fear, every doubt, every ghost from my past seemed to have retreated, silenced by the raw, undeniable connection forged between us in the dim light of this hidden place.

Then, my stomach betrayed the peaceful silence with a loud, embarrassingly coarse growl. Hunger, sharp and demanding, suddenly asserted itself, a stark reminder of our predicament now that the intensity of our passion had subsided. My body clearly remembered its needs. Vida stirred against me, laughter bubbling softly in her chest. She hugged me again, seemingly amused.

"Seriously," I murmured against her hair, my own voice rough, "it's time we found something to eat."

"Oh really?" she teased, tilting her head back to look up at me, her turquoise eyes soft now, the usual warrior's sharpness momentarily veiled. "You survived seven days without food or drink. Surely one more day fasting won't matter?"

"Those seven days are a different story!" I protested, grinning down at her. "I was unconscious! Now I'm awake... and other activities expend energy."

"I think it is the same," she countered, her eyes dancing with mischief.

"Hmm." I sighed dramatically, stroking her bare back. "This is clearly a very unhealthy relationship beginning here. Starvation and teasing."

She laughed again, the sound bright in the enclosed space, and I joined her. The easy laughter felt precious, fragile. We fell silent again, just holding each other, kissing gently, savoring the lingering warmth, the quiet comfort.

I glanced towards the waterfall curtain. Rain still streamed down outside. No chance of hunting or fishing yet. Another night here, it seemed. Likely without food. My stomach growled again, protesting the idea.

"William," Vida's voice beside me was suddenly serious again, pulling me from thoughts of hunger. "Who *are* you, really?"

Her question caught me completely off guard. Did she suspect something? Sense something different about me, something connected to my Hualeg blood? Did she somehow *know*? I looked at her face, searching her expression, but she wasn't looking directly at me now, tracing patterns idly on my chest. Maybe... maybe it was just a casual question, born of intimacy and curiosity.

"Me?" I tried for a light tone, deflecting. "I'm no one important. Just a failed blacksmith's apprentice from the south..." I paused, letting my eyes linger on her face, "...who somehow got lucky enough to meet a beautiful, fierce warrior girl like you. Why do you ask?"

"Nothing..." she murmured, still not looking at me.

"Why?" I pressed gently.

"Hmm..." She hesitated. "I just... feel... you are no ordinary man."

I laughed, trying to dismiss her seriousness. "Why would you think that?"

"Well," she finally looked up, her gaze thoughtful, analytical, "for one, you are very strong. Stronger than you look, even. And you fight... differently. Not like a southern soldier. More like... like Hualeg, but wilder somehow. Unpredictable."

"Oh." I shifted uncomfortably. "Well, I still lost to you that first time, remember? Fainted like a babe afterwards."

"That was because you were not fighting seriously then," she stated confidently.

"I *was* serious!"

"No, you were not," she insisted calmly. "Not like you fought the Logenir. That was different." She paused, her gaze intensifying slightly. "Second... your body... it is like fire."

"Oh dear," I tried another joke, feeling increasingly awkward. "What does *that* mean? Am I going to burn you?"

"No. It is not like that." She frowned slightly, perhaps frustrated by my attempt at humor. "I mean... warmth. Unusual warmth. When I... when I am near you... I do not feel the cold. At all."

"Isn't that... normal? When two people are close?"

She looked up sharply then. "Have you slept close with many other southern girls, William?"

"Hey!" I protested, feeling my own face flush now. "I said 'two people'! Just... generally!"

Vida glared, though maybe with less heat than before. "Keep your voice down. Do you want someone outside to hear you?"

"There's no one out there!" I insisted. "We're safe here for now—"

"Hey!" she cut me off, putting a finger gently against my lips. Then she withdrew it quickly, as if burned.

I laughed again, enjoying her rare flash of discomposure. She silenced me with a soft kiss this time, lingering just long enough to make my pulse race again before pulling back. We looked at each other, the air thick with unspoken things. I felt my own desire rising, ready to forget food, forget danger, forget everything but her... for another day... but she gently pushed me back.

"I mean it," she said, her expression serious again. "Your body's heat... it is different. Stronger. Especially when you are... aroused." She gestured vaguely towards my lower body, then quickly looked away, shaking her head slightly. "It is just... how you are. Like fire."

"If I'm like fire," I asked softly, intrigued despite myself, "does that mean I hurt you?"

"No," she said quickly. "Not hurt. It is... good warmth. Like... if you stood among people freezing in the snow, they would not need a bonfire if you were there."

I grinned. "No need to exaggerate, Vida."

"Why? It might be strange, but it is true," she insisted stubbornly. "And third."

"There's more?"

"Yes." Her voice dropped, becoming low, intense. "And this is the most important thing. Something I must show you."

She carefully eased away from me, moving across the cave to where her travel bag lay in a dry corner. My curiosity spiked. What was so important she had to show me now? She rummaged inside the bag for a moment, then drew out something wrapped carefully in a piece of soft, dark cloth. Returning to my side, she knelt before me, the wrapped object held gently in her hands.

Slowly, she unfolded the cloth. Resting in her palm lay a black stone, about the size of my outstretched hand. Smooth, dark, yet... not entirely dull. It seemed to absorb the dim cave light, and deep within it, I could almost imagine faint, shimmering veins pulsing with a light of their own. It felt... strangely familiar. As if I'd seen it before, held it before. But where? When?

"What kind of stone is it?" I asked, reaching out instinctively to touch it.

Vida pulled her hand back slightly. "You do not remember?" she asked, her voice barely a whisper, her eyes searching mine intently. "Not at all?"

I frowned. "No. Should I?"

"That," she said, holding the stone out again, though not letting me touch it this time, "is the stone you found in the cave. After you killed Ethrak."

I froze, staring at the stone, then at her face. "I... I found this? I don't remember."

"After the beast died," Vida explained patiently, "you knelt beside it. You saw this stone lying near its mouth." She paused. "I do not know if it was there during the fight, or if... if it came *from* the beast somehow. But you saw it. You picked it up." Her voice grew quieter, more serious. "And this stone, William... this is the object I have been seeking all this time."

My mind reeled. The stone... the thing she was hunting... the reason for this whole dangerous quest? "And... you've had it all this time?" I asked, feeling a surge of bewildered anger. "Since the cave? You kept it hidden?"

"I am sorry." She reached out again, this time stroking my cheek gently, her touch sending shivers down my spine despite my confusion. "As I told you back at Helga's cabin... I could not speak of this with the others there. They would not understand. Or perhaps, they would fear it too much."

"You also said," I reminded her, my voice sharper than I intended, "that you wouldn't explain until we met the wisewoman. Why tell me *now*?"

Her gaze softened. "After... after this morning... after what we shared... how could I keep secrets from you now, William?"

Her honesty disarmed me. I nodded slowly. "Okay. What *is* this stone? Why were you looking for it?"

"Do you remember Freya's story? The legend of Ethrak guarding the weapon of Anthor, the thunder god?"

"Yes. Anvasar, the hammer." Then realization dawned. "But... when I asked you in the cave if you found the weapon, you said no. You let me believe the legend was wrong, that there *was* no hammer." My voice hardened again. "You lied to me then."

"Yes," she admitted quietly, meeting my gaze without flinching. "Then, I lied. I am sorry."

"At least you are honest *this* time," I muttered, though the anger was fading, replaced by intense curiosity.

"I am trying to be," she replied softly. "If it seems I lie again... just hit me."

I couldn't help but grin, shaking my head. "I think I can find better ways to punish you than that."

"You pervert," she retorted instantly, though a tiny smile touched her lips before she quickly suppressed it, pouting slightly instead.

"What? Why pervert?"

"May I continue my story?" she interrupted firmly.

"You called me a pervert! Now, I must do something to you!" My fingers rubbed her inner thigh, creating a circle.

"Hey! Stop it! ... William!"

I laughed. "Fine! Go ahead. Tell me."

"My story will be long," Vida shifted slightly, snuggling closer. "So I hope you have patience." She took a deep breath. "Freya told you the common legend, the one most Hualeg know, about Signar seeking the god's weapon. Now I will tell you another story, much older, known only to a few. It is up to you if you believe it, but I heard it from Helga, and *I* believe it."

She began, her voice low and mesmerizing, pulling me back across millennia. "It is a story from the beginning of time," Vida recounted softly, "when our people were one, not yet divided into many tribes. Our first ancestors, Madnar and Fyrsta, came not from this earth, but from Himinar, the sky-world. The gods, angered by some mistake made in the heavens, sent them here as punishment, casting them down onto the northernmost glacier of this world."

I listened, picturing that desolate icy landscape.

"But the gods did not leave them entirely without aid," Vida continued. "They gifted Madnar and Fyrsta a pair of black stones, imbued with celestial power, meant to unite them, give them strength, bind their spirits together. With the power of these stones flowing between them, they survived the killing cold of the great glacier. Yet, after they had children, offspring born in that harsh land, they began to doubt. Could their people truly endure forever on the ice? Fearing for their descendants, they journeyed south, eventually reaching the lands we now call Hualeg. Here, they encountered the ancient tribes who already lived within the deep forests. Our ancestors settled, multiplied, their blood mingling with the forest people, growing stronger, more numerous."

She paused, shifting slightly against me. "Madnar and Fyrsta themselves, the legends say, had only one child born purely of their sky-blood: Ardnar. But Madnar took a second wife, Erena, a woman from one of those ancient forest tribes, and with her, he had five more children. All their descendants, mixed blood and pure, became known as the Hualeg people." Her voice dropped again, becoming more serious. "But the secret, the true nature and power of the two black stones... that knowledge was kept hidden, known only to the direct descendants of Madnar and Fyrsta through Ardnar's line. It was passed carefully down through the generations, only from the chief – the *Hardingir*, we call him – to his chosen successor."

I processed this. Hardingir. Chief. And the stones... a secret lineage. "Passed from chief to chief," I murmured. "But you heard this story from Helga. How could she tell it, if she is not Hardingir?"

"I heard..." Vida hesitated slightly, "...that Helga *was* Hardingir once. Briefly. In my grandfather's time. Then she relinquished the title, passed it to her younger brother... Radnar."

Radnar. Just another name from the past... I tried to file it away as Vida continued, her voice low and serious, drawing me deeper into the ancient history.

"Some time after Ardnar," she said, "during the reign of Hardingir Hednar, a struggle for power began. Hednar had twin sons, Hinnar and Godnar. Both were strong, both capable warriors, both respected. Hednar loved them equally and could not choose between them as his successor. In what seemed a wise decision then, but proved disastrous, he divided the territory of Hualeg – east and west. And he separated the twin black stones, giving one to each son, hoping they would rule together in harmony."

She sighed softly, the sound barely audible over the waterfall's roar. "It was the beginning of all our sorrows. After Hednar died, Godnar, perhaps listening to jealous subordinates whispering poison in his ear, attacked his brother Hinnar without warning."

"Hinnar," Vida's voice grew harder now, filled with the echoes of ancient grief and anger, "survived the betrayal. Filled with vengeance, he turned to arts forbidden by the gods. He took his own black stone, the one given by his father, and forged it into a sword of terrible power." She paused, her eyes meeting mine, dark and intense. "We call it Grokhark. The Bearer of Hatred."

"Wielding Grokhark," she continued, "Hinnar struck back. He attacked Godnar's holdings, killed his own brother cruelly on the battlefield, slaughtered nearly all of Godnar's followers, and took the second black stone – Godnar's stone – for himself, reuniting them briefly through bloodshed."

"But the gods," Vida whispered, glancing upwards as if fearing eavesdroppers even now, "were angered by Hinnar's cruelty, his breaking of kinship, his forging of their sacred gift into a weapon of hate. They sent four executioners against him – the Four Calamities – monstrous beasts summoned from the corners of the world." Her voice listed them like a grim chant: "Rokhan, the Ice Tiger from the Great Glacier north beyond Hualeg. Amerik, the Shadow Wolf from the endless western forests. Ondhar, the great River Serpent from the southern swamps. And Ethrak, the Mountain Bear, from these very eastern peaks."

I listened, spellbound, picturing the apocalyptic conflict.

"Hinnar gathered his remaining warriors," Vida said, "and met the Four Calamities on the Holy Land, the plains south of here where the first Hualeg settled. Wielding Grokhark, he fought like a madman. He killed Amerik the Wolf and Ondhar the Serpent." She shook her head slightly. "But Rokhan the Tiger, slyest and strongest of the four, wounded Hinnar grievously and snatched the sword Grokhark from his failing grasp, fleeing back towards the northern Ice Lands. Some tales say Rokhan drowned in the frozen sea, losing the sword forever in its depths. Others... are unsure."

"And Ethrak?" I prompted softly.

"Ethrak the Bear," Vida finished grimly, "found the wounded, disarmed Hinnar and killed him. The beast then took the remaining black stone – Godnar's stone, the one Hinnar had stolen back – and retreated deep into its mountain lair here in the east, guarding it for centuries. The war was over. Hualeg was left shattered, leaderless, broken into the warring tribes we know today."

She fell silent, the weight of the ancient tragedy heavy in the small cave. "So Signar, centuries later," she connected the legends, "heard the whispers of Ethrak guarding great power. He mistook it for Anthor's hammer, but it was always Godnar's stone." She finally looked at the wrapped stone beside her. "The stone that grants power, but poisons any who touch it... unless they carry the true blood of Ardnar."

"So *that's* why," I breathed, relief mixing with a new layer of unease about the stone itself. "Why I fainted..."

"Yes," Vida confirmed, her expression grave. "An ordinary man... touching it might have died instantly. But your body resisted, William, somehow. It is so strong, stronger than you ever know. But the shock still overwhelmed you." Her hand came up, gently touching the bruise still fading on my jaw. "I... I feared you were dead. Truly. When I felt your pulse still beat... I knew I had to bring you to Helga. Only she might understand the stone's effects, heal any hidden damage."

"You already told me that part," I said,. "It's okay, Vida. You don't need to apologize. Helga... she can examine me. But believe me, I feel fine! Nothing bad will happen."

"Until Helga tells me you are truly unharmed," she insisted fiercely, her grip tightening slightly on my arm, "I will not calm down."

"Alright," I conceded, strangely comforted by her fierce concern. "But if I'm really sick, how could I have exhausted *you* so thoroughly since this morning?" I tried a teasing grin. She responded with a light punch to my arm.

"Could you be serious?" she retorted, though her lips twitched.

"I *am* serious!" I pulled her closer again. "Okay then. So, your mission... you found the stone Ethrak guarded. Is it over now?"

Vida looked down at the wrapped stone beside us, her expression turning serious again. "Finding *this* stone was only the first part." My heart sank slightly. Of course, it wouldn't be that simple. "There is one more thing," she continued, meeting my eyes. "When I first came to Helga, seeking guidance long ago, she recognized me... recognized the bloodline, the descent from Ardnar, of course. And she said... if I truly wished to do what was best for *all* Hualeg, not just the Vallanir, then my path, my responsibility, was clear."

"Responsibility?" I prompted gently.

"To reunite the two lost black stones," Vida stated, her voice low but firm. "The one Ethrak guarded," she touched the wrapped object, "and its twin – the one Hinnar forged into the sword Grokhark, lost centuries ago when Rokhan the Ice Tiger carried it north." She took a deep breath. "Helga said this task should have been taken up by my predecessors, but they failed, or feared to try. She said it now falls to me." Her gaze held a heavy weight. "At first, I hesitated. The legends are dark, the quest sounds impossible. But... I accepted the charge. So I came east, first, to seek the stone Ethrak held. Now that I have it..." she looked north, towards the unseen icy wastes, "...I must journey to the Ice Lands. Find Grokhark."

A descendant of Ardnar? Tasked with reuniting mythical stones? "Wait," I interrupted, trying to process it. "You... Ardnar's line... that means you are... the daughter of the chief? Of the Vallanir Hardingir?"

"Hmm... yes," Vida admitted quietly. "I thought perhaps you would have figured it out by now."

I nodded slowly, bewildered. Of course. That explained her authority, why Svenar and the others obeyed her without question, even Freya's deference beneath the teasing. Daughter of a chief... which meant she likely knew many people back in Vallanir. Knew their histories. Did she perhaps know the name Vilnar? Know of my father? The question burned on my tongue. Should I ask her now? Find out if she knew his story, the quarrel with his brothers Mom mentioned?

But no... safer not to reveal my own connection yet. Safer to understand the landscape first.

I pushed the thought aside, focusing on her quest. "What happened," I asked instead, changing the subject slightly, gesturing to the stone wrapped in cloth beside her, "when *you* touched the stone? Back in the cave? Did you feel anything?"

She looked down at it, her expression clouded with doubt. "I felt...

nothing," she admitted, her voice uncertain.

"Nothing?" That seemed strange. "Are you sure this is the right stone then?"

"It is," she insisted, though without full conviction.

"Maybe," I speculated, "you need to combine it with the other stone first? The sword? Before you can feel the effect?"

"I guess so." She carefully re-wrapped the stone, tucking it securely back into her leather bag.

I pulled her close again, hugging her tightly, suddenly aware of the immense burden she carried, the incredible danger she planned to face. "After this," I murmured against her hair, "you will continue the journey? North? To the land of ice?" The name alone sent shivers down my spine. "This Rokhan tiger... legends say dead, yes, but Ethrak was supposed to be just legend too, wasn't he? Vida, are you sure you want to go there? It sounds far worse than these mountains."

"The legend says Rokhan is dead," she repeated stubbornly. "I only need find the sword."

"Legends can be wrong, Vida! Your journey will be even more difficult! More dangerous!"

"I have promised Helga," she stated simply, her voice resolute. "I *will* carry out the mission."

Her determination, her quiet courage... it settled something within me. "Then I will accompany you," I said, the decision feeling absolute, necessary.

Vida looked up at me, her turquoise eyes wide with surprise. "William... I have promised you. Before. That I would let you go home."

"Well," I smiled down at her, stroking her cheek, "after today, the situation has changed! How can I possibly let you face that danger alone?"

Her breath hitched, her chest rising and falling quickly against mine. "Maybe... maybe it would be best if we..."

"Vida," I interrupted gently but fiercely, holding her gaze. "I told you I love you! And I meant it. I will come with you to your village. I will speak to your... family. I will make you my wife, if you will have me." My heart pounded at my own words. "Why are you still doubting? Still afraid? Who are you afraid of? Freya? Are you afraid of hurting her feelings? Or," I asked softly, searching her eyes, "are you choosing to hurt your *own* feelings?"

"Why are you blaming *me* for being afraid?" she whispered, pulling away slightly, turning her face. "These feelings... they are mine. I do not wish to deny them." She looked back, pleading now. "Stop it, William. Do not push me."

"Okay," I said softly, respecting her turmoil, though my own heart ached with uncertainty. I hugged her gently, kissing her forehead.

We sat in silence for a long time, the only sound the roar of the waterfall outside, the air thick with unspoken emotions. Finally, Vida spoke again, her voice low, hesitant, muffled against my chest.

"I was thinking... what if... what if we separate? For a while?"

38

A Better Plan

Vida's words hit me like cold water. Separate? Now? After... this? It felt like a joke, a cruel one.

"Relax, William, don't be mad," she said quickly, sensing my sudden tension. "I'll explain."

"About what will happen," she began hesitantly, "in my village. When we arrive. If we go there together now... I fear it will not be easy. For you. Freya's claim... the customs... you are a stranger. Your position is not favorable. I... I will help you, of course, but my own standing is... complicated. Not as strong as it should be yet." She met my gaze, her eyes filled with worry. "That is why I thought... perhaps it is better if we part ways now, just for a time. Secretly. Without Freya or the others knowing. I know where Helga used to hide rafts further upriver. We take two. You head south, back towards Thaluk. I go north, continue my quest for Grokhark alone. When my task is done," her voice grew softer, "when my position is stronger, truly secure... I *will* come south. Find you. Then... then we can be together. Properly. For the rest of our lives." She looked at me anxiously. "What do you think? It seems... a sensible choice?"

I stared at her, stunned, processing her words, her fear *for me*. Sensible? Perhaps. But the thought of leaving her, of her facing the dangers of the Ice Lands alone... it felt unbearable. "Does that mean," I asked slowly, "I don't have to go see your shaman anymore? Well, I'm glad for that part.

But Vida..." I shook my head. "If something happened to you out there alone... hunting that sword... I would regret letting you go for the rest of my life. No. I won't leave you. I *will* go with you."

An idea sparked, a different path. "Or... listen. How about this? We forget separating. We forget Vallanir village for now. We go *together*, you and I, straight towards the Ice Lands *right now*. Find Grokhark. Bring it back. *Then*, you take the stone and the sword to your village, secure your position. *Then* I return south. When everything is truly settled, *then* you come south to meet me. What about that? Sounds better, doesn't it?"

Vida didn't answer immediately, her brow furrowed in thought as she stared at me. "Go quietly... north now... past my village, past the watchers... all the way to the Ice Lands... without being noticed?"

"Do you think it's impossible?"

"The chances are slim. They *will* know eventually."

"But even if they knew, could they physically *stop* us once we are far north, heading into the ice?"

She considered. "Perhaps not. If we move swiftly..."

I grinned, feeling a surge of hope. "Then we can do it, can't we?"

"But..." she frowned, "...if Freya finds out we bypassed the village, went north together alone... she might follow us again."

"Will she? Why is she always following you everywhere?"

"She once told me... that I am everything to her," Vida explained softly. "Sister, friend, teacher. She loves me greatly, more perhaps than our parents. She wishes to be like me, follow my path."

"Well, I can see that. But she can't follow you forever."

"Yes. But now you perhaps understand why I cannot hurt her," Vida murmured, looking down. "She likes you, William. Greatly. She wants you. Thinks custom gives her the right to claim you. But I... her sister... her protector... I took you from her."

"You talk as if you and I have no feelings, no choice!" I retorted, frustrated again. "We are two people, Vida! She is one! She needs to learn, to accept! I will talk to her when the time comes, explain respectfully. If she still refuses to understand... well, maybe I *am* guilty by your customs, maybe I deserve punishment. But I still cannot be *forced* into marriage!"

"I do not want anything bad to happen to you..." Vida whispered, repeating her earlier fear.

"I can take care of myself!" I insisted. "What? Do you *still* want us to part ways? Because I don't!"

Vida lifted her face, studied mine for a long moment, then finally, slowly, nodded. "Alright, William. We will not part ways. Not yet." Relief washed over me. "We will try your plan. Tomorrow, we find Helga's hidden raft. We travel north together, as quietly as possible. We seek Grokhark in the Ice Lands. *After* we find it... *then* we separate, for a time. You return south. I return to Vallanir with the stone and the sword. Once... once my position is secure, my duty fulfilled... I will come south again. To meet you."

"Good plan," I smiled, pulling her close again. "A much better plan." I pictured it – us, together. "I imagine we could stay by the river somewhere, if you don't want to live too far south. Find a hidden place like... like the house where we first met. Build our own cabin. Forget about tribes and politics and everyone else."

Vida laughed softly against my chest. "A person like *you*, William? Not caring for other people? Living quietly? I think that is not possible."

"Why not?"

"Because," she tilted her head back, her eyes serious again, "as I said before, you are not ordinary. Your life... it will not end quietly beside a river with just me. One day, you will become a very important person. A great man."

I shook my head dismissively. "I don't even want to think about that."

Vida smiled sadly. "I only mean to say... on our journey, in our lives... many things can happen. Good, bad. Things different from our plans, our desires. We must be ready to accept that. I will be ready." Her eyes held mine. "And may the gods be on our side."

"Vida," I murmured, "I don't want to think about what might happen yet."

"William..."

"You," I interrupted gently, pulling her face closer to mine. "I just want to think about you. Right now. I want *you*."

We looked at each other, lips slightly parted, the air thick with anticipation. Tomorrow, the dangerous journey north, the uncertain future... it could wait. This moment, tonight, still belonged only to us.

We made love again then, slowly this time, cherishing every touch, every kiss, every shared breath. Afterward, exhausted, utterly content, we finally fell asleep wrapped in each other's arms before midnight even struck.

Dawn came too soon. We woke together, the intimacy of the night replaced by the urgent need for practicality. After ensuring the area outside the waterfall was clear, we left the cave, shared another brief, fierce embrace on the riverbank, then quickly found fish in the stream for a hurried breakfast. As the sun climbed higher, warming the forest, we set off, heading west through the trees, following Vida's unerring sense of direction.

Later that day, we reached the banks of the wide Ordelahr River again. Then, following the shoreline north, walking through woods and across rocky outcrops, we eventually came to the place Vida sought – a small, dark cave hidden beneath tangled tree roots near the water's edge, overgrown with brush. Vida pushed the brush aside, revealing a small raft tucked inside, crafted crudely from lashed logs, along with two rough oars.

"There is only one raft," Vida noted, pulling it out.

"We only need one," I replied. "Shall we pull it to the water now?" I glanced around. The wide river looked peaceful here. "Seems safe. No sign of Logenirs."

Vida shook her head, though her eyes remained watchful. "Safe for now. But that could change quickly. Their departure after our battle at the hut... it might mean Vallanir patrols are around here already. They might spot us in daylight on the open river." She looked towards the setting sun. "Better we hide here until full darkness, then row through the night. Safer that way."

I nodded agreement. Moving unseen was crucial now. We concealed ourselves in the small alcove with the raft. It was less comfortable than the cave behind the waterfall, certainly less private, but it didn't matter. We rested, ate the last of our fish, and waited.

As soon as true darkness fell, we dragged the raft to the river's edge, pushed off, and began rowing north, staying close to the right bank where the trees offered the deepest shadows. We moved quickly but cautiously, oars muffled, eyes and ears straining against the darkness. So far, so good. We passed the spot where we'd landed two days ago. Vida expertly steered the raft close to the bank again, into a section where thick willow leaves drooped low over the water, concealing us completely.

"We will soon be nearing the main Vallanir watch posts," Vida whispered, her voice tense. "The village itself will be on the left bank ahead. The river widens there, maybe thirty meters across. If we stay moving on the right, in the darkness, we should pass unseen."

I wasn't so sure. My unease returned, a prickling sensation on my skin. Luck, as Rogas always said... it felt like ours might be running out.

Far ahead, tiny pinpricks of orange light appeared, flickering in the distance. The Vallanir village. Home... for her. A place of danger and uncertainty for me.

Suddenly, a clear shout echoed across the water from behind us, startlingly close. "Vida! William!"

Vida went rigid beside me, peering back through the darkness. I did the same, my heart sinking. A boat, approaching fast, a single torch burning bright at its prow, revealing the figures within. And that voice... unmistakable. Freya.

"How?" I whispered incredulously, staring at the approaching torchlight. "How could she possibly see us from back there? In this darkness?" Another flash of her strange sensing ability?

Vida shook her head, her voice tight with frustration. "We must have... become careless. Shown ourselves somehow..."

"So what now?" I asked grimly. Our plan to slip past unnoticed was ruined.

Vida looked puzzled for a moment, then sighed in resignation. "We meet them. What else can we do?"

"We keep going north!" I argued desperately. "Pretend we didn't hear them! We can still make it!"

"No kidding," she retorted flatly, dismissing the idea.

"Vida..."

"We go out, William," she stated firmly, already steering the raft out from under the willow leaves. "There is nothing else *to* do now."

"Nothing? What about our plan?"

"I have not forgotten our plan!" she snapped back, annoyed now. "But now we meet them." She lowered her voice, urgently. "Please, William. No rash actions now. Do not say anything to make Freya suspicious. It will only make things worse. Just... follow my lead. Trust me. There may be... another way."

Another way? My mind raced, filled with unease. We were heading straight back into the heart of the Hualeg world, straight towards the confrontation over Freya's claim. But looking at Vida's set face, her plea for trust... what choice did I have? I took a deep breath, trying to regain composure.

We brought the raft out into the main channel and waited. Freya's boat pulled alongside moments later. And behind it... four more longboats, filled with maybe fifty armed Vallanir warriors, their faces grim in the torchlight. My stomach plummeted.

"Hello!" Freya's smile was blindingly wide as she easily stepped from her boat onto our small raft.

Vida stood to meet her, instantly reverting to her formal, slightly stiff leader persona – the playful intimacy of the cave completely gone. William followed suit, moving onto Freya's larger boat. The raft was quickly secured and taken in tow by one of the warrior boats.

"Where did you come from?" Vida asked her sister.

"Hunting Logenir!" Freya replied brightly. "We crossed the river yesterday, headed south, trying to catch uo with the enemy. But," she shrugged dramatically, "they got away. So we turned north again this morning. I just *knew* I would find you two somewhere along here tonight! And here you are!" She beamed at both of us.

"Do you know what happened to us?" Vida asked carefully.

"We found Helga's hut yesterday afternoon," Freya nodded. "Burned to the ground. Found two Logenir bodies inside. We were afraid... afraid it might have been you. But I was sure you were safe, hiding somewhere." Her gaze swept over me, concerned. "Then this morning we saw dozens more Logenir heading back west, downriver, trying to escape in two boats. We chased them, but they were too fast. We pursued as far as we dared without getting too close to their territory, then stopped late this afternoon. We rowed back north until we finally found you just now." She smiled again, then eyed us both shrewdly. "Are you two alright? Where *have* you been hiding all this time?"

"In the forest," Vida replied. "We are fine. But... Helga? I feared the Logenirs who attacked the hut might have harmed her."

"Helga is fine!" Freya reassured her quickly. "She's safe. In Vallanir."

Vida looked utterly shocked. "In the village?"

"Yes! When I returned two days ago to gather the warriors, they said Helga had just arrived too! I didn't see her myself, but she's unharmed."

"That is... good news." Relief washed over Vida's face. "She must have sensed the Logenir approach and fled before they reached her hut." She turned to me then, her expression practical again. "Helga can check on you tomorrow then, William."

"Whatever," I shrugged. "I don't really care."

"Cheer up!" Freya beamed at me. "I am sure there is nothing wrong with you!" She leaned closer, her eyes sparkling with excitement. "But tonight... tonight you meet my father! It is almost midnight, I know, but he will still be awake, waiting for us! You will like him, William! And I am *sure* he will like *you*!"

39

No Longer Yours

Stepping onto the Vallanir dock felt like crossing an invisible line, violating a sacred trust. *Never go north,* Mom had pleaded with her dying breath. Yet here I was, setting foot in my father's homeland for the first time. Anxiety warred with a strange sense of defiance, a feeling that fate, or perhaps just Vida's relentless quest, had pushed me here despite my promise. What awaited me now? What consequences would follow such a transgression? Would Mom and Dad scold me from the afterlife? The thought was both absurd and deeply unsettling.

I pushed the feelings down, focusing on the present as I followed Vida and a still-chattering Freya up from the river landing. We walked along wide paths paved with flat river stones, winding between sturdy timber longhouses. Torches flickered on posts, casting pools of warm light against the deepening twilight. People emerged as we passed, drawn by Freya's cheerful greetings or perhaps just curiosity about the stranger – me. Their faces in the torchlight were varied. Some remained expressionless, watching silently. Others smiled warmly, likely just glad to see Vida and Freya returned safely. But a few, mostly older men and women, stared openly, their mouths slightly agape, expressions of shock or perhaps recognition that made my skin crawl. *Gods, don't old people here ever sleep? It's nearly full night!*

Their intense scrutiny made me deeply uncomfortable. Why had I even agreed to come up to the village proper? I should have stayed on the raft, hidden. This welcome, this attention... it was for Vida and Freya, the daughters of the tribe, returned from a dangerous journey. I was just an outsider, baggage they'd brought along.

We reached the base of a low hill dominating the village center, where a truly massive longhouse stood. This had to be the chief's dwelling. I followed the sisters up the wide wooden steps onto a large stone terrace. Two imposing guards flanking the entrance opened the huge doors – carved timber, easily four meters high – revealing a vast hall inside, brightly lit by scores of torches set in wall sconces.

Three figures waited near the far end, seated on high-backed chairs upon a slightly raised platform. A man in the center exuding quiet authority – Freya and Vida's father, the Hardingir? To his right sat a woman with striking auburn hair, still beautiful despite her years. To his left, another woman, equally striking, her hair the same spun-gold as Vida's. Their mothers? One of them? Both? Hualeg customs were still a mystery to me.

"Father!" Freya dashed forward without hesitation, throwing her arms around the seated man's neck. He chuckled, returning the embrace warmly. She then hugged both women with equal affection before stepping back, beaming. Vida followed, offering a more reserved, respectful embrace to each.

I hung back near the entrance, feeling out of place, unsure of protocol, not daring to approach the seated figures uninvited.

"Were you well while I was gone, Father?" Freya asked anxiously. "Still coughing at night?"

"I am fine, little spark," her father replied, his voice deep and resonant. "Worry more about yourselves. I suspect you gave your sister a difficult time on this journey south, eh?" He glanced towards Vida with questioning eyes.

"Not truly, Father," Vida answered politely, her tone formal now. "Freya made much noise, as usual, but caused no real trouble." Her expression turned serious. "We did encounter Logenirs near the southern border. Clashed with them. We lost some men, but it had nothing to do with Freya.

I will speak with their families tomorrow, arrange compensation."

My mind raced. She spoke of losing *her* men to Logenirs... but made no mention of the Vallanir warriors *I* had killed near my father's house, before Freya's capture. Was she deliberately omitting that? Protecting me? Or was it simply not relevant to this report?

"I always trust your judgment, Vida," the chief said, his brow furrowed with concern. "But Logenirs... I warned you to be careful, stay clear of them."

"I apologize, Father. It was my mistake," Vida acknowledged calmly. "Mornir led a large war party south, raiding villages. The situation... was difficult. I chose not to stand aside while they committed such acts."

"I heard rumour Mornir lost many warriors," the chief said, his eyes sharp. "Was that your doing, daughter?"

"We accounted for a few only," Vida replied carefully. "Most were killed by southerners defending their homes."

"Truly?" Her father looked surprised. "The southerners fielded an army against them?"

Vida shook her head. "Only villagers, Father. But... there was one among them. A warrior of great skill. He alone killed perhaps half the men Mornir brought."

"One man?" the chief asked, clearly shocked now. "Who?"

Vida finally turned, gesturing towards me where I stood awkwardly near the door. "This man, Father. His name is William." She beckoned me forward. "He journeyed east with us, seeking the mountains. He aided us against Ethrak. Afterwards, we traveled together to Helga's hut seeking her counsel, but found it burned... Logenirs had been there..."

Her voice trailed off. I realized, stepping forward hesitantly, that her father and the two women were no longer listening to her explanation. They were staring at *me*. Not with curiosity now, but with a strange, unnerving intensity, their eyes wide, searching my face as if seeing a ghost.

Feeling suddenly exposed, deeply uncomfortable, I remembered my manners and bowed my head politely.

"You..." the chief's voice was barely a whisper, strained. "Your name...

what did Vida say it was?"

I lifted my head, meeting his intense gaze. "William, Hardingir."

"And you are from... where?"

"A town called Ortleg, sir. In the kingdom of Alton, to the south."

He continued to stare, silent, his expression unreadable. The two women beside him mirrored his intense scrutiny. My heart began to pound. What did they see? Did they somehow know? Recognize something? This felt far beyond simple curiosity about an outsider. I cursed myself again for coming here. *Should have stayed on the boat!*

"I brought him here!" Freya suddenly announced cheerfully, breaking the heavy silence, seemingly oblivious to the strange tension. "William helped us greatly, Father! Saved Vida, even! I want him to feel welcome while he is here! Can he stay in our house, Mother? Father? We have that empty room..."

"Of course..." her father murmured, nodding slowly, finally breaking eye contact with me, leaning back in his chair as if suddenly weary.

"Welcome to our home, William," the red-haired woman said then, her smile warm and seemingly genuine like Freya's. "We are glad you have come safely to Vallanir. There is much to discuss, I am sure. But it grows late. I will have the servants prepare a room for you immediately, so you may rest."

"Welcome, William," the yellow-haired woman added, her voice cooler, more reserved than the other woman's. She turned to the chief and the redhead. "Perhaps the guest house would be better, though? More privacy for him. It is quieter there than here, with people coming and going constantly."

The red-haired woman nodded thoughtfully. "That is true. You would likely rest better there, William."

"Thank you," I replied gratefully, eager to escape their intense stares. "I apologize if my arrival has disturbed your evening."

The red-haired woman summoned a servant, gave quiet instructions. The servant beckoned me to follow. Vida and Freya remained with their parents as I was led out of the great hall.

Part of me didn't mind leaving Vida and Freya behind for the night. I needed space, needed time to think. Their parents... they looked like good people, welcoming enough on the surface. But that *stare*... it had felt like they were looking straight through me, seeing things I didn't even understand myself.

The guest house was comfortable enough, located near the river a short distance from the main longhouse. I was given a clean room with a window overlooking the dark water. Exhausted from the journey and the strange, tense welcome, I fell onto the sleeping furs almost immediately.

When I woke the next morning, sunlight streamed through the window. Someone had left breakfast on a small table near the door – smoked fish, fresh bread, creamy milk, even some honey. A feast compared to our recent trail rations. I devoured it hungrily.

After eating, I sat on the small terrace outside my room, looking out at the wide, powerful flow of the Ordelahr River, enjoying the crisp morning air. My thoughts turned to Vida. We needed to see Helga. I hadn't seen Vida or Freya yet this morning, and despite needing time to process last night's strange encounter, I felt a pang of... missing her. Missing Vida. Deciding I couldn't just wait here all day, I stood up, intending to head towards the chief's longhouse. Just as I reached the path, however, Vida herself appeared, walking towards me.

"I am sorry for the delay," she said as she approached, her expression serious. "I had to meet with the families of some of the warriors we lost."

A pang of guilt shot through me. "Are their families... okay?" I asked.

"They grieve," she replied quietly. "But they understand the warrior's path. I have arranged compensation according to our custom."

"Did they ask...?" I hesitated. "Did they ask how those men died? Or who...?"

Vida looked at me intently, perhaps sensing the direction of my thoughts. "Why do you carry this specific worry, William?"

"I killed those men, Vida. You know how I feel. It was a fight, but still... Don't you think it would be better if I talked to them, explained what happened, and apologized?"

"There's no need. Forget it."

"But..."

"Forget it, William," she repeated, her gaze steady. "Or the guilt will crush you. What happened then was battle. Survival. Mistakes were made, blame is shared across many events on this quest. If punishment is deserved for any of us, let the gods decide our fate." She drew herself up, changing the subject decisively. "Now, let us go find Helga. Before Freya realizes we are gone and comes looking for us. Or," she raised an eyebrow slightly, "do you wish her to accompany us?"

"No," I shook my head quickly. Dealing with Helga felt daunting enough without adding Freya's unpredictable energy, or worse, discussions about marriage customs, into the mix.

We set off immediately, heading south out of the village along the riverbank, then turning onto a less-used path leading into the hilly forest. The house was small, secluded, nestled deep amongst ancient pines about a hundred paces from the nearest trackway. It looked... forgotten.

"This is Helga's old house," Vida whispered as we approached. "She has not lived here for many years."

Vida knocked softly three times, then called out, "Helga? It is Vida. May we enter?"

After a moment, the door creaked open just a crack. An eye peered out. Then the door opened wider. An old woman stood there, tall despite a slight stoop, her long white hair unbound and wild around a face etched with countless wrinkles, yet dominated by sharp, startlingly intelligent eyes the same turquoise shade as Vida's and Freya's. Helga. She glanced briefly, assessingly, at me, then focused on Vida, beckoning us inside.

We sat cross-legged on worn floor mats around a low, scarred table while the old woman watched me intently, saying nothing. The air inside smelled strongly of dried herbs and something else, something sharp and ancient.

"Helga, this is William," Vida introduced. "He's from the south. A few days ago, we visited your hut. Since you weren't there, we spent the night. But the Logenirs came and attacked us. We escaped safely, but I was worried something might have happened to you. I'm glad you're here."

"My house burned down?" Helga asked, her voice raspy but calm.

"Yes," Vida confirmed. "Did you know that? Did my sister tell you?"

Helga shook her head. "I could sense it. The disturbance. The fire." She shrugged dismissively. "It's all right. The house was old and will be rebuilt. I can also make my potions again."

"What brought you back *here*?" Vida asked. "Did you sense the Logenirs would attack the hut?"

"I sensed their evil intentions from afar," Helga replied, her sharp eyes settling on Vida. "Did you provoke them during your journey south, Vida? They seemed filled with unusual hatred, seeking revenge. You should have been more careful."

"I was careful," Vida defended herself. "Their path crossed ours unexpectedly." She changed the subject, drawing the wrapped stone from her bag. "Anyway, I got this." She placed it on the table. "We killed Ethrak in the mountains far to the east. We found this near the beast. Now I must go north to find Grokhark."

Helga's ancient eyes fixed on the stone, then flicked towards me, then back to Vida. "Did you touch the stone, child?"

"Yes," Vida admitted quietly.

"And you felt...?"

"Nothing," Vida confessed, sounding frustrated, uncertain. "I am... not sure."

"If you cannot feel its power," Helga stated bluntly, her voice surprisingly strong, "then you will *not* retrieve Grokhark."

"Does that mean... I must wait? Until I *can* feel it?" Vida asked anxiously.

Helga shook her head slowly, her gaze shifting, pinning me where I sat. "Grokhark... its fate... its responsibility... is no longer yours." Her eyes narrowed, focusing entirely on me now. "It falls now... to this young man." She pointed a bony finger directly at me. "You. What is your name again?"

"William," I answered, my throat suddenly dry.

"You feel it, don't you?" the old woman demanded, her eyes boring into mine.

"Feel what?" I objected, confused, alarmed, shifting uneasily. What was she talking about?

"Helga," Vida interjected quickly, seeing my distress. "I brought William here for *you* to check him. Yes, he touched the stone after killing Ethrak. I was too late warning him." Her voice filled with anxiety again. "Because he is from the south... not... not like us... I feared the stone harmed him! He was unconscious for seven days, Helga! If he falls ill..."

"He is not ill," Helga interrupted dismissively, never taking her eyes off me. "His body is strong. Unusually so. It is fine."

"But you said only Ardnar's descendants could touch it without dying!" Vida protested.

"Anyone *can* touch the stones, child," Helga replied patiently, as if explaining to a slow learner. "But only those who carry the true blood of Ardnar can *survive* it. And perhaps... gain something from it."

Vida's eyes widened as the implication hit her. She turned slowly, staring at me with shocked comprehension.

"Hey, look," I said quickly, getting increasingly nervous under Helga's intense scrutiny. "I'm definitely not sick. Maybe slightly confused after sleeping for a week, but fine! Can we just forget about stones and gaining things? Vida?"

"Who are your parents, boy?" Helga's sharp question cut me off.

I swallowed hard, feeling cornered. Why did everyone keep asking this? "My parents... are from the south," I repeated the half-truth.

"That is your mother's origin, perhaps," Helga stated calmly, as if reading my mind. "And your father? Do you know who he is?"

I hesitated. "I... I never met him."

Helga nodded slowly, patiently. "Did your mother ever speak of him?"

"Yes."

"What did she tell you?"

"She said... he was a northerner." My voice was barely a whisper now. "A Hualeg."

"And?" Helga pressed gently, leaning forward slightly. "What else?"

"That... that is a private matter," I mumbled, feeling annoyed.

"Do you know his tribe, boy?" Her voice was insistent.

"Yes." I looked up defiantly. "Vallanir."

"And his name?" Helga's ancient eyes held mine.

I took a deep breath, steeling myself. There was no escape now. "His name... was Vilnar."

The name dropped into the sudden silence of the small hut like a heavy stone. Beside me, Vida cried out, a sharp, broken sound, covering her face with both hands, her shoulders shaking.

My head snapped towards her, shock ripping through me. "Vida? Why? What is it...?" Then, seeing the utter devastation on her face, the dawning comprehension in Helga's knowing eyes... it hit me. The connection. The reason for Vida's strange reactions, her guardedness, her intense interest in me. "You... you know my father?" I whispered, looking back and forth between the weeping girl and the ancient wisewoman. "You *both* know him! Who *is* he? Who *was* Vilnar... to you?"

I received no answer. Vida scrambled to her feet and fled from the hut, disappearing into the forest outside.

40

Unexpected Visitor

"Vida!" I shouted, scrambling to my feet, ready to run after her, needing to understand, to comfort her, to figure out what her reaction meant. But Helga's sharp voice stopped me cold.

"My grandson, Vahnar."

I froze, turning slowly back to face the old wisewoman. Grandson? *Vahnar?* My head spun. She knew that name, the one whispered in hushed tones by my mother, the one synonymous with my father's lost northern life. "You... you know that name?" My urgency to chase Vida warred with a sudden, desperate need for answers right here, right now. I sank back down onto the floor mat opposite Helga. "You know my father. Who... who is he to you? Please, Helga. I have to know."

Helga closed her ancient eyes, letting out a long, weary sigh. "Yes, boy. I know Vilnar. I was the midwife present when his mother brought him into this world." She opened her eyes again, their turquoise depths seeming to pierce right through me. "He was... an extraordinary young man. Headstrong. Passionate. And his face..." Her gaze lingered on mine. "...it is startlingly similar to yours. From the moment you appeared at my door, Vahnar, I knew who you must be."

My mind struggled to absorb this. Helga knew him, delivered him. Knew me on sight. "Do you... do you know what happened to him? My mother... she told me my father was dead."

"Dead?" Helga froze, confusion clouding her features.

"You... you didn't know?" I asked.

"Some tales say he perished in the south," Helga murmured thoughtfully. "Others whisper he still lives, wandering far lands under a different name. The truth... has been lost to us here for many years."

"But *what* happened?" I pleaded, leaning forward. "Who *was* he? Why did he leave? Why did my mother warn me never to come back here?"

"Vahnar, listen to me." Helga's voice regained its stern authority. "I could explain the past, tell you the stories. But on reflection... not now. It is not the time." She gestured towards the door Vida had fled through. "You and Vida... you have more immediate matters between you, born from this revelation. Go to her first. Speak with her. Understand her feelings, reconcile this shock between you. *Then*, when hearts are calmer, perhaps you may return, and we will speak of Vilnar."

"But I was going after her!" I protested, jumping up again, frustrated. "You stopped me!"

"Yes." Helga nodded slowly. "It was... an unexpected moment. Minds thrown into turmoil cannot think clearly. I spoke impulsively, perhaps unwisely. I wished to say more. But now... now I believe it is best to wait. Let the immediate storm pass. Speaking more now might only cause greater harm."

"I don't understand any of this," I muttered, shaking my head, feeling lost and angry. "But I *am* going to talk to Vida. Find her. And after that, I *will* come back here for answers."

"Do not return until you have spoken with her," Helga insisted, her gaze firm.

With a frustrated sigh, I ran out of the small hut, sprinting across the small yard and down the rough path towards the main trackway. Reaching the fork, I hesitated, scanning the trees. Which way had Vida gone? Left, back towards the village? Or right, deeper into the concealing forest? Damn it! Why hadn't I followed her instantly? And why had she cried like that, run like that, just from hearing my father's name?

It had to be connected. Vilnar... was he an enemy of her family? Mom had said he quarreled with his brothers, left his tribe under a dark cloud. Had Vida just realized she'd brought the son of a family enemy, maybe even a traitor, into the heart of Vallanir? That would explain her tears, her flight. And that would explain why Mom warned me never to return – to avoid exactly this kind of disaster.

Fear, cold and sharp, pierced through my confusion. What if Vida's father, the Hardingir, recognized the resemblance too? What if he knew the name Vilnar, knew the story? What would happen to me then? I still desperately wanted to know the truth about my father, but maybe... maybe finding out now was too dangerous?

"William!"

Freya's cheerful voice shattered my anxious thoughts. She came running up the path from the village, her red hair flying, a bright smile on her face, seemingly oblivious to the turmoil I felt.

"I've been looking for you!" she puffed, reaching my side. "Did you see Helga? Is she alright? Where's Vida?"

"I..." I hesitated, unsure how much to reveal. "I saw Helga. She's fine. But Vida... I don't know where she went. She just... left."

"Left? Why?" Freya looked momentarily confused, then shrugged it off with characteristic speed. "Never mind her for now! Come with me!" She grabbed my arm, pulling me along.

"Where are we going?"

"Just follow! You'll see!"

She led me back towards the main settlement, but instead of going down into the village proper, she turned onto a narrow, winding path leading up the side of the hill that overlooked the longhouses. The path grew steeper, rockier, eventually ending at a dramatic stone outcrop at the very summit. We stepped out onto the flat rock, and the view took my breath away. Below us lay the village, nestled beside the river. Beyond it, the vast, rolling green expanse of the northern forest stretched out as far as the eye could see, until it met a distant line of stark blue and shimmering white on the far horizon.

"What... what is that?" I asked, pointing towards the horizon, awestruck.

"The blue line?"

"The northern ocean," Freya announced proudly, sweeping her arm wide. "And the white beyond it... that is the Great Glacier. The beginning of the Ice Lands." She grinned at my expression. "Beautiful, isn't it?"

"Amazing," I murmured, shaking my head. I'd seen snow-capped mountains in the south, but never anything like this – an actual ocean, stretching to meet a land of permanent ice. "I've never seen the sea before."

"I wanted to bring you here," Freya said softly, moving closer. "Ever since we started north. I knew you would appreciate the view. Even though the sea looks small from here, it holds a certain majesty, don't you think?"

"Have you... have you ever been there? To the coast?"

"Once," she nodded. "Years ago. Father took Vida and me north, visiting the Andranir tribe who live by the sea. It is beautiful, but freezing cold. Only hardy fishermen dare sail those waters." She turned to me then, her eyes sparkling with sudden enthusiasm. "Do you want to go there, William? We could go together! See the ocean up close!"

I smiled, touched by her offer, but my mind was still reeling from everything else. "It sounds interesting, Freya. Let me... let me think about it."

She studied my face thoughtfully. "I wonder what you are truly thinking about right now."

I sighed. "A lot of things." What could I tell her? "What do you want to know?"

"For instance," she began, her gaze direct now, though her tone was light, "if I asked you to go with me, say, on a journey just the two of us... would you be happy? Or would you just think I was being strange?"

I understood immediately where this was heading. Freya, unlike Vida, rarely hid her intentions. That teasing question on the boat... Vida's warning... it was all culminating here. If she wanted to ask me to be her husband, this was likely the prelude. Better to face it now, get it over with, gently if possible.

"I wouldn't think you were strange, Freya," I replied carefully. "We aren't children anymore. There's nothing strange about asking someone if they'd like to... spend time together."

She turned her head, looking straight at me again. "So... would you be happy?"

"That depends," I answered honestly, meeting her gaze, "on what you truly meant. What you truly wanted... by asking me to go with you."

"I want you," she said softly, but with unwavering conviction, "to be my husband." She held my gaze, searching my reaction.

Silence hung between us for a moment, broken only by the sighing wind. I had to answer. Had to be clear, for her sake, for Vida's, for mine. "Freya," I began gently, "we've known each other... what? A month? Maybe a little more? Yes, I like you, you're brave, cheerful, kind... but to be husband and wife... surely it takes more than liking? More time than we've had?"

She laughed softly, a sound tinged with sadness, turning back to look out at the distant ocean. "So you believe time is the only barrier? That we cannot know our hearts so quickly?" She glanced back at me sideways. "Aren't you lying to yourself, William?"

I exhaled slowly. "What do you mean?"

"You like Vida, do you not? More than just a friend." Her words weren't an accusation, just a statement of fact. "You have known her no longer than you have known me. Perhaps even less. So why does time matter for us, but not for you and her? Why lie to me about the reason?"

She saw right through me. "Yes," I admitted quietly. "You're right. I haven't been honest. I'm sorry, Freya. I just... I didn't want to hurt you."

"Lying hurts more in the end," she replied simply, without bitterness.

"Now that you know the truth... are you angry?"

"Angry?" She shook her head, turning fully towards me again, her expression surprisingly calm, though tinged with melancholy. "How could I be angry? Not truly. Not with you, not with Vida." Her voice softened. "She is my sister. My everything. The best person I know. I love her more than anyone. I only want her to be happy." Her gaze drifted past me for a moment. "But... isn't it normal for me to wish for my own happiness too?"

"Can you truly be happy," I asked softly, "if achieving it means others cannot be?"

"Time, they say, can change many things," she replied, a familiar Hualeg fatalism creeping into her voice. "Perhaps one day your feelings for me will grow. Perhaps your feelings for her will fade. Perhaps *her* feelings for you will change." She looked directly at me. "Do you truly think that is impossible, William?"

"I... I don't know," I admitted honestly. "Maybe. But what purpose does thinking about that serve now?"

"Do you want to marry my sister, William?" Her question was blunt, direct.

"Yes," I answered without hesitation, meeting her gaze firmly. "If she will have me. Perhaps not immediately – she has her own path, her mission. But yes. If we can make it work, that is what I desire."

"It *cannot* work," Freya stated flatly, "if I do not agree."

"Why not?" I already knew the answer from Vida, but I needed to hear Freya state the custom herself.

"Because you have been *mine*," she declared, her chin lifting slightly, "since the day you took me from the riverbank."

Short. Concise. Clear. The weight of Hualeg law settling between us. I didn't react outwardly, just held her gaze.

"You do not look surprised," she observed quietly. "Did Vida tell you?"

"Yes," I confirmed. "She explained the custom."

"She told you." Freya nodded slowly, absorbing the implication. "That means... she feels something for you, too. To reveal such things..."

"Yes," I said softly. "She loves me. As I love her."

Freya nodded again, her lips trembling slightly as she fought for control. I could see the hurt in her eyes now, raw and deep. "So... you both understand the situation. The law. My right. Yet... you do not care." Her voice cracked slightly. "*She* does not care."

"Do not blame her, Freya," I said quickly.

"She is Vallanir! She knows the rules better than anyone!"

"Yes! But is she truly breaking them by having feelings? By choosing? What will you do, Freya? Force her to deny her heart? Force *me* to deny mine?"

She shook her head, turning away again to face the wind. "No. I do not wish to force anything." Her voice was quiet now, laced with a surprising maturity. "With the power I hold by law... I *could* force you. Compel you to marry me today. Vida... Vida would eventually have to consent, for the sake of peace, for custom. But I will not do that." She turned back, her eyes glistening but resolute. "I will wait, William. I will wait until you are ready. Until your feelings change. Until you can finally see me, like me, the way you see Vida now. I will wait. Forever, if I must."

I shook my head, frustrated, saddened by her determination. "Freya... what if that time never comes? What if my feelings don't change?"

A bitter smile touched her lips. "Then... then I suppose I truly will be the unlucky one."

"You shouldn't do that to yourself..."

"So you wish me to simply give up?" she challenged softly. "Give up the man I want? The man I saw in my dreams?"

"Freya," I sighed, "our lives... your life... it's still long. One day, you will find someone else. Someone right for you."

"*You* are the one," she whispered fiercely. "Not someone else. Like I said... I saw us. Together. Happy."

"Freya, it was just a dream!"

"It was my dream that saved your life once," she reminded me quietly. "Remember? When Mornitz captured you? Vida came because *I* saw your danger."

My stomach clenched. She was right. I owed her. "That," Freya continued softly, pressing the point, "is another reason you should return the favor to me now."

"Freya, don't..."

"You are right," she interrupted suddenly, shaking her head as if clearing it. "Forget it. It was just a dream. I will not bring it up again." She took a deep breath, forcing a brighter smile. "Again, William, I will not force you. I just... hope. Hope that one day you will accept me. That is all."

I shook my head again, speechless, trapped by her hope, her claim, her kindness. She stood beside me for another moment, looking out at the distant sea ice. The wind whipped strands of her red hair across her face. My own thoughts felt chaotic – Freya's impossible hope, Vida's sudden flight, my father's shadowed past, Helga's cryptic words... It was all too much.

"I think," Freya said finally, her voice carefully cheerful again, "it is time we returned to the village." She held out her hand invitingly. "It is well past noon. Will you come with me now?"

I took a deep breath. "I... I think I'll stay here a little longer, Freya. Alone. If that's alright?"

She nodded, her smile faltering slightly but holding. "Of course. I will wait for you back in the village then. Come to our house later... join us for the evening meal? Do not be late."

She turned and walked back down the path, leaving me alone on the windy hilltop.

I stared out at the blue ocean horizon for a long time, the vastness somehow both calming and terrifying. What a mess. What was I supposed to *do* now? Taking deep breaths of the cold northern air, I tried to sort through the tangled mess in my head.

Late in the afternoon, feeling no clearer but knowing I couldn't stay up there forever, I finally headed back down towards the guest house.

Sitting on the small wooden veranda outside my room, watching the river flow endlessly northwards, I tried again to make sense of it all. Freya... her claim was serious, rooted in their laws, strengthened by her feelings and, damn it, by the fact I *did* owe her my life. But I couldn't marry her. Not when my heart belonged entirely to Vida.

Vida... where had she run? Why? Just hearing Vilnar's name had shattered her. What was the connection? Was she safe? The urge to find her was overwhelming, but I had no idea where to even start looking. I had to trust she'd reappear, trust what we shared meant she wouldn't just abandon me here.

And my father... Vilnar. Helga knew him. Vida knew him. His past was clearly a source of pain, maybe danger, within his own tribe. Should I even pursue it? Mom's warning echoed louder than ever. But Helga had called me *Vahnar*. Grandson. The need to know, to understand my own identity, felt stronger than the fear.

So many problems. Which one first? Vida was the most important. Finding her, understanding why she fled. But I couldn't search blindly. Freya... I could only wait, see what she did next, prepare to state my case clearly when the time came. Which left... my father. Maybe finding answers about *him* was the only thing I *could* actively do right now. Helga wouldn't talk yet. But the chief... Freya's father... he must know the story. He received visitors daily, Vida had implied. Maybe I could just... visit him? As a guest? And carefully ask? Yes. That felt like a plan. The best one I had.

Filled with renewed, if shaky, purpose, I stood up, ready to head towards the chief's longhouse. But as I turned, I stopped short. Standing quietly on the steps leading up to my veranda was the yellow-haired woman from last night. Vida's mother, I believed.

"Good afternoon... Ma'am," I greeted her, feeling hesitant, unsure of the correct address or the reason for her visit.

"Good afternoon, William." She smiled gently, stepping onto the terrace beside me. It was Vida's smile, but softer, less guarded. If only Vida could smile like that more often...

"How are you finding your stay?" the woman asked politely. "I hope the guest house is comfortable? We apologize if our northern ways seem rustic compared to your southern home."

"Ma'am, your hospitality is generous," I assured her quickly. "The room is very comfortable, much larger than my own home. I am very grateful."

"I am glad to hear it," she replied, her eyes studying my face kindly. "I hope you will continue to be comfortable here."

"I hope so too."

"I heard you took a walk earlier today," she commented casually.

"Yes. Vida took me to meet Helga this morning, and then... Freya showed me the view from the hilltop."

"Ah, yes." She smiled again. "The girls seem quite taken with you. Happy to have your company."

I grinned awkwardly. "Yes, it's... strange, perhaps, that they wish to spend time with someone like me."

"Not strange at all," she countered smoothly. "You seem a kind and capable young man. Attractive, too."

"Thank you, Ma'am." I felt my cheeks warm slightly.

Her expression shifted then, growing more serious, her gaze direct. "William," she asked, her voice quiet but carrying weight, "how long do you plan to stay here in Vallanir?"

Her question hung in the air, simple on the surface, but I felt a sudden prickle of unease. Was this just polite conversation? Or was she probing, testing, perhaps connected to Freya's claim, or the mystery surrounding my father? I tried to guess her intention, unsure how to answer.

41

Family

"I don't know yet," I replied cautiously to the yellow-haired woman; her question about how long I planned to stay hanging heavily in the air. "Maybe a few days. I'm just... visiting." Visiting felt like a pale, inadequate word for the complex web I felt myself stumbling into.

"I wish you could stay longer," she said, her smile gentle but her eyes holding that same intense, searching quality I'd seen in her husband, the chief. "As long as possible."

A strange thing for her to say to a near stranger. Why would she care how long I stayed? I nodded noncommittally, feeling increasingly uneasy.

"William," she continued, her voice dropping slightly, becoming more serious, "I have something I must tell you. Something important, I think."

"Okay." I glanced around the open veranda. "We can talk here?"

She shook her head quickly. "No. It requires privacy. A place where no one else might overhear." Her gaze was insistent. "If you do not mind... perhaps in your room?"

It felt strange, inviting the chief's wife into my temporary quarters, but her urgency was palpable. Secrets? Already? Perhaps this was about Vida? Or Freya? "Alright," I agreed hesitantly.

I led the way back into the guest room, closing the door behind us. The small space suddenly felt charged with tension. We sat on the simple wooden chairs near the door, facing each other. She looked nervous now, her hands clasped tightly in her lap.

"I am sorry," she began, her voice low, "for asking this of you, meeting in this way."

"It's alright," I waited, my own nerves fraying.

After a long silence, she finally spoke again, seeming to gather her courage. "Before I continue... perhaps I should properly introduce myself. My name is Tilda. I am Vida's mother."

"I... I could guess that," I admitted, managing a small grin, trying to ease the tension. "You look very much alike." The grin faded as the thought struck me: *If I somehow end up marrying Vida... this woman would be my mother-in-law.* Rudeness wasn't a good start.

Tilda offered a faint smile in return. "And I am sure you must resemble your father, too."

"Oh... yes. So my mother used to say."

A shadow crossed her face. "How are they, William? Your father? Your mother?"

I fell silent, meeting her gaze directly.

"They are dead, Ma'am."

Her face crumpled, genuine shock and sorrow replacing her earlier tension. "Dead? Both? When? How?"

"My mother... passed away almost three months ago now. Just before I left Ortleg." The grief felt fresh again. "And my father... my mother told me he died when I was just a baby."

"What happened to him?" Tilda whispered, tears welling in her eyes.

My own breath caught. She knew him.

"I... I don't know yet," I admitted truthfully.

"William," she leaned forward slightly, her voice urgent now, "do you know... your father's name?"

There it was. The question lurking beneath the surface since I arrived. Helga knew. Vida knew. And now Tilda. Why had she brought me here to ask this? Was it a secret? Something dangerous? But this was my chance. The chance I'd journeyed north for, perhaps without even admitting it to myself. To find out about my father.

"His name was Vilnar," I confirmed, watching her reaction closely.

Her breath hitched. "And... do you know who he is? Where he came from?"

"My mother told me," I said slowly, carefully, "that he was from Hualeg. From the Vallanir tribe."

Tilda's composure broke completely then. Tears flooded her eyes, streaming down her cheeks, yet she was smiling, a radiant, tearful smile. She reached across the small space between us, clasping both my hands tightly in hers, her grip surprisingly strong. "Yes," she whispered. "Yes, Vilnar was Vallanir. Born here, raised here." Her eyes searched my face eagerly. "His wife... her name was Ailene. And his son..." she squeezed my hands, "...*your* name... the name Vilnar gave you... is Vahnar."

"You... you know all of us?" I stammered, unsure how to react to her intense emotion, the warmth of her hands engulfing mine. A part of me felt elated, found. Another part felt wary, uncertain. Should I trust this so easily? Was there something I would regret?

"I have known your father since we were children," Tilda explained, her voice calmer now, though tears still shone in her eyes. "He was... quiet as a boy, smaller than his brothers, perhaps appearing weak. His three older brothers," she smiled faintly, "Kronar, Tarnar, Erenar... they were always loud, boisterous, playing dangerous games. Vilnar often stayed apart. I used to watch over him sometimes. Like a big sister. But as he grew into a man... gods, he grew strong. Fierce. Became one of our finest warriors. He fought many battles beside Kronar. Then..." she sighed, "...then Tarnar persuaded him on that ill-fated raid south. He rebelled. Refused an order to kill innocents. He fought his own brother. He returned home, ashamed but defiant. The council... they ruled he broke warrior law. He was punished. Exiled for three years." Her eyes held mine. "Many of us knew he acted rightly, honorably. But Hualeg law is rigid. He had defied his kin in a raid. There was no other choice for the council, for his father." She paused. "Then, we heard... later... that he met and married your mother in the south. That you were born, Vahnar." She looked at me intently. "Did your mother tell you any of this? Of the exile? The reason?"

"She only told me my real name, Vahnar, just before she died," I admitted. "She said my father never spoke of his past in Hualeg. She respected his silence, never asked. She felt the past didn't matter."

"Do you believe that?" Tilda asked. "That it does not matter? That it is okay not to know?"

I shook my head firmly. "No. I want to know."

"Then I will proceed," Tilda said gently, her eyes holding mine. "I have a feeling you have wanted to know this for a long time, so I will tell you what I know." She took a steadying breath. "You three were returning to Vallanir – your father bringing you and your mother home – to visit your sick grandfather, Radnar. But something bad happened shortly after. Your father's eldest brother, Kronar, died in a battle." She paused, sorrow clouding her face again. "Then, while your father was briefly away traveling north, another tragedy struck. Your grandfather died. They said he fell down the stairs in the longhouse. When your father came home, he clashed with Tarnar. The reasons... grief, old wounds, suspicion perhaps... I do not know for certain. In order not to make the situation worse, your father secretly took your mother and you away one night, heading back towards the south."

"We were all shocked by his sudden departure," Tilda continued, her voice low. "Tarnar... he suspected your father was somehow responsible for all the bad things happened in the village. He sent warriors south to pursue Vilnar, to arrest him. For days we waited. Then... terrible news reached us. Tarnar, and all thirty warriors with him... found dead beside the river, far to the south. Killed, we assumed, by Logenir raiders who must have ambushed them." Her eyes filled with fresh tears. "And of you three... your father, your mother, yourself... nothing. No word. No sign. For all these years... we believed you lost too. Killed by Logenir, perhaps, or vanished into the southern lands." She squeezed my hands again. "Until now."

I sat there, stunned, trying to digest the enormity of her story. It explained so much, yet raised a thousand more questions. And the timeline... it didn't quite fit with Mom's story of Father dying when I was a baby. Unless... unless Mom didn't know the whole truth herself?

Tilda took a deep breath, composing herself. "Your mother was probably right, Vahnar," she said, her smile widening now, filled with warmth and perhaps relief. "In the end it no longer matters what happened in the past. It's much more important that you're finally home again, in your true homeland. Here in the land of Vallanir."

Her words felt... kind, but didn't fully resonate. Was this my true homeland? The words felt strange. Ortleg was home. The southern forest was home. This place... felt like a dangerous, complicated inheritance. I nodded slowly, not wanting to argue, not wanting to voice the conflict I felt.

"Now that you know all this," she continued, her eyes shining, "you know how important you are to us. You're part of our family. Tonight, when you eat with us, I'll tell my husband who you really are, and he'll be as happy as I am. Although," she added with a knowing look, "maybe he could have guessed who you were from the beginning. And tomorrow we will announce it throughout the land that Vahnar, the son of Vilnar, has returned at last."

Announce it? Tell her husband – the chief? A sudden thought struck me, sending goosebumps prickling across my skin. "Just a moment," I interrupted gently. "Your husband... you mean the chief, right? I'm sorry, but... there was another woman there last night besides you. Sitting beside him. The one with the red hair. Is she...?"

Tilda smiled patiently, seemingly unsurprised by my question. "Me and Meralda are both wives of the chief. She is the First Wife, so her position is higher than mine." Two wives. Another Hualeg custom. Tilda continued, gesturing slightly as if clarifying a family tree, "It is Meralda's daughter, Freya, who carries the main line now and would later succeed the tribal chief." She paused, then added the crucial detail, "Oh, and one more thing I forgot to explain: The current chief's name is Erenar. He is your father's third brother."

My uncle. The chief. Meralda was his First Wife, Freya his daughter. That meant Freya... was my first cousin. The realization hit me – marriage between us would surely be forbidden, just as it would be in the South! A surge of unexpected relief washed through me regarding Freya's earlier 'proposal'. There must be a clear reason, a tribal taboo perhaps, why it could never happen.

Tilda went on, unaware of the turmoil her words caused, "I am his second wife. I married him some years after my first husband died." She looked at me kindly. "So Vida is not the chief's daughter; she is my first husband's child. But of course," she added quickly, "Erenar loves her anyway, like his own daughter."

Vida isn't Erenar's daughter. The words echoed in my head, drowning out almost everything else. She was Tilda's child by a *different* father. Not Erenar. Not directly from the line that connected *me* to Erenar and Freya through my grandfather Radnar. A wild, illogical hope surged through me. If Vida wasn't Erenar's daughter... wasn't my cousin through *that* line... then maybe...? Maybe the connection wasn't forbidden? Maybe there was still a chance for us? My heart hammered against my ribs with sudden, desperate happiness.

But then came Tilda's final words, delivered softly, shattering that fragile hope instantly.

"In case you didn't understand," she clarified gently, "my former husband... Vida's father... was Kronar. Your father's eldest brother. So Vida, just like Freya, is a close relative of yours, too. She is your first cousin."

* * *

Vida, my first cousin. Just like Freya. The revelation crashed down on me, shattering the world I'd started building in my mind, the future I'd foolishly allowed myself to hope for just moments before. It all made a sickening kind of sense now. Why Mom warned me away from the North, from my father's past. Knowing the truth only brought pain, confusion, heartbreak. Vida's tears when she heard my father's name, her sudden flight from Helga's hut... it wasn't just shock, it was the horror of realizing who I was, who *we* were to each other. Shame, hurt, the violation of kinship... she must have felt it all far more keenly than I did. Everything between us – the closeness, the passion in the cave – felt tainted now, wrong, impossible. Over.

Could she even bear to look at me again? I doubted it. And yet... gods help me, despite knowing it was forbidden, wrong, impossible... the thought of her, the memory of her touch, still sent an ache through me. Maddening. Vida had indeed driven me completely crazy.

Dread filled me as I walked towards the chief's longhouse for the evening meal later. How was I supposed to act? How could I sit near her, knowing what I knew now? Knowing *she* knew?

Tilda greeted me warmly at the door, seemingly oblivious to the devastation her words had caused me earlier. "Vahnar," she smiled, using the name that still felt foreign, "we have been waiting for you."

I followed her numbly into the great dining hall. The long table gleamed with polished wood, laden with platters of roasted meats, fish, breads, fruits – a feast fit for a Hardingir's family. Normally, the sight and smell would make my stomach rumble with anticipation. Tonight, it just felt like ashes in my mouth.

Six people were already seated. Erenar – my uncle, the Hardingir – sat at the head. To his right sat Meralda, the red-haired First Wife. Tilda took her place at Erenar's left. Beside Meralda sat a boy of about ten, and opposite him, a little girl maybe six years old, both with Meralda's reddish hair – must be Freya's younger siblings, Rennar and Vaya. Freya herself sat next to the boy, and she offered me a bright smile as I approached.

And across from Freya... Vida. She didn't look up. Didn't acknowledge my presence at all. Tilda gestured for me to sit in the empty place between the two sisters. Between the cousin who wanted to marry me by right, and the cousin I loved but could never have. Wonderful. I sat down stiffly, acutely aware of Vida beside me, staring fixedly down at the wooden trencher, her face pale and unreadable.

Erenar eyed me as I sat, and I returned his gaze with a respectful nod, trying to mask the turmoil inside me. Did he know yet? Had Tilda told him who I truly was?

Apparently not, because Tilda cleared her throat slightly and addressed the table. "Before we eat, I have something important to tell you all. Wonderful news." She glanced towards her husband. "Of course, if you do not mind, my husband?"

I saw Freya's expression shift instantly – surprise, yes, but also a flicker of annoyance? She darted a quick look at Vida, then at me. Did she think Tilda was about to announce something about *us*? About Vida wanting me? Did Freya feel betrayed already?

I knew better, of course. Tilda's news was far more shocking, far more complicated than Freya imagined. I risked a glance at Vida. Still nothing. Utterly still, face averted. Gods, it hurt to see her like this. This morning... everything felt so different. Now... shattered. And maybe, I realized with a fresh stab of remorse, it was my fault. If I'd just told her my father's name from the start, back in the South, back before... before the cave... maybe none of this pain would have happened. Maybe that would have been better for both of us.

"I do not mind," Erenar replied easily to Tilda, then turned to his First Wife. "What do you think, Meralda? Should we hear this wonderful news now, or after we eat?"

Meralda smiled graciously. "If the news brings joy, Tilda, why make us wait?"

"That's right," Erenar agreed, settling back in his chair.

"Thank you." Tilda nodded, taking a steadying breath before addressing everyone, her voice warm but carrying weight. "This is unusually joyful news, and very important to our family." Her eyes met mine briefly. "A long time ago, when Vida was just a small child, and before Freya, Rennar, and Vaya were even born... your father," she indicated Erenar, "had a younger brother named Vilnar. He journeyed south, lived there for some years, married, and had a son. For many years, we did not know what became of them, feared them lost to us. But today... today I learned the truth." Her smile widened as she looked around the table. "Your uncle Vilnar and his wife have passed on to the gods. But their son... he lives. He has grown into a fine, strong young man. And he has returned." Her gaze settled on me again. "This young man, whom you have known as William... is Vahnar. Son of Vilnar. Your lost cousin."

Clatter. Freya dropped her spoon onto the table, staring at me, her face draining of all color. Disbelief warred with shock in her eyes. Her gaze darted wildly around the table – at Meralda, at Erenar, at Tilda, then piercingly at Vida's still-averted face – before snapping back to me. "That means..." she whispered, her voice trembling, "that means... you've been lying? All this time? You lied to me? And to Vida too?"

"I didn't lie, Freya," I replied quietly, meeting her distraught gaze. "I only learned the truth myself today."

She shook her head violently, squeezing her eyes shut as if trying to block it out. Her breath came in short, quick gasps. When she opened her eyes again, they blazed with accusation. "You lied!" she attacked, her voice rising. "I think you knew! Knew you were Vallanir, knew your father was Vilnar! But you hid it! From all of us! You lied to *me*! You let me... you let me think..." Her eyes filled with tears, but she laughed then, a terrible, broken sound. "No wonder! Look at her!" She pointed a shaking finger at Vida. "Look at my sister! Pale as a corpse since you arrived! You, William... Vahnar... whatever your name is... *you* did this to her!"

"Freya..." Meralda started gently, reaching for her daughter, clearly understanding now that something much deeper than frustrated affection was at play here.

Erenar and Tilda looked equally stunned by the raw emotion, the implications of Freya's outburst.

"Or maybe you're lying *now*?" Freya cried, ignoring her mother, rounding on me again, almost hysterical. "After our talk on the hill today? Is *this* your way out? Avoiding my claim by lying to Mother Tilda? Pretending to be our uncle's son?" She turned desperately to Tilda. "He could be, couldn't he? Lying to you? Claiming kinship he doesn't have?"

Tilda shook her head softly, her voice calm but firm, filled with pity for her step-daughter. "No, Freya. He does not lie. He is Vahnar."

Freya seemed to deflate at Tilda's quiet certainty. She nodded slowly, tears flowing freely now. "Yes," she whispered. "I... I am sorry, Mother

Tilda. I did not mean..." She couldn't finish. Pushing back violently from the table, she turned and fled from the dining hall, her heartbroken sobs echoing behind her.

A heavy, suffocating silence descended on the room. The two younger children stared wide-eyed at the empty doorway where Freya had stood.

Then Vida moved. She rose silently from her seat, her face still pale and expressionless. She bowed her head slightly towards Erenar and Meralda. "Forgive me," she murmured, her voice barely audible. "I must go. I cannot stay for the meal."

"Vida..." Tilda reached out a hand towards her daughter, but Vida was already turning, walking quickly, silently from the room.

Tilda watched her go, looking utterly lost and confused, then wordlessly rose and followed her daughter out as well.

I sat there, stunned, amidst the ruins of the family dinner, alone with Erenar, Meralda, and the two wide-eyed younger children. I laughed bitterly in my heart, though no sound escaped my lips. A disaster. An absolute disaster. And all wrong from the very beginning. Maybe following Vida north, maybe falling in love with her... maybe *that* had been the biggest mistake of all.

"Love," Erenar commented quietly into the silence, startling me back to the present, "can be a terrible, destructive force indeed." He looked across the table at Meralda. "Perhaps you should go speak with your daughter, my dear."

Meralda nodded, rising gracefully. She paused beside my chair, placing a gentle hand on my shoulder. "William... Vahnar," her smile was kind, filled with sympathy. "I am sorry this night has been so... difficult. Unexpected. Do not dwell on it. Freya... she feels things deeply. It is... just a misunderstanding that time will heal." She patted my shoulder again. "And from now on, please, do not call Tilda or myself 'Ma'am'. We are your aunts. You should call us 'Mother', as is our custom. Do you understand?"

"Yes... Mother," I managed, the word feeling foreign, lodging in my throat.

The red-haired woman nodded politely and left the room, presumably to find Freya.

Erenar chuckled softly, turning his attention back to me, his expression surprisingly relaxed. "And from now on," he said, a wry grin on his face, "you should also call *me* 'Father'. Seems strange to southerners, I know, but here... uncles are fathers, aunts are mothers. Keeps the family bonds strong, warm. Isn't that right, Vahnar?" He winked, then turned to his young son and daughter who were still picking uncertainly at their untouched food. "And you two, Rennar, Vaya! Eat up! Don't waste good food like your older sisters just did!"

The two children nodded obediently, focusing instantly on their plates. I managed a faint smile for them, grateful for the small pocket of normalcy in the midst of the emotional wreckage. Erenar, it seemed, possessed a remarkable ability to remain unfazed by drama. His relaxed manner, his easy acceptance of me despite the chaos, helped settle my own frayed nerves slightly.

When the children finally finished and were excused, leaving just Erenar and me alone at the long table, I felt less nervous, though still deeply unsettled. He spoke bluntly, leaning back in his chair, regarding me thoughtfully.

"So," he stated, more observation than question. "Both my daughters have fallen in love with the same person. With you." He grinned wryly. "Cannot say I am surprised. You look much like your father did at your age. Vilnar... he had the same trouble. Always turning heads, breaking hearts without meaning to." He chuckled. "Lucky for me, my own looks are merely... average." He laughed again.

I managed a weak grin back, still feeling off-balance by the whole situation.

"Before you ask about Vilnar," Erenar continued, perhaps sensing my unspoken questions, "let me speak plainly. Your father... my brother... was two years younger than me. Handsome, strong, righteous, brave, smart... almost perfect, as young men go. But," he sighed, his expression turning serious, "he had his flaws. Reckless, often. Reacted too quickly on pure feeling, acted sometimes without thinking things through fully. I would not be surprised," he added, his gaze sharp, meeting mine directly, "if some of that same impulsiveness has passed down to you."

"Yes..." I admitted quietly, thinking of my impulsive return to the tavern in Ortleg, my fight with Rogas, maybe even following Vida north. "It looks like I cannot hide much from you... Father." The address still felt strange.

"But, Vahnar," Erenar leaned forward again, his expression keen, "I am curious. If Freya's accusation held *some* truth... if perhaps you suspected your heritage, knew your father was Vilnar, knew he was Vallanir... why come all the way here with them? Why hide your identity from them for so long?"

I met his gaze, choosing my words carefully, needing him to understand, perhaps needing his protection. "I only knew my father's name was Vilnar, and that he was from Vallanir. Nothing more. I did not know he was the Hardingir's son, your brother." I explained about my mother's dying warning, her vague story of a quarrel between Vilnar and his brothers. "I decided... if I traveled north with Vida and Freya... I had to understand the situation first. Understand the nature of that quarrel, see if revealing myself would bring danger, or just reopen old wounds. So I waited."

Erenar listened intently, then nodded slowly, thoughtfully. "Your mother spoke of a quarrel? Yes, that is true. The last time Vilnar left... he argued fiercely with Tarnar. Over the southern raid years before." He waved a dismissive hand. "But Vahnar... if you have siblings, you know such quarrels are normal between brothers. Fire flashes, then cools. We are family. Bound by blood. In the end, family must stand together. Especially now. We have dangerous enemies outside our borders."

"The Logenir?" I asked.

"Exactly," Erenar confirmed grimly. "They have always been our enemies, and they grow stronger, bolder under Malagar's leadership. We cannot afford carelessness now." He looked at me intently again. "Yesterday, Vida told me briefly of the battle you aided her militia in, down south near Thaluk. How many Logenirs did your combined forces kill there?"

"Approximately one hundred and fifty," I confirmed.

"That many?" Erenar looked impressed, but also concerned. "A significant blow. But they still have their main army far to the west. Five hundred warriors at least, perhaps more if their own allies join them. We Vallanir, with our closest allies like the Brahanir and Drakknir... maybe eight hundred, if all answer the call. But our allies are distant. It takes time for them to gather. If the Logenir strike hard and fast..." he left the implication hanging, "...we might have to rely only on our own strength."

"You mean... if war comes... we could lose?" The thought was sobering.

"Vallanir *never* gives up," Erenar stated fiercely, his eyes flashing. "We never truly lose. But yes," he admitted frankly, "this time, their chances look better than they have in generations. Which is why," his gaze sharpened again, locking onto mine, "your presence here, Vahnar, your return... it is invaluable."

"When I came here..." I protested honestly, feeling uncomfortable again, "...I wasn't thinking of war..."

"Vida said you came seeking answers, helping her hunt Ethrak. The quest for the hammer failed, she told me." He shrugged. "No matter. Because we found something far more valuable." He leaned forward, his voice dropping, filled with conviction. "You, Vahnar. Fate, the gods, the spirits... they guided you back to Vallanir. Back home. To protect us."

"Isn't that... exaggerating things?" I shifted uneasily. "I still struggle sometimes just to protect myself."

"Vida believes in your abilities," Erenar stated simply. "She judges warriors well. And I always trust her."

"After tonight..." I muttered, thinking of Vida fleeing the room, "...I am not sure she believes in me much anymore."

Erenar actually laughed then, a short, sharp sound, shaking his head. "Yes, I can see that. Your... situation... with my daughters... it looks pretty complicated indeed." He paused, then added, his tone softening slightly, though his words felt like another blow, "Talk to her, Vahnar. Give her time. Hearts heal. I am sure Vida... she will eventually accept you..." He paused again, then finished, his gaze meeting mine with casual certainty, "...as her brother."

Brother. The word landed like a physical punch, stealing my breath, crushing the last, foolish ember of hope that maybe, somehow... My heart felt like it was cracking inside my chest.

"I..." I swallowed hard, unable to find words. "I'll think about it," I replied quietly, dropping my gaze, feeling utterly defeated.

Erenar nodded, seemingly satisfied, oblivious to the devastation his words caused. "Do not think too long, Vahnar. We need you. Now. You are Vallanir's best hope." He stood up, signalling the end of our conversation. "Starting tomorrow, you will join me. Meet the elders properly. I will introduce you to our people as Vahnar of Vallanir." He placed a heavy hand on my shoulder. "And starting tonight, you move your belongings into this house. Your place is here now. No longer the guest house." His grip tightened slightly. "You are not a guest, Vahnar. You are family."

42

Watch Over Her

Sleep offered little escape that night. I lay stiffly on the sleeping furs in the room Tilda had said was once my father's, staring up into the darkness. My thoughts chased each other in circles. This house, this village... it felt both strangely familiar and utterly foreign. Opening the window earlier, looking out at the dark southern woods, I'd imagined my parents standing there, maybe gazing towards the life they'd left behind. I understood that longing now, more than ever. Ortleg, Bortez's forge, even the dusty roads I'd walked with Muriel... it felt like another lifetime, though barely two months had passed since I fled. How was Muriel now? Was she safe under Horsling's protection? Did she ever think of me?

Then my thoughts inevitably circled back to Vida. Cousin. The word was a physical pain, a barrier of blood and custom that made the closeness we'd shared in the cave feel like a transgression. Was it truly over? Had that one revelation erased everything? I knew I shouldn't think about her, shouldn't hope. I *had* to forget, move on. But how? Her face, her fierce eyes, the unexpected softness in her touch... it was seared into my mind. It was maddening.

I needed to talk to her. Needed to see her, gauge her reaction now, after the initial shock. Her room was likely just down the corridor. But what good would it do? What could I possibly say? What answers could I hope for? That she was fine? That we were just family now, nothing more?

That the love I felt, the love I thought she returned, meant nothing? No. I couldn't face those answers. Better to just... let it lie. Forget it. Or go crazy trying. Sleep eventually came, but it was shallow, filled with uneasy dreams I couldn't recall upon waking.

I rose before the first hint of dawn, restless. The longhouse was silent, the other doors along the corridor firmly closed. Downstairs in the great hall, candles still burned low, casting long shadows. I helped myself to some fruit left on the massive dining table, the memory of last night's disastrous meal making my stomach clench. Needing air, needing action, I unlatched the heavy front door and stepped out onto the stone terrace.

Two guards sat huddled against the morning chill, the same pair from yesterday, I thought. They scrambled respectfully to their feet as I emerged.

"Good morning," I nodded. "Edril? Adrag? Am I right?"

"Good morning. Yes, sir... Lord Vahnar." They still looked slightly nervous around me.

"Just William is fine," I sighed. "Or Vahnar, if you must. No need for 'sir' or 'lord'."

"Alright... Vahnar."

"Is it always this quiet?" I asked, looking out at the sleeping village. "Did I wake too early?"

"Not really," Edril replied. "Hunters, fishermen... many leave before dawn. You would see them down by the river docks now."

An interesting thought, maybe a distraction. But no, mingling with villagers wouldn't help me forget Vida, or the tangled mess my life had become. "I think I need something else," I said. "Is there... somewhere here to practice? With a sword?"

Adrag pointed towards the back of the longhouse. "Behind the house, Vahnar. A training field. Quiet this early, no one will disturb you. There's an old weapon shelf on the back wall – blades are old, mostly, but some still have a good edge. Or... you could borrow ours, perhaps?"

"The weapons there will be fine," I said quickly. "Thank you."

I walked down the terrace steps, around the side of the immense longhouse, and found the field they'd described – a large, flat expanse of packed earth surrounded by tall pines. Against the back wall of the house stood an old, weathered shelf holding an assortment of practice blades, shields, and spears. I ran my hand along the sword hilts, testing weights, checking balance. Being a blacksmith gave me an edge here; I knew good steel, knew how a weapon should feel in the hand. I selected a longsword that felt solid, balanced, its edge worn but serviceable.

Then I began to practice. Back in Ortleg, Bortez always disapproved of my interest in swords, wanting me focused on the forge, but I'd practiced forms on my own whenever possible, occasionally testing my skill against Rogas or some of the retired soldiers in the village who humored me. Since fleeing north, since the river ambush, since Thaluk... there had been no time for disciplined practice, only desperate fighting for survival. My skills felt raw, instinctive, honed by necessity rather than proper training. If I didn't work at it, that edge would dull quickly.

I moved through the basic forms I knew, then shifted to the more aggressive Hualeg style I'd seen Vida and her warriors use, adapting it, making it my own.

Sweat poured off me as I pushed myself harder, faster, channeling all my frustration, my grief, my confusion into the movements, the blade whistling through the cold morning air. I lost track of time, lost in the rhythm of attack and defense, until the sky began to lighten and the sun's first rays pierced through the pines.

Lowering the sword, breathing heavily, I sensed I wasn't alone. I turned. Erenar – my uncle, the Hardingir – stood near the edge of the field, flanked by the two guards, Edril and Adrag. They were watching me, Erenar's expression thoughtful, unreadable.

Wiping sweat from my brow with my forearm, I walked over, placing the sword carefully back on the shelf. "Father," I inclined my head respectfully.

Erenar shook his head slowly, a strange look in his eyes – admiration? Calculation? "Vahnar," he said, his voice filled with something akin to awe. "What... what *was* that we just witnessed?"

"What do you mean?" I asked, catching my breath.

"Your movements. So fast. Precise. No wasted energy. No flaw I could see." He shook his head again. "No wonder... no wonder the Logenir fell before you like dry leaves."

I laughed softly, deflecting the praise. "Just shaking off the stiffness. It has been a while since I practiced properly." I changed the subject. "You are heading out early?"

"Yes. There is a meeting at the village hall. Important news arrived late last night." His expression turned serious. "I was planning to gather the elders this afternoon, introduce you formally. But this news... it requires immediate attention."

"Do you wish me to come?"

"Of course," Erenar replied immediately. "Your insight, your experience against the Logenir... it is needed." He glanced at my sweaty state. "Or do you wish to eat first? Your... Mother Tilda has prepared breakfast, I am sure."

Mother. The word still felt alien. "I ate some fruit earlier," I replied. "I am ready now."

"Good. Then come with me."

We walked down the hill towards the village center, Edril and Adrag following a respectful distance behind. The village was coming alive now, people moving through the lanes, smoke rising from chimneys, the sounds of the market near the hall growing louder. Heads turned as we passed, eyes fixing on Erenar, then flicking towards me with open curiosity. Some people even broke off from their tasks and began following us towards the hall, sensing something important was happening.

The village hall was already crowded when we arrived. Warriors, elders, clan leaders milled about, their faces grim, voices low and urgent. Most stood near the back, leaving a clear space around the central fire pit where about a dozen figures were already seated in a formal council circle. My eyes scanned the seated figures, stopping as they found her. Vida. She sat straight-backed, staring into the fire, her expression shuttered, revealing nothing. To her left, an empty chair – Erenar's place, presumably.

"Bring another seat," Erenar commanded sharply as we entered, his voice cutting through the low murmur. "Place it beside my daughter Vida.

For my son, Vahnar."

More murmurs rippled through the hall – surprise, confusion, maybe resentment? Son? Placing me, the newcomer, the southerner, in a seat of honor beside Vida? Erenar was making a clear statement. A chair was quickly brought and placed to Vida's right. Erenar gestured for me to sit.

Trying to appear calm, masking the sudden pounding in my chest, I walked forward and took the seat. Vida didn't look at me, didn't acknowledge my presence in any way. The tension felt thick enough to cut. Erenar took his own seat between us.

"Before we begin," Erenar announced loudly, his voice silencing the room, "I have an announcement." He gestured towards me. "I wish to introduce this young man properly to you all. Vahnar, son of Vilnar, my lost brother."

A wave of excited whispers swept the hall.

Erenar continued, his voice resonating with authority. "Some of you older ones may remember my brother Vilnar, who left us many years ago. His wife and he perished in the south, but their son, Vahnar, has returned to us. He has already proven himself a warrior of exceptional skill against our enemies." He looked directly at me. "He will be of great help to us in the days ahead. More importantly," Erenar declared firmly, "my brother's son is *my* son now. In battle, in council, in all matters, I expect you to listen to his voice as you would listen to my own daughter, Vida." He let his gaze sweep the room, challenging anyone to disagree. "That is my announcement."

He paused, letting the weight of his words settle, then turned to business. "While this is cause for celebration, a darker matter requires our immediate attention. Krennar," he nodded towards a sturdy, middle-aged warrior with golden hair and beard seated opposite us, "explain briefly."

Krennar stood up, his face grim. "Hardingir, Elders. Scouts returned this dawn. The Logenir... they have made their move. They have crossed the western border, occupied the northern hunting grounds near the Ash River pass. In force."

Murmurs of anger and concern filled the hall.

Krennar continued, "We do not have exact numbers, but the scouts report seeing banners not only of Logenir, but of the three western tribes allied with them. They mean business, Hardingir. This is no mere raid for territory. They seek to conquer."

"We cannot let that happen!" Drinar, a thin elder with sharp eyes and grey hair, interjected forcefully, rising partly from his seat. "The division our fathers made was just! The Logenir are never satisfied! Give them the hunting grounds, they will demand the river next, then the forest, until they stand at our gates! Their claims are lies! They seek only our destruction!"

"Have they sent envoys? Requested a meeting?" Erenar asked calmly.

"Once their position is stronger, perhaps they will mock us with demands," Drinar spat contemptuously. "Why talk? They have already invaded our land! Our history with them is written in blood! Open war is the only answer!"

"I agree with Drinar," Krennar stated firmly. "Talking is pointless. It is time to fight. We must act swiftly, gather our strength, meet them before they advance further. We cannot wait for distant allies this time. We defend Arthark Pass," he slammed his fist on his knee, "and counter-attack with all our might!"

Erenar nodded slowly, then turned his gaze pointedly towards Vida. "Daughter? Your thoughts?"

Vida looked up from the fire, her face composed, the mask of the warrior firmly in place. "Prepare the soldiers," she said, her voice clear and steady, ringing through the silent hall. "I will lead them."

My breath caught. Lead them? Into battle? Against potentially a thousand enemies?

"Who leads the Logenir force?" Erenar asked Krennar. "Is it Mornir?"

"We do not know for certain yet, Hardingir," Krennar replied. "But given the scale and audacity, it seems likely."

"Mornir," Erenar mused grimly. "Reckless like his father. He just returned from his failed southern raid, losing scores of men, yet he attacks again so soon?"

"If his army is large enough, Hardingir, perhaps it is not madness, but confidence," Drinar cautioned.

"That is what troubles me," Erenar admitted, looking around the circle. "The Vallanir have never lost a true war. But the Logenir grow stronger each year. Their alliance now... their numbers may surpass ours significantly if the Andranir and others do not arrive swiftly." He turned his gaze back to me, his expression intense. "Which is why I have hope now, Vahnar. You faced Mornir's warriors near Thaluk. You defeated them against odds. I hope... you can do so again. Here. Will you accompany Vida? Fight beside her?"

Go with Vida? Into battle? My heart leaped at the thought, despite the danger, despite the impossibility hanging between us. To fight beside her, protect her... Yes. Without hesitation. I opened my mouth to agree, to accept—

"No." Vida's voice cut across the hall, sharp and cold, before I could utter a sound. "I do not want him to come with me."

The rejection hit me like a physical blow. I stared at her, stunned, hurt, confused. Everyone in the hall turned to look at her, surprised by her flat refusal.

"Vida..." Erenar began, his tone laced with warning.

"Father," she retorted, meeting his gaze defiantly, "do you think I cannot defeat Mornir myself? Do you doubt my ability to lead our warriors?"

"Daughter, I am merely concerned," Erenar replied patiently. "This is not some border skirmish. This is war."

"Yes! A war I have prepared for!" Vida insisted fiercely. "I will fight them. I will face Mornir myself. And I *will* kill him before all his warriors!" Her eyes flashed with fire.

Erenar studied her for a long moment, then asked quietly, "Are you certain this decision is purely tactical, daughter? Or does it stem from... your personal issue with Vahnar?"

"Father," Vida's voice was dangerously low now, "I ask only one thing. Trust me."

The silence stretched again, thick with tension. I held my breath, watching them.

"Okay," Erenar finally conceded with a heavy sigh. "Vahnar will not accompany you."

Relief seemed to wash over Vida, though her expression remained hard. "Then gather all the warriors," she commanded Krennar immediately. "Prepare weapons, armor, supplies. We march before midday." Krennar nodded respectfully and hurried out to relay the orders.

Vida rose, bowed stiffly to Erenar, and walked out of the hall without another word, without even glancing in my direction.

I sat there, feeling numb, angry, deeply disappointed. Rejected. She didn't want me. Didn't need me. All our plans, the tentative hope for a future together... meaningless now, apparently.

Shortly after Vida left with Krennar and the other war leaders, Erenar dismissed the remaining elders and turned to me, his expression sympathetic but firm. "Vahnar," he requested quietly, "I want you to follow our troops. Secretly."

I looked up, surprised, hesitant now. My enthusiasm had vanished with Vida's rejection. "What... what do you want me to do, Father?"

"I want you to protect her," Erenar said simply, his eyes holding mine. "From behind. Watch over her. Ensure no treachery befalls her from within our own ranks, perhaps. Or intervene if the battle turns truly desperate. Can you do that for me? For her?"

Protect her? Even after she rejected me? A part of me wanted to refuse. But looking at Erenar's worried face, thinking of Vida facing that horde alone... "Okay," I agreed, though my voice felt flat. "But who watches over *me*?"

Erenar managed a faint smile. "If your skills are truly as remarkable as reported, perhaps you will need no one."

"That's nonsense," I grumbled under my breath. "But yes. I can do it."

"Trust me, Vahnar," Erenar said softly. "She will appreciate your presence in the end. Even if she does not know it."

Really? I wasn't so sure about that at all.

That afternoon, clad in dark, inconspicuous clothing, carrying only my sword, dagger, and a small pack, I slipped out of the village unnoticed and began trailing the main Vallanir war party as they marched west towards the Arkhark Valley. I kept my distance, moving through the trees parallel to their path. The warriors in the rear guard saw me, nodded grimly – Erenar must have instructed them – but made no sign, keeping my presence secret from Vida marching confidently at the head of the column.

We traveled through the rest of the day and into the night, stopping only briefly. After maybe a third of the night had passed, the army halted at the edge of the forest overlooking a wide, shallow valley. They made a cold camp, resting before the dawn.

In the grey light just before sunrise, they moved out again, descending into the hilly lowlands of the valley. From the soldiers' low talk drifting back to me, I gathered this was the Arkhark, the contested hunting ground the Logenir now occupied. The valley floor was wide, crossed by a small stream running north to south, bordered by more forests and rocky hills to the west where the enemy presumably waited.

The Vallanir army stopped again near the eastern bank of the stream. I watched from the concealment of the trees as Vida quickly, efficiently deployed her forces. Three hundred warriors moved forward, crossing the shallow stream, spreading out in a battle line – three ranks deep – facing the western forest. The remaining two hundred formed a reserve line behind them, near the edge of the eastern forest where we'd emerged. Vida herself took position at the very center of the front line, sword drawn, shield raised, calm and imposing.

I remained hidden behind the trees, my own hand tight on my sword hilt, feeling the familiar tension coiling in my gut. I scanned the western forest opposite them. All seemed quiet. Too quiet. But then my ears picked up a faint noise, a distant murmur that grew rapidly louder, resolving into shouts, war cries, the harsh clang of weapons being readied. They were coming.

Screams and guttural roars echoed through the trees as the first wave of enemy warriors burst from the western forest, brandishing swords, heavy axes, and crude spears, shouting challenges as they charged towards the stream. Logenir? Or their western tribal allies? Hard to tell from this distance, but they looked fierce, hungry for blood. Maybe two hundred of them in this first wave – fewer than Vida's front line, but charging with reckless abandon.

How would Vida respond? Would she hold the line at the stream?

She didn't hesitate. As the enemy warriors splashed into the shallow water, Vida raised her sword high. Her voice rang out, clear and commanding, screaming a Vallanir battle cry that was instantly answered by her own warriors. Shields locked, spears lowered.

The western warriors hit the Vallanir line like a tidal wave. The battle began instantly – a brutal, bloody collision in the middle of the stream. Swords flashed, axes crunched against shields, spears thrust. Hualeg fighting was raw, merciless. Men screamed as limbs were severed, skulls crushed. Bodies began to fall, staining the clear stream water red. My heart pounded, my eyes fixed desperately on Vida in the chaotic center of the melee.

She fought like a storm unleashed. Fierce, fast, deadly. Her sword seemed everywhere at once, parrying, thrusting, cutting down every enemy foolish enough to engage her directly. She moved with a deadly grace, seemingly untouched amidst the carnage. Watching her, a surge of fierce pride mixed with relief went through me, though my fingers still itched to draw my own blade, to be down there beside her. But I held back. This was just the beginning, I knew. I had to stay hidden, stay watchful.

My fears were confirmed moments later. Another wave of enemies burst from the western forest – maybe a hundred more warriors, roaring as they charged, heading straight for the weakened center of Vida's line, clearly targeting Vida herself.

The Vallanir reserves reacted instantly. With answering shouts, the two hundred warriors held back near the eastern forest charged forward, splashing into the stream to meet the second enemy wave head-on, blocking their path to Vida's main line. A larger, even more chaotic battle erupted across the width of the stream, casualties mounting rapidly on both sides as the reserves clashed furiously with the fresh enemy troops.

My knuckles were white on my sword hilt as I watched, restraining the urge to charge down the slope. I scanned the swirling fight, trying to assess the numbers. Maybe five hundred warriors engaged now on each side? It was hard to tell precisely amidst the chaos, but the Vallanir, despite being potentially outnumbered overall, seemed to be holding their own, perhaps even gaining a slight advantage due to their discipline and Vida's fierce leadership at the front.

But then I remembered the discussion back in the village hall. Krennar and Erenar had estimated Malagar's total force, with allies, could be as high as *one thousand* warriors. If that was true... where were the remaining five hundred? Why hold back half their army? Were they lying in wait further back in the western forest? Or worse... circling around through the hills to attack the Vallanir flank or rear? If *that* happened, Vida's forces, caught between two attacks, could be annihilated.

My eyes scanned the surrounding hills, the edges of the forests, searching for any sign of movement, my initial relief replaced by a cold, growing dread. Where were they? And when would they strike?

43

A Gift From the Enemy

From my hiding place among the eastern pines, I watched the brutal chaos unfold across the shallow stream. My eyes tracked Vida constantly amidst the swirling melee in the center column. She moved like a whirlwind, her sword flashing, holding her ground fiercely against the waves of attackers. Further north, Krennar's column seemed to be pushing their opponents back slowly. But to the south... worry clenched my gut. Our warriors there were clearly struggling, giving ground step by painful step, their line buckling inwards. A dangerous gap was opening up, threatening to expose Vida's flank.

My gaze flicked towards the western forest edge closest to that vulnerable southern flank, scanning the shadows between the trees. Waiting. Anticipating. My instincts screamed danger. And they were right. One by one, then in a sudden flood, more enemy warriors burst from the woods, maybe another hundred or more, charging not towards the main fight, but directly at the weakened southern end of the Vallanir line, aiming to roll them up and hit Vida from the side.

Anyone else might have panicked, shouted a warning that would be lost in the din. But seeing the threat materialize exactly where I feared, a cold, hard clarity settled over me. Erenar wanted me to protect her from behind? Fine. This was how.

Before the Vallanir reserves could fully react, before the southern column completely collapsed, I exploded from my hiding place. Roaring a wordless challenge, I charged down the slope alone, straight into the flank of the advancing enemy horde.

I hit their front ranks like a thunderbolt. Surprise was my only shield. My sword became an extension of my will, a blur of lethal motion. Parry, thrust, slash, spin. Down, down, down. The first few fell before they even realized they were attacked from the side. Screams of pain and horror erupted as I carved a bloody path deeper into their formation. Blood sprayed, splattering my face, my clothes. I didn't care. All thought vanished, replaced by pure, focused combat instinct. Kill anyone close. Keep moving. Keep killing. Don't stop. If a Vallanir warrior stumbled into my path in the confusion, they might get slashed too – there was no time for careful distinction, only for maintaining momentum, destroying the threat.

How many fell before my blade? I lost count. Dozens, surely. The pile of bodies grew behind me as I relentlessly pushed forward, a lone figure driving a wedge deep into the enemy's flank attack. The effect was devastating. Warriors who had been charging forward moments before now hesitated, faltered, their eyes wide with terror as they saw the whirlwind of death cutting through their comrades. Fear, sharp and contagious, spread through their ranks.

Those nearest me broke first, turning and scrambling back towards the safety of the western forest. Their panic infected others. Soon, the entire flanking force, which had seemed poised to crush the Vallanir line, dissolved into a routing mob, fleeing back into the woods, leaving behind a carpet of their dead and dying. The immediate threat was broken. The battle at the stream, seeing their flankers routed, seemed to turn decisively; the remaining Logenir and their allies began to fall back in disarray.

I stood panting amidst the carnage I had wrought, sword dripping red, chest heaving. Around me, the surviving Vallanir warriors near the southern flank stared at me, their expressions a mixture of stunned amazement and perhaps fear. Further off, cheers rose from the main battle line as they saw the enemy fleeing.

I lowered my sword slowly, looking around the gruesome scene – the bodies strewn across the grass, floating in the blood-stained stream. More brutal, more savage than anything I'd seen even in the fights near Thaluk.

Then, a sudden, cold thought pierced through the fading battle haze. *Vida.* I hadn't seen her go down, but in the chaos... where was she? My eyes frantically scanned the victorious Vallanir warriors regrouping by the stream.

"Vida!" I shouted, my voice raw. No answer, just confused looks. Panic seized me, cold and absolute. "VIDA!" Was she among the fallen? Lying somewhere amidst the bodies? No. It couldn't be. Not like this. I started forward, ready to frantically search the piles of dead myself. "No! It wasn't supposed to end like this!"

"William! William!"

I spun around. Svenar, Vida's huge, bearded warrior, was running towards me from the center of the battlefield, his face grim, breathless.

"Svenar! Where is she?" I demanded, grabbing his arm.

"I know where she is!" he panted. "One of Krennar's men... dying... he told me just now. He saw Vida fighting Mornir himself, near the northern flank during the worst of it."

Mornir? *Here?* I hadn't seen the Logenir chief in the melee. "She fought Mornir?"

"Yes," Svenar confirmed grimly. "And Mornir... he captured her, Vahnar. Dragged her away. Into the western forest."

A roar of pure fury escaped me. Mornir. The bastard who'd attacked Thaluk, who'd likely ordered the ambush on me near Helga's hut. Now he had Vida. Captured. I knew Vida was skilled, maybe more skilled than Mornir in a fair fight. But he must have tricked her, trapped her, used his men... The thought of what he might do... Fury warred with sickening fear. I should have been down there! I should have protected her!

"Gather two hundred men!" I roared, shoving Svenar towards the regrouping warriors. "The strongest who can still run! We go after them! NOW! We have to get Vida back before Mornir reaches Logenir territory!"

Night was falling quickly now, shadows lengthening across the blood-soaked valley. Tracking them in the dark forest would be difficult, dangerous. We had no time to waste. As Krennar and other leaders quickly organized the pursuit force, reports trickled in – Vallanir losses heavy, maybe one hundred fifty dead or seriously wounded. But the enemy had suffered far worse – three hundred dead confirmed on the field alone. And we hadn't spared the wounded.

We plunged into the western forest, following the trail of broken branches and blood left by the main retreating Logenir force. Throughout the chase, we encountered stragglers – wounded Logenirs unable to keep pace. There was no mercy. Our warriors cut them down where they found them. The enemy was clearly disorganized, their command broken after Mornir's capture of Vida and subsequent retreat.

By the time true night fell, deep in the forest, we tracked the main body of survivors – perhaps two hundred Logenirs – to the base of a steep, rocky cliff face. They were trapped, too wounded or exhausted to flee further west, trying to establish a defensive position among the boulders littering the slope. We quickly surrounded the hill, sealing off any escape routes.

"We should attack," Krennar, the Vallanir war leader, suggested grimly, joining me at the foot of the slope. "See if Vida is up there, or if they sent her back towards Logenir already."

"I suspect Mornir himself is here," I replied, scanning the dark cliff face. "They said he was wounded fighting Vida. He wouldn't have traveled far. And if *he* is here, she is likely here too."

"Then we go up," Svenar growled beside me, hefting his axe. "Finish them off."

"There are many wounded up there, yes," Krennar cautioned, shaking his head. "But they hold the high ground. Attacking uphill into rocks in the dark... we would take heavy losses ourselves. Vahnar," he turned to me, "do you have a plan? A way to draw them down?"

Rage still burned hot within me. "I want to burn this whole gods-damned hill," I snarled, gripping my sword hilt. "Smoke them out like rats."

Svenar grunted approval, but Krennar looked shocked. "Burn them? Vahnar..."

"But that could hurt Vida," I admitted, forcing the rage down, thinking clearly again. No. There had to be another way.

"Then we wait," Krennar concluded. "Surround them. By morning, hunger, thirst, their wounds... they will have to come down or surrender."

"No!" I refused flatly. "I will not wait! I have to get Vida back *tonight*!"

Ignoring their cautious advice, I stepped forward, closer to the base of the cliff, cupping my hands around my mouth. "MORNIIIR!" My voice roared into the night, echoing off the rocks. Silence answered. "MORNIIIR! ARE YOU UP THERE, YOU COWARD?" Still silence. "MORNIIIR! COME DOWN! Or I swear by Odaran's eye, I will climb up there myself and rip your heart out!" Silence. "MORNIIIR! Send Vida down! Release her NOW! If one hair on her head is harmed, I will butcher you piece by piece before I let you die!" Silence. "MORNIIIR! Come down! Surrender! I will spare your men! Stay up there, and I will kill every last one of you! DO YOU HEAR ME?!" Silence. "MORNIIIR! YOU BASTARD! COME DOWN!" Silence. "MORNIIIR!" Silence. "MORNIIIR!"

All through the long, cold night, I stood there, calling him out, challenging him, threatening him, pleading for Vida's release. My voice grew hoarse. My men watched silently from the darkness behind me. Madness? Foolishness? I didn't care. I had to do *something*. If he wouldn't answer, wouldn't come down... then I *would* climb up. Kill them all myself if necessary.

Finally, as the first hint of grey touched the eastern sky, just as my patience completely snapped and I prepared to scale the rocks, a voice answered from the clifftop above.

"Vahnar!"

I froze. That voice... rough, strained, but recognizable from the brief glimpse on the river weeks ago. Mornir. And he knew my name. Vida must have told him. Which meant... she was still alive! Hope surged through me, fierce and bright.

"Vahnar!" Mornir called again. "I recognize your voice! We met briefly, south of here! I am ready! Ready to come down! Deliver the girl! On one condition! You let me, and all my surviving men, return safely to Logenir!"

"COME DOWN!" I roared back. "RELEASE HER NOW!"

"If she is safe," I shouted, needing confirmation, "unharmed... then I give my word! You and your men may leave! That is my promise! Now bring her down!"

"Let all my soldiers descend first!" Mornir countered. "Let them pass safely west towards Logenir! Once they are gone, clear from your sight, *then* I will come down with the girl!"

I hesitated. Could I trust him? A Logenir's word? But Vida's life hung in the balance. It seemed I had no choice. "Do it!" I yelled back finally.

One by one, figures began scrambling down the rocky path from the clifftop. Logenir warriors, many wounded, limping, supporting each other. They looked terrified, glancing nervously towards me and my silent warriors as they passed the base of the hill and disappeared westward into the forest. We let them go. My promise held. I counted them as they passed. One hundred eighty-nine.

When the last one had vanished, Mornir's voice came again from above. "They are gone! Now I come down with the girl! Do you still keep your promise, Vahnar of Vallanir?"

"Bring Vida here," I called back, my voice tight, "and you can go."

"Send your soldiers away first!" he demanded. "All of them! Back to the forest edge! Until I cannot see them!"

I turned to Krennar, who stood grim-faced beside me. "Do as he says. Move the men back. Now." Krennar nodded curtly and relayed the order. Our two hundred warriors melted back into the trees surrounding the clearing at the base of the hill.

Satisfied, Mornir finally appeared at the top of the path, nudging Vida roughly ahead of him. He held a rope tied tightly around her wrists, the other end looped in his hand. He pressed the tip of his sword against her back, forcing her to walk slowly down the rocky track towards me.

My hand tightened on my own sword hilt, every muscle tense, ready to spring if he made one wrong move. Vida walked stiffly, her head held high, her face pale but defiant in the pre-dawn light. She looked exhausted, maybe hurt, but alive. That was all that mattered.

Just as she reached the bottom of the path, nearly within my reach, Mornir spoke again, halting her. "Stop. Stop there." He kept the sword point pressed against her back, his eyes fixed on me.

"Don't do anything stupid, Mornir!" I growled, taking a cautious step forward.

I saw Vida's eyes flash with anger, saw her body tense as if preparing to fight him even bound.

"Calm yourself, Vahnar!" Mornir replied, though his voice held a tremor of fear beneath the bravado. "I just... I wish to say thank you. If this works out as promised." He attempted a smile that didn't reach his eyes. "You seem... an honorable man. For a Vallanir." He paused. "We are enemies, yes. You hate me, I hate you. But perhaps... perhaps we can trust each other in this, just this once. I respect your strength, Vahnar. Therefore... as a sign of respect... I wish to give you a gift. Information. If you will truly forgive me, my soldiers, for this trouble."

A gift? Information? From him? I didn't believe him for a second. He was stalling, planning something. "Just say what you have to say, Mornir," I replied coldly.

"You, Vahnar," he began, his voice dropping slightly, becoming conspiratorial, "are the son of Vilnar. Grandson of Radnar." He paused, watching my reaction. "Now I will tell you of your father. Tell you what *really* happened to him. How he truly died."

My breath caught. This man... knew about my father's death? "Tell me!" I demanded, my voice hoarse, forgetting caution, needing only the truth.

"Can you promise again? Let me go safely after I tell you?"

I hesitated, glancing at Vida, who stood rigid between us. Her safety was paramount. "Yes," I nodded grimly. "My promise holds. Now tell me!"

"Then listen closely," Mornir said, lowering his voice further, though likely still audible to Vida standing right beside him. "I will not shout it for your warriors in the trees to hear. This is... a gift. Between us."

I felt deeply uncomfortable, suspicious, but curiosity, the burning need to know about my father, overrode everything else. "Continue," I commanded.

"Our tribe, Logenir," he began, his tone turning bitter, "always despised by yours. Robbers, murderers, savages – the names your Vallanir throw at us. You never care how *we* live, how we struggle, though we have families, children, homes to protect, just like you. We want a better life, just like you. Maybe we are *already* better than you in some ways! Do you think we grew strong just by being backward? No! But you Vallanir... always think you are superior."

"Hey!" I shouted, my patience snapping. "Enough! I understand your grievances, Mornir, justified or not! But save the tribal politics for another time! Much of what you say is just self-pitying bullshit! Remember *your* raids south! Remember why I killed so many of your men near Thaluk! And I will do it again if I must, no matter what tales you spin now! Stop wasting time! Tell me what you know about my father, or this truce ends *now*!"

Mornir grinned mirthlessly, seeming almost impressed by my outburst. "But what I say *is* connected, Vahnar. Because of your tribe's arrogance, your prejudice... you blame Logenir for everything bad that happens. Like sixteen years ago. When your father Vilnar fled Vallanir with his wife and son – with *you*." Did I know about that? He assumed I didn't. "He left because of a dispute with your uncles, Tarnar and Erenar. Over an attempted assassination against your father himself, up north somewhere. And also over who should succeed your grandfather Radnar. Vilnar suspected his brothers were behind the assassination attempt. They denied it. Rather than spill kin-blood, your father left."

He paused, letting that sink in. "But what happened next? Your uncle Tarnar gathered thirty warriors, pursued your father south, intending to kill all three of you. Days later... Tarnar and his men were found dead by the river." He leaned forward slightly. "And do you know what your *other* uncle, Erenar, told the Vallanir elders when he became the new Hardingir? He claimed *Logenir* warriors ambushed and killed Tarnar! A lie! A convenient lie that fueled hatred against us for years!" His voice dripped with resentment. "We tried to deny it, sent messengers. Erenar killed them, suppressed the truth. He *needed* us as the enemy to secure his own power, gain support from allies. In the end, we stopped trying. If Vallanir wants us as enemies, fine. We will fight you. Forever."

I stared at him, stunned into silence by the torrent of accusations. Erenar... lied? Blamed Logenir for Tarnar's death? Used it to gain power? Could it be true?

"How?" I finally managed, my voice hoarse. "How do you know all this? Why should I believe *you*?"

"We have eyes and ears in Vallanir," Mornir shrugged dismissively. "As your tribe likely has spies among us. It is the way of things. We kill them when found, or feed them lies. But this truth... it serves me now to tell it to *you*. Think, Vahnar! Your tribe's recent history... built on lies. Erenar, your wise Hardingir... an impostor."

Beside him, Vida gasped softly, trying to pull away, her eyes flashing with anger towards Mornir, maybe towards me too for listening.

Mornir roughly pulled her back. "Hey, Vida, easy now. Just telling truths. Nothing will happen. Right, Vahnar?"

"Whatever you believe," I said carefully, my mind racing, trying to process the implications, watching Vida's distress, "Erenar is still our chief." Doubts swirled, but Vida was still in danger. I couldn't afford to provoke Mornir now.

"And if he did these things... perhaps for the good of the tribe?" I asked, testing him, playing devil's advocate. "Why should we protest now?"

"Is that so?" Mornir sounded genuinely disappointed. "You would accept such dishonor? Hmm. Less like your father than I thought." He paused, then leaned closer again, his voice dropping to a deadly whisper. "Would you still feel that way, Vahnar, if you knew it was Erenar himself who planned Tarnar's pursuit of your father? Planned it so they would likely kill each other? So that *all* his rivals – Kronar already dead, Vilnar and Tarnar destroying each other – would conveniently disappear, leaving *him* free to rise as Hardingir, unchallenged?"

My blood ran cold. Erenar... capable of such cold-blooded betrayal? Against his own brothers?

"Simple, isn't it?" Mornir smiled cruelly. "Smart and simple." He jerked his head towards the south where Tarnar had died. "Do you understand now, Vahnar? It was not *my father's* warriors who killed Tarnar and his thirty men downriver sixteen years ago. It was your father. Vilnar. He fought them all, alone, and killed every last one of them."

"By the gods!" The words were ripped from me, filled with horrified disbelief. "If you lie now, Mornir, I swear I will kill you where you stand!" My hand tightened on my sword, shaking with rage and confusion. "My father... killed them all? Then ran away? He's still alive?"

"No," Mornir replied flatly. "He did not run. Your father was mortally wounded in that fight. He tried to reach your mother's boat – she had gone south first with you – but his strength failed him. He died there, alone, on the river."

"How...?" My voice broke. "How do you know this?"

"Because," Mornir stated calmly, delivering the final, devastating blow, "I met someone later. Someone who traveled those southern rivers soon after. The one who found your father's body floating adrift in his boat... performed the rites... burned him... sent his soul to Valahar."

"Who?" I whispered, dreading the answer.

"A shaman," Mornir replied, his eyes glinting with malicious satisfaction. "*Your* shaman. The wisewoman named Helga."

44

How the Gods Punish Us

Lies. Lies seemed to be everywhere in this northern land, maybe everywhere in the world. Anyone could commit them. Gods know *I* had lied – hiding my identity, maybe even lying to myself about Vida. So why should I be surprised others lied to me? But Mornir's words... they felt significant, twisting things I thought I knew. Had Erenar truly betrayed his brothers? Had my father killed Tarnar? Had Helga kept secrets about his death? It left me feeling foolish, exposed, and utterly alone. Who could I possibly trust now? Erenar, my uncle, the chief? Tilda, my newfound aunt? Helga, the wisewoman? Even Vida... she had lied about the black stone, hadn't she? And now she pulled away, distant. Could I be sure she wouldn't lie again? Did she truly know nothing of my father's past, of Erenar's alleged deceit? Right now, it felt hard to believe anyone.

Mornir's story was explosive, affecting everyone here. It could be true. Or it could be a lie, a fabrication designed to shatter the Vallanir from within. And Vida had heard it all. Now, what would she do? Was she on the side of truth, or would she protect her family at all cost, protect the lies Erenar might have built his power upon? I didn't know. I only knew I had to be careful now. Watch everyone. Trust no one fully. And lie myself, if it meant surviving this. Maybe the only weapon against lies was more lies.

But before that, Mornir had other sentences. "Do you know *why* I am telling you this, Vahnar?" he asked, his voice lowering again, though still carrying clearly. "Do you know why I did not want your soldiers to hear? Because I want *you* to know the truth about your father. And I want *this girl*," he gestured towards Vida with his chin, "to know what *her* father, the chief of your tribe, truly did in the past. I want you both to *think.*"

He straightened up slightly. "I'm gonna tell you how my tribe is, so you can understand. We are ready to fight, always. To be honest, I came here ready, confident I could defeat your Vallanir forces. I believed it was time for Logenir to rise, for Vallanir to fall, for *us* to take care of the other tribes. But then..." his gaze fixed on me again, "...then I met *you*. In the south, briefly. Here, today. You ruined everything. You destroyed my warriors, not just physically, but mentally. We Logenir are not cowards, Vahnar! So why did we become so fearful before you? So desperate? So stunned with disbelief?"

He paused, as if genuinely pondering the question himself. "While I was trapped on that hill tonight, I thought about this. Why is this happening? What is wrong? And then I realized. This is the way the gods have shown us. It is not *I* who am destined to lead Hualeg. It is *you*. What happened today proves it. You can be a destroyer, yes," he glanced towards the unseen battlefield, "but you were also a forgiver, letting my men go." His voice rose slightly. "You were meant to be the leader of *all* of us, Vahnar! *You* deserve to be Hardingir of the Vallanir, not Erenar, that impostor!"

He took another deep breath after his long, passionate speech, then concluded firmly, "This is what I wanted to tell you. Be the leader of your tribe now. Take the responsibility that is yours by right, by strength, perhaps even by destiny. I promise you, Vahnar, if that happens... if *you* become Hardingir... we Logenir, and all the tribes of the West with us, will submit to your rule. We will follow *you*."

I stared at him, utterly speechless for a long moment. His words – about my father, Erenar, Helga, destiny, leadership, even Logenir submission – swirled chaotically in my head. It was too much. Lies? Truth? Manipulation? Sincere belief born of defeat? And he expected an answer now?

My mind settled on one overriding feeling: exhaustion. And distrust.

"Go," I said curtly, dismissing him, dismissing everything he'd just said.

Mornir held my gaze for a second, perhaps surprised by my flat rejection, then nodded slowly. "I await your answer," he said cryptically.

He patted his chest once in that strange gesture of respect, then turned without another word and walked quickly after his soldiers, disappearing into the darkness of the western forest.

I watched him go until he was completely out of sight, my mind still reeling. Then, feeling numb, I walked over to where Vida stood pale and silent, and cut the rope that bound her wrists.

"Thank you..." she whispered, rubbing her skin.

I just nodded, unable to speak. The urge to pull her into my arms, to feel her warmth, to reassure myself she was safe, was overwhelming. But Mornir's words lay between us like a poisoned blade. Erenar's betrayal. My father's death. Our kinship. The responsibility Mornir tried to thrust upon me. It was too much. I turned abruptly and walked away towards the regrouping Vallanir troops waiting by the eastern forest edge.

"William," Vida called out behind me, her voice small, anxious. "I hope you don't believe what Mornir said. He's a robber, a murderer, a swindler."

I kept walking, ignoring her words, needing distance.

"William!" she shouted again, louder this time, desperation in her voice.

I stopped, turning back slowly, letting my own confusion and hurt harden my face. "What?" I snapped back. "I don't care what he said. Do you think I trust *him*? What difference does any of it make now? No. I have nothing to do with any of this Hualeg mess. I'm not staying here long. I've done enough in your country, risked enough. When we get back to the village tomorrow, I'm leaving. Going straight back south. Alone."

Vida stared at me, her eyes wide, blinking rapidly as if I'd struck her. She looked utterly lost, confused, hurt. She opened her mouth, perhaps to argue, perhaps to plead, then seemed to think better of it, closing it again, taking a small step back.

I watched her for a moment, the silence stretching between us thick with unspoken pain. So many things I wanted to scream, to ask her... but what was the point now? What future, what plans could we possibly have together? Cousins. Lies. Betrayal. It felt hopeless. There was nothing left to talk about. Without another word, I turned away again and walked towards the waiting soldiers.

They cheered softly as I approached, relief evident on their tired, bloodstained faces. I barely noticed, walking past them towards the edge of the camp. They were Vida's troops, Krennar's troops. Not mine. My brief leadership during the chase felt meaningless now. My only goal was getting back to the village, confronting Helga, and leaving.

After walking for several hours, weariness finally forced a halt. At midnight, Krennar called for a rest at the edge of a dark forest. The soldiers collapsed gratefully, building small fires, tending wounds. I found a spot apart, leaning against the rough bark of a pine, trying to force my aching body to relax, trying to escape the thoughts chasing circles in my head. It was difficult. Mornir's words kept replaying. *Erenar... Father... Tarnar... Helga... Lies... Destiny... Leader...*

What should I do next? I *had* to talk to someone, had to confirm the truth, or dismiss the lies. Helga? She knew something, found my father's body. Confront Erenar directly? Accuse the Hardingir based on Mornir's word? That felt impossibly dangerous.

Footsteps approached. I looked up. Svenar. He sat down opposite me without invitation, offering a chunk of roasted meat on a broad leaf and a waterskin.

"For you," he rumbled. "You have not eaten or drunk yet."

"Thank you." I accepted gratefully, tearing into the meat.

Svenar took a sip from his own skin, watching me silently. He clearly had something to say.

"Speak, Svenar," I said finally, "if there is anything."

He nodded. "How do you fare, Vahnar?"

"I'm alright," I replied. "And you?"

"Very well. Spirits are still strong." He paused. "Vida asked us to collect the bodies of our fallen comrades properly at first light. We will carry them all on stretchers back to the village. We plan to leave after sunrise, if that meets with your approval."

"Why should I approve or disapprove?" I asked tiredly.

"Well... because..." he shifted slightly, "...we listen to you now, Vahnar. As the Hardingir commanded."

"My approval isn't needed," I repeated. "Did Vida send you to talk to me?"

"No," he shook his head. "She did not send me directly. She merely... asked *through* me... if you were well."

So, still keeping her distance, but asking about me indirectly. It didn't clarify anything. "Tell her I'm fine."

"Okay." Svenar nodded again.

I went back to eating. After a moment of silence, thinking about the battle, I asked, "Our fight today, Svenar. By the stream. Do you think... the losses were too heavy?"

"Yes," he nodded solemnly, his gaze distant. "So many have died. It was the biggest battle I have known in my entire life. Sometimes," he sighed, "I cannot believe there are so many people willing to die, willing to meet Odaran so soon."

"If they had a choice," I countered quietly, "perhaps they would choose a different path."

"Maybe," he conceded. "But, as I have said, we are fighters. It is our way. We fight..."

"Until the next life," I finished wearily. "Yes, Svenar, I get it." I took another drink, the sentiment feeling bleak.

Svenar looked at me then, that long, knowing smile touching his lips again. "Do you realize yet, Vahnar, what you truly did today?"

"What do you mean? I'm drinking."

"In the battle," he clarified patiently. "When you charged the flank alone. Do you know how many Logenir you killed?"

I took a deep breath, the memory a chaotic blur. "Dozens..." I guessed.

He shook his head slowly. "A hundred," he stated quietly but firmly. "Maybe more."

A cold shock ran through me. A *hundred*? I stared at him, swallowing hard, trying to comprehend ending that many lives. I shuddered involuntarily.

"Now," Svenar continued, leaning forward slightly, his voice low, intense, "to these men," he gestured subtly towards the sleeping warriors, "you are... something else. Something more. They saw you today. They respect you. They fear you. Some... perhaps they worship you already. Call you Anthor's incarnation. They will follow you anywhere now, Vahnar. Fight for you without question. Die for you. All because of one battle like this. You made them that way." He paused, letting the weight sink in. "Do you understand that? After today, legends about you will spread throughout Hualeg. Your life... it turns onto a path you could not have predicted." He studied my face again in the firelight. "The question that comes after this is, are you ready?"

Ready? For legends? Worship? It felt absurd, meaningless. My mind was filled with my father, with Erenar's potential betrayal, with Vida... This situation Svenar described... it felt hollow. My personal matters felt far more important. Avenging my father, if Mornir spoke true... *that* felt real.

"Are you ready," Svenar pressed softly, "for the responsibility that will surely come your way? Ready to make mistakes upon mistakes? Because you *will* make them. Yes, that's right, mistakes." He chuckled humorlessly. "Do you think the gods themselves don't make mistakes? Oh, their mistakes are many! Look at Anthor – leaving his hammer behind! A great error!" He took another sip before looking at me again, continuing his grim philosophy. "How you are judged, Vahnar, will not be by today's glory, but by how you face your mistakes later. How you correct them. Will you fix them yourself? Or will you let others suffer for them?"

I managed a weak grin. "You don't have to worry about that, Svenar. I'm not a god. My mistakes shouldn't cause *too* much trouble."

"Do not be so certain," he warned, his tone gentler now. "Something we think small can be very significant to someone else. I have warned you." He stood up then, stretching his massive frame. "Rest now, Vahnar. You have earned it. May Odaran watch over your sleep."

"You too, Svenar," I replied quietly. "And... thank you. For the warning."

He nodded once and left me alone by the fire. Thankfully, that was the last deep conversation of the night. His words gave me much to think about, another heavy layer on top of Mornir's revelations and my own tangled feelings. Exhausted, my mind buzzing, I finally managed to fall into a heavy sleep.

I woke later than usual, just before sunrise, feeling surprisingly rested despite everything. Around me, the camp was already stirring, warriors preparing the stretchers for the dead, packing the few remaining supplies. Someone had left another piece of roasted meat beside my sleeping spot. Svenar again? Or maybe... I looked around and saw Vida approaching, walking towards me from where she'd been speaking with Krennar. My heart did that familiar, painful clench seeing her.

She stopped a few paces away, her expression carefully neutral, formal, though perhaps a hint of weariness showed in her eyes. "Krennar will lead the main party back to Vallanir now with the fallen," she stated. "There is no need for you to hurry with them. Eat first."

"You can all go ahead," I replied, matching her cool tone, the distance between us feeling vast. "I will catch up later."

"I thought..." she hesitated slightly, glancing away for a moment before meeting my eyes again, her voice softer now, uncertain, "...perhaps I would travel back with you? If you do not mind?"

My breath caught. Travel with me? After last night? After everything? "Okay," I managed, trying to keep the surprise, the sudden, irrational flicker of hope, out of my voice.

She nodded curtly, then turned away as Krennar gave the signal for the main party to depart. I ate quickly, my mind racing. What did this mean? We watched the somber procession carrying the stretchers disappear eastward into the forest. Then, Vida returned to where I stood waiting. We started walking together, following the trail at a distance behind the main party.

We walked in silence for a long time. The forest felt heavy with unspoken words, with the chasm that had opened between us. I didn't know what to say, how to act around her now. Perhaps she felt the same.

Finally, after maybe an hour of walking, she broke the silence, her voice low, still not looking directly at me. "Is it true, William? What you said yesterday? That as soon as you reach the village... you intend to go straight back south?"

Hearing her voice, soft and uncertain after the cold formality earlier, made my heart ache. Relief warred with caution, but the wall I'd tried to build crumbled. "Perhaps," I replied honestly.

She glanced at me then, her turquoise eyes searching mine. "You... you no longer wish to accompany me north? To the Ice Lands? To seek Grokhark?"

I stopped, turning to face her fully on the narrow path. "Do you still *want* me to accompany you, Vida?"

"Yes," she whispered, looking down at the fallen leaves at her feet.

"As what?" I pressed gently, needing clarity, needing something, anything to hold onto. "As friends? Or..."

"What do *you* want us to be, William?" she countered, still not meeting my eyes.

I let out a short, humorless laugh. "Are we competing now? To ask each other back?"

"You did that first," she mumbled.

"I still love you, Vida," I said softly, the simple truth cutting through all the complications, all the prohibitions, all the lies we'd been told.

She was silent again for a long time, walking slowly beside me, head bowed. Finally, she replied, her voice thick with unshed tears. "We are cousins, William."

The word hung between us, cold and absolute. I didn't care. Not about customs, not about laws, only about what I felt, what I saw in her eyes despite her denial. "And you still love me, too," I stated quietly, knowing it was true.

She didn't answer, didn't deny it, just walked on thoughtfully.

"I would accept it," I continued, needing to break through her silence, needing her honesty, perhaps, "if you told me you didn't love me anymore. But I think you still do. I can still feel it."

Vida stopped then, shaking her head, finally looking up at me, her eyes glistening with tears she refused to let fall. "Yes," she finally choked out, the word barely audible. "Yes. I still love you." Then her head snapped up, anger flashing through the pain, directed perhaps at fate, at the gods, at the impossibility of it all. "How could I *not* love you anymore? Are you crazy?"

A faint, sad smile touched my lips. Hearing her admit it, even in anger, even knowing it solved nothing fundamental... it eased the crushing weight in my chest, just a fraction. "Thank you," I whispered.

She turned away, frowning, confused. "Why do you thank me?"

"It just... makes me feel better," I admitted honestly. "To know the truth. Even though I know... I cannot hope for more."

"Yes..." she murmured, sounding utterly weary. "...Me too."

I took a deep breath, the forest air cold in my lungs. "If I could wish for anything right now," I said softly, "it would be to turn back time. Just a few days. Back to the cave behind the waterfall. Before Tilda spoke. Before we knew. I would tell you then... tell you we didn't have to go back north at all. We could just take the raft south together, find our own way, without ever needing to know who our fathers were."

Vida shook her head sadly. "William... that changes nothing. We would still be cousins. Ignorance does not erase truth."

"But if we didn't *know*," I argued, perhaps foolishly, "would it be a problem? Would the gods truly punish ignorance?"

"Perhaps," she conceded doubtfully. "Or perhaps not. Perhaps they would understand." She sighed. "But I would still have declined your invitation then, William. I still had my duty, my quest. And if you had not come north with me, if you had not fought yesterday... perhaps Vallanir would have lost. Perhaps *I* would be dead now. So," she looked at me, her expression filled with a strange mixture of sorrow and acceptance, "I must be grateful for the path Odaran showed me, even this painful one. And I hope... I hope you know that too. This... this is the best we can get now."

Was it? Maybe she was right. Thinking about it now, if I hadn't come north... I would never have learned the truth about my father. Bitter knowledge, yes, gained at terrible cost... but knowledge I had craved my entire life. Knowing, even with this unbearable pain, felt strangely better than the aching emptiness of not knowing at all. I nodded slowly, accepting her painful logic.

"So," I asked quietly, the question heavy with unspoken meaning, "you want me to forget you after this?"

She was silent for a long moment, then shook her head slowly, decisively. "I will never forget you, William."

"Me too," I whispered back. "How could I?" A wave of profound sadness washed over me. "But that means... our lives will be filled with this ache, this regret. Perhaps... perhaps *this* is how the gods punish us."

"Or perhaps," Vida offered softly, that Hualeg fatalism surfacing again, "this is how the gods brought us together in *this* life, to face these trials, to learn something beyond simple happiness. Who knows?" A flicker of something – hope? faith? – touched her eyes. "In our next life... perhaps things will be different. Perhaps then... we can truly be together."

Next life? The idea felt cold, distant, offering little comfort for the pain of *this* life. Could I truly believe in such a thing?

"But that is for later, William," she said firmly, meeting my gaze again, her strength returning, the warrior resurfacing. "Not now. We still have much to do in *this* life. Stay strong. The gods will judge us by how we endure this hardship, how we fulfill our duties despite the pain. They *will* do what is best for us in the end. Trust me."

45

Totally Stupid Boy

We walked the rest of the way back towards the Vallanir village in silence, the weight of our acknowledged, impossible love heavy between us. Vida's words echoed in my mind – *We are cousins... next life... stay strong...* Cold comfort. My own heart felt like a raw wound.

As we neared the village outskirts, she spoke again, her voice carefully neutral, pulling me back to the immediate, dangerous present. "About your father, William. What do you think now, after hearing Mornir's story?"

I shrugged, kicking at a loose stone on the path, wary of revealing too much. Mornir's words had shaken me, planted seeds of doubt about everyone, even potentially Vida if she was protecting her stepfather, Erenar. "What do *you* think?" I countered. "Is it all true?"

I knew I had to be careful. Vida seemed honest, just, but Erenar was chief, her mother's husband, the man who had apparently treated her like his own daughter. Her loyalty would likely lie with him.

"I was... puzzled," she admitted slowly, choosing her words with care. "Perhaps parts held truth. But then I remembered who spoke them. Mornir. He killed his own brother for power. He lies, robs, cheats – it is his nature. I cannot believe his words. He spoke only to make us restless, suspicious, to turn us against each other. He hopes to destroy Vallanir through discord, since he failed in battle." Her voice grew stronger, filled with conviction. "My father... Erenar... he is *not* like that. I know him. He is kind. He has protected our family, our tribe, all these years."

"He is not your real father," I pointed out quietly.

"He *is* my father now," she insisted firmly.

"So," I pressed, needing clarity, "you want me to simply ignore everything Mornir said? Forget it?"

"I..." she hesitated, then sighed. "I want you to be *careful*, William. Do not let Mornir's poison twist your feelings, cloud your judgment."

"That's not an answer, Vida."

She looked stunned for a moment by my bluntness. "Don't believe his story," she stated finally, decisively.

"Okay," I replied curtly, though my mind remained unconvinced.

"Don't think about it anymore," she urged. "Once we reach the village, just... come with me."

"Where to?" Suspicion flared again.

"To the Ice Lands," she said quickly. "To find Grokhark. It is best we leave soon. And... I only want *you* to go with me."

"And then?" I asked. "What happens after?"

"What do you mean?"

"When your quest is done," I clarified, needing some vision of the future, however impossible, "and I return south, as I must eventually... will you follow me? Or will you stay here, in the north?"

Vida sighed heavily, turning away slightly. "William... why must we discuss this again? We *cannot*..."

"Then just say it!" Anger surged, fueled by the emotional rollercoaster, the confusion, the impossible situation. "Say you'd rather live here! Say we part ways when this is done, goodbye, farewell! Say you don't want to see me again! It's simple, isn't it? Just say it!"

"Why are you so angry?" she asked quietly, turning back, her eyes wide with surprise, maybe hurt.

"Why *can't* I be angry?" My own emotions boiled over, raw and uncontrolled. "After everything? After learning who I am, who *you* are, what Mornir said... I'm just supposed to ignore it all? Forget everything? Fine!" The words tumbled out in a bitter rush. "Don't worry about me! As long as I am here, your quest, your safety... it's still my priority. I will help you. Anything you need. Go to the Ice Lands? Fine! Sacrifice my life for you? Gladly! Go back south alone afterwards because that's what you truly want? Fine! We won't talk about it anymore! Just tell me when you want to leave for the north. I will be ready."

I stormed ahead then, leaving her standing silent on the path. We continued the rest of the way to the village without another word exchanged between us.

As we entered Vallanir proper, the tense atmosphere from the war council was replaced by something else, something equally heavy but different. Grief. Families of the seventy warriors lost in the battle wept openly in the lanes, while others embraced returning soldiers with tears of relief. The victory felt overshadowed by the cost.

They were already building the cremation tower by the riverbank. By nightfall, all the bodies, including those brought back on stretchers earlier, were prepared and placed upon it. The entire village had gathered around the silent tower. Torches flickered everywhere, casting long, dancing shadows, illuminating faces etched with sorrow. The women and elders stood closest, holding flaming brands ready. I saw Vida standing near her mother Tilda, her face pale and withdrawn in the flickering light. Pradiar the shaman stepped forward, his voice raspy but strong as he chanted the ancient prayers to Odaran Sky Father.

"Take all the souls of these brave people by your side!" he cried, raising his arms to the dark heavens. "Those who came to join all our predecessors! Let their bodies be ashes and let their souls be your faithful guardians until the end of time! In Valahar, eternal glory be with you, O Odaran!"

At his signal, the waiting torches were thrown. Flames instantly licked at the dry firewood beneath the tower, catching quickly, roaring upwards, engulfing the pyre and the bodies upon it. Heat washed over us as the fire raged, sending sparks and thick black smoke swirling into the night sky, carrying the ashes, uniting the spirits of the fallen with the wind and the stars.

After the solemnity of the funeral, the mood shifted jarringly. A victory, however costly, demanded celebration, demanded thanks to the gods. Bonfires were lit in the main square before the village hall. Barrels of ale and strong northern spirits were rolled out. Huge haunches of venison roasted over open pits. Hundreds gathered – warriors, families, elders.

Songs began, loud and boisterous at first, then shifting to mournful chants for the fallen, then back to defiant war songs. Stories of the battle were told, growing grander with each retelling, fueled by grief and ale. And, as Svenar had warned, the stories quickly began to focus on me. Vahnar, the returned son. Vahnar, who killed a hundred Logenir single-handedly. Vahnar, who faced down Mornir and granted mercy.

It felt exaggerated, unreal, disturbingly similar to the way my reputation grew in Thaluk after the first Hualeg attack. But here, in Hualeg itself, where strength and battle-prowess were valued above all else, the effect was magnified tenfold. Men clapped me on the back, offered me endless cups of potent drink, called me hero, champion, even... Anthor's Incarnation, one drunk warrior slurred.

I didn't want it, tried to deflect it, but the drink flowed freely, and the constant praise, the feeling of acceptance (however misplaced), began to wear down my resistance. The alcohol numbed the ache in my heart, softened the sharp edges of confusion and suspicion. Why fight it? I *had* fought bravely. I *had* survived. Why not embrace the moment, let go of the worries, just for tonight?

"Actually, I am confused!" Krennar, the war leader, declared loudly, drawing the attention of the group clustered near the main bonfire – Erenar, Drinar, Svenar, Vida, me, and several others, all well into our cups by now. Vida too, I noted detachedly; she'd matched the warriors drink for drink, her usual reserve seemingly washed away by grief or perhaps the need to forget.

"Why," Krennar demanded, swaying slightly, "did Vahnar not just kill Mornir up on that hill? Finish all the Logenir dogs right there? He could have done it himself!"

"Because Vida was hostage!" someone shouted back immediately. "He had to be careful!"

"No! Not the *only* reason!" Krennar grinned slyly, clearly enjoying holding court. "Mornir deserves worse than a quick death! He should die slowly! Before the widows of the men he killed! Lose face! Cry like a babe before Vahnar here dismembers him! *That* is what our Vahnar must have planned, eh?" He looked directly at me, his eyes gleaming in the firelight. "You have a plan to attack Logenir itself, yes? Teach them a lesson they will never forget?"

Fueled by the drink, by the flattery, by the simmering rage beneath the surface, I laughed recklessly. "Why not?" I slurred, raising my mug. "Yes! Let's chop them all up! Hands and feet first! Hang their bodies from the trees for the crows! Let them die!"

A roar of drunken approval went up from some of the warriors. Krennar laughed heartily. "Oh, Vahnar! By Anthor's hammer, you are terrible!"

"And after that," I continued, caught up in the morbid fantasy, "we go home! Wait twenty years for their children and grandchildren to come take revenge, dismember *us*! Then *our* great-grandchildren go back and dismember *them*! Ha!"

"Hey!" Svenar's booming voice cut through the laughter. "You are too drunk, Vahnar!"

"Really?" I drained my mug defiantly, slamming it down. "Is anyone here *not* drunk?"

"But it's true!" another warrior shouted, pointing towards me. "Vida was up there! If *we* had rushed the hill, Mornir would have hurt her!"

"Who told *you* to go up?" someone else retorted. "*Vahnar* would go up! Kill Mornir! *You* go up, you just die!"

"I needed no help!" Vida suddenly shouted, startling everyone. She swayed slightly, her eyes blazing with drunken anger. "None of you needed to go up! *I* could have killed Mornir myself! Bastard! Who doubts me? Who?!"

"No one doubts you, Vida..." several voices murmured placatingly.

"But Vida," another warrior ventured hesitantly, "you looked... different... when fighting Mornir before. Slower. Weaker, maybe. That is why he captured you."

"Weak?" Vida shrieked, trying to draw her sword, fumbling with the hilt. "You think I am weak? Come here! Fight me! Prove it!"

Before anyone could react, I slammed my own empty mug down on the rough table so hard it bounced. "Who here," I roared, my own drunken fury surging, "wants to hurt Vida?" My eyes swept wildly across the startled faces. "Goddamn it! If *anyone* dares disturb her, dares insult her... I will kill them myself!"

"Hey! Hey! Vahnar! Calm down! Please!" Several hands grabbed my arms, restraining me. "It was just drink talking! A joke! No one here will hurt Vida! No one dares!"

"Looks like we have *all* had too much drink tonight," Erenar's calm voice cut through the commotion.

My head snapped towards him, sitting there calmly on the Hardingir's seat, watching everything. Suddenly, Mornir's accusations, fueled by the alcohol, roared back into my mind. "Oh, Chief!" I slurred, pulling away from the restraining hands, staggering slightly as I faced him. "*You* should have been there too! With me! Listening! Mornir... he said many important things! About the past! About my father!" My voice rose, heedless of the consequences. "About how my father was *murdered*! He said *you* knew all about it! Said *you* were the cause! Is that true, Uncle? Is it?!"

A shocked silence fell over the gathered crowd.

"Vahnar!" Krennar shouted, jumping to his feet, his face flushed with anger. "What nonsense are you speaking?"

"Who speaks nonsense?" I retorted hotly, glaring at Krennar. "Mornir said it!"

"He is a swindler! A liar! You should not have listened to his poison!" Krennar insisted furiously.

"Hey, hey, calm down now," Erenar said smoothly, raising a placating hand, though his eyes were hard as he looked at me. "It seems Vahnar is truly overcome by drink and grief. He should rest now." He turned towards the edge of the firelight. "Svenar? Could you please escort Vahnar... escort my nephew... back to my house?"

Svenar nodded silently, approached me, and placed a heavy hand on my shoulder.

"I can go myself!" I snarled, slapping his hand away, though my legs felt unsteady beneath me.

"Let me take care of him," Vida's voice said softly beside me. Suddenly she was there, slipping her arm around my waist, supporting my swaying weight.

I leaned against her gratefully, the world tilting. We walked away from the firelight, away from the stunned silence of the crowd. I didn't know what was happening, my mind fogged by drink and emotion, but as we stumbled towards the longhouse, I heard Vida whisper fiercely close to my ear.

"Stupid boy. Can you *never* shut your mouth? Totally stupid."

Then the world swam, darkness rushing in, and I lost consciousness completely.

* * *

The next time I surfaced, it was to an incredible, pounding headache and a churning stomach. I was lying down, unsure where. My own room in the longhouse? It felt... wrong somehow. Darker. Colder. I kept my eyes closed, trying to drift back into oblivion, wanting only for the pain to stop. But sleep wouldn't come again. Instead, a voice began whispering in the darkness of my mind, insidious, persistent, seemingly coming from nowhere, yet echoing my deepest, rawest grief and anger.

"Kill him..." it whispered. "Kill him... Kill him... He killed your father... Kill him..."

Revenge. The thought filled my heart, thick and black, bubbling upwards like swamp gas.

I forced my eyes open. My vision swam, blurry at first, then slowly focused. A man sat on a stool beside the sleeping platform where I lay. Watching me. Erenar.

Instinct took over. Kill him! My mind screamed the command. I tried to lunge, tried to summon the strength that had served me so well in battle...

but nothing happened. My body wouldn't respond. Hands, feet, head... utterly immobile. Panic flared, cold and sharp, cutting through the vengeful rage. I could only move my eyes, darting them around the small, unfamiliar room. Trapped. Helpless. What had happened?

"What...?" The word was a weak croak, relief flooding me that I could at least make a sound, but terror quickly followed. *Bastard! Who did this? Erenar? Did he do this to me?*

"Vahnar," Erenar said calmly, his face impassive in the dim light filtering from a high, barred window.

I glared at him, trying to pour all my hatred, all my fear, into that look.

"I am sorry I had to do this to you," he continued, his voice even. "I am... merely afraid you would hurt us all in your anger. Yourself included. If that happened, I am certain you would regret it greatly later."

"Did you... paralyze me?" I managed to force the words out, my voice a strained whisper, anger mixing with the rising tide of fear.

"For a while only," he reassured me calmly. "Until you have calmed. Until we can speak reasonably."

I wanted to scream, to roar, but my throat wouldn't obey. "Should have... killed you... last night..." I hissed, the words barely audible.

Erenar just shook his head sadly. "That was three days ago, Vahnar. You have been... asleep... recovering. And I am sure, if you *had* killed me then, you would indeed regret it now. The pain in your heart might be momentarily eased, yes, but you would unleash a new pain – a cycle of vengeance and hatred – that would consume not only you, but many others around you. Our family. Our tribe." He sighed heavily. "So once again, I am sorry for inducing this sleep, for binding you like this. Do not worry. The effect of the herbs is only temporary; you will be fine soon. I am doing this only so you can truly *hear* what I must say."

"You killed my father," I retorted, pouring all the hatred I felt into the whispered words, my tongue and lips slowly regaining movement. "You planned it all. You incited Tarnar... to attack Father... so they would kill each other! That is how you became Hardingir! You lied to everyone! Made them believe Logenir killed Tarnar! You deserve to die! I *must* kill you!"

Erenar didn't flinch. He just watched me, his expression filled with a profound weariness, a deep sorrow. He heaved another long sigh. "Vahnar," he began, his voice low, heavy with regret, "I made a grave, unforgivable mistake in the past. Yes. And not a single day has passed since then that I do not regret it. The faces of my brothers... Kronar, Vilnar, even Tarnar... the face of my father... they haunt my sleep whenever sleep comes at all. For sixteen years, I have not known a single night of true peace." His voice cracked slightly. "This is how Odaran punishes me in this life, before the spirits claim my soul for judgment in the next. I can only hope... hope that my brothers, my father... can somehow find it in their hearts to forgive me then, accept me into Valahar. But if they will not, I must accept that too. That is my deserved punishment." He looked directly at me then, his eyes filled with pain. "I cannot truly apologize to *you*, Vahnar. Words are meaningless for such a wrong. But still... I must try. For what happened to your father, for the life you lost... I am sorry. Truly sorry."

I shook my head weakly against the furs, rejecting his words. "I... won't forgive you."

Inside my head, the insidious voice whispered again, louder now. *"Kill him. Kill him. Kill him!"* My body felt strangely warm. I felt... a tingling... in the tips of my fingers. They moved! Just slightly, but they moved!

"I will kill you," I whispered, feeling a surge of vengeful strength return.

Erenar just nodded sadly, accepting my hatred. "Vahnar, it is natural you feel this way. But think! Think what will happen to Vallanir if you strike me down now! Everyone here... they will turn against you. They see me as Hardingir, the one who brought stability after years of loss. Killing me, no matter your reasons, no matter the truth of the past... it will destroy this family. Destroy Tilda, Meralda. Destroy Vida and Freya, who both care for you, despite everything. Destroy the fragile peace I have worked sixteen years to build." His voice grew stronger, pleading now. "What I did... it was wrong. Evil, perhaps. But if you repeat that cycle of kin-strife now, Vallanir *will not survive*. We are not Logenir, Vahnar, thriving on betrayal and bloodshed! We are Vallanir! We value kinship, honor, love!"

"Kill him! Don't let him affect you!" The voice hissed in my mind. I could

move my fingers more freely now. My toes. Yes!

"I built this tribe back from the ashes of my brothers' wars," Erenar continued urgently, perhaps sensing the change in me, the returning strength fueled by hatred. "Built alliances based on kindness, justice, forgiveness where possible. That is how we have survived, how we have defended ourselves against the Logenir all these years! What happens when you kill me? Our allies will scatter. No one will trust Vallanir leadership again. One by one, the western tribes, the Logenir... they will pick us apart. Or we will destroy ourselves from within! Do you want that, Vahnar? Is *that* the legacy you wish to claim?" He leaned closer, his eyes pleading. "I know my past sins are unforgivable! But look at what we have now! Look at the future I have tried to build! A future I wished, eventually, to leave to the *next* generation! To *you*, Vahnar! To your children, your grandchildren! I say this because I *do* believe in you! Despite everything! I have thought long on what is best for Vallanir... and I truly believe I want to leave its future in *your* hands..."

His words barely registered. The potion... the paralysis... it was fading completely. Strength surged back into my limbs, fueled by the burning desire for revenge, amplified by the hateful whispers in my head. With a roar, I broke free, throwing off the furs, lunging from the bed. I grabbed Erenar – my uncle, the chief, my father's murderer – by the throat, slamming him hard against the wooden wall of the room.

"*Kill him! Kill him! Kill him!*" The voice screamed triumphantly in my mind.

I glared into Erenar's startled, fearful eyes, tightening my grip. "Do you think," I snarled, my voice raw with hatred, "all the good you claim you've done can *ever* cover the evil of the past? No! You pay now! You get what you deserve!"

He didn't struggle, just looked at me with a terrible sadness, seemingly resigned, ready to die. That was right. He deserved it!

"You're dead!" I roared, drawing back my other hand to strike...

"William! Stop it!"

Shouts erupted from the doorway. Suddenly, the room was filled with people – Freya, Vida, Tilda, Meralda... How had they gotten here so fast? They rushed forward, grabbing at my arms, trying to pull me away from Erenar.

But none of them could move me. Their hands felt like flies buzzing against my skin. My strength, amplified by rage and maybe something else... felt immense, unstoppable.

"Kill him! Kill him! Kill him!" The voice urged, louder, dominating everything else.

I tightened my grip on Erenar's throat, ignoring the desperate pleas of the women, the shouts of the warriors. He deserved to die! He had to die!

"You're dead!" I roared again, ready to deliver the final blow...

Then something hard, impossibly hard, slammed into the side of my head. Pain exploded behind my eyes. The voices, the faces, the room... all dissolved into swirling darkness once more.

46

Nightmare

This time, I woke to darkness and pain. My head felt like it had been split by an axe and roughly bound back together. Every muscle screamed in protest as I tried to shift, only to find I couldn't move my limbs freely. Panic flared as I registered thick ropes biting into my wrists and ankles, securing me spread-eagled to heavy iron rings set into... wooden bars? A cage? A cell? I blinked, trying to focus in the gloom. A small, damp room, heavy air, the only light a thin slit above a heavy wooden door opposite me.

My last memory... roaring Erenar's name... grabbing him by the throat... the shouts... the figures pulling at me... then a blinding pain in my head... I looked down at myself. No new wounds from beating, thankfully. Just the aches from the battle and the lingering throb in my head. But attacking the chief... gods, what had I done? That crime surely deserved death here. Would they torture me first? Or wait until I'd fully recovered before the execution?

Tears of frustration and anger welled up. I wept silently in the darkness, cursing my stupidity. Why had I lost control like that? It was madness! Now I was trapped here, helpless, likely facing death for my outburst. And Erenar... Erenar still lived. He had won. Fool! Idiot!

No. A cold voice whispered in the back of my mind, chillingly familiar now. *Don't give up. Not yet.* A spark of defiance rekindled. I *could* still kill him. If I got out. I *was* strong enough. *Kill him. Kill him. Kill him.* The litany fueled a cold, simmering rage beneath the fear.

Footsteps approached outside. I tensed, holding my breath, then forced myself to relax, closing my eyes, feigning continued unconsciousness. The door creaked open. Light spilled in, momentarily blinding me. Someone entered quietly, sat down cross-legged on the floor just inside the doorway. I risked opening my eyes a fraction.

Vida. Her face was pale, shadowed, her eyes red-rimmed, wet with tears she wasn't bothering to hide.

"William..." she whispered, her voice thick with sorrow.

"Vida," I croaked, relief flooding me just seeing her, despite our impossible situation.

"How are you?" she asked softly.

I let out a harsh, bitter laugh. "How do you think? Tied up like a beast." My eyes narrowed. "Was it you? Did you hit me back there? Knock me out?"

She looked down at her clasped hands. "Yes," she admitted quietly. "I am sorry."

"It's okay," I sighed, the anger fading again, replaced by weary confusion. "I'm fine." Physically, at least.

"You should not have been so stupid," she whispered, shaking her head.

"Maybe," I conceded. "But it felt like it had to be done. He deserved—"

"Please..." she interrupted, looking up, pleading in her eyes. "William, listen first. I have just come from the council. My father... Erenar... and the elders." Her voice trembled. "What you did... it was serious. Attempted murder of the Hardingir. The law demands... the death penalty."

My blood ran cold again. Death. So soon.

"I defended you," she rushed on, leaning forward slightly. "I told them... you were sick. Still recovering from the cave, the lost time. Drunk from the feast. Grieving. Not thinking clearly. I argued for imprisonment, time for you to calm down." She shook her head sadly. "The elders refused. They fear you now, William. Your strength, your rage... they think you are too dangerous." She took a shaky breath. "But then... Father... Erenar... he intervened. Reminded them you are Vilnar's son, his nephew, his son by custom. He... he is willing to forgive you. He persuaded the council to grant you one chance."

One chance? After trying to kill him? I stared at her, amazed. "I... I can be set free?"

Vida nodded slowly. "Yes. One chance. Tomorrow, you will be brought before the council again. You will speak." Her eyes implored mine. "If you show true remorse for attacking Erenar... if you swear a solemn oath, by Odaran, never to repeat it, never to raise hand or voice against the Hardingir or this council again... then they will forgive you. Release you." She leaned closer, her voice urgent. "But William... if you refuse... if you show no regret... the death sentence will be carried out. Immediately."

I understood. Lie. Apologize for something I didn't truly regret, swear loyalty to the man who likely killed my father, and live. "You think I regret trying to kill him?" I asked bitterly. "My only regret, Vida, is that I *failed*!"

"William, please..." she begged, tears spilling over now.

"But you said... I get a chance to talk to them?" The thought sparked again – a chance to expose Erenar publicly?

"Yes," she confirmed. "Tomorrow. Before the elders."

"And Erenar suggested this?" I scoffed. "Isn't he afraid? Afraid I'll stand up and tell everyone what Mornir said? Tell them Erenar instigated Tarnar? Lied about his death?"

Vida sighed, looking utterly weary. "William, think! Who would believe Mornir's word against the Hardingir's? It cannot be proven! And... have you considered? By saying Vilnar killed Tarnar and thirty Vallanir warriors... you destroy your own father's name! Turn their families against his memory! Is *that* what you want?"

Her words hit home. Disgrace my father?

"So you want me to just forget it all?" I asked bitterly. "Let Erenar escape? Let the truth stay buried?"

"Yes," she whispered, looking down again. "Maybe... maybe that is what we must do now. For peace. For your father's honor."

"I can't forgive him, Vida! I won't!"

"Can you not do it... to protect your father's name?" she pleaded.

"My father would be disappointed if I didn't avenge him!"

"How do you know?" she cried, suddenly emotional again. "How? What if he'd be disappointed seeing you throw your life away now? Seeing you destroy his tribe? Fine!" Her voice broke. "You cannot do it for your father! Then what about me? Can you not do this *one thing*... for me?"

I looked down, away from her tear-streaked face, torn apart inside. Revenge... justice... Vida's safety... my promise to her... "I... I can't expect anything more from you anyway, can I?" I mumbled miserably. "Not in this life. Cousins..." I lifted my face, forcing a bitter smile. "So if I have to die tomorrow, then..."

"Stop thinking like that!" Vida surged forward, grabbing the bars near my head, her face close to mine, tears flowing freely now. "I want you to live, William! Do you hear me? LIVE! Even if... even if I can only see you from afar, even if we can never be together... I still want you *alive*! Can you not understand that? Can you not... can you not do this... for *me*?"

Her raw anguish, her desperate plea... it shattered my remaining resistance. Looking into her eyes, seeing the love and fear warring there... how could I refuse her this? How could I choose vengeance over the life she was begging me to keep?

"Alright, Vida," I sighed finally, the fight draining out of me, leaving only a heavy weariness. "Alright. I'll do it. For you. Tomorrow... tomorrow I will say I am sorry."

Vida nodded, relief washing over her face, though the tears still flowed. She wiped at them furiously with the back of her hand, managing a watery smile. "Thank you..."

"Hey," I replied softly, a foolish request rising despite everything. "Can't you... kiss me now?"

"Oh, William," she sobbed, shaking her head. "Don't make me cry more..."

"Please? Just once..."

She looked at me, her expression filled with love and unbearable pain, then leaned forward hesitantly. "Tomorrow," she whispered, her lips brushing mine, feather-light, gone too soon. "If... if everything truly goes well tomorrow... I promise you. I will give... everything... to you then." She pulled back quickly, stood up, her face determined again, though her eyes still glistened. "Rest now."

She turned and left, the heavy door closing behind her, plunging me back into near darkness. I lay there, bound and aching, Vida's promise echoing in the silence. A promise for tomorrow. It felt like a fragile lifeline, warming my heart against the cold despair, making me believe, just maybe, that something good could still come of this. The resentment, the urge for revenge... they were still there, humming beneath the surface. But Vida's promise... right now, that felt like what I needed more.

That night, sleep came fitfully, filled with troubled dreams I couldn't recall. The next morning dawned grey and cold. Hunger gnawed at me – I hadn't eaten since yesterday morning's hurried breakfast. Would today be my last day? Or would Vida's promise hold true?

Waiting in the silence of the cell, doubts returned. Could I really trust Erenar's offer? Was this hearing a genuine chance for reconciliation, or just a trap? A way to make me confess guilt publicly before executing me? My body grew warm with returning anger. Erenar... why hadn't I killed him when I had the chance? Why let myself be stopped?

"*Kill him. Kill him.*" The voice whispered again in my mind, insidious, persuasive. Yes. I could still do it. If I got free...

The cell door opened abruptly. Six heavily armed guards entered. My heart pounded. Was this it? Two nervously held swords towards my neck while the other four swiftly untied my hands and feet from the bars, only to immediately bind my hands tightly behind my back. Heavy iron chains were fastened around my ankles, connected by a short length that forced me into a clumsy shuffle. Overkill. Did they truly fear me this much? Even bound like this? If I were truly free, I had no intention of fighting *them*.

They marched me out, down the short corridor, and into the main village hall. It was packed, just as Vida had said. Elders, warriors, families lined the walls, their faces grim, eyes fixed on me. Erenar sat on the Hardingir's seat, flanked by Krennar, Drinar, and other elders. Tilda and Meralda sat nearby. And across the room... Vida and Freya, standing together, Vida pale and tense, Freya looking anxious.

I was pushed roughly into a heavy wooden chair placed alone in the center of the room, facing Erenar and the council. The heavy ankle chains clanked loudly in the sudden silence.

Drinar, the thin elder with sharp eyes, stood up to lead the proceedings. "Vahnar, son of Vilnar," he began formally, his voice echoing in the tense hall. "You are brought here to answer for your actions three days past. You stand accused of the attempted murder of Erenar, Hardingir of the Vallanir tribe. For this, our law demands the sentence of death." He paused, letting the words hang. "However, Hardingir Erenar, exercising his right as chief and acknowledging your kinship and recent service, offers mercy. You have this one opportunity now to apologize before this council, and to swear a solemn oath, by Odaran, that you will not repeat such actions. If we find your regret sincere and your oath binding, we will consider reducing your sentence. If you show no regret, if you refuse the oath, the sentence of death stands. Do you understand?"

"Yes," I replied, my voice hoarse.

"During this proceeding," Drinar continued sternly, "you will show respect. Any disruption, any further threats, will revoke your right to speak, and the sentence will be carried out immediately. Do you understand?"

"Yes."

"Vahnar," Drinar concluded, gesturing towards Erenar, "you may speak now."

This was it. My chance. Remember Vida. Remember her tears, her plea. Remember her promise. Just say sorry. Swear the oath. Live. For her.

I looked directly at Erenar, sitting impassively on his high seat. My uncle. The man who might have killed my father. "What do you want me to say?" I asked, my voice dangerously quiet, ignoring Drinar. "Something you *need* me to say? Or the truth?"

"Vahnar! I warned you!" Drinar rebuked sharply.

"I'm sorry," I began again, forcing the words out, closing my eyes, picturing Vida's face. "And I swear... by... Odaran?" I glanced at Drinar for confirmation.

"Yes, by Odaran," he snapped impatiently.

"Okay." I shrugged, trying to appear compliant, trying to swallow the rage threatening to choke me.

"Are you *really* sorry, Vahnar?" Drinar pressed, clearly unconvinced.

I closed my eyes again. *Sorry. For Vida.* But seeing Erenar's face in my mind's eye brought back the flood of betrayal – Father dead, Mother warning me away, Tarnar's attack, Helga's lies... Erenar instigating it all... *Kill him!* the voice screamed inside my head.

"Vahnar!" Drinar's voice was sharp. "Are you sorry? This is your last chance!"

I opened my eyes. Looked straight at Erenar. The apology shattered. The promise to Vida forgotten in a surge of uncontrollable fury. "Yes," I heard myself say, my voice chillingly calm now. "I *am* sorry." I paused, feeling the hall hold its breath. "Sorry... if Erenar *also* regrets that he instigated Tarnar to attack my father sixteen years ago with the intention of killing both my father *and my mother!*"

Gasps exploded around the room. Erenar's face went rigid with shock and fury.

I didn't care. The dam had broken. "You, Erenar!" I surged forward in the chair as much as the chains allowed, pointing at him. "You did it so your brothers would die, leaving *you* free to become chief! Then you spread lies! Blamed the Logenir for Tarnar's death to gain sympathy, gain support! You built this tribe on lies! Hid the truth!" My voice rose to a roar. "A swindler! A murderer! *You* are the one who deserves to die! And *you* sit there judging *me?*"

My chest heaved, raw emotion tearing through me. Then, confusingly, tears pricked my eyes again. Why? Why was I doing this? Destroying my only chance? Breaking my promise to Vida? *Oh, Vida... where is she?* I looked wildly around the room, searching for her face through blurred vision. Everyone stared back, speechless. Not angry, but... pitying? Why pity *me*? Erenar was the criminal! Were they all blind? Did the past mean nothing? Would they let this evil stand?

"Vahnar," Drinar finally spoke, his voice heavy with grim finality. "We gave you a chance. You cannot do it. With this council as my witness—"

"Bastard!" I roared again, cutting him off, refusing to hear the sentence. "I will *never* forgive any of you!"

Something snapped inside me then. An incredible energy, raw and powerful, exploded outwards. With a shout that seemed to shake the hall, I surged against my bonds. The thick ropes binding my hands behind my back *snapped* like rotten cords.

Screams erupted. People scrambled backwards in terror. Warriors drew swords.

Ignoring them, I grabbed the heavy wooden chair I'd been bound to, hefted it like a mere stool, and hurled it straight at Erenar. He dodged aside with surprising agility as the chair smashed against the wall behind him. Lunging forward, ignoring the heavy chains hampering my legs, I aimed to crush his skull.

Danger flared from the side. A guard thrusting with a spear. I twisted, letting the point scrape past, grabbed the shaft, yanked the guard off balance, and smashed my free fist into his face, sending him reeling. Another guard swung a sword from my left. I ducked under the blow, punched him hard in the stomach, kicking him away as he doubled over. Nobody could stop me. My eyes found Erenar again, scrambling terrified on the floor.

Yes, the voice hissed in triumph. *Be afraid. Before you die.*

"Nooo! Everyone! Please, stop! Williaaam!"

A desperate cry pierced through my rage. Arms wrapped around me tightly from behind, trying to hold me back. Small arms. A soft body pressed against my back.

Then, simultaneous with the cry, came another sound – a sickening *thud* – and a long, high-pitched scream of pure agony ripped through the air.

"William... please..." A choked whisper, right beside my ear.

The voice... Vida's voice... laced with unbearable pain... it somehow penetrated the red haze, cooling my fury just enough for me to freeze, to turn my head.

I turned. Saw Vida's face, inches from mine, pressed against my shoulder.

She was smiling, a strange, heartbreakingly sad smile. And there was... blood... suddenly blooming on her lips, trickling down her chin. Red against her pale skin.

My eyes dropped lower. Saw the dark, broken wooden shaft of a spear protruding from her stomach, piercing her clean through from behind. A guard's spear. Thrown wildly in the chaos. Meant for *me*. Striking *her* as she threw herself between me and the blow.

My heart shattered. Everything stopped. Sound, sight, breath... all ceased. This couldn't be real. A nightmare. It *had* to be a dream.

"Vida?" The name was a choked whisper, disbelief warring with horror. "VIDAAA!"

Her arms around me weakened, began to slip. I caught her, holding her up as her legs buckled, sinking slowly to my knees, cradling her against me. Trying desperately, impossibly, to hold her together, to stop the life flowing out of her. *What have I done? Oh, gods, what have I done?*

"Hug me... William..." she whispered, her voice fading, blood staining her lips, her eyes fluttering closed. "Hug me..."

Crying, sobbing uncontrollably now, I held her close, burying my face in her hair, rocking her gently, trying to ease a pain far beyond easing.

"William..." Her eyelids flickered open one last time, her gaze finding mine, filled with love and sorrow.

"Yes, Vida... I'm here..."

"I... love you..."

"I love you too, Vida," I cried, tears streaming down my face, mingling with the blood on hers.

Then I let out a long, agonized scream that tore through the stunned silence of the hall as I felt the last breath leave her body, felt her go limp and still in my arms.

47

Forgiveness

Why Vida? The question echoed in the hollow space where my heart used to be. Why her? Of all people, why did *she* have to be the one who die? Why not me? I was the one consumed by rage, the one who deserved punishment. I should be the one lying broken, not her. Only me.

Later, standing on the dark shore of the Ordelahr as dusk settled completely, I stared numbly at the pyre where Vida's body burned. Smoke curled towards the starless, overcast sky, carrying her spirit away – to Valahar, to rest in peace, as Pradiar the shaman had prayed. That's what their beliefs said. For everyone else weeping silently around the fire, Vida was perhaps the purest soul among them, the most deserving of that peace.

The entire village mourned. How could they not? Vida, fierce and disciplined, yet possessing a hidden warmth... she was respected, admired, perhaps loved by many in ways I hadn't fully understood. Death always seemed near her, a warrior constantly challenging danger, but no one, least of all me, expected it to come like *this*. My fault. The thought was a relentless hammer blow against my skull. My rage, my loss of control... I had caused this. All of it. Tomorrow, when I joined her in the afterlife, I would apologize. Maybe she wouldn't forgive me. But I had to say it.

Heavy iron chains bound my wrists and feet again, biting cold against my skin, pulled much tighter than before. It felt unnecessary. The fight had drained out of me completely when Vida fell. I wouldn't run. Wouldn't resist. I had fully accepted my fate now. Let them sentence me tomorrow. If I could die sooner, tonight even, and perhaps find her again, wherever souls went... that would be better than enduring this night, this unbearable, crushing pain alone in the darkness. This, I supposed, was my punishment in this world.

The night deepened. The funeral fire died down to glowing embers. The mourners drifted away, leaving the riverbank silent save for the soft whisper of the water. Vida's ashes mingled with the dust, blown away by the cold wind. Someone approached through the darkness, sat down on the ground in front of me. Other figures stood silently nearby, shadows against the dying firelight.

I didn't look up, didn't care who they were. Guards, probably, come to take me back to the cell. Fine. Let them. If I had a choice, I'd die right here, by the river where her ashes scattered. But it wouldn't be that easy, would it? Maybe they meant to torture me first. I deserved that too.

"Vahnar."

The voice startled me. I lifted my heavy head. Erenar. My uncle, the Hardingir, sat cross-legged before me. Behind him stood Tilda, Meralda, a pale but composed Freya, and several of the tribal elders, including Krennar and Drinar. Their faces were etched with sadness in the dim light, tear tracks glistening on some cheeks. What more could they possibly want from me?

"What?" I asked dully, looking back down at the ground.

"It is... a very sad day," Erenar whispered, his own voice heavy. "The burden feels... immense. Hard to carry. Especially," he glanced back towards Tilda, "for Vida's mother."

My gaze lifted involuntarily, meeting Tilda's eyes. They were red, swollen from weeping, but held a profound depth of sorrow rather than accusation. Seeing her grief mirrored, magnified my own. Fresh tears welled in my eyes, hot and shaming. How could I face her? Vida's mother? After what my actions had cost her? I looked away again quickly, unable to bear her gaze.

"Ma'am... I am so sorry... Truly sorry..." Tears flowed freely down my

FORGIVENESS

face.

"Vahnar," Tilda's voice was surprisingly gentle, though thick with tears. "Why do you call me that again? You are still our son, Vahnar, no matter what has happened." She knelt beside Erenar, reaching out a hand towards me, though she didn't touch my chains. "Today I lost my child. Do you truly think I wish to lose another? Please," her voice broke slightly, "do not blame yourself alone. We *all* made mistakes. Perhaps mine, perhaps Erenar's, perhaps the elders'... mistakes bigger than yours led us to this terrible place. We are all just as sorry, Vahnar. Just as heartbroken." She took a shaky breath. "My husband... Erenar... wishes to speak with you. I beg you, listen to him now. This is the worst day Vallanir has known in memory. But we must endure it. For the future. For our children, our grandchildren who remain. Please, Vahnar. Listen."

I nodded numbly. "I am listening."

Erenar cleared his throat. "Vahnar," he began, his voice low, filled with a weariness that seemed bone-deep, "earlier today... after you were taken away... I spoke long with the elders. With my wives. With Freya." He looked me straight in the eye. "I told them everything. About what happened between me, Tarnar, and your father, Vilnar, sixteen years ago. I admitted my part. Instigating Tarnar's pursuit out of spite, out of ambition." He swallowed hard. "Like I told you... in your room... I am sorry. Truly sorry. Not a day passes I do not feel the weight of that guilt. But for sixteen years, I hid it. Fear kept me silent. Fear of losing my position, fear of retribution, fear that people would forget any good I tried to do for Vallanir." He sighed heavily. "But I know now... I cannot hide any longer. Today, I confessed everything to the council, to my family. I have prayed to the gods for mercy, though I likely deserve none. I pray my father, my brothers... especially Vilnar... can somehow forgive me in the afterlife. And now," his gaze held mine again, filled with shame but also a strange sort of relief, "I apologize to you, Vahnar. I know... I know it may be impossible for you to forgive..."

"I forgive you," I heard myself say, the words quiet but clear in the stillness.

My quick reply seemed to stun everyone. Erenar stared at me, bewildered.

Tilda gasped softly.

"The mistakes you made," I continued, looking down at my chains, a bitter calmness settling over me, "they were terrible, yes. But they were not as great as the mistake *I* made today. My rage... it cost Vida her life." The admission felt like tearing open my own chest. "I would be ashamed indeed if I could not find forgiveness for you, when my own actions are beyond forgiving." Maybe... maybe forgiving him was the first step towards finding peace myself. If I was to die tomorrow, better to die without this hatred consuming me.

Erenar nodded slowly, seeming to accept my words, his own eyes glistening now. "We... we have all forgiven you too, Vahnar." He raised a hand. One of the guards who had stood silently behind me stepped forward, knelt, and began unlocking the heavy iron chains on my wrists and ankles.

I looked up at Erenar again, confused. "You... you let me go?"

"Yes," he confirmed gently. "You are free now."

Free? The word felt meaningless. "But... why?" I shook my head sadly, the fight completely gone from me, replaced only by despair. "What good is freedom now? Can it bring Vida back? Can it let me see her smile again?" My voice broke. "I don't want it. Take me back to the cell. Let the sentence be carried out tomorrow. Let me die..."

"Vahnar! Stop it!" Tilda exclaimed sharply, cutting through my despair. "Do you truly think Vida would like seeing you like this? Wallowing in misery? Wishing for death?"

I looked down again, unable to answer, tears blurring my vision. "I loved her..."

"And she loved you," Tilda insisted, her voice softening again, kneeling beside me now, placing a comforting hand on my shoulder. "Do you think she would want you to throw your life away now because of a terrible accident? Because of grief?" She gently tilted my chin up, forcing me to meet her tear-filled but steady gaze. "She would want you to *live*, Vahnar. To be strong." Her grip tightened slightly. "You know her. You know her spirit. You must know what she truly wanted, what she was fighting for. Now that you are free... you have a chance. A chance to do something *for* her. Do you understand?"

Her words pierced through the fog of my grief. What did Vida want? Beyond our impossible love?

But then another fear surfaced. "If you release me," I asked hesitantly, looking from Tilda to Erenar, "won't you... won't you be afraid of me?"

"What do you mean?" Tilda asked, puzzled.

The elders murmured uneasily behind them.

"My anger... the rage..." I struggled to explain. "I couldn't control it yesterday. In the hall. It... it just took over. There's something... wrong inside me. In my head, my body... it makes me do terrible things. What if it happens again? I could hurt you. Hurt anyone."

Erenar nodded gravely. "We are aware of the danger, Vahnar. What we witnessed in the hall... it was not natural warrior fury. That is why," he added firmly, "we do not believe punishing you further is the answer. This is... an affliction, perhaps? A imbalance caused by... recent events?" He glanced towards the river where the pyre still glowed faintly. "We cannot condemn a man for a sickness of the spirit. But neither can we ignore the danger. We must face it, understand it, find a solution." He met my eyes again. "I have spoken with Helga. She... she knows what happened in the east. She understands what may be affecting you. Tomorrow," he stated calmly, "you *will* talk with her."

I nodded slowly. Helga. Maybe she *could* help. Explain the whispers, the rage, the lost time... Maybe. It was a sliver of hope.

"Do you know, Vahnar," Tilda asked gently, "what you will do now? After you speak with Helga?"

I shook my head wearily. "I don't know yet. I... I was thinking... maybe just go back south. Leave Hualeg behind again."

"Your home is *here* now, Vahnar!" Tilda's voice rose with surprising passion. "Your family is here!"

"I'm sorry, Mother Tilda," I mumbled, "but I don't know... I don't know if I can stay here. Not without... not without thinking of Vida every day..."

"Are you truly going to leave us, Vahnar?" Meralda, Erenar's First Wife, spoke for the first time, her voice filled with quiet disappointment.

"I... I don't know..." I repeated helplessly.

"That means," Erenar's voice cut through my uncertainty, firm and decisive again, "it is time to move on to the next agenda."

I looked up at him, confused. Next agenda?

Erenar stood, drawing himself up to his full height, addressing not just me, but the gathered elders. "Vahnar," he began solemnly, his voice ringing with formality now. "After confessing my past misdeeds to the council, I told them also that the Vallanir tribe must endure, must look to the future, no matter the pain of the present. Given my mistakes, the shadows they cast... I feel I no longer deserve to lead as Hardingir. I am not worthy of the full respect, the full trust, required to protect our people in the dangerous times ahead." He paused, his gaze sweeping the faces of the elders, who nodded gravely. "We have all discussed this at length. We are unanimous in our agreement on who *is* best suited. Who has the strength, the courage, perhaps even the destiny, to take on this responsibility." He turned back to me, his expression serious, unwavering. "We have chosen *you*, Vahnar. You will be the next Hardingir of the Vallanir."

I stared at him, utterly, completely shocked. Me? Hardingir? After everything? It made no sense.

Before I could even form a protest, Erenar continued, raising his voice so all could hear. "All of you here are witnesses! By Odaran, I, Erenar son of Radnar, step down this night as Hardingir of the Vallanir! And I appoint Vahnar, son of Vilnar, grandson of Radnar, as my successor! May Odaran bless us all!"

I sat frozen on the ground, shivering uncontrollably now, though not from cold. *Hardingir? Me? What is happening?*

Erenar stepped towards me, reached down, took my right hand, and clasped it firmly between both of his, nodding respectfully. "Accept this responsibility, Vahnar," he urged quietly but intensely. "Lead us well. Take good care of us all."

Then he stood beside me. One by one, starting with Meralda, then Tilda, then a tearful but resolute Freya, then the elders, Krennar, Drinar, then Svenar, other warriors, even villagers who had gathered silently behind...

they came forward. Each took my hand, clasped it briefly, murmured words of respect, allegiance, hope. Some of the older women even kissed my hand. It seemed endless, this procession of expectant faces, this sudden, overwhelming weight of leadership settling onto my shoulders. Numbly, dazedly, I accepted their gestures, tried to nod, tried to force a smile that felt impossibly difficult.

"How long will this last?" I whispered desperately to Erenar, who stood steadfastly beside me throughout.

"Long enough," he replied with a faint smile. "Live with it, Vahnar. It is a moment that comes only once in a lifetime."

"But... why?" I asked again, feeling completely lost, uncomfortable. "Why do this to me?"

"It is the only way we can keep you here, in Vallanir," he answered honestly.

"But why do you *want* me here?" My voice felt thick.

"Because we *need* you," he stated simply, his gaze unwavering. "All of us. After today... after yesterday... there is no one more worthy, no one stronger, to protect us now."

I froze, finally understanding the weight of their decision, the burden they were placing on me. "What... what do you want me to do now? After this?"

Erenar shrugged slightly. "Anything you think is good for us. Lead the council. Prepare our defenses. Make peace, or make war. You are Hardingir now. You will have to figure it out for yourself."

"And what about you?"

"I will stay," he replied readily. "Rest in my own longhouse. Offer counsel if you seek it, stay silent if you do not. Unless," he added quietly, "you wish me punished further? Banished? Killed? I will accept your judgment, Hardingir."

"I told you," I said wearily, "I forgive you." The words felt true now, strangely enough. The immediate, burning need for revenge had been overshadowed by grief, by this staggering responsibility. "Stay in the village. I... I may need your wisdom."

"Yes, Hardingir," he nodded, stepping back respectfully.

The procession finally ended well before midnight. The villagers dispersed quietly to their homes. The elders murmured final respects and departed. Soon, I was left standing almost alone by the dying embers of Vida's pyre, the heavy weight of the Hardingir's cloak, hastily retrieved by Tilda, settling on my shoulders.

I returned to the main longhouse, no longer a guest, but its master. As I walked past the closed door of Vida's room, the reality crashed down again. Hardingir. Alone. Without her. The sadness, the loss, felt unbearable. I stumbled into my father's old room – *my* room now – and finally let the tears come again, crying silently in the darkness for Vida, for myself, for the future I never wanted.

The next day, after a short, troubled sleep, I ate breakfast alone in the great hall, the silence oppressive. Then, steeling myself, I prepared to visit Helga. Erenar had said she knew why I lost control, why the rage consumed me. Maybe she held the answers. Maybe understanding *that* was the first step in figuring out how to be the leader these people suddenly expected me to be.

Walking through the village in the quiet early morning light, trying to avoid the respectful, curious glances of the few villagers already about, I heard my name called softly.

"William..."

I turned. Freya stood there, looking hesitant but determined, her eyes still showing traces of yesterday's sorrow. She managed a small, tentative smile.

I simply nodded a greeting, unsure what to say to her now.

"Are you... are you going to see Helga now?" she asked quietly.

"Yes."

"Allow me to accompany you." It wasn't a question, more a statement of intent.

I stared at her for a moment, surprised by her insistence after the previous night's drama. Part of me wanted to refuse, to face Helga alone. But looking at her pale, determined face... perhaps she needed this too. Needed answers.

Needed... something. "That is unnecessary, Freya."

"William, please," she insisted, her voice trembling slightly but firm. "Allow me. Let me... share your burden. That is what I can do now. As your sister," the word still felt strange, jarring, "and as your friend. Perhaps I cannot help much, but... maybe you will feel better not facing her alone?"

Her quiet plea, her offer of simple companionship... it touched something in my weary soul. I finally nodded. "Okay, Freya. You can come with me."

We walked together towards Helga's old house in silence. When we arrived, I knocked on the weathered door.

It opened almost immediately. Helga stood there, her ancient eyes sharp, studying me intently for a long moment before nodding slowly. "Hardingir," she greeted formally, her voice raspy. "Welcome. Come in. You do not mind talking inside?"

"I don't mind," I replied, stepping into the familiar herb-scented room. "Sorry if I disturb you."

"I was waiting for you," Helga said simply, gesturing for us to sit on the floor mats around the low table. She glanced briefly at Freya, then focused back on me, taking a deep breath that seemed to rattle in her chest. "It would be better, perhaps, if we could meet in happier times. I am... sorry... about what happened yesterday, Vahnar. About Vida." Her voice cracked slightly on her grand-niece's name.

"Yes," I said quietly, the pain fresh again. "I am sorry too. Vida... I know she was close to you."

"Vahnar," Helga continued, her gaze sharp again, "what we must discuss now... it will likely bring more sadness, more difficulty."

I nodded grimly. "We have to get through it."

Helga nodded back. "You are Hardingir now. You *must* lead your people through difficult times. That is the path laid before you."

I took a slow breath myself, accepting the weight. "Yes."

Helga glanced towards Freya again, who sat quietly beside me, watching us intently. "And you do not mind your sister hearing this conversation?"

"No problem," I replied firmly, meeting Freya's grateful gaze briefly.

Freya smiled, a quick, nervous flash.

"Okay, if you say so." Helga looked slightly incredulous but finally nodded agreement. She straightened her old body, fixing her piercing eyes on me. "Vahnar. Let us begin. Have you recognized yet that something is... wrong... within you?"

"Yes," I admitted readily. "My emotions... anger, rage... I cannot control them sometimes. It makes me do... terrible things. Unforgivable things." Vida's face flashed before my eyes.

"Do not dwell only on what happened," Helga cautioned gently. "Regret is a swamp that drowns the spirit. Our task now is to find the answer, the cause. Do you know what caused this loss of control? And how long... how long have you felt this imbalance growing within you?"

"Since I came to Vallanir, I suppose," I replied honestly. "Maybe... maybe I have been cursed by your gods? For disobeying my mother? For returning here? Maybe this is all disaster brought by my return?"

"What foolishness is this?" Helga's voice rose sharply, offended. "The gods do not curse mortals so! They test us, yes! Guide us, yes! Punish hubris, perhaps! But they do not inflict uncontrolled rage as some petty vengeance! Think carefully, Vahnar! *When* did this truly start? Was it here? Or perhaps before you arrived? Ask your heart. It remembers, even if your mind forgets."

Her words were like a key turning a lock. My mind flashed back – not to Vallanir, but further back... to the cave. The beast. The dizziness *after*. The lost week. The strange fluency in Hualeg. The whispers... The black stone. "That stone," I whispered, realization dawning with chilling certainty. "The black stone from the cave."

Helga nodded slowly, her expression grave. "Yes. The stone." She leaned forward. "In the old legends, Vahnar, it is always thus. When one of the twin stones of Madnar and Fyrsta is held alone, separated from its other half... it grants great power, yes, enhances strength of body, mind, spirit. But it also amplifies *weakness*. It strengthens *all* emotions – the good, and the bad. Love grows stronger, yes, but so too does hate. Belief becomes easier, but doubt harder to overcome. Reason gives way to passion. Slowly, subtly at first, then more powerfully, the stone makes the bearer lose balance, lose

FORGIVENESS

control, allowing base emotions to surge upwards until, eventually..." her voice dropped, "...they destroy the soul from within. That is what happened to Hinnar, to Godnar, long ago. And now... it happens to you."

Vida's words echoed in my mind – *Maybe something happened to you... something we cannot see...* My own insistence that I felt fine... Fool! "So everything Vida said was right," I admitted, my voice heavy with fresh regret. "There *was* something bad inside me. Growing. And I... I didn't believe her."

"It was my fault as well," Helga replied quietly. "I did not realize the effect would manifest so strongly, so quickly, in one who touched it unprepared. I thought... given your lineage, perhaps... you would be fine. I was wrong."

A terrible thought struck me then. "The stone... could it have affected Vida too?" I asked urgently. "She touched it later, after I fainted!"

"Why would it?" Helga looked surprised. "You were the one who touched it first, Vahnar. Took the full force of its power awakening. You received the... effect. Vida touched it later, after its initial surge perhaps, and told us she felt nothing, did she not?"

"That's what she said," I conceded, doubt nagging at me. "But what if she *did* feel something? Something that weakened her? Maybe she didn't tell us, didn't want us to worry?" I remembered the warrior's comment at the feast, Vida looking slower, weaker fighting Mornir. "Maybe that's why she was captured? Maybe the stone... maybe *I*..." My voice trembled with frustration and a new wave of guilt.

"Vahnar, that is merely guessing," Helga responded gently but firmly, unconvinced. "Grief seeks reasons where none may exist. It is unlikely the stone affected her so."

"I am sure of it!" I exclaimed desperately, needing something, someone else to blame besides my own rage. "The stone is cursed! All of this... Vida wouldn't have died... none of it would have happened if you hadn't told her to seek it in the first place!"

"William..." Freya whispered beside me, her voice filled with fear at my outburst.

"And now you blame *me*, Vahnar?" Helga asked, her voice dangerously quiet, her ancient eyes challenging mine. "Will you let your amplified emotions rage again now? Hurt an old woman who tries only to help you understand?"

Her words pierced through my rising anger. I stared at her, stunned by my own accusation, ashamed. "I... No..." I looked down, struggling for control. "Forgive me, Helga. I... I misspoke." Taking a deep breath, I forced myself to meet her gaze again. "I just meant... I made mistakes. So many mistakes. It was my fault Vida... My fault. I should have listened to her warnings. Been more attentive."

"By Odaran's missing eye, boy, stop blaming yourself for everything!" Helga retorted sharply, though her tone held more exasperation than anger now. "Yes, you made mistakes. So did Vida. So did I. So did Erenar, Tarnar, Kronar, Radnar before us! Life is filled with mistakes! Instead of dwelling only on the darkness, why not acknowledge the light as well? If I had not sent Vida on her quest, yes, perhaps she would still live. But *you* would never have met her. You two would never have known each other, never shared those moments together, however brief." She held my gaze. "Is *that* what you would prefer, Vahnar? To have never known her at all? I do not think so."

She was right. Again. Those moments with Vida... they were the most precious thing that had ever happened to me. Worth any pain? Perhaps.

"What... what do you want me to do now, Helga?" I asked finally, feeling weary, lost.

"First," she said pragmatically, "the black stone you possess. Where is it now?"

"Vida had it," I replied. "In her bag. It should still be in her room in the longhouse."

Helga nodded gravely. "You must retrieve it. Take good care of it, Vahnar. Guard it closely. I am not yet certain of its full effect on you, especially now... after Vida. But if your earlier hunch held truth, if it *can* somehow affect others nearby, weaken them perhaps... then no one else must know of it. No one must touch it. You must keep it safe, hidden, for the rest of your life. Until you die... and pass the stone, and its burden, to your own successor."

"I will take care of it," I promised grimly. I turned slightly, looking at Freya beside me, her face serious, attentive. "And Freya," I added, making a decision, "will help me watch over it. Especially if I must be absent."

Freya met my gaze, understood the trust I was placing in her, and nodded firmly. "Yes, William... Vahnar. I will."

"In the meantime," Helga continued, her voice urgent again, "you *must* obtain the second stone. Grokhark. As soon as possible. The legends are clear – the longer the stones remain separated, the stronger the imbalance grows within the bearer of one. Your emotions, your strength... they will become harder and harder to control. You could hurt more people, Vahnar. Unintentionally. You must find the second stone, reunite them, restore the balance – for your own sake, and for the safety of everyone around you."

"And for Vida's sake," I added quietly, the purpose solidifying within me now. This *was* what I had to do. For her. "Helga, I intended to do this anyway. It was Vida's quest, her dream. She believed reuniting the stones could unite the Hualeg people, bring peace." My own skepticism felt petty now in the face of Vida's sacrifice, Helga's certainty. "Even if the dream seems impossible, I must try. For her. I just... I do not know where exactly to look for Grokhark."

"You must journey north," Helga stated simply. "To the Ice Lands. Where exactly the sword lies hidden... perhaps the legends hold clues. Or perhaps," she added, her gaze intense again, "your own heart will guide you now, thanks to the black stone you carry. It will call to its twin." She leaned forward. "But be warned. It is not an easy place. Killing cold. Endless darkness in winter. Creatures of ice and shadow dwell there. Ordinary men cannot survive long in that realm. But you, Vahnar... thanks to the stone you now bear... you may have something inside you, a strength, that could help you endure."

Her words echoed Vida's strange comment about my body being like fire. "Vida said something like that too," I murmured, understanding dawning. "She... ah..." Realization hit me again – how much Vida knew, how much she tried to tell me, guide me, that I hadn't understood until now. I shook my head, pushing down the fresh wave of grief and regret. I took a deep breath. "Okay. I understand. Thank you, Helga." I looked at her, then at Freya, my resolve hardening. "I will go north. Tomorrow. And I hope... I hope everything goes well."

"May Odaran protect you and bless your quest," Helga replied solemnly. "But, Vahnar," she held up a cautionary hand, "one final thing you may not yet understand, and I must remind you again. The true history of these stones... it is a deep secret. Known only to the Hardingir line, passed down carefully. Even then, not all chiefs learned it immediately; often only near the end of their lives, to keep the secret safe. I know because I *was* Hardingir briefly. Radnar knew, as my brother. But Erenar..." she shook her head, "...Erenar does *not* know the full truth, the true nature of the stones."

I nodded slowly. "I will keep it secret from him."

"But," Helga continued, "we *can* share the secret, if reason demands it. I told Vida, because the task fell to her, because I trusted her above all others. Vida then told you, because you touched the stone, became bound to its fate." Her sharp eyes turned to Freya. "Now... I hope you have good reason, Vahnar, the new Hardingir, for letting young Freya here know these deep secrets as well."

"Yes, Helga. I do," I replied firmly, meeting her gaze. I looked at Freya, saw the understanding and perhaps trepidation in her eyes, but also her unwavering loyalty. I gave her a small, grateful smile. "If what you say is true... my journey north will be incredibly difficult. Dangerous. I may get lost. I may fail. I may even die there." I took another breath. "And I am prepared for that. If... if that happens... I want Freya," I looked directly at her now, ensuring she understood the weight of my words, "to succeed me as Hardingir of the Vallanir. And I want her to inherit the black stone, to guard it, perhaps even to continue the quest in my place, if she chooses."

48

Heiri Hardingir

The small boat felt terribly fragile as I rowed away from the shore, leaving the last trace of Hualeg lands behind, heading north across the vast, cold ocean towards the land of ice. A journey no one took. Madnar and Fyrsta, our first ancestors, had fled *south* from the glacier; survival lay away from that frozen waste, not towards it. Yet here I was, rowing north, directly against my mother's dying wish, chasing a mythical sword to perhaps save my own soul.

Leaving Vallanir had been... difficult. Predictably, almost everyone objected. Erenar pleaded responsibility, Tilda wept openly – having lost one daughter, how could she bear losing another son? – Meralda cautioned wisdom, even Freya, despite her promise to help me, had begged me not to go, tears streaming down her face. It had taken all my newfound, unwelcome authority as Hardingir to insist. I told them simply that this journey *had* to be undertaken, that Helga herself had decreed it necessary. If I didn't return, I told them, accept it as the will of the gods. I repeated my decree: Freya would succeed me, guard the stone, lead the Vallanir. Her tearful acceptance, her promise to pray for my return while bearing the burden I placed on her... it was a heavy weight to carry north.

But all that was behind me now. No point dwelling on it. Days blurred into a rhythm of rowing, resting briefly, rowing again. The blue sea stretched endlessly, reflecting the pale, low-hanging autumn sun. Icebergs, colossal white mountains adrift, began to appear, silent sentinels guarding the approach to the northern realm.

Finally, the ice itself. A vast, blinding white expanse stretching to the horizon under a sky that never seemed fully light or fully dark. I pulled my boat onto the frozen shore, leaving it behind and began to walk.

Where was I going? I had no idea. Helga said my heart would lead me. So I walked, putting one fur-wrapped foot in front of the other, trusting... something. Trusting Vida's quest, perhaps. Trusting Helga's wisdom. Or maybe just trusting the faint warmth that seemed to emanate from within me, pushing back the unnatural cold, the strange fire Vida had spoken of. It kept me alive, kept me moving, though I knew it had limits.

Days passed. Or maybe hours? Time lost meaning in this endless twilight, this landscape of white upon white. I walked north, west, east, south again, searching for... what? A sign? A feeling? A path? There was nothing but ice, wind, and a profound, soul-crushing silence.

I ate the last of my dried meat, melted snow for water. Exhaustion became a constant companion. Hope dwindled. Despair began to creep in, cold as the ice itself. Why was I doing this? For Vida? Was avenging her, fulfilling her quest, worth dying alone in this frozen wasteland? Collapsing onto the ice, too weary to take another step, I closed my eyes, ready to give up.

"Maybe you should stop asking questions."

The voice, soft and familiar, startled my eyes open. Vida. Sitting beside me on the ice, smiling gently, her turquoise eyes filled with warmth, looking more beautiful, more real than memory.

"Vida?" I whispered, tears instantly freezing on my cheeks. Was this death? Had I finally crossed over?

"Yes, it's me," she replied, her voice like a gentle melody. "You push yourself too hard, William. At some point, you must stop thinking so much. Stop burdening yourself with guilt. Stop blaming yourself for everything." Her spectral hand seemed to reach out, though I felt no touch. "Stop looking outside yourself for answers."

"Stop looking?" I asked, confused. "You mean... stop searching for Grokhark?"

She smiled again. "Maybe you do not need to look so hard, when what you seek is already here." Her gaze drifted across the icy expanse. "All around you. Inside you. Your heart knows the way, William. You just need to accept it. See it." Her form shimmered slightly. "This place... it is where it all began. Where *we* all began." She seemed to point, though her hand remained beside her. "Do you see, over there? Where the ice remembers a shoreline? The tall man, sitting before his house? That is Madnar. And the beautiful woman beside him? Fyrsta. And the little boy, laughing as he slides on the ice near that frozen lake? That is Ardnar, their son. He loved to play there. Sometimes," her smile widened, "he played with Rokhan, too."

"Rokhan?" The name from the legend.

"The great white tiger," she confirmed. "Can you see him? Just there, hiding behind that pressure ridge, pretending to stalk the boy?"

I squinted, and impossibly, through swirling ice-mist, I thought I *did* see them – faint, ghostly images superimposed on the desolate landscape. A house that wasn't there. A frozen lake. Figures from myth. And a massive white tiger playfully stalking a laughing child. "Are they... playing hide and seek?" I breathed, awestruck.

Vida laughed, a clear, joyful sound. "Is it so different from children everywhere?"

"No difference?" I shook my head, a disbelieving laugh escaping me. "Please, Vida. No child I knew played hide and seek with tigers! We don't even *have* tigers in the south!"

She laughed again, freely this time. "I have never seen a true tiger either, William, only heard the legends."

"Me neither," I admitted. "Just stories. Always figured if you met one, running was the only sensible plan."

Her laughter warmed me more than any fire. Seeing her like this, happy, free from the burdens she carried in life... it eased some of the ache in my own heart. "I'm glad," I whispered, "so glad to see you again, Vida."

Her spectral smile softened. "Me too, William."

"Is everything... alright? With you? Where you are?" The question felt clumsy.

"I am happy now, William," she reassured me gently. "Truly at peace. So please, take away your sadness for me. Not everything that happened was your fault." Her form began to shimmer more brightly. "Alright," she said softly, "I will forgive you your part in it, if hearing it helps your heart rest."

"Thank you..." I choked out.

"Now that you have seen this place, seen the beginning," she continued, her voice starting to fade slightly, "I must go."

"No!" Panic seized me again. "Don't go! Please, Vida, stay!"

"You do not need to be afraid anymore, William," her fading voice whispered. "You will be fine."

"It's not that!" I cried out to the empty ice. "I just... I want to be with you!"

"You need to get back on your feet now," her voice echoed softly around me, already distant. "Do what you must do. Finish the quest. Live. Don't worry, William. I will always be near you, in your heart, even when you cannot see me."

"Can I... can I see you again?" I pleaded to the wind.

"Maybe," came the faint, fading reply. "I do not know the paths ahead. But no matter what happens, do not lose faith in yourself. Live your life, William. Live it as best you can. And after that... you will see."

"I love you, Vida..."

"I love you too, William."

Then she was gone. Leaving me alone again on the vast, empty ice, the ghostly vision faded, my heart aching with loss, yet strangely... lighter. Filled with a renewed sense of purpose.

The lake. Ardnar's playground. Rokhan's haunt. My heart knew it now. I stood up, my strength surprisingly returned, and looked around. The landscape was still just ice and sky, but now I saw it differently. Over there... yes, where the ice dipped slightly, remembering the curve of a shoreline Madnar's house might have stood upon. And to the right... a vast, flat expanse, smoother than the surrounding ice... the frozen lake.

Staggering slightly at first, then walking with growing confidence, I made my way towards it. Using my axe, I began chipping away at the surface ice. It was thick, ancient, but I worked relentlessly, driven by the certainty Vida's dream-guidance had given me. Over and over, I struck, until finally, the ice fractured, cracked, broke open, revealing dark, impossibly cold water beneath.

The lake looked deep, black. What waited below? Fear warred with faith. Vida's words echoed: *Live your life as best you can... you will see.* My heart, Helga had said, would guide me. Taking a deep breath, pushing aside all doubt, I jumped.

I slid into the frigid water, the shock stealing my breath, then swam downwards through the crushing darkness, drawn by an undeniable pull from the depths. Deeper and deeper I swam, until faint light began to bloom beneath me.

The bottom of the lake wasn't dark mud, but smooth, pale stone, glowing with its own internal luminescence. And sitting there, calmly, seemingly waiting, as if carved from the ice itself, was a creature of myth. A tiger. Immense, terrifyingly beautiful, its fur the colour of fresh snow, its eyes burning like twin red coals in the underwater gloom. Rokhan.

"It has been a long time, Ardnar," the tiger's voice echoed not through the water, but directly inside my head, ancient and impossibly clear. *"You took so long to find me. This time... you have lost."*

I hovered in the water before the massive creature, awestruck, yet strangely calm. "I am not Ardnar," I replied, surprised my own voice sounded equally clear in my mind.

The tiger's red eyes narrowed, boring into me. *"Who are you then? Do you dare play games with Rokhan?"*

"I am Vahnar," I stated clearly. "Son of Vilnar. Son of Radnar." I hesitated, then added honestly, "Son of... many fathers back to Ardnar, whose names I do not yet know."

Rokhan seemed to ponder this, silent for a long moment, his gaze unwavering. *"Vilnar's whelp,"* he rumbled finally, a flicker of recognition, perhaps even sadness, in his ancient eyes. *"Radnar's grandson. Yes... back* to Hinnar the Slaughterer himself." The growl returned. *"Are you the chosen one then? Ardnar's chosen? Hmm. I see him in you, yes. In the spirit, if not the face. You are crazy indeed to dare come here."*

"Master Rokhan," I said respectfully, sensing no immediate hostility now, "do you know why I have come?"

"Of course," the tiger replied, weariness tinging his mental voice. *"You seek the sword. Grokhark. The Bearer of Hatred."* His gaze dropped slightly. *"Take it, then. But first... answer me truly. Why do you want it? Are you like Hinnar, seeking power through vengeance and slaughter?"*

"That's two questions," I noted automatically, then answered honestly, the words coming clear and certain now. "I need the sword, Master Rokhan, to save my own soul. To restore balance within myself, so I do *not* become like Hinnar."

Rokhan froze, his massive head lifting slightly, his red eyes widening in surprise. Then, a deep, rumbling sound filled my mind – laughter. *"Is that it? So simple? No grand claims of uniting the tribes? No vows of righteous duty? No lust for power?"*

"All of that..." I admitted truthfully, "...honestly, seems too large for me to even imagine right now."

"Well said!" Rokhan's laughter rumbled again, shaking the water around me. *"Good enough! I like your answer, Vahnar Vilnarson! Honesty! Acknowledging your own weakness! Yes! Better by far than grandiose lies! Ardnar chose well! The gods chose well! I need not worry then, need I?"*

"I suppose not..." I replied, bewildered by his sudden good humor.

"Then take it!"

"Take... what?"

"The sword! Grokhark! Take it!"

"Where is it?" I looked around the glowing lake bottom.

The great white tiger sighed, a sound like shifting glaciers, and slowly, painfully, raised his massive right foreleg. My breath hitched. Embedded deep in the thick white fur of his chest, angled upwards beneath the ribs, was the hilt of a sword. A black hilt, strangely familiar, matching the description of...

"Why...?" I whispered, horrified. "Why is the sword *there*? Who did this?"

"*Who else?*" Rokhan growled, the pain clear in his mental voice now. "*Hinnar! The Slaughterer himself! Centuries ago! In our final battle! His cursed blade struck true, even as I took it from him. It has remained here ever since, pinning my spirit, preventing my final journey to Odaran, while my brothers Amerik and Ondhar feasted in Valahar without me! And Ethrak...*" He shuddered. "*Ethrak slept, until you woke him, killed him! So now my time comes! Finally! I can wait no longer! Once all four Calamities are truly gone from this world, perhaps Odaran will have need of us again in the next. Do you understand?*"

I nodded slowly, beginning to grasp the ancient sorrow, the long waiting. "Yes, sir."

"*Then do it, Vahnar Vilnarson! Pull it free!*"

I stepped forward hesitantly, reaching towards the black hilt embedded in the tiger's chest. I lifted my face, meeting his ancient red eyes one last time. "I am sorry, Master Rokhan."

"*Yes, yes, yes! Enough sorrow! Just do it!*" he urged impatiently.

Taking a deep breath, I grasped the cold, strangely resonant hilt of Grokhark with both hands, braced my feet against the glowing lake bottom, and pulled. Pulled with all my strength.

The sword resisted for a moment, then slid free with a terrible sucking sound. Instantly, a blinding white light exploded outwards from Rokhan's chest, engulfing everything, accompanied by a deafening bang that seemed to tear through the very fabric of reality. Consciousness fled once more.

***

When I woke again, I was lying face down on the ice beside the hole I'd cut, gasping, shivering uncontrollably. In my right hand, heavy, cold, humming with a barely contained power that resonated deep in my bones, was the black sword, Grokhark. I stood up shakily. My body felt weak, dizzy, drained, but... whole. Unwounded. I looked down at the hole in the ice. The glowing light from the lake bottom was gone. Only darkness remained below. Rokhan was free.

Carefully, reverently, I strapped the ancient, terrible sword to my back alongside my own familiar blade. Then, turning away from the now-silent lake, I began the long walk south, feeling a new, strange strength slowly returning to my limbs, guided now not just by hope, but by the heavy weight of destiny on my back.

It took only a day to reach the coast where I'd left my boat hidden amongst the ice floes. Pushing it back into the freezing water, I began the arduous journey south across the northern ocean. Days later, weary but alive, I saw the familiar coastline of the Andranir lands emerge from the sea mist.

To my surprise, as I approached the main Andranir docks, a large group was waiting on the shore – Federag himself, along with elders and warriors. They must have seen my small boat from afar, but their presence felt... expectant. Formal.

As I stepped onto the pier, securing my boat, Federag strode forward, his expression serious, almost awed. He stopped before me and bowed deeply from the waist. "Heiri Hardingir," he greeted me, his voice filled with reverence, using the ancient title for the High Chief, the King of *all* Hualeg.

Around him, every Andranir warrior, every elder, every villager followed suit, bowing low. "Heiri Hardingir." The words washed over me, echoing strangely in the cold sea air.

I stood frozen, stunned. *Heiri Hardingir? Me? How...?* They couldn't know what happened at the lake, surely? But then my eyes fell on the black sword hilt protruding over my shoulder. Grokhark. The Bearer of Hatred. But perhaps also... the symbol of unity? They must have recognized it. Or sensed its power.

"Please," Federag gestured towards the village, still bowing slightly. "Rest with us, Heiri Hardingir. Allow us to offer hospitality."

"Thank you, Federag," I managed, still feeling uncomfortable with the title, the deference. "I need only... eat a little. Drink. Maybe rest for a while. Then I must return to Vallanir immediately. If you do not mind."

He looked taken aback. "By Odaran, you may eat your fill! Stay forever if you wish! We would be honored!"

But I insisted. All I needed was strength for the final leg of the journey. Federag quickly provided roasted meat, strong ale. I ate quickly, then requested leave to depart, asking only to borrow a boat suitable for the river journey back to Vallanir.

Federag wouldn't hear of me rowing myself. He insisted on providing not just a sturdy river boat, but thirty of his best warriors to man the oars. "That is unnecessary," I protested. "I can row myself."

"Please, Heiri Hardingir," Federag insisted respectfully but firmly. "Allow us this duty. Allow us to escort you home properly."

Seeing his insistence, and feeling the deep weariness in my bones, I finally agreed. After brief farewells, I boarded the large Andranir longboat. Letting his warriors handle the oars allowed me to rest, truly rest, perhaps for the first time since a long time ago. I slept deeply, securely, rocked by the rhythm of the oars carrying me home.

Two days later, we arrived at the Vallanir docks. And this time, the welcome was overwhelming. It seemed the entire village had gathered – warriors, elders, women, children – shouting, laughing, weeping with joy. News of my return, perhaps even rumors carried on the wind about the sword I now bore, must have preceded me. I stepped onto the dock and was engulfed by the crowd, embraced, clapped on the back, hailed as Vahnar, as Hardingir, as hero. I hugged them back as best I could – Tilda, Meralda, Erenar (his relief palpable), the children Rennar and Vaya, Freya (her eyes filled with complicated emotions), Krennar, Drinar, Svenar... so many faces, filled with relief and hope.

But one face was missing. Vida. Amidst the joyous chaos, her absence was a sharp, deep ache in my heart. Even now, even knowing the truth, even hailed as chief... without her, the victory felt incomplete. All I could do now was cling to the memory of her, hold it close.

That evening, during the celebratory feast in the great hall, I sat mostly silent, listening as my family – my aunts Tilda and Meralda, my uncle Erenar, my cousins Freya, Rennar, Vaya – told stories, laughed, tried to include me in their warmth. Freya, seeing me quiet, eventually asked gently about my journey north, her eyes filled with curiosity.

I just smiled, shaking my head slightly, unsure how to even begin explaining the dream, the lake, Rokhan, Grokhark. It all felt too strange, too unreal, too dreamlike itself now. "Everything is fine, Freya," I said simply. "We will all be fine now." They seemed to accept that, nodding, believing, perhaps needing to believe.

The next day, the true weight of my new reality arrived. Chieftains from across Hualeg began arriving – Federag from Andranir first, then chiefs from the Brahanir, the Drakknir, the smaller eastern tribes. They came to pay respects, to see the wielder of Grokhark, the prophesied uniter. Then, most surprising, most significant of all, came the delegation from the west – Mornir, his face impassive now, alongside the Hardingirs of the other western tribes, the ones who had allied with him against us just weeks before.

The villagers watched nervously as they approached the longhouse where I sat in the Hardingir's seat, flanked by Erenar and the Vallanir elders. Hatred still simmered between East and West, generations deep. But I had given my word to Mornir, and perhaps more importantly, the presence of Grokhark hanging on the wall behind me commanded a new kind of respect, a new kind of fear. I nodded a silent welcome as they entered.

Mornir, his face unreadable, walked to the center of the hall, stopped before me, and knelt, bowing his head low. Many gasped. Around him, the other Logenir and western chiefs followed suit, kneeling, bowing.

"Heiri Hardingir," Mornir's voice was rough but clear, devoid of its earlier malice.

"Hardingir Mornir," I replied formally, acknowledging his rank.

"May Odaran bless you, and grant you long life to lead all of us."

I nodded slowly, looking out over the assembled chiefs, east and west, kneeling together before the Vallanir hearth for the first time in centuries. "May Odaran bless us all," I replied, my voice gaining strength, authority.

On that day, the old hostilities paused. On that day, all the tribes of the northern lands, without exception, offered homage, declared allegiance,

however tentatively, however fearfully, to the Heiri Hardingir.
To the King of the Northmen.

* * *

Winter arrived, deep and white, blanketing Hualeg in snow and ice. In past years, this meant isolation, hunkering down, enduring the cold darkness. But this winter felt... different. Vallanir village thrived with a strange new energy. People travelled between longhouses even after dark, paths kept clear, torches burning bright. Markets stayed open late, taverns bustled with laughter and song until midnight. Children, bundled in furs, shrieked with joy sledding on the frozen river, seemingly immune to the biting cold.

There was a warmth here now, something beyond the hearth fires. A feeling of unity? Of hope? It drew people. Visitors came from other tribes, experienced the change, and many asked permission to stay, to settle, swelling our numbers. Would this last? Would it bring prosperity? Or just new problems? I wasn't sure. But if it brought happiness, fostered peace, even for a time... maybe it was a path worth walking.

I sat alone by the window in my chamber – my father Vilnar's old room – gazing out at the silent, snow-covered forest stretching southwards. The old question, the one that always lingered beneath the surface, returned. If I could find peace, happiness, purpose *here*... why should I ever leave? Why yearn for the South? Maybe my place *was* here now, in the North, forever.

But did I truly feel that way? Was this feeling – acceptance, duty, the respect of a people – the same as happiness? Or was happiness still... elusive?

Mom's voice echoed in my memory: *Don't look back, Vahnar. Look forward. Happiness lies ahead.* Her advice felt wise, kind. But how could I find true happiness without understanding where I came from? Without acknowledging the past, the mistakes – mine, my parents', my ancestors'? Only by facing those shadows, accepting them, could I learn. Learn to live well. Learn to stay strong. Learn to keep faith.

After that, Vida's voice whispered in my heart, *who knows what the future holds?*

This is how the gods brought us together, she'd said. *This is the best we can get.* Maybe she was right. Maybe happiness wasn't a destination, but the journey itself – the struggle, the learning, the enduring.

Is happiness already here? Or still waiting to be found? The answer, perhaps, was both. Happiness *was* here, in the fragile peace, the tentative unity, the hope for a better future for these people I now led. But it was also something out there, something ahead, something I had to keep searching for, striving for, as long as I lived.

IV

Epilogue

49

Coming Home

The Ordelahr just keeps flowin'. Always has, always will. Seen gods walk this land, seen 'em leave. Seen kingdoms rise and fall further south. Seen boys grow into men, seen men carried away by war or time. River don't care. Just keeps runnin' north, same as it always has. Life's like that, I reckon. Can't stop it. Try dammin' it up, it just finds another way 'round.

This afternoon, the sun felt weak through the thick leaves overhead down by the pier. Sat here alone, watchin' the current, thinkin'. Mostly thinkin' about folks gone by. Stories told around fires, faces laughin', faces grievin'. My own wife... gone these many years. And my son...

Strange Moor ain't here pesterin' me. My younger brother. Only family I got left in Orulion now. Why's he still here, anyway? This village... ain't the same place we grew up. Feels foreign sometimes. Moor should've left, like the others. "Maybe we're both just lazy old fools, Root," he always says when I ask him. Maybe he's right. Laziness runs deep sometimes.

Didn't run in my Boot, though. Not lazy, my son. Lively lad he was. Brain maybe not the sharpest hook in the tackle box, face plain enough, but stubborn? Persistent? Aye. Girls seemed to like that fire in him well enough. An' that stubbornness... maybe that's what made him surprisingly handy with a sword, though I always wished he'd stuck to nets.

Reminds me... that other lad. The tall one, come through a few months back. "Tuck," he called himself. Stayed just one night, him and his brother

"Dall." Young Tuck... somethin' about him put me in mind of Boot. Naive, maybe? That fierce youthfulness burnin' under the surface? Now the stories comin' downriver... they're callin' him a hero.

"A hero? That boy?" I still find it hard to believe.

"Aye, Root! A proper hero!" young Pekkar shouted at me in the tavern last week, spillin' his ale. "Leader of Taupin's army now! Killed hundreds o' Hualegs himself, they say! Drove 'em clean back to the ice!"

"Hundreds?" I scoffed. "By himself? Lad, d'you know how tough a Hualeg warrior is? Takes three good men to bring one down! One boy killin' hundreds? Impossible!"

"So? Just proves men like William Tuck exist!" Pekkar insisted stubbornly.

"Aye, maybe," I'd grumbled, swallowing my drink. "Met him once, you know. Stayed the night." A mistake sayin' that. Ever since, can't drink my ale in peace without someone askin' 'What was he like, Root? Tell us about Tuck!' What's to tell? Stayed one night! Quiet mostly, polite enough. Worried about somethin'.

The stories get wilder every telling. Beat the Hualegs, drove 'em north. Made friends with some Hualegs too, they say now! Took one o' their women for a wife! Some whisper Tuck himself *is* Hualeg blood! Hard to know the truth from river gossip. Latest news is, Tuck's vanished again. Disappeared up north somewhere.

"Normal," Jorg the tavern keeper said, polishin' his counter. "Mercenary type. Job's done, money's paid, he moves on."

No. Don't feel right. Heroes shouldn't just vanish like morning mist. Makes him sound like that knight everyone talked about after the Elniri war years back... the one who saved the day then disappeared too. An' what about Tuck's brother? Dall? No stories 'bout him bein' a hero? Or disappearin'? Don't seem fair.

Still... Taupin's little village army is famous now. Did what no king's soldiers ever managed – beat the Hualeg raiders proper. Heard tales o' Hualeg trouble since I was a boy, since Alton kings stopped carin' much 'bout us up here on the Ordelahr. Some say the raids started long before even that...

Aaaah! What use is an old fisherman knowin' such things? Ain't important...

My thoughts drift back again, always back, to my own son. Boot. Oh, lad, where did life take you? Did you find glory as a soldier? Did you find happiness? Did you meet your mother again, beyond the veil? Why'd the news stop, son? Why'd the coins stop comin'? Just wait for me, boy. Won't be long now, I feel it in my bones. Old Root's comin' to join you both. Ten years since he marched south, full o' hope. More'n eight since the last letter, the last bit o' coin...

Footsteps behind me on the pier. Heavy tread. Stopped nearby. Gods, can't an old man sit in peace? Felt annoyed. What business could anyone have with me now?

"Father?"

The voice... young, hesitant, but familiar beneath a strange accent... it sent a jolt through me. I gasped, turnin' my head slow, afraid of what I might see, afraid of foolish hope.

A man stood there. A soldier, by his worn uniform, though the Alton crest was faded. Leather backpack slung over one shoulder. Face... gods, the face was familiar, the shape of the jaw, the set of the eyes... but thinner, harder, etched with lines of hardship, marked by scars I didn't recognize. And his hand... his left hand... half the pointer finger was gone, just a ragged stump.

"W-what?" I stammered, my old heart poundin'. "Who... who calls me Father, son?"

The soldier looked nervous now, fidgeting. "Father... it's me! Your son! Boo—"

"I-I HAVE NO SON!" The words ripped out of me before I could stop them, harsh, defensive. A wall built over years of grief and forced acceptance. "My son is long dead! Died a soldier for the King! Eight years ago!"

The man flinched back, shocked by my reaction. His mouth opened, closed again. His eyes blinked rapidly.

Why'd I say that? Shame washed over me. Always hidin' feelings, that's me. Keepin' it locked inside. Now look. "My son is dead!" I insisted again, louder this time, though my voice cracked. "Who are you? What do you want?"

"It's Boot! I *am* your son!" the man insisted, his voice thick with emotion.

"Lies!" I cried, turning away, staring hard at the river. "My son wouldn't forget his own father! Wouldn't vanish for eight years without a word!"

"Th-that... there's a reason, Father! Please! Listen!" he stammered, taking a step closer. "That's *why* I came back! Because I still can... I still want to be... a dutiful son!" His voice broke. His eyes looked wet now.

I kept my gaze fixed on the swirling water, refusing to look at him, though my own tears were starting to flow freely now. "P-proof?" I demanded stubbornly, my voice trembling. "What proof have you that you're my son? I remember my boy... died a hero!" Even as I said it, my heart leaped, wanting desperately to turn, to embrace this stranger who looked so much like...

The man – Boot? – was silent for a moment. Then he fumbled in the pouch at his belt. "I... This..." He held something out. A bottle. Dark glass, fancy label, sealed with wax. Expensive southern wine.

My eyes widened. Memory flooded back – Boot, young and eager, boasting before he left... *'One day, Father, I'll bring back enough coin for you to drink fancy wine every night!'* We'd laughed then. Now... Between my own tears, a choked laugh escaped me. Louder, then louder still, until I was roaring with laughter, tears streaming down my face, the sound echoing over the quiet river. Ten years, maybe twenty, seemed to fall away from my shoulders.

"Son!" I finally choked out, turning, grabbing him in a fierce hug. "You remembered! You truly did it!"

He hugged me back just as tightly, burying his face in my old fishing tunic. "No, Father," he mumbled sadly, pulling back slightly. "This... this is just a gift. Strange story. Tavern owner back in Ortleg... forced me to take it. Made me think of you, of my promise." He shook his head. "Only bottle I have now. But... I *do* have some money saved. Enough to buy more wine, maybe."

I just smiled, clapping him on the back, tears still flowing freely. My son. Home. We sat there on the quiet pier as dusk settled, passing the expensive bottle back and forth, savoring the rich taste. I asked him about his strange way of talking now. And slowly, hesitantly at first, then with growing confidence, Boot began to tell me his extraordinary tale.

Kidnapped, not two years after leaving home. Betrayed by fellow soldiers, sold like cattle to some criminal merchant up in Nordton. Slavery. Running. Hiding. Never daring contact home for fear of bringing trouble down on us. "Got tired o' bein' their victim!" he snarled, glancing at his mutilated hand. Living hand-to-mouth, wandering, eventually falling in with... Elniri? A noble hired him?

"Ooooh! Elniri?" My eyes widened. Pride surged. "Met them, did you, son? True they're all dark-skinned giants?"

He explained then, patiently, something about everyone technically being Elniri now, by decree of some High Highness Quazar. Didn't make much sense to my simple mind – Boot looked the same colour as always – but I nodded along. "Then what happened?"

"Got a job, Father. Official work. For the Elniri government." He explained being sent back into Alton lands months ago, late last spring, part of a secret team searching for certain people. "A mother and her son," he said. "Traveling alone. Might have remarried, changed names." They'd split up the search across different regions. He'd requested this northern area, hoping for a chance to come home. The trail led him to Ortleg, near Prutton. "Heard rumors there of folk like them," he said. "But the trail went cold. Mother died recent. Son vanished. Couldn't be sure it was them anyway."

"Names?" I asked. "Didn't you know their names?"

"No. Maybe they weren't using real names."

"I see."

"The real problem," Boot continued, taking another swig of wine, "was my contact. An officer, liaison between the search teams. Supposed to meet me in Prutton this summer. Give me my pay, funds to return to Danqs – that's where the Elniri base is. But he never showed! Waited weeks in Ortleg. Money ran out." He sighed heavily. "Couldn't get back to Danqs.

Couldn't stay in Ortleg forever. Heard Alton and Tavarin might go to war again, borders tightening. So... figured it was finally time. Time to come home. See if you were still... here." His voice softened again, tears welling in his eyes. "Was afraid, Father. Afraid I'd come back and find you gone too."

"Oh, son." I was moved beyond words, understanding finally the hardship, the loneliness, the fear he must have carried all these years. Considering his pride, his stubbornness, I just hugged him again. Then I chuckled, wiping my eyes – must be the wine making me leak like this. "Well, don't be sad anymore, lad! You're home now! Safe!" I clapped him on the back. "Strange how fate works, eh? Sure they won't find you here?"

Boot shrugged, managing a weary laugh. "If they look, let 'em come. I'll handle it."

"That's the spirit!" I grinned. "But when it comes to the women, son, don't run! Still gotta take responsibility! If need be, you can always join Taupin's famous army!"

"What?" He looked horrified. "Join an army again? Never! Not strong enough anymore, Father!"

We both laughed then, long and loud, the sound echoing happily over the darkening river.

Since that day, old Root's become famous in Orulion, haven't I? Aye. Hosted the hero Tuck, they say. And now my own son's back, scarred maybe, but full of tales no one else can match. Still many things I don't understand, about Elniri and kings and such. But Boot's home. That's what matters. We'll make the best of the time we have left. Life goes on, like the river. No use being tied to the past.

Just hope... hope that young lad Tuck finds his way home someday too. Finds his own peace. Wherever he is now.

50

I'll Wait Forever

The rain drummed against the workshop windows again this afternoon. It felt like it had been raining for days, a persistent, dreary drizzle that matched the mood hanging over Ortleg since... well, since William left. Winter was long gone, supposedly spring now, nearly summer even, but the wind still carried a chill that seeped into the bones, especially at night. I coaxed the fire in the living room hearth back to life, grateful for its warmth, then curled up in Father's big chair with one of the books Master Benzo sometimes lent me. Reading helped pass the time, helped keep the worried thoughts at bay.

I'd barely finished a page when a sharp knock echoed on the main door. I looked up, startled. Not Father – he was visiting cousins in the next village today and wouldn't be back till late. He never knocked anyway, just came right in bellowing a greeting. Who could it be? Customers rarely came this late, especially in the rain. Neighbors? My stomach tightened slightly. Neighbors usually only knocked if they brought bad news. Had something happened to Father?

No. I shook my head, pushing the thought away. He was fine, just a short trip. Don't borrow trouble, Muriel. Taking a breath, I went to the door, peering cautiously through the small crack in the window beside it.

A man stood on the porch, huddled inside a heavy, dripping raincoat, his face hidden in the deep shadow of his hood. My hand instinctively went to the heavy forging hammer I kept propped just inside the doorframe – a habit I'd picked up since Father insisted on Mr. Horsling's 'protection'. I glanced quickly across the muddy street. Max, the big, quiet man Mr. Horsling paid to sit outside his shack and 'watch' our house, was still there, hunkered down on his stool, seemingly relaxed, his gaze steady on my porch. If Max wasn't alarmed, the visitor likely wasn't dangerous. Not one of those bandits William fought, then. I didn't need to be afraid.

Still, a shiver of unease went through me. I opened the door just a crack, keeping my hand near the hammer. "Yes?"

The man lifted his head slightly. Rainwater streamed from his hood, but even in the gloom, I recognized him instantly. That swagger, that annoying, self-assured grin that always seemed out of place. Sometimes, that grin scared me more than an open threat.

"Rogas." The name came out flat, cold. I took a deep breath, trying to keep my voice steady. "What are you doing here?" My fingers tightened on the hammer handle. "Where's William?"

"Whoa there, lass! Didn't come looking for trouble, don't worry," Rogas said quickly, holding up his hands in a placating gesture, somehow knowing exactly where my hand was. "Your watchdog knows I'm here." He jerked his chin towards Max across the street, who gave no reaction.

I ignored his attempt at reassurance. "Where's William?" I demanded again.

His grin flickered slightly. "He's fine."

"*Where* is he?" My voice rose, sharper this time.

"Up north! Still up north! In some village," he elaborated vaguely. "He's alright, Muriel. Doing well."

"Doing well?" My grip tightened on the hammer. "Then why did you leave him there? Why aren't you with him?"

Rogas shifted his weight, looking momentarily doubtful before the confident grin returned. "Let's just say... he's needed up there right now. I'm... not so much."

"Needed for what?"

"Well," he puffed his chest out slightly, "turns out those northern villages needed some proper soldiers to help 'em against the Hualeg raiders. William and me... we stepped up. Done pretty well so far, chased 'em off a time or two." He chuckled. "We're a good team."

My blood ran cold. "Hualeg raiders?" I stared at him, horrified. "Aren't they supposed to be giants? Savages? Dangerous?" My fear for William boiled over into anger. I shoved the door open wider, stepping onto the porch, raising the hammer slightly. "You took him north claiming it was for *refuge*, to *hide* from those bandits! And now you tell me you left him behind to fight *Hualegs*?"

"Hey! Calm down! Put the hammer down, eh?" Rogas backed up a step, holding his hands up again, his grin finally faltering. "Listen, William can take care of himself! Trust me! He's... different now. Not the same lad who left Ortleg. Still a good kid deep down, yeah, but... harder. Stronger. I'd bet good coin the Hualegs are more scared of *him* now than he is of them!"

I shook my head fiercely, not believing him, not wanting to believe William had changed that much. "When is he coming home?"

"When the business up there is done," Rogas said evasively. "Soon, I hope."

"Are you sure?"

He tried a cocky grin. "Wanna bet on it?"

"What about your enemies?" I pressed, ignoring his attempt at levity. "The ones from the south? Those bandits? Are they still after him? After you?"

"Them?" Rogas grimaced, looking genuinely uneasy for a moment. "Done with, far as I know. Dealt with." He shrugged. "But... still gotta be careful in life, right? Always gotta be ready for the unpredictable."

"You're hardly fit to be quoting wisdom!" I grumbled, lowering the hammer slightly but keeping it ready.

He actually laughed then. "Just repeating what my favorite young philosopher told me! William himself said something like that last time we talked!"

"William did?" I asked, confused.

"Who else?" Rogas grinned again. "Anyway, look, Muriel. I mainly came by to pass on the message. Tell you he's alright, so you wouldn't worry yourself sick. Now, I really must be going."

"Going where? I thought you were staying here? Waiting for him?"

"Wait here? In Ortleg?" He looked genuinely surprised. "Gods, no! Need to earn some coin, girl! And my luck's always been better down south. Time to head that way." He turned, starting down the porch steps into the rain.

He paused at the bottom, turning back one last time, his expression strangely serious for a moment beneath the dripping hood. "You know, Muriel... you, me... we're both lucky folk. Lucky to know someone like William." He held my gaze. "Won't say why exactly, but... don't you worry too much about him. We'll see him again. Maybe soon, maybe... maybe after a very long time." He shrugged again, the casual gesture somehow chilling. "Go ahead, you can wait for him if you want. Wait right here." His grin returned, thin this time. "But remember what the philosophers say... life goes on. Always other things to do, eh? More important things, maybe."

And with that, he turned and walked away quickly down the street, his figure swallowed by the rain and the gathering dusk.

I stood frozen on the porch, his parting words echoing in my ears. *Wait if you want... may take a very long time... life goes on...* Why had he said that? Did he mean William *wasn't* coming home soon? Did he know something more? What really happened up there in the North?

Slowly, feeling a cold deeper than the rain, I closed the door, barred it, and went back to the chair by the fire. I stared into the flames for a long time, Rogas's words churning in my mind. Then, resolutely, I picked up my book again.

I'll wait, I told myself fiercely, ignoring the doubt, ignoring the fear. *Forever, if I have to.*

But forever felt terribly long. The seasons turned. Autumn faded, winter locked Ortleg in snow and ice, then spring returned, melting the rivers, greening the hillsides. And still, William didn't come back. Almost a year now since he'd fled north with Rogas.

Rogas had been wrong about William returning soon. But perhaps right about life going on. Father needed help in the forge; orders still came in, metal still needed shaping. Chores needed doing. Master Benzo still lent me books, and I studied, trying to fill the empty hours, trying not to count the passing days, weeks, months.

What was I even waiting for anymore? Did William even think about Ortleg? About Father? About... me? Maybe Rogas was right about that too. Maybe there *were* more important things than waiting for someone who might never return.

One clear morning, late in spring, after breakfast, I took the familiar path up the quiet hill south of the village. Under the shade of the old oak tree stood the simple, elongated mound of earth where we had buried Mrs. Elise. No headstone marked the spot, but I knew it well. I came often, keeping the weeds clear, sometimes just sitting quietly. Kneeling beside the grave now, I patiently began pulling away the fresh spring weeds that encroached on the bare earth.

A soft footstep behind me made me stop, turning quickly, my breath catching. Someone stood on the path not far away, watching me.

An old man, thin and slightly stooped, dressed in a long, dark robe like a traveling scholar or priest. His hair was thin and grey, his face clean-shaven, kind eyes regarding me calmly. He carried a small leather satchel over his shoulder and leaned lightly on a long, sturdy walking cane. A traveler, clearly, come from far away.

My first thought was: customer? Then: robber? My hand instinctively dropped to the small knife I always carried tucked in my belt now. Where was Max? I scanned the base of the hill quickly – no sign of him. Panic flickered briefly. I was alone up here. But I could defend myself if needed. I was skilled with the knife. Still... Max should have been nearby.

"Good morning, child," the old man greeted me politely, his voice soft.

"Good morning, sir," I replied, forcing my voice to sound steady, trying not to betray my sudden anxiety. I stood up slowly. "Are you looking for the blacksmith's workshop? You've taken the wrong path. Down on the main road, turn left, about a hundred paces."

"Oh, no, child. Thank you, but I came specifically to visit this grave."

He smiled gently. "In fact, I was standing back amongst the trees for a while before you arrived." He took a step closer. "Forgive me, I haven't introduced myself. My name is Pyrlik. I have journeyed from Alton city."

"You came... to visit this grave?" I asked, surprised, still wary. "But... it has no name, no stone. How could you know who rests here?"

"I asked in the village," he explained simply. "Described who I sought. They guided me here. You... you have been tending the grave? All this time?"

"The woman buried here... Mrs. Elise... she was a close friend to my father and me," I said, feeling protective of her memory. "So yes, I tend her grave."

The old man looked at me intently then, his gaze deep, searching. "She passed from this world about a year ago now, am I right?"

"Yes. Last autumn."

"And you knew her only as Elise?"

"Yes. That was her name. Did... did you know her, sir?"

Pyrlik nodded slowly. "I knew her, yes. Long ago. Under a different name." He paused, then asked gently, "Does she... did she have children?"

I hesitated for a moment, suspicion warring with curiosity. Who was this man? But Max would surely be watching from somewhere nearby. And the man seemed harmless, gentle. "Yes," I nodded finally. "A son. Two years older than me."

"His name?" Pyrlik asked, his eyes sharpening slightly. "And where is he now?"

"His name is William," I answered, then hesitated again. Should I tell this stranger where William went? What if he *was* connected to those bandits? But perhaps not. Perhaps just an old friend of Elise's, wanting to reconnect. I decided to offer only the basic truth. Max was likely close. "He... he went north," I said carefully. "Shortly after his mother died."

"Why?" Pyrlik asked quietly.

"I don't know," I replied honestly.

He seemed to sense my lingering suspicion, my reluctance to say more. "You have nothing to fear from me, child," he reassured me kindly. "I hold no ill intentions. I simply knew the woman buried here many years ago. A brief acquaintance, but memorable. I had hoped, perhaps, to meet her son."

"I don't know when he'll be back, sir," I said, my own worry surfacing again, sharp and familiar. "Or... or if he will come back at all." My voice trembled slightly. "The North... it's a dangerous place. He shouldn't have gone there. It was foolish."

Pyrlik smiled sadly at my fierce protectiveness, my poorly hidden annoyance. "Then let us both pray for his safe return, child." He reached into the satchel at his side, drawing out a small, stoppered glass vial. "And when he does return," he held the vial out to me, "can you do an old man a service? Give this to him?"

"What is it?" I asked, taking the vial cautiously. It felt cool in my hand.

"It is... important," Pyrlik replied cryptically. "Important for him to finally know who his mother *really* was."

"Who his mother really was?" I frowned, confused. What did he mean? She was Elise.

But before I could ask more, he nodded, seemingly satisfied. "I will give it to him," I promised, tucking the strange vial safely into my own pocket.

"I thank you, child," Pyrlik said gratefully. "And I thank you also, for tending this place with such care." He bowed his head respectfully. "I hope our paths may cross again someday. Goodbye."

I returned the greeting, watching as the old man turned and walked slowly back down the path towards the village, leaning heavily on his cane, until he disappeared from view. I never saw him again.

The months continued to pass. The vial remained tucked away, waiting. And I continued to wait too.

Printed in Great Britain
by Amazon